# UNQUIET MINDS

## RONNIE BROWN

CRANTHORPE
MILLNER
PUBLISHERS

First published by Cranthorpe Millner Publishers (2024)

ISBN 978-1-80378-193-8 (Paperback)

www.cranthorpemillner.com

Cranthorpe Millner Publishers

Printed and bound by CPI Group (UK) Ltd, Croydon, CR0 4YY

*For my brother, Eric.*
*You're not alone in your aloneness.*

*Pressed by the Moon, mute arbitress of tides,*
*While the loud equinox its power combines,*
*The sea no more its swelling urge confines,*
*But o'er the shrinking land sublimely rides.*

Sonnet XLIV *Written in the Church Yard at Middleton in Sussex*
(Charlotte Turner Smith), 1789

*I stand amid the roar*
*Of a surf-tormented shore,*
*And I hold within my hand*
*Grains of the golden sand –*
*How few! yet how they creep*
*Through my fingers to the deep,*
*While I weep – while I weep!*

*A Dream Within a Dream* (Edgar Allan Poe), 1849

# Chapter I

On the corner of Water Lane and Dam Street stood a doughy-white police tent. Lit inside by white LED lamps, ghostly masked, gloved and overly suited-and-booted forensic teams collected samples. In the hope they might find smears of blood containing DNA traces of the killer, they scraped, collected and bagged from the splatters and drag marks everything they could, samples of blood, dirt and a broken green fingernail.

Gemma, aged twenty-three, had been walking her dog, a fluffy reddish-coloured hybrid of the 'doodle' family. The attack was vicious and inhuman. She died from her wounds. Unable to speak, she wrote down two and a half sentences before she died of her injuries; two and a half sentences ending in 'werewolf'.

Whispered home-grown reports mentioned cannibalism and said her throat had been torn out. More accurately, though equally ghastly, the police coroner reported multiple claw marks and bites on the body, indicating the ferocity of the attack. The press did not yet have the details. The dark shadows of superstition, familiar to the area, required merely a hint of tales of lycanthropy, and mass panic or vendettas in the wider community would ensue.

The other sentences scrawled on an available notepad read: 'It was small or crouched down like an animal... It came from behind...'

Forensic guesstimates confirmed the assailant as not much over 1.52 metres.

Alfie, the Labradoodle, was still missing.

## Chapter 2

Chief Inspector Saida 'Dawn' Raed abandoned her scrutiny of Richard Hart's papers to focus on the werewolf attacks.

Gemma, the victim, had been a Bateman. Raed was party to the knowledge of an ongoing feud between Gemma's family and the Bowers. Had this simmering hatred boiled over into vicious recrimination? Her available staff were out making cautious enquiries with the locals, including members of both families. The run-ins were legendary. She spoke with Stan, the head of the Bateman clan. He berated them for not doing anything while his opposite number, Geoff Bowers, was unperturbed by it (on the surface, at least). Beneath, she discerned, he was badly shaken. The hostility between them was going to be an issue.

The previous victims were Sara Bowers, aged nineteen, and Matilda Smith, who went by her pet name Matty. Both Sara and Matty, a non-clan member aged eighteen, had survived. Both young ladies were hoping to go to university. The attacks in early September had put paid to that. Geoff, Sara's granddad, said she would have been the first in the family to go to university.

The bitterness that consumed these rivals was apparent. The attack on Matty Smith questioned the police theory of a turf war. One Bateman, one Bowers. Yet the simple explanation was too obvious. Smith was not a member of either family.

Raed was tearful. Tears turned to anger. The climate of fear was something she knew well. The unrest in her hometown of Bradford during the riots in July 2001 and the ensuing drugs wars and related racial anxiety, were a suitable yardstick for measurement. This murder was vile in the extreme. She considered her new colleague, Hart, in the adjoining room. His work was piling up. It would take his mind away from his brooding.

The night closed in and darkness descended on Loftus. The bad weather wasn't helping police work. Raed and Hart arrived to oversee the collection of evidence. The blood smears indicated that Gemma had crawled a yard or so before passing out. Another dog walker had discovered her. Dried blood smudged the paving stones, and a distinct handprint showed where she had taken her hand from her throat while trying to crawl. The sad, green-painted fingernail was hers. Raed thought the handprint resembled a cave painting; a woman's handprint, the colour red; women the first artists.

A small group of onlookers gawked and huddled together, as if waiting for something else to happen. The white light from within the tent silhouetted them and obscured detail giving their presence an eerie blackness and a hazy aura.

As Hart emerged from the tent, Raed noticed him falter. His gaze went beyond the group of local onlookers. His head went down and then from side to side as if trying to shake off a gnat. His shoulders slumped. He jerked his head back and glared into the darkness, his concentration disturbed. He froze.

She followed his gaze. Behind the gaping locals two men stood in the shadows. As she peered into the gloom, they turned and walked away.

## Chapter 3

As the autumn sun set on the damp, grey streets of Leeds, the first signs of winter were already beginning to show in the gathering windswept leaves and mouldering conkers. Ron I Penny was walking to the local store. His sabbatical year not yet over (the university still deciding what to do with him) he didn't know what he wanted.

The wet roads reflected the lights from the supermarket, cafés and bars, and offered respite from the half-lit slate skies and matching Yorkshire stone walls to which the oncoming winter months brought an overall grimness. The taillight of a dark lorry created a colour field in the puddles: fuzzy greens; manic reds swimming in a disembodied black.

Dusk offered him anonymity, a grey in between breathing space from the dark events of his experience in The Tableau Case – the horror of Annabelle and Peter Burns's gallery. He wondered how Hart was. Trying to see more in the landscape, he examined the reflections in the puddles that the full moon helped to paint. He recalled Andrew Gifford's sensitively painted images of Headingley and Bradford. The artist captured Headingley's twilight mood perfectly in his contemporary works. In the form of a lecture, Penny addressed an imaginary audience along the way, studying the puddle paintings as he went. He rubbed his chin and began:

"In contrast to Gifford's contemporary landscapes, Atkinson Grimshaw's paintings romanticised the grey townscape. Anything can be romanticised along the way. Take for example the current reception of the sepia-tinted photos of Quarry Hill in Leeds, once an open choleric sewer. Or how people now see Sutcliffe's photos of Whitby – a place of dire poverty and hardship!" The lecture ended. Reflection ensued, trauma.

He thought of Grimshaw's later industrial landscapes, lit by pale moonlight or soft yellow gas lamps, casting artificial warmth on the chill. That warmth was missing in Headingley, sucked out by personal traumas.

Perhaps rain could wash away the stifled feeling, the claustrophobic indoors, the pensiveness and, momentarily, the vivid flashbacks of restless souls. He tried to recall his thoughts of hope. There was none. He glanced over his shoulder.

**Chapter 4**

Raed looked intently to her right through the plate-glass partition through to the next office and across into the corridor.

Outside Hart's office, two men sat. One was thick set with a beard, the other tall and gangly. The taller man was wearing a beret. They waited patiently. Raed peeked at them through the glass. Neither of the men moved. They appeared amicable. What were they doing here? The police station at number six The Yard was open for operational use only. Her preference would be to have it accessible to the public; closure could only lead to further alienation. Counters had fallen across the country from nine hundred in 2010 to around five hundred in 2019. Raed disliked the lack of physical accessibility, online contact had its merits, response could be quicker and victim support enabled.

A brief and judicious assessment told her that the shorter one could handle himself. He was battle-scarred and fit. The taller of the two had an interesting face, and extraordinary lavender-blue eyes. That he was unreadable puzzled her; that they were together was odd. Yet there appeared to be a strong bond between them. She clicked her tongue to chide herself for guessing and making assertions about male bonding. She returned to her files. As she turned away, the smaller one leaned over towards the other and spoke. It couldn't have been more than two words. In response, the other removed his beret to reveal a mop of dark curly hair.

Raed turned the page. On the top in bold it read: *The Tableau Case: Debrief.* Carefully she read through the case notes of the crimes the twins Annabelle and Peter had committed. She scanned the photos of the bodies resembling works of art, took in the role of Hart. The story read very differently from the tabloid representation. Their given title The Tableau Twins had stuck in both non police and police circles.

Her concentration faltered as Hart stood, sat down again, scrunched a piece of paper, threw it across the room, and jerked his head sideways as if suffering from DTs. She put her notes down. She stared at Hart.

His nose twitched like a small rodent. Raed contemplated having a quiet word with her new colleague. She heard him cursing; the F-word followed by what might be a person's name beginning with an explosive P, sounding like a microphone popping. She got to her feet to call next door. Then the abuse subsided.

He was glowering at the seated pair. Both looked straight ahead, both appearing unmoved. She studied them for a moment. The smaller one could have been asleep while the tall one held his beret between his knees, like a schoolchild waiting to see a headteacher. The 'headteacher' was showing signs of stress. She turned back to her notes. *Who were they?* Not locals.

DI Hart was stomping up and down as if possessed. Raed considered the idea that Hart was unhinged. His behaviour and vulgar language cut the ground from under his biodata, as she called it: his rapid promotion, his master's in forensic science and criminology. The walls were thin, the language offensive.

"That fucking P—" The name escaped her as he went to open the door.

She had avoided profanity throughout her career. An Asian colleague had once asked her why she didn't speak fucking English like the rest of the force. There was, she recalled, no ready-made answer.

Her take on the Bradford Riots had added to her popularity in certain quarters, and her recognition of the underlying drugs turf wars that pitched Asian against Asian, Asian against Caribbean, and English dealers against both. The reality contradicted the slanted sociological and political explanations of racial analysis and prejudice favoured by academics and government analysts – all of which was duly amplified by the media.

She was promoted for her 'excellent work' and sent away for her 'unfaltering war against the criminal classes'. A thank you can take differing forms. Her move took her temporarily to Loftus.

She was happy with her new posting. She liked the North Riding, although it appeared to lack the community spirit of the West. Time would tell. She missed the busy character of her home: the Victorian buildings, its hectic shopping centre, trips to Saltaire, walks above Ilkley, the bustle of Skipton market, and her family. As compensation, the Cleveland Hills and walks on the coast made her feel like she was on holiday. The nearby golden sands and clifftops added to this; the shopping in Middlesbrough was cheap and cheerful. Yet the honeymoon period was a short one.

Hart was stock still, his face like a death mask. From the few conversations she had had with him, she gathered he saw his move to the area as a condemnation, a demotion. He was staring down at the floor.

Outside, dense louring clouds warned of a storm. Autumn was coming in fast and slipping readily into a northern winter. She switched on her desk lamp as the place darkened. Hart, she concluded, reading well below the subtext of his data, was too good to be true. In a short addendum committed to memory, she noted the issue of his demeanour for her first briefing. He, she concluded, appeared to be a very unhappy man, an unquiet soul. As she read, the grounds for his twitchy manner became apparent.

Her detailed analysis of The Tableau murders highlighted the cause of his wounds. Hart's emotionally charged recollections of the house at Carshalton would, according to police psychological reports, wear off in time. Strung throughout the report, like a warning red light, was *Penny*. The explosive P…

## Chapter 5

Mass panic, Hart conjectured, would be difficult for the stoical residents of Loftus. His common sense told him it was more likely that vigilante repercussions on anyone different would ensue. He thoroughly checked out family ties and feuds, Gemma Bateman's family first. It would require a local insider to gain accurate information. This was the murder of a young woman. Surely they would talk.

The previous attacks involved serious mauling, with both female victims taken by surprise. Both Sara and Matty escaped with their lives. Sara's statement insisted that the attacker was 'wrapped in blackness and came out of nowhere'. Neither Sara nor Matty could recall anything of relevance to the police. Acute stress meant Matty's GP prescribed medication; Sara's depression was manifest in her over concern with morbid thoughts of further attacks and fitful nights. Both needed help. It was awful for Hart to see these youngsters so troubled.

What had they really seen? The bridge between the seen and the unseen was familiar territory to Hart. Understanding the nature of anxiety in victims, he realised the need for clinical intervention. It was not readily available. The budget was meagre. He appealed to Raed for help and she did her best. Nothing in the kitty was the answer from above.

*Is this about me?* he asked himself. He began to believe it was. He glared at the men outside.

One thing was for sure: these offences were committed by a human a malevolent human being. Familiar with mythology, Raed recognised that much. She accepted that physical reality wasn't the only reality. The person who committed these crimes might be waiting at the bus stop discussing the weather with a neighbour or chatting over the fence, but still be a demon.

Abdullah, her eldest brother, had delighted in terrifying his little sister, Saida with tales of the Si'lat – the djinns and devils from pre-Islamic times. With the wind they travelled on, they scavenged and brought disease. Her haunted dreams of these dark creatures provoked her – not into terror, but to declare war on them. Abdullah got his comeuppance at the hand of his cute little sister, and a bucket of evil-smelling liquid that took days to completely scrub off.

Raed took time off from the harsh reality of her job and Gemma's death then returned to mull over the crime. The savagery of the mutilation corresponded with the work of a djinn, or a treacherous spirit (a Si'lat), part of the imaginal realm. They were fiction. This was real. She was going to lock this person away for a long time.

Gemma was a popular young lady, liked by all (though one might exclude the Bowers). She was open, gregarious, and engaged to be married. During Raed's visit to the family, Gemma's mum showed her Gemma's wedding dress. She lifted it from the wardrobe and, in tears, placed it back again.

Gary, Gemma's fiancé, was working away, as was the case with so many young men in the area. He was flying back from the rigs. He wanted to track down this killer and exact revenge. He wasn't the only one.

## Chapter 6

Penny began philosophising. Common sense and common knowledge was his target, which he argued wasn't common. Indeed, it was nonsensical. Parents tell their kids a load of shite, he concluded. Kids reach adulthood, then spend huge chunks of their lives finding out that one or both parents were insane, seriously prejudiced, wrong and/or grossly misinformed. He kicked a bundle of soggy leaves. Aimed at blocking dark thoughts, his meandering worked only for so long. His own shadow overtook him, and he jumped.

He turned into Meanwood Road. The question of what was factual and what belonged to a prejudicial fantasy world was an issue, and a lifetime task to answer – if it could be done. He now knew that Roman Catholics could be quite nice. The interrogation and torture by what some referred to as the 'Papes', Roman Catholics that is, hadn't extended to Glasgow in the twentieth century. One might assume so, if the doctrine according to his Calvinist mother was to be adhered to. Latterly, her way of thinking was that they worked surreptitiously, by taking over 'the council' – the new inquisition. His own upbringing was one of 'facts', rumours, gossip, and a hateful collection of encyclopaedias.

Then there was murder and Brownleigh's carcass. If he tried to shake off the hopelessness, Brownleigh's flayed corpse returned.

His father's memories of the unsolved Green Lane Case rose to the surface. A walker found Linda Cook's body in the lane; surgical cotton wedged in her trachea. Throttled asphyxiated... Then there was the Sutton Bank body – The Nude in the Nettles case – also unsolved. An anonymous caller phoned in the crime and claimed he could not give his name due to 'national security'. The former occurred in Redcar in the early 1960s; the latter in the Hambleton district of North Yorkshire in the 1980s. DNA testing was not available and the cases went cold. He wanted to solve them.

Penny's grandparents were living around the corner from Green Lane at the time of Linda Cook's murder. Years later, he quizzed his granddad about the homicide.

"Someone must've seen or known something," he conceded. "Mind you, folk round here don't talk."

Penny may have read it wrongly, but his granddad's voice implied he spoke the last sentence with pride. But so much was mythologised in the town. The stone in number five's garden was a meteorite. That was a myth. Running into the kid next door on a return trip home, he recalled the meteorite.

"Do you 'member' the meteorite round the corner Ronnie?"

Penny mentioned that meteors did fall in the area in the late eighteenth century, but "They missed Dormanstown council estate."

He was nearing the store, his mind flitting from therapeutic anecdote to despondency. He recalled his dad's attitude to bad language. His dad swore only when he referred to his mam's cooking. The expressions 'boiled to buggery' and 'burnt to buggery' led the youthful Penny to believe buggery was something to do with cooking. At senior school he learned that in past times it was a crime. Prison followed. In terms of a reference point that wasn't a bad idea. His mam's cooking was criminal. He tried to smile. Thoughts poured in and ran out. The night wasn't cold but he shivered. The light had changed to an eerie green.

His dad also told him that a smart Alec had said that a rumour without a leg to stand on will find a way of getting around. He was dead right. Uncertain truths were to plague him over the next few months.

As the interior of the store lit up and warmed the inner chill, he checked in his pocket for his money and dividend card. Here in the shop, he would find peace in the form of shopping, the end of his philosophising and the arduous task of thinking. He picked up a basket and walked further into the store.

In Cleveland, Gemma Bateman was lying in the morgue.

When post-mortem examinations were complete, her body was released. The family gathered at Upleatham crematorium for the funeral. It was a downcast family that huddled in the chapel. The priest was at a loss. His comment that God was with her when she died incensed one or two of the mourners. Gary's short eulogy moved them to tears. Then it was back to The Arlington Hotel.

Notably, the members of one local family failed to attend.

## Chapter 7

Dove and Periwinkle were all Hart needed at this moment in time. He had nothing personal against them, except their friendship with Penny. The four men had worked well together in the past.

Hart's self-awareness had grown. He was a frustrated academic, Penny a frustrated detective. He wondered if Penny had learned from his experience? His own critical facilities had heightened. Had Penny learnt anything from him, his skills of detection sharpened during The Tableau Case? He probably thought so. Hart wasn't convinced. He was bargaining with his sanity; he was on high alert. At times, his anger ran away with him.

His workload was huge, though he tackled it with his usual energy. He had interviewed Sara Bowers and Matty Smith. Matty's acute anxiety meant her memory was poor. Sara made light of it. Hart surmised; a delayed response would occur. He was right. Her parents confirmed she found it difficult to focus.

Middlesbrough, Redcar and Cleveland's diabolical nature increased by the minute. Middlesbrough extended its hellish tendrils along the Cleveland Way, tainting everything in its path with fire and brimstone.

"Or should that be limestone?" he joked in a lighter moment. Those moments gave him a glimmer of a return to normality.

He liked the address of the police station. On one occasion he picked up the phone and said, "Hart of the Yard!"

Scotland Yard it wasn't.

To make life worse, he now faced the incomers from the south: Penny's abominable mates. In his office sat Dove and Periwinkle, the latter smoothing his beret and staring out of the window. Was Penny close by? He balked at the idea, yet wondered how he was.

Dove tried a discrete professional smile as they entered Hart's office. They hadn't come about the werewolf attacks, but a seemingly unrelated issue. Hart seethed and screeched something unintelligible. The werewolf killing was foremost in Hart's mind. Once again fiction was becoming a fact.

The amicable response from Hart never came. Hart eyed Periwinkle as he gazed out of the window at the near-derelict factory buildings opposite. Hart's demeanour was randomly oriented; icy and silent one moment then unsettled and gushing the next.

Hart inspected the floor as he spoke. "Not only have I got werewolves on my patch, but now you." Anger was boiling over into hysteria.

Periwinkle turned his attention away from the crumbling buildings.

Hart opened his mouth to speak again. For a moment, his mouth remained agape and nothing was said. They hung back.

Hart finally spoke. "What the hell are you two cowboys doing here?"

His perceived failures during The Tableau murders and the university embezzlement case, not to mention the macabre death of his paid informant, had prompted the Met to cast him out into the far and desolate north, a vile wilderness that served up hardship on a daily basis. With this move, his ambitions for a career in the metropolis were thwarted. He could not see it as a positive loan (in the sense young footballers undergo) to gain strength and experience. Dove, Periwinkle and, to a degree Penny, were innocents, a reminder of something he wanted to avoid: a stimulant. Irritability, flashbacks and sleepless nights accompanied a feeling of detachment and desperate loneliness. He reflected on whether Penny might be in a similar place. He didn't want to see people at all, yet he knew the efficacy of company.

Hart took a second then resumed his tirade. "I want you out of here, back in the south where I belong."

Dove acknowledged Hart's slip with some sympathy. Hart was suffering.

Drawing on his academic studies in criminology and an uncomfortable though erroneous feeling he was a source of amusement he assumed a composure fitting his rank and an erudition that caught Dove unawares. Yet, he seemed to be addressing another audience, one that wasn't present.

"One would think that historically serial murders may have promoted such fantasies as lycanthropy! The dismemberment or awful wounding of fellow humans may have been hard to take in, and thus monsters were created. What we can't understand, or cope with, we invent other mechanisms for – symbols if you like. The werewolf may be one such symbol; dragons another."

Dove tried another smile, one of approval. He felt unable to broach the subject they had come to talk about. He never did for somewhere in the mechanism of Hart's tortured mind a switch was thrown. He moved from Freudian analysis to fucking and blinding.

"All we know is Gemma was barely alive and that she claimed to see a werewolf. After a friggin' night out in these parts it's hardly surprising-it's like a fuckin zoo." He apologised to his imagined audience. "Sorry, it's horrible – on a par with The Tableau." He could barely say the last word. His wounds were open and obvious.

To help him find a bridge Dove stepped in. "What has pathology or forensics got to say?"

This was not the best case for him to be involved with at any level.

Hart didn't reply. Hart wasn't listening. He wasn't going to answer. Instead, he said, "The killer is extremely fly, cunning as hell."

Then with a cracked throat he told them to leave.

Raed watched as the men exited. Their body language implied it had been a wasted meeting.

Hart caught a glimpse of his new boss. Her face showed concern.

He was sitting stock still, shamefaced, frozen in situ. She couldn't be sure, but was that a tear in his eye?

## Chapter 8

Penny was in exile, though he had capitalised on his experience by publishing an art historical potboiler. His memory faltered at times and his motivation shifted rapidly from full-on to full stop. Halfway up the stairs he would forget what he was going for. He started to make lists before shopping. On his return he would unpack the groceries to find key items he'd forgotten. Sometimes he went back, at others he sat in the chair.

His book, *Dark Art*, owed much to an early conversation with Hart, and paid lip service to the Dark Art movement. He credited Hart and others, as well as Gallery X in Dublin and the online Macabre Gallery.

Situating snippets from The Tableau Case alongside gothic representations – vampires, witches, monsters, werewolves in folklore history – he pitched it down, spiced it up, threw aside academic jargon, and had a money-spinner. A reviewer described it as: 'Stephen King for pseudo-academics without the moral underpinning'. The reviewer giveth and taketh away. It was publicity.

His main thrust was the representations of demons that haunted his painted world and, more recently his dreams;

fiends and fallen angels, demons that lived across the road, representations of the monsters and the weird that have filtered into popular culture. Shapeshifters were everywhere. It was tempting to throw in a prime minister or two – they changed so fast. The Tory Party seemed to have had as many leaders in the last few years as Middlesbrough Football club had had coaches and managers. A fan suggested revolving doors for both the manager's office and for Number 10.

His book. He wanted a wider meaning of art and its history, ditching notions of good, bad, high and low, was a prime mover. He directed his gaze towards tabloid journalism and sensational Victorian images from such as *Illustrated Police News*. Art is omnipresent, its purpose and reception manifold.

The theme of murders most foul and suicide helped to sell it. The frontispiece – a woodcut of a man laid below a suspended guillotine burning through the rope with a candle challenged the boundaries between fact and fiction, the exciting and the dreadful. The victim becomes a fiction. Two images were from the twin's files.

So far, the police hadn't examined the provenance of the images. Hart's copy with a personal thank you was still in the wrapping, unsent. Penny made great store of the fact they had solved The Tableau Case, and that representations convey meanings not immediately apparent. Meaning has to be teased out.

He included images from the *Garden of Earthly Delights*: aspects of becoming animal, metamorphosis, the weird, the diabolical; Spring-heeled Jack vomiting blue and white flames; gory woodcuts from *The London Illustrated News*, and penny bloods (or penny-dreadfuls) that due to inflation, now sell for 65p. The editor advised he delete the last sentence about inflation. Transgression, he argued in his opening words, was familiar to art and artists. He deleted it.

The publisher accepted *Dark Art* as a teaser and hyped it up as the forerunner to his big book on The Tableau Case.

All the pieces had come together, production planning had been smooth, and in nine months *Dark Art* was in the shops. Writing helped alleviate the repeated graphic recollections of the twins' gallery with its display. Dead art, dead bodies. Not really nightmares – they belonged to his day, powerful photographic flashes.

The advance for The Tableau work, his lived thriller, bothered him. He was struggling, but the publisher's patience held out. Draft chapters, which required editing, began to take shape. He had all his material and hoped for a first draft ready within six months. His obsessive rate of work surprised them. It avoided him having to go out.

Penny worked at it in fits and starts. The fits were manic, the starts stressful, the stops unsettling. The material supplied by the twins was enough to go on. In fact he had more than the police. He needed a moratorium, a gap between the event and the writing. The editor, a war films geek, remarked that there was a period of quiet after World War Two then a massive upsurge of books and war films from around 1950 until 1971. They began with escape stories such as *The Wooden Horse* and ended with *Zulu* which heralded a different world. The analogy was apt and appreciated. The publisher couldn't wait five years.

His agent had advised he played up the tell-all aspect. The elevator pitch with its art-criticism-meets-true-crime-slant, and emphasis on his lived experience of real horror was a selling point. The writing experience was both upsetting and a release.

## Chapter 9

Hart's old work partner, Lucy Freeman, called Penny to talk about the university fraud case. Her take on the fraudster case was that it wasn't exactly Nick Leeson or Crazy Eddie who they'd copped; rather it was a middle-aged woman, a university administrator. The press gained no access to detailed information. The big boys and girls who had ignored the embezzlement escaped with early retirement, while those at the top received a large pay-out. Freeman mentioned in glowing terms his colleagues Dove and Periwinkle.

The fraud case. He's almost forgotten this earlier case, the evidence left in his pigeonhole, the problems caused by holding onto the file, and finally his novel way of solving it. Detectives Freeman and Hart were still in the dark he suspected and her call was aimed at a possible slip up or confession that would incriminate him. Do the police ever take time off?

Freeman passed on to the new investigators cases that carried rewards and information. To reciprocate, they turned out to be considerate with their intelligence.

Dove and Periwinkle's new careers meant that they had found a niche that gave their experience and contacts an outlet.

"We don't spy on adulterers unless we want to nail them for other reasons."

That was good news.

She said little about the fact that Dove and Periwinkle had access to the underworld and upwards; networks that reached across the differing stratum or castes of society. She chatted. They'd resolved a case involving the selling of chickens and turkeys as organic, when the truth lay in an abysmal crowded farmyard shed in 'Hantsharing' (Penny assumed that was Periwinkle's word). Dove was a key witness. The verdict was guilty. Fittingly, the law cooped the farmer up like his hens as a resident in one of Her Majesty's overcrowded prisons. Dove said banged up. The Animal Welfare Act saw to his cruelty.

The farmer had threatened them. "I'll see you fuckers off when I get out."

Freeman assessed that the scally had best do his homework on Dove during his time within before he attempted anything as silly. Penny considered warning him. She lamented the problem of prison. The turkey man's incarceration would help build his competencies in crime, upgrade his résumé, and prepare him for better and more lucrative jobs. If he were wise, Freeman added, he'd forget his threat and draft a book.

Pleased to hear from Lucy Freeman, he suspected the call was aimed at digging information. He was more pleased he didn't slip up.

## Chapter 10

*'I would like to say to those who think of my pictures as serene*
*[...] that I have imprisoned the most utter violence in every inch*
*of their surface.'*
(Mark Rothko)

Only after his shopping trip to the store did the effects of Penny's diagnosed trauma – the numbness, vivid clicks, the disconnected damaged feeling, and irritability that had flowed back and forth – begin to ebb away. It would return, but he felt he'd turned a corner. The Rogerian therapy and counselling hadn't worked; the writing of his little book was more efficacious.

He was grateful to his doctor for allowing him the counselling experience gratis. The counsellor was another story. The self-medicating was fun for a while, but that had to stop.

In the future he would undergo therapy to help him chase out the devils, or at least some of them. Others he wished to remain. The open spaces between shelves, the bright lights and people milling around offered a kind of security. Here was sanctity. A visit to the Tate Modern helped, too. There, he bathed in the colour and serenity of the Rothko paintings. What lay beneath? Demons? Art was the way forward.

A new Penny was going to emerge from the store. All the counselling in the world couldn't have achieved what Betty and Rita at the tills enabled that day. Therapy could indeed take differing forms. He expected Rogers would have agreed that the criterion could change. Where Jeanine, Rogers's advocate, failed, Betty and Rita gave him hope. The university faded away; the visions of the carcasses, and The Tableau killers' art, lessened in strength, though the pathetic image of Brownleigh stayed.

Combined with running miles, arguing with everyone, binge-drinking (effective in suppressing the nightmares and desires), he was also overeating. The new authorial Penny would have surprised Dove and Periwinkle with his take on werewolves, his theories on the lunar month, and menstruation. His nightmares weren't as erotic as Fuseli's; more in keeping with Cranach's crawling werewolf carrying off a child – bestial, horrid, unforgiving. But was it really a werewolf, or a man banished? Insane? A cannibal?

## Chapter 11

Hart closed his office door behind him. Then he changed his mind, opened it again, and went back inside. Raed had left the office to attend some awful function. Is that what promotion offered? Endless handshaking with officials, bureaucrats, councillors, all the while smiling?

He opened the beginnings of his personal file on Gemma Bateman. Here was violence, real violence, yet a theatrical component existed. In Hart was a desire to create a more peaceful world. Just a few years since, people had fainted while watching *Titus Andronicus*; people had walked out during Sarah Kane's *Cleansed*. He loved the theatre – the Greek dramas with their off-stage violence – Euripides, Sophocles.

He watched *Cleansed*. Incest, electrocution, forced sex reassignment and other atrocities. The playwright Sarah Kane committed suicide at twenty-eight years old.

The content was what he saw as a part of his job. He wasn't sure he had the stomach for it. He read up on the play and on Kane. He felt worse. The voice in his head was telling him to walk away. The voice was persuasive, corrosive.

He needed to confront these issues. At that moment he closed the files and walked around the town, and out towards Magpie Wood. He turned there rather than walk to the cliffs. The towering cliff frightened him. Did the heights worry him? He didn't want to test out his theory. He turned there and past the Animal Rescue Centre. A notice outside said: *A pet might help*. He paused and then went back to his digs.

\\\

The store awakening heralded a chain of events which led both to recovery, more bad dreams (though bad dreams as a product of writing and desire rather than desperation), a change of direction, and a new murder case. Penny was hungry for a challenge.

He browsed the drinks section. A notice read: 'Chablis. Buy two bottles and get fifty per cent off a third.' Two bottles went into the basket. His search for a third proved futile: no more Chablis. Two went back on the shelf. Back in the fruit and vegetable section tomatoes on the vine were £2 – expensive. However, a note stated: 'Buy one and get a cucumber free!' Beneath a poster stating 'Eat Sensibly' were the tomatoes. The tomatoes went into the basket. The cucumber rack was empty. The tomatoes went back on the shelf.

Wandering aimlessly, Penny picked up a stick of natural liquorice and headed for the check-out. The queue was long; two check-outs available. There were Betty and Rita (it said so on their badges). They rotated away from the customers and adopted a position comfortable for conversation with each other.

"So you heard about it, Betty?"

"I did, Rita. He should be put away. The police do nowt!"

"I know what I'd do to him."

Penny trembled; his curiosity aroused. As they spoke, the queue built up behind him. He began to feel uncomfortable. To allay such a feeling, he envisaged what their take might be on what they'd do to the criminal. What atrocious torment did they have in store for the anonymous deviant? Waterboarding was current and popular, and nasty in the extreme. He eyed the natural liquorice in his basket. It was fuzzy. Should he turn back? The pressure of a queue was building behind him and held him in situ. He leaned forward and drummed on the belt to emphasise his desire to pay for it and leave. Panic ensued. His drumming stopped, his chest tightened, his breathing became shallow and cold beads of sweat ran down his sides.

Betty wasn't finished conversing. Her cold stare warned him off. She turned her head back to Rita. Penny placed his tongue on the roof of his mouth and breathed deeply through his nose. One, two, three in, hold for four, one, two, three, four, five, out.

With a hand gesture that said not yet to the customer in front, she continued, "She was a nice girl."

"True. She wouldn't harm a soul."

The tall thin woman with a long, cream-coloured Macintosh at the front of Rita's queue left her shopping on the belt and walked out. Agitated flitting between queues followed; not alarming, though nerve-wracking.

Turning away from Betty, Rita snorted at the arsy cow and cleared her shopping away. Penny wondered if he, the perpetrator, would survive their planned and systematic torment (which might include queuing endlessly in the shop while they nattered) or aiming to find the cut price Chablis to the other two, the cucumber with the tomatoes. He began to question whether the conversation was actually happening. Then, having cleared the belt, things settled down.

Betty wheeled her chair round to face Penny and said, "Next."

He thought of a Jacques Brel song and its lyrics. His knees were turning to jelly. He placed the liquorice and his membership card on the empty belt. With hindsight, he claimed that it was her frostiness that brought about a renewed sense of reality in him, one of being back in the real world, a world of co-operative vengeance, one of retaliation by ordinary people out to right the wrongs of the really unpleasant. Magical reality it wasn't, but was it fiction? He paid; he left. That night he would go without a drink.

Back at home he ate liquorice. For the first time in weeks he enjoyed listening to music.

Outside the window the moon was full, the sky a sorry patch beckoning more rain. He turned the volume up and listened to the global sound of a Leeds-based group called Samay. The rhythms fascinated him, the blend of classical India and jazz. He clicked his tongue along with the intricate sound of the tabla. Fiction was the way forward.

## Chapter 12

Without speaking, Periwinkle and Dove strolled back to their digs. For professional reasons, illness, or spite, Hart had blocked the opening of any meaningful conversation, and in doing so, any communication that might have helped his case and theirs. The information that they wished to share remained unshared.

A dying moon barely lit the terraced streets but offered a friendly light. The air was damp and a sea fret coming in.

Periwinkle broke the quiet: "Hart hasn't learned from his experiences. This is an awful business, and he's not ready for it." He adjusted his beret on his head. "Do you think we should call Penny?"

Dove wasn't quite sure.

Periwinkle wondered if Penny, might welcome putting his intellectual self to work on lycanthropy. He too might be suffering. It could be chancy.

Dove thought about it. "His pastoral experience might come in handy with Max?"

Dealing with young adults wasn't their thing. They decided for the time being to wait.

In the uncomfortable damp of that evening, another attack occurred.

Unperturbed by the changing weather, Dove and Periwinkle had crossed the fields to the clifftops above Hummersea Scar. Dove spent time staring out at his precious mother ocean. While judging wind speeds and wave swells, the North Sea weather responded with maximum force, and retreat from the precarious tops became inevitable. Before they headed across the fields away from the storm, he admired the swelling tide.

"We return to the sea!" The swirling wind snatched his words and swept them far out across the tide. Periwinkle guessed the faint noise he heard was to do with the sea and nodded approvingly.

The distressed woman bleeding from the throat found them. She saw Dove first as she staggered out of a field on their left by a farm. He went to help. She was holding her neck with one hand. There were dark patches of blood on her coat and hand, which she refused to take away from her throat. Dove called an ambulance. It went somewhere else. Locals arrived to help and to ogle.

She appeared incapable of speech. Her coat was moist with fret and blood-spattered. He placed her in her late fifties, smartly dressed, her coat an indistinguishable colour in the dark. The blood Dove observed was beginning to dry.

He calmed the lady. The paramedics arrived as one woman suggested calling the air ambulance. They whisked her away, ensuring she had hospital care.

Dove noticed one or two onlookers smiling. Was it schadenfreude or something deeper? He shrugged it off. Probably relief. It could've been him. Then he thought maybe not.

Raed joined the volunteers with two uniformed police and introduced herself to all present with a sturdy handshake. She marked out an area for a search as soon as it was light. Dove gave a statement.

Focussing on Dove, she asked, "Can you and your colleague join me tomorrow in my office, at ten a.m.?"

Dove heard it as an instruction – civil, but a command, nonetheless. He saw no reason to countermand it. He thought she was sound. "Be there at ten, ma'am."

She found Dove's gruff manner personable. She needed to find out why they were in Loftus.

The group dispersed shortly after muttering to each other. Weather reports showed no letting up. The night had descended into a misty jet black as Raed walked to the yard. In her office, damp and defeated by the hindrance the weather had caused, she asked for a cup of tea, changed out of her sodden clothing, and put on warm tracksuit trousers and a woolly jumper worn over a t-shirt. Then she called Hart's mobile. His answerphone was on.

Raed's reputation was not one earned for simply kicking criminal butt. Fair, but exacting, her own colleagues needed to beware if they fouled up.

"Hart, I want you in my office first thing."

Once inside their digs, Dove and Periwinkle continued their conversation on the inclusion of Penny.

Periwinkle led. "It's just an idea – talking to the young girls and boys who might know Max, or anything, might well fit within his skills and competencies."

He could, of course, cause mayhem.

Periwinkle's slant on Penny's teacherly language raised a smile. The fact remained he could do it. They had not discussed their reasons for being there. Dove knew that could, and would, lead to more misunderstanding. That Hart hadn't asked them formally why they were in the area was out of character.

Jack, an old mate, and an ex-navy master-at-arms had written to Dove to say he was anxious about Max, his teenage son. Max was ill at ease, behaving oddly. Adolescent problems were not Dove's forte but his willingness to help an old comrade was. The spur – that Max might be involved with strange goings-on and drugs at school – clinched his interest. Jack, a retired naval police officer (a 'crusher') could spot the signs of drug use. He wasn't sure Max was on anything.

"If it is a bit of dope, then so be it." He described his son as a chatty lad who had recently been uncommunicative. Age, of course, might be a consideration. Jack was of a liberal disposition, despite his military background. "It isn't bullying. I just know. Max is showing signs of withdrawal. He is anxious about going to school. He is frightened, or guilty of something." With hesitation, he finished, "I'm keeping an open mind."

The chance to catch up with an old friend prompted Dove to sign up.

Jack's briefing ended with the following, "Not sure if you've seen any coverage of the so-called werewolf attacks in the area? I suspect that Max knows something about these weird goings-on. He seems drawn to the shadow side."

"Werewolves, you say? I'll see you as soon as." This was different to their normal PI stuff. They could poke around and see what came up.

On arrival, they called in on Jack. Max appeared and said a quick hello then disappeared just as quickly upstairs to his room. He was pleasant enough, though eager to get away. That was in keeping with lads his age. To the boy they would be old codgers. Jack offered them a room. Dove thought it better to be elsewhere. They found digs in a four-bedroomed house.

They were still debating Penny's inclusion. Both had misgivings. The plus was that he knew the area. He had knowledge of lycanthropy. Periwinkle treasured his gift of *Dark Art* and had read it more than once. It wasn't long, and the pictures enthralling.

After the events of the evening they were already involved. He kept his inner thoughts to himself, but a can of worms came to mind. In that respect he was close to Hart's thinking.

Should they get back on a train? Dove began to think he was a suspect. If they left, would they be hauled back?

✸

Dove tried ringing Penny again. "C'mon pick up you get."

The phone clicked and a familiar voice said hello.

"Ronnie-boy. Dove here of Dove and Periwinkle, private investigators."

"Ah Dove." Penny's melodramatic tone spoke of superior officers addressing the 'men', that is in the theatre of plays rather than war.

Dove fought against saying 'ah, Penny dear boy', and won. He kept it straightforward. "We are in your old neck of the woods, the northeast-a place called Loftus." He hung back. He waited for a briefing on Loftus and environs. It never came. He decided on a prompt. "Have you read about the Werewolf Case?"

"No."

The answer was too brief. "We're here helping Jack, an old colleague. His young son Max has problems." Dove explained Max might be involved in, or know about, the werewolf killing.

No reaction.

He tried assertive. "If you're busy I can call another time? Periwinkle sends his regards." About to hang up he got a result.

"Can you imagine a group of retired gentlefolk killing people out of boredom?"

Enough was enough. Dove replied, "If you can't be arsed, we'll leave it."

"What you up to?" Penny asked.

Dove explained again, spicing it up for Penny's benefit. His manoeuvring and patience paid off, sort of.

"Historically, lycanthropy goes back a long way. It is mentioned in Burton's *Anatomy of Melancholy* in 1621. It has roots in medieval Europe. Loftus has a long history, in the alum and jet industries, and ironstone mining. That brought about the birth of Middlesbrough – and it's subsequent death! It goes back a long way, Anglo-Saxon times. Archaeologists uncovered a princess's grave there. Interesting place. It's between Carlin Howe and Skinningrove. Key place in the birth and history of biostratigraphy."

He finished on a crescendo, an exclamation perhaps, but to Dove he didn't sound interested at all.

Dove's grasp of cheap psychology came into play, his ace up the sleeve… a joker more like. "You'll never guess who is on the investigating team."

Penny was mumbling so Dove soldiered on.

"Hart and a policewoman, who is without doubt his superior in rank and class."

"I expect Hart is unaware of her value. Is he okay? He knows about werewolves. Does he know that people up there don't talk, and I don't mean they're non-verbal unless the police are involved."

"Hart's struggling and he's resentful."

"What can I do?"

To Dove it sounded like a defeated man talking. "Your pastoral skills would come in handy" Dove's creeping appeal to Penny's life skills fell flat. He decided to stick to threats and drop any psychological tactics in future.

Penny underwent a moment of anxiety as he weighed up the notion of pastoral skills, managing behaviour, safeguarding, speaking, leadership and spiritual skills. Others too came to mind. He wondered if he could take advantage of them for his own issues.

"Yes, that's fine," Penny said eventually. "See you in a couple of days. I've got something urgent on."

Dove wasn't sure at all where Penny was coming from. He decided to keep it simple. "Be good to catch up. Bring warm gear. The winter's setting in already. I'll text you the address. Can book you a room if you wish?"

"Yes, that's fine." He rang of.

Dove threw the phone on the couch and addressed Periwinkle. He was about to say he wasn't sure at all it was a good idea to bring Penny in. He wasn't sure if his success was a victory or a curse.

He chose to express his mixed feeling inadvertently. "Penny is coming up." Then, after a delay. "He sounds different."

The conversation with Penny had been a strange and disjointed experience. Probably wise not to analyse it.

Penny, self-styled sleuth, up-and-coming novelist and literati, authority on anything including Loftus and lycanthropy, was facing early 'retirement'.

The new universities promoted staff to upper management, or lecturers to readers, to get them out of the way or amend a cock-up – usually theirs. Early retirement got rid of thorns in their side or alternatively, in his opinion, remove those who were successful. Following a template employed by the recent government and their reshuffles, the idea was to keep the inadequate.

Retirement was what he needed, but it didn't help. It hurt, though it was exactly what this thorn wished for. He wouldn't miss the admin – the tedious meetings, the preparation, the marking. The offer was on the table. Brigid, head of fine art and now deputy dean, called to ask how he was. No doubt Brigid would chase it up.

She said thanks for his little book. "I love it." She tried hard to keep it light-hearted.

To his ear, Brigid's Ulster Scots voice meant that little sounded jovial.

"The degree show was a mess," she continued. "The conceptual piece involving a faux boa constrictor, a whale's penis, and a sealed box labelled *killer bees* that buzzed loudly went horribly wrong on the opening night. Actually, it started before that on the bus as the student brought the box of killer bees down for the hanging."

Penny missed the mayhem, though a day later, he'd forgotten about the university. His ability to focus came and went. The cold nip brought out his jumper and beloved scarf collection. He began to think of writing. He'd wanted to author a novel for years to add to his academic profile.

In his mind the store had been a revelation and he was willing to accept that it all really happened. He looked at the receipt. He turned it over and read slowly: *liquorice*. Then he turned it back and crossed out *theophany*. That was the day of revelations, the day of Betty and Rita. In the hall mirror he noticed his eyes were bright, his face flushed. He switched on his laptop with intent. He thought of killer bees.

He opened a new document, typing *Wholesale Slaughter* at the top. He centred it, then moved it right.

He sat back, bit into the last of his liquorice and gazed blankly out of the window at the white orb of the moon. He moved his title to the right. Then he wrote. As he wrote, the effects of the panic attack he felt in the shop dissipated. Here was a way forward. His protagonist would resolve his dilemmas. Oldman – the name was a done deal – would enable his escape.

*Oldman awoke to hear his favourite song by The Platters; his daughter's shrill soprano murdering the tune. He tried to smile. The muscles on his face wouldn't form the necessary shape. He tried to move his mouth – nothing. He couldn't speak.*

*The coffin was spacious.*

*John and Yoko's* Imagine *preceded the* Cantata Herz und Mund und Tat und Leben, *which was played at his wedding. It faded, and there was quiet. Was it the Westminster choir that sang it so well? Lastly, Cat Stevens's version of* Morning has Broken *trilled around the crematorium, which he could not see. He assumed it was a crematorium, in keeping with his last wishes.*

*Familiar and unfamiliar voices joined in. The eulogy was touching. His daughter Bridie's voice sounded muffled but demonstrated wit and grace. He wanted to applaud. She highlighted things he'd quite forgotten about during his time as a dad, before he and Helen split up, and he became a non-person. It was all over with no audible sobs. He prepared to travel into the flames…*

Penny coughed. "Far too Poe." It wasn't Poe and he wasn't C. Auguste Dupin, Poe's fictional detective, though he was working on it. His credentials were quite thin, his enthusiasm boundless.

He crumpled the printed page and threw it across the room directly into the small waste bin, taking pride in the fact his aim was accurate. Old skills were finding their way back. He turned back to his laptop, deleting the introduction, then went across to the bin, rescued it, smoothed it out, and placed it under a paperweight. He started again.

A tale unfolded of killing; a co-operative involved in bumping bad people off. He was barely into his introduction when he hit a major snag. How does one remove people 'officially'? Kill them, then obtain death certificates, get administrators to accept the documents before burial, clear an autopsy, sort out wills and probate?

The kin must notify family doctors immediately. If death was unexpected, or happened outside of care or a hospital, the police contacted; the local registry office within five days; a funeral arranged within five days of the date of death?

Who were the perpetrators? Pensioners – bored pensioners. No, retired professionals; early retired, still mentally and physically active, still wanting a challenge and well-to-do. They were all in a residential home. No, posh sheltered accommodation, apartments in a country house.

*Reynold's Hall was an old family seat divided into superior apartments, the interiors in keeping with the magnificent eighteenth-century building set in parkland.*

Too cosy. Yet, soft focus crime fiction was in. The only way forward for his plot was to have the doctor, the lawyer, the civil servant *et al* as killers, or party to the killing. The professionals had to do the work. Include a military man with contacts, or those with a professional network. It was fiction, and stranger things happen.

They would be involved in the removal of nuisances, not all of them nuisances, just the bad ones rather than those who caused annoyance. Mortality displacement of a kind?

Oldman, his hero, an ageing professional, a man of integrity and pure intelligence, would go undercover. He could become a cooperative member. No, that wouldn't work.

The phone rang. He ignored it. It was the damned university. Human resources had called him about his retirement, and did he need help over any financial issues? He left it.

He was excited about his new venture. He was hungry and went downstairs to eat. He didn't bother to check the caller's ID.

## Chapter 13

Oblivious to the cold snap, three t-shirted teenage boys were hanging out in Loftus market square, their bikes thrown randomly on the ground. A police officer pulled over, parked, and moved them on. He checked, in a good-natured way, to see if they were carrying tinnies in their packs. Their past experience meant they didn't give him any lip.

"No, sir." Kyle, the smallest one, a sandy-haired boy, spoke for all. In a gesture of openness, he began to unzip his bag.

A tall pale-faced boy never spoke.

George, with longish hair, grinned obligingly and offered his backpack.

"No worries, boys."

They picked up their bikes and straddled them. About to move off, Kyle addressed George. "Wonder where Max is." He sounded worried.

"Don't know, Kyle. Think his dad's grounded him for crimes against the state. Maybe sorting his life out?"

The tall, thin boy straddled his bike. He knew the name Max. He couldn't place him. As the other two rode off toward Hummersea Lane, the boy pushed his bike off and followed, catching them up easily and easing off the pace.

Max was the boy whose voice talked to him when he was in his room alone. Initially, he forgot Max as he cycled along, riding into his latest BMX challenges. Then it came back: Max was one of his computer games, or something to do with the Olympics. He didn't ask the others.

Pulling their bikes off the road into a field, they sat down. George had some grass in the small pocket on top of his backpack that they shared. Then they cycled back home. The temperature was plummeting as they rode. The tall, pale-faced boy wanted to get home to the security of his laptop. He felt threatened and couldn't suss out the reason.

Max, his homework done, had been watching *Lost Boys,* a vampire movie from the 1980s. He had his pyjamas on and was ready for bed. He appeared amicable enough, engaging Dove and Periwinkle in a short conversation with a hint of sardonic humour regarding their relationship with his dad, a humour that evidenced his knowledge of naval catchphrases. Max was comfortable dealing with adults, that was for sure.

Jack explained to Dove that he allowed him to watch it and saw no point in banning stuff. Max had been having restless nights, talking in his sleep, but in the mornings as fresh as a daisy and ready for school – until recently.

"He loves all that horror, blood and guts. Can't see anything in it myself and never have." Jack looked to Dove for agreement.

Dove wasn't sure. The boy seemed confident. What then was disrupting his sleep?

## Chapter 14

Penny picked up *Dark Art*. He opened it and read: *Dedicated to Lillian*. He scanned a short passage on shapeshifters in the visual arts, from medieval graphics to Mystique in *X-Men*. Finally, he felt that compulsion, the one that led him to investigate The Tableau murders; that feverish buzz that told him he was onto a story; the desire to outwit Hart. He could collaborate with his mates again.

Dove's invite hadn't curtailed his daydreaming or his isolation, the intrusive thoughts, the moments of irritability with inanimate objects. It sent him off on another tack.

The follow-up to *The Tableau Twins* – *The Werewolves of Loftus*.

Penny was staring intently at the opening lines of the first chapter of his great novel. It began:

*The undercover work at Reynold's Hall was handed to me by my boss, Griggs. I was to infiltrate after the second suspicious death.*

He crossed out the letter I and then moved his text into the third person. I, he mused, was another shifter.


*Oldman was in Griggs's office. The boss looked stern. The briefing was short. He handed Oldman a file.*

*"Their profiles are in there. All upstanding citizens."*

*"What am I chasing here?"*

*"An informant. It's odd, Oldman. We had a list delivered with five names on it of victims and of suspected perps. All the former scallies – to use current parlance – the latter respected citizens. Two of the former are dead. Post-mortems revealed nothing. Neither was ill."*

*Griggs picked up a memo from his desk.*

*"Death one: a dodgy dealer on the periphery of politics. Death certificate states heart failure. No sign of toxins barring his politics and views on gender." Griggs didn't smile. "Boys play with trucks, girls: dolls." He paused. "Everything was in order. In truth a nasty creep of a man that had no obvious ailments. Death number two: a member of the press, an investigative journalist Mary McKean."*

*Oldman recognised the name. McKean was a female Theroux who took the right wing to task.*

*"McKean choked on her own vomit."*

*"What was she investigating?" Oldman asked.*

*"Her laptop, her notes are missing. McKean was a light drinker. She had consumed a good bottle or more of Scotch. We can assume she was going to blow the cover of yet another army of idiots."*

*Oldman considered the two. There was no pattern, and with only two a pattern could not be discerned. But it did seem odd.*

One complete ne'er do well and a fairly well-respected member of the press, a freelancer.

"And you believe the informant came from inside?"

"Oldman, these people are killers – the residents Bingham, Fielding, Stead, and Jack David. They're smart. They're our suspects. Unusual suspects in this case, but don't underestimate them. And yes, I do."

"If they are responsible, why don't we simply pull them in for questioning?"

"They don't pull the trigger, as it were. They're planners." Oldman avoided a negative comment about policy and planning but paused to write something down. "Someone up there in the system is working it. I intend find out who. Below them is another tier who do the dirty work and clean up. I have my suspicions. There are fresh faces up there with Lawson, people I don't know. I'll dig around. Someone among those musketeers has a conscience. Find out and blow their game apart."

"Reynold's Hall sounds very posh," Oldman mused. Before Griggs could reply, he continued. "Who authorised this job?"

Griggs looked uncomfortable. "I did, though Lawson, top man as he will be, briefed partially." Griggs avoided any further explanation. "It is posh. You'll move into an apartment in the west wing. We'll furnish it as best we can. I'll send an inventory. Oh, and here are the estate details – the usual estate agent speak."

"And contact?"

"With me only. Any techy stuff contact Hayley. Report back with a no-contract phone. There's something amiss here, Oldman, and it's coming from upstairs. People lobbying for power. None of this gels."

Oldman felt a twinge of distrust. In his estimation Lawson was a slippery customer. Griggs's discomfort was apparent. Griggs terminated the meeting by handing him the keys. Oldman left with more than a bad feeling. He went to view his new home.

Reynold's Hall was indeed splendid, the facilities and services excellent. The interiors were complementary; the high-end kitchens redundant for most as the dining room served great food. The list went on: private bar, gym studio, and what the twelve current residents dubbed 'the games room', in effect a lounge. The view of the Downs was breathtaking. Oldman paid cash. That might have been a mistake, a breach of protocol. Protocol was news. He hated the word. The residents didn't do cash.

He had never seen the like. The interiors were in keeping with the majestic Palladian front and gardens. Symmetry abounded and though internally modernised in terms of function it nodded towards a classical past. Ornate cornices and panelling everywhere.

He pulled in in his battered Tahiti-blue Triumph TR8, the English Corvette, and watched a funeral cortege go past. The residents (he assumed they were residents) wore black and slow marched past him with a coffin to a burial ground, to 'shake hands with dust and call the worm his kinsman'. Oldman felt good about recalling Blair's graveyard poem, yet curious about the funeral. He wasn't keen on Blair's writing but liked Blake's illustrations to the text. The bone orchard didn't appeal at all, and if it was a portent then it was well timed.

Odd coincidence, he thought, counting the mourners and aiming to clock faces. No one looked his way and he went inside.

The hall was empty. He scouted around, checking the rooms, and matching them with his shortlist: Fielding, Bingham, Jack David and Stead. It didn't feel right. Then he went to his own *room. He shook the bad feelings off and settled in a comfy chair. Security cameras abounded outside but nothing showed internally, at least nothing he could suss. Ivy clung to the outside and around the tower, its tendrils seeking small cracks in the structure. Most likely it held the building together.*

*Resident thirteen felt uneasy. Who was responsible for the leak? He couldn't beat a confession out of twelve retired gentlefolk. Could he?*

Penny was still working on the details of how a group of killers could circumvent the law. What drove them to kill? Was it Ealing revisited? Was Ealing for the twenty-first century a bit cheesy? Murder was a serious business, and Stead, the designated leader, was a strong, complex and tricky adversary according to his notes. The rose-tinted domestic 'noir' was current. He had something more sinister in mind.

## Chapter 15

All was quiet in Loftus over the next few days. Reports filtered in of the sightings of monstrous beings, but no criminal actions.

Raed found Hart's opinions intolerant. To him, finding any individual in an area that was full of grotesques was like finding a needle in a haystack. Raed had other ideas and an open mind. The people around there were badly done to by governments and southern-based economies. That was ongoing. Despite his bad start, Hart showed a good side. Her detailed reading of his profile pointed to an honest police officer – educated, correct – at odds with the force as she knew it. Three negative points had surfaced: he could bear a grudge, he wasn't comfortable in teams, and he held onto information. Time would tell.

The man, Penny, who had brought The Tableau Case to an end, held her attention. He sounded impish. She decided there and then if she were ever to meet him, she would keep him at arm's length. His profile was extensive, both in police files and in academia. Press articles on him abounded, and reviews of a little book. At a glimpse *Dark Art* suggested a morbid nature.

The attacks and murder all happened around dusk, not too late at night. They had the hallmark of a prank gone horribly wrong. Bearing in mind Hart's reticence to share, she mentioned her findings and thoughts in their meetings. She considered sending Hart to Middlesbrough, his hell on Earth, where a backlog of cases filled the in-trays. Middlesbrough was reputed to be the most dangerous town in the county. That would keep him occupied and away from his folktales and fiction. The local force was pleasant, hardworking; she liked the people. On the face of things, the north cared for its elderly, an integral part of her Islamic culture. The downside of her promotion was endless deskwork and an onerous social calendar when a return to active police work was beckoning. Things got in the way.

She stayed.

So did Hart.

Head down, Hart was leaving Raed's office when Dove and Periwinkle arrived at ten o'clock sharp. He cut his eyes to their attempt to be convivial, pushing past them as their heads bobbed a hello.

After signing in, they entered the small office. Both said, "Good morning, ma'am," and shook her hand.

The general public rarely addressed her as ma'am. She decided to be cautious.

Periwinkle led. "Grateful you could see us. It won't take long."

He told her of their reasons for being in Loftus. He filled in the details of why Hart resented their presence. He told her of Jack's concern for Max, and their connections to an old colleague. He left nothing out. Max, he concluded, knew something and it was troubling him.

She listened without responding. She imagined the touchline was a difficult one for these men. Raed's eyebrows furrowed when it clicked who they were. That aroused her inquisitiveness. She mentioned The Tableau murders and alluded to Penny.

"It was a troubling case for us and for the public. Your colleague has a certain reputation in the gutter press." She scanned the room. "Did you tell DI Hart why you were here?"

"We tried. Our case seemed small in contrast to the werewolf murder. We thought there might be a loose connection to the werewolf attacks."

"Periwinkle—?" She paused, waiting for a first name. She gestured to Dove for help. Periwinkle it was. She continued, "Adolescents could be party to the werewolf incidents. A death has now occurred – a murder. This is not a schoolkids' jape. It's a murder."

Periwinkle reported what they knew of Max. Dove filled in the gaps. She listened. Hart was silly to disregard these men.

In what appeared a throwaway remark, Periwinkle added, "It seems a shame in the circumstances, and somewhat counter-productive, that we are being tailed by your chaps."

Raed found it funny that the two men were aware of the fact. That bolstered her first impression of them: honest, forthright, and sharp. How did they become mixed up with that dreadful man, Penny?

Dove and he wanted space to manoeuvre, a day or two to speak to the boy. Raed didn't respond at first. She had grounds to talk to Max herself.

"From what you imply the boy is troubled." She was of the conclusion that she, with care, should start asking schoolkids specific questions.

The call came in while they talked, a conflab extending well beyond Raed's allotted time.

Dove's phone rang three times before he apologised and took the call. "It's Jack."

Jack was desperate. "Max has gone missing. He left early and didn't arrive at school. Dove, I'm really worried. This is not the boy I know."

Raed picked up her phone and began issuing instructions to staff. She terminated their meeting and asked Periwinkle to come in around lunchtime the next day, adding after a moment, "Both of you."

A respectful formality remained. The coincidence of their presence in Loftus bothered her. And she must check files on both, especially the one called Periwinkle.

\\\

While Raed put available constables out to search for Max, the mercury in the barometer dropped further and the fret thickened. They checked known schoolmates' houses; they skirted the district. The sea fog clung to their clothes, soaked them through and dampened their spirits, adding to the misery.

A small group of volunteers – friends of Jack's, including Dove in a greatcoat, and Periwinkle in an immense naval duffel coat – set off despite the inclement weather.

Raed talked to Liz Trout, the local headteacher. Max had been to see her the day or so before his disappearance, with something urgent to discuss. She was busy. The boy had then gone away and left the school before time. Raed and Liz accepted that schoolyard subcultures blocked information. All Liz could offer was that Max was a capable student; she doubted it was his work.

Raed looked at Liz. "Why did Max's visit stick in your mind?"

"Oh, that's simple. In an unprecedented move, Jim, my husband, had arrived at the school without notice. It was a first." Jim apparently attended only the necessary functions.

Raed listened carefully to her explanation. Jim had come to tell her he needed to go away for an emergency job in the Gulf.

"Max was outside my office when Jim arrived."

Raed imagined the kid was keen to impart something.

"Jim was only there ten minutes or so. When he left, the boy had already gone."

"Where in the Gulf was Jim off to?"

"The Gulf was all he said. A plumbing job. He even asked about the boy."

"Did he know him?"

"I doubt it. Jim was a rare sight at the school. He asked what was wrong with the kid."

Strange that his wife didn't ask where in the Gulf he was off to. She checked out Jim's status – self-employed plumber. Then she was sidetracked. Following Jack's guidelines, she coordinated the search: the local hangouts for kids his age, those public spaces and less public gang haunts and dens evidenced by the discarded empties, roaches, and pizza cartons. Signifying claimed territory and alliances, those youthful haunts bore their relevant graffiti tags. In red, *The Clan*, and *Death to the Five*, and in bright purple, *Death to the Clan*. In those confidential adolescent spaces tucked away from parents and prying adults, the youngsters swapped stories – strategic, heroic, and romantic; smoked, toked, and drank.

The police searched alongside civilians. Hart maintained a social distance from Dove and Periwinkle. The search was fruitless. Raed thanked everyone and called the search off. She forgot to look up Periwinkle.

## Chapter 16

*The residents treated Oldman to a polite reception: nibbles, good wine and an introduction. The four he had listed stayed on the fringes and studied him closely. They were private people. He chatted to all, including the four suspects: Stead, Jack David, Fielding and Bingham. They listened like hawks to his every word. He decided at that moment to take his time to build 'friendships' around the hall initially, then with the four, though that might seem deliberate. A man named Ken Briggs gave him his first opportunity.*

*Ken, ex-military and all tweed and brogues, was eager to talk. Introductions formed with the briefest of icebreakers. "I was a—"*

*One of the women, Luna, a colourful figure, declined to say anything about her past. No second name was offered, only that she liked food, hated the dark and confined spaces. "They tease me and call me Nightlight." Blue frock, pink cardigan and red boots topped by a yellow beanie; Luna looked magnificent. The beanie was a permanent feature. Wisps of blonde hair stuck out. The smile radiant. Luna Nightlight was lovely.*

*Ken was more gregarious. "Must give you my mobile number, old man." He did – a card with his rank and something about a* consultancy. "Still do military training weekends. One never knows who will invade from without or within."

"The Territorial Army?" Oldman's first question.

"Something like that." He winked as he spoke.

Oldman had to find a source of information in the small crowd that gathered. One of them had leaked the information. After two or three glasses, he thanked them all and excused himself. It was around seven o'clock. Bingham handed him his last glass, which he drained.

Bingham was a strange woman to him, clearly top-notch though dressed dowdily in a loose woolly pullover, and frayed jeans, her crowning glory a mass of reddish hair flecked with grey in a permanent tangle.

Tired, Oldman excused himself and escaped to his room, where he fell asleep for hours. He awoke muddle-headed and blurry-eyed. It was just short of midnight. It was wet and windy but weather doesn't cause mental uncertainty. Or perhaps it does. His phone lay by the bedside, and a text from Ken lit up the screen.

He also had the sense that he'd had a visitor. Things seemed out of place, if only slightly. Strong wine? He didn't remember giving Ken his number.

He dozed off again. Up early, he took a shower and sat down to think. Outside the window, the sun was breaking through. The view of the countryside retained a glow; his head still felt woozy.

That his arrival at the hall coincided with a funeral bothered him. Who had died? What of?

## Chapter 17

Walking to their digs, Dove and Periwinkle saw a lone figure cycling – a tall skinny kid. It was, in Dove's estimation, way past his bedtime.

"You ready for a nip, Periwinkle?"

"Cocoa will be fine."

They parted company. Periwinkle went inside and removed his glistening duffel coat and hung it to dry; Dove went to the pub seeking information, gossip, and a glass.

∖∖∖

Penny gazed from the train window at the changing landscape between Middlesbrough and Saltburn with affection, dampened by a personal sense of loss and anger. He thought of Dove and Periwinkle to whom he owed so much. He examined his own ability to steal the limelight and promised to try harder not to…

No black smoke belched from the coke ovens; the cooling towers on the right of the Trunk Road had gone. Coke ovens and cooling towers do not speak… voters do. The Tories still hadn't got the message. Yet they were running the country

– the people had spoken. The landscapes he envisaged on his last visit were destroyed, an act of iconoclasm. The blast furnace still stood for the time being, the wealth of England elsewhere. What art would it inspire? More artists, more words. He'd read that somewhere. Where was the revolution now, industrial and artistic? The train passed The Riverside, football, money.

He texted Dove to say he was in Saltburn. On the train he had read up on lycanthropy and was in a flutter. After dropping in on a friend, he would be in touch. It wasn't quite the truth. The dizziness that was manifest as he sat staring at his hometown; the sadness and joy he felt in equal quantities was replaced by hopeless emptiness. He rushed off the train at Saltburn and walked until he felt tired. It was difficult to concentrate, but as he walked, ignoring the scenery, he gradually began to focus on Oldman, his leading character and friend. He talked to himself, unaware of his declarations and their effect on passers-by. With Oldman as an imaginary friend he felt safer.

His personal distrust of folk was against the grain, and though partially aware it was a traumatic symptom, it felt real. He stopped talking.

In the police station, Raed made Dove and Periwinkle welcome.

In stereo they said, "Morning, ma'am."

There was gruffness in the smaller one's voice, his brusque manner contrasting with his melodic and well-spoken friend.

Dove's accent was one she couldn't pin down. He was from the south coast. His vocabulary, though clipped, was erudite. Dove, she judged, was always searching.

Raed began to like the two men. She wished they were with her as colleagues and was pleased they weren't against her. In her estimation, they were professionals. She formed her point of view quickly, though she was prepared to change her mind. Dr Death was lucky to have Dove and Periwinkle as friends. There must be more to the man to have such allies. Fact one: the media foisted the title on him, just as they did her own ass-kicker tag. Fact two: the media weren't to be relied on for the facts. Unfortunately, their importance meant they often worked together in a distrustful marriage of inconvenience.

Her inner dialogue on Penny remained an open issue. It was not as if he'd practised germ warfare like his namesake, Dr Death, the chap in Project Coast, or had breached medical ethics. Ethics however, she cautioned herself, were a problem for Penny. Hart's notes implied so. Stitched in and out of the minute details were hints of malpractice, though the indicators of collusion were speculative. It was enough having to build trust among the locals and elsewhere with a police force tainted by recent incidents, raising standards with a much-reduced force imperative. She chose her words carefully and noted her thoughts on stitching. Depends, she decided who was doing the sewing.

Tea came in a brown ceramic teapot. Raed had considered vanilla but decided on cardamon. Periwinkle was full of praise for her subtle choice.

Jack had already been in and offered a list of hideaways, the home addresses of aunties and uncles where Max might turn up. None had seen or heard from the boy. Jack wasn't the most talkative of folk, but plain-speaking and frank in his discussion of his son. Jack's fears had grown. Raed had stayed at the station late into the night and dealt with most calls herself. She was tired but she was still alert. Liz had volunteered a statement. Max's missed appointment nagged the headteacher. It nagged Raed, too. Raed checked her statement that she had had to go to a staff workshop. It all tallied.

Liz confirmed that Jim's testiness with the boy was unusual, probably due to him being called away at short notice. The fact that Jim had spoken crossly to the boy aroused Raed's curiosity. Liz's assertion that such was out of character was her word only. This was a woman who didn't know where her husband was working.

In half an hour Raed, Dove and Periwinkle were in accordance with one thing: that youths were involved, but not guilty of the werewolf crime itself, nor Max's disappearance. Nor were they party to information, or linked in. Raed was still cautious. The Max affair and the Werewolf case might be interconnected. Dove recalled the tall thin boy cycling home after ten o'clock at night after the attack on the 'old dear'.

"Would you recognise him?"

"I guess so. The bike was clearer than the boy." He growled *bike* and *boy*.

"Can you say more?"

"The bike appeared to be white and black. It was yellow and black, a BMX type. The boy was tall and skinny."

Raed smiled approvingly and picked up the phone. Speaking to the staff she said, "Keep an eye out for a tall skinny kid on a yellow and black BMX bike. He was out late in the evening when the attack occurred. No need to apprehend. Identify him if you can, nothing more. Report back to me."

Two boys were missing from school the next day. Max, and a tall thin boy who was playing games on his laptop, alone, lost in imaginings. He remembered the voice of Max now and how it spoke to him. Max's voice wasn't there anymore. His pale face was colourless in the artificial light cast by the green screen, the curtains closed. The game was on. As the colour drained further from his already pallid face, he chased his own ghost.

## Chapter 18

The biting cold was like a slap in the face as Penny stepped off the bus. He'd walked to Skelton from Saltburn, then felt okay to mount the next X4 bus. In a charity shop, he bought an oversized woolly jumper. He put it on in the shop, leaving the tag hanging outside the sleeve. Not bad for a fiver. Saltburn had been breezy and distinctively chilly. Loftus was dank and chillier. Visibility was poor. All he had was his backpack with his laptop, a book, basic essentials, and his green scarf looped around his neck in the manner of Aristide Bruant. Green rather than red, it was Penny's cabaret scarf.

On the bus from Skelton, a single streak of light had broken through the coastline mist and formed a narrow line between the cloud layers and the Cleveland Hills. The silvery light and warmth from the bus heaters provided a false sense of the weather. In his bag was *Medieval Monsters*, an old picture book that still attracted rave reviews. On the way to the pub he thought folk eyed him with suspicion.

He met Dove and Periwinkle at one thirty p.m. in The Arlington. The briefing was short; Penny said little.

His proposed pastoral role with Max had become needless. There remained the concern that his reputation might hamper things.

"We will need to let Raed know you are here." Dove said, reluctant to send Penny home.

It would have been a waste of time. Penny wasn't going anywhere.

Dove drove him to Skelton to get warm clothes from his cottage. At least that would stop Penny's teeth from chattering.

Back in the pub, Penny's lack of focus was apparent. A pint of beer loosened his tongue. "I read that the brewery has closed The Green Tree pub. Years ago, it was one of the best pubs in the area. The lads and I used to take the bus up there from Redcar and stagger back through Saltburn Valley Woods past what was the site of the old Marske Mill. That was spooky. A landmark demolished. It's tragic!" He dried up and stared around furtively. Artfully avoiding the issue of his academic and pastoral skills, Penny explained why Marske Mill was in Saltburn.

Dove assessed rightly: Penny knew the locale and understood the people's silence.

From there he went on to the parable of the police dog, the one that disappeared during a raid in Loftus. The dog ended up guarding a local's prize leeks on his allotment. Apocryphal or not, it spoke volumes. His telling of it lacked his usual elaborations; he was reciting it verbatim. His usual claim on a story was missing. And in Dove's opinion he was avoiding something.

Penny considered the importance of schoolkids to the case. He had to help. He clearly didn't want to go home. The digs offered a safe haven. His pals were there, the property owner up above. Days later Penny informed Dove that he had an idea. He refused to open up about it. His closing statement baffled Dove.

"If Oldman can do it then so can I!"

Anxious energy fuelled Penny's infiltration plan. His one day a week throughout the winter term at the local school was a shock to Dove. He rang the university and asked for permission to offer study skills and tutorials at the school, with a view to promoting pathways to higher education. Manic, wired, and conscientious, he felt worthy again. In addition, he might tutor students in the history of philosophy. He persuaded the university to call the school to set it up. The carrot came at the end of his request: he would like to do this before early retirement. Brigid was on to it.

He hadn't accepted the retirement deal. Despite his growing publications and popular toxicity, the university wanted him out of the way. Three temps had replaced him. In his red notebook he wrote: 'constructive dismissal leading to constructive action!'

Before the Monday appointment, he researched Liz's background and called her at home. Jack informed him the kids called her Liz the Destroyer. His accent, spiced with a friendly amalgam of local speak for the occasion, was strong. He recollected her old girls' grammar school headteacher, an eccentric woman (mad). Growing bolder by the second, he had claimed over the phone to be an honorary pupil at her school, an aside which had caused her to giggle. Resisting his desire to dip into his new gender-inclusive glossary, he kept it simple.

Down to business, he floated the idea of his philosophy tutorials, his Plato to NATO course. They could use *Sophie's World* as a reader. Digging deep to find humour, he told her he'd been raised in a leper colony on the outskirts of Redcar – Dormanstown. The thick fog outside and within his brain caused him to refer to Loftus as Antonio Bay, a reference to the horror movie *The Fog*. The demons surfaced from the deep in his case were internal, the fog real. His slanted remark was portentous.

They met Monday shortly after the university had called to arrange things from their end. The art detective was back in business. He felt nervous. Liz was a curious woman with a depth that defied simple analysis, and bonny, too. Tricky, so like the local area: full of secrets, full of riddles. For the time being he was going to work for her. Youthful satire or not, the Destroyer tag plagued him. His brief was one day a week to tutor small groups of six or seven in Year Eleven. That would allow him to meet the students of Max's age.

## Chapter 19

The latest werewolf victim, the lady from the field, was known as Wee Granny Bowers to the locals. Though suffering from shock, she was home. She wasn't willing to talk to the female constable sent around to her house. In fact, she told her from behind closed doors to go and shag herself with a ragged drift. The constable couldn't grasp it. Raed asked her to try.

"It sounded like raggy drift, ma'am."

Raed sent Hart to have a go. He was more successful.

"Don't be fooled," one of the locals volunteered, looking over his shoulder. "She's sharp as a bloody razor. Two pence short, but canny."

Meanwhile, Liz gave Penny his own room. His new office was the broom cupboard. The windowless room added gloss to the clandestine nature of his purpose and heightened the high-risk romantic image he held of detection. He met the staff who, barring a couple of cynics, went along with the sudden arrival of a teacher with his own room. Welcome to the asylum was the common greeting. Cynicism was always agreeable. It was for him a great starting point for sound politics. Another aspect crept in. He felt protected surrounded by these people and in the cupboard.

Dove and Periwinkle combed the countryside with Jack. No joy. The magnificent panoramas offered by the clifftops was negated by the weather. It was a grave situation. It was apparent no one knew anything. Or they just didn't talk. In circumstances such as these Periwinkle thought that doubtful. Local people would be concerned. They didn't want to admit it but the boy might be dead.

Gran Bowers told Hart a long hairy figure had risen out of the grass at the side of the path and tore at her throat with something sharp, like a claw. She had lashed out at it and managed to run away. It had screamed like an animal. She had run from the path to the road, whereupon she lost track of things.

"I think that's when I ran into yer' man, Dove."

Hart jotted notes down; at that point more to avoid disputing her story than recording the facts. He did have one query. And he did point out that Dove was not his man.

"What were you doing in the fields near Rose Hill Farm at night?" he asked her.

Gran didn't know. Hart's intelligence in the town told him that Granny Bowers was not well-liked. Gran Bowers was a witch. His education forbad such finality and difference. In his notebook, he recorded her ramblings, and his guesswork. Ms Bowers was a marginalised figure, an outsider, a casualty of deviancy.

Gran liked Hart and fed him endless cups of tea and cake. His personal austerity measures (he referred to them as his big haircut) were a naive product of listening to, and believing, politicians along with his own sense of self-punishment, his denial defeated by currant cake.

At first, he bought into it and then grew to detest the conveyor belt of goodies. The liquid was starting to affect his bladder. The slabs of currant cake laid heavily on his mind and stomach. He carried on, failing to realise the self-defeating nature of his programme of austerity, and the fact that creating demand may well have been a way forward. Was it a smoke screen? A cake screen?

"The figure didn't speak, Inspector Hart." She let inspector roll off the tongue then clipped it at the end. "It growled. It smelled of dead meat."

His avoidance of speech wasn't for the lack of trying. A mouth crammed with fruitcake forbad anything articulate. He made copious notes. His neat script detailed the woman's description of Fenris, the wolf-monster, breaking out from the bowels of the earth. Words like annihilation spiced the text along with gibberish about devouring the sun, the end of the world. He found it enthralling. That was what witches did…

Back in his office, the Internet confirmed the Nordic gods and the myth of Fenris. He read with interest the folktales and their comic versions. He doubted Ms Bowers read *Captain America* comics or Kay Scarpetta novels. Who had fed her this? The myths may well have been a part of north-eastern Viking heritage, along with dragon stories. Scaw the Serpent Slayer was local to Loftus's mythical past. Given free time he would go to Handale Woods, the location of the buried hero. He read that the dragon slayer's sword was four-foot long.

She was barking mad. In her house, there was no evidence that she read, no laptop visible. She burbled on. His notes, which would need stringing together, mentioned something about the chaotic – something about shackles. Was it chaos that needed the shackles? He wasn't sure. If it was, he agreed. He had a specific person in mind, one whose personal anarchy plagued him.

The designated deity of mischief was working his own personal chaos. Cleveland was home to Penny, Vikings, Normans, and Danes – fighting people, men and women, especially on Friday night. Fridays used to be wear-a-tie night, get-pissed night, get-into-a scrap night. One had to dress for the occasion.

"Did you know that Marske volunteers kicked Roundhead arse in a skirmish on the beach?"

Whether it was mods or rockers, whatever, Dove was not really concerned. "Were they wearing ties?"

Penny's feverish multi-tasking self was writing his fiction in note form, working chapters of his manuscript, developing short study skills exercises for students, and wandering about chatting without apparent aim to all and sundry – students, staff, and the janitor, Phibes. Penny set aside his impending retirement. He was hyper, obsessive; in between. listless.

Phibes was John Petit, an ex-Durham University student, better qualified than all the staff put together. He felt happy doing an honest job. Penny liked him instantly and called him 'me old mate Phibes'. His description of the job as truthful refracted on Penny. Phibes's reading of *Dark Art,* a gift from Penny, led him to wonder what he was doing there. A Dali

74

fan, he found it provocative. A visit to the Macabre Gallery was on the cards.

Penny's fictional hero, Professor Oldman (the promotion sounded better than doctor), retired, super-agent, quidnunc (better than gossipmonger) and *resident-terrible* (Penny's French was terrible) was now firmly ensconced in the splendid west wing of Reynold's Hall.

*Apart from stopping for occasional small talk, he chose not to mix with the suspects, the gang of four (part of the plan). The residents were getting curious. That too was part of the plan. They too had plans. Griggs had made sure he had a landline but was not to use it to contact him or his daughter. The residents were checking him out.*

In the school staffroom, the maths teacher, Baron von Strucker was discussing Penny.

"He's a snooper, a spy! He's up to something clandestine. Part of a new Ofsted ploy. Is he an Ofsted government agent? I know the name from somewhere."

In total fear of von Strucker, the French language assistant, Marie-Claire, sat quietly and surrendered to his denunciation. If Strucker had been listening carefully, he might have heard the occasional *merde*, referring both to him and his hypotheses on the new incumbent. 'Pinkie' Gray, the PE teacher, stuck his head in at the Ofsted moment, and upon hearing the O word disappeared again. He didn't much like Strucker and considered his facial scarring was not simply horrid; more a symbol of what lay beneath. No one dared ask how or who. In the yard, where Gothic horror and slasher movies prevailed, duelling was the moderate explanation. Others ranged from beasts tearing his face off to torture in a Japanese prisoner-of-war camp. That Strucker was no older than forty had escaped their attention.

## Chapter 20

The gardens were magnificent, in keeping with the great era of the country house. Missing was the art, the family portraits, the ornate furniture. The rooms boasted huge windows and mirrors. Light was abundant.

The funeral – he chatted to one of the Hall's cleaners, making friendly enquiries about the death.

"Mrs Smythe, taken in the night. Suddenly."

He contacted Griggs. Privacy was important. It was early days. He talked to the gardener, Boyce, who added to the tale.

"Gladys Smythe? Nothing wrong with her, fit as a flea."

He met Ken in the bar and kept it chatty; Luna too would meet over a coffee. His first impression was that no one in the hallowed hall was going to inform – no one. He noticed a certain chariness about Ken with other residents and between Ken and himself too after he mentioned poor Ms Smythe.

Luna dropped in for a glass one night, a gin and tonic. It was to be an eye-opener. Ken teased her about the beanie. Ken had access to her fears. Moreover, he enjoyed pressing buttons. That Luna was scared of the dark amused him and he kept on about it until Oldman said:

"Enough."

The usual 'just joking' excuse followed but Oldman could see Ken was miffed. He chose not to cite the Roseanne Barr cases and her history of offensive tweets. Ken's ribbing was merciless and unkind.

Luna Nightlight, he used her playful nickname, switched in his conversation from playful to hurtful. Teasing was like that.

Ken was cruel. Luna left whispering an apology to Oldman. Oldman thought of testing Ken out in the same sarcastic vein, but his position there relied on some expedience. Calling the man a short arse wouldn't help. Teasing could be educative too. In this case social relations were strained to the limit.

Ken swapped spit about his time in the army. He was an engaging man with a past, though he left huge gaps in his stories. He had an annoying habit of calling him 'dear boy'. Not far beneath the posh accent were traces of someone extremely working-class, lumpenproletariat, and a man with something to hide. It rankled Oldman. He pushed Griggs for feedback on Smythe.

"And while you're onto it, check Luna Winter and Ken Briggs."

Ken had been something in military intelligence, an oxymoron, Ken joked, then added a vindictive comment about morons. Oaf would have paired up better with 'dear boy'. When Ken came down to the dayroom he did so with a Daily Mail and sat on his own.

In the quiet of his room Professor Oldman paused his reading of Get Shorty, placed a marker in the page, and began writing a letter to Bridie. It spoke not of boredom, though a hint of the lack of challenges in his retirement, and his affection for Elmore Leonard's work:

'One never knows who the good guy is. Everything about Reynold's Hall is tasteful: the décor, the service and, to date, the people. I note that they play bridge and other games which I have never attempted. I can, for the first time in my life, leave my door unlocked.'

Not for long.

A knock on the door interrupted his thoughts. He peered through the peep hole. A man in grey overalls stood in the corridor.

"Just here to check your electrical supply."

Oldman let him in; studied him. The man busied himself. He looked around, checked everything thoroughly – far too thoroughly. He kept looking at the door. Oldman clocked his face and stored it somewhere in his inferior temporal cortex. He never forgot a face – names, yes – and he read New Scientist.

He left the man to work and wandered down to the small library and book exchange in the lounge. Get Shorty would be exchanged. His donations of New Scientist were well thumbed. He picked up a large book and glimpsed at some of the illustrations. Oldman looked at the cover. He turned it over. Another tell-all memoir. About to put it back, he noticed a small Rennie Macintosh marker in one page. He opened it and read:

'Our childhood dreams ended that day. We knew our snowman was just the beginning. We grew up, we read. Nothing we did fitted the bill. We loved, we had morals, we learned, and we listened to others. When we were allowed, we mixed with them. We enjoyed others' company. Often we were alone. Being grounded for a dressed-up snowman seemed unfair.'

He looked at the cover. The case had made the international press. Curious at this point, he flicked through the illustrations. The inclusion of others in this way indicated difference. He wasn't convinced. True horror had been a part of his life. About to put the book down, he thumbed through a few pages.

'The day Peter was diagnosed with stage four liver cancer we went for a run. We ran; we cried together through the old pine wood, our route, the one we explored as children, running past our secrets we shared together. Nothing was said. We heard the strange art historian on the wireless that evening and we knew what to do. We both knew we had to go public! Suicide, and suicidal it was, but that day we were both dying.'

He read on, examined the planning for the first public showing of their work. He was familiar with the language, that of military decision-making, though the orders were not received from above, unless one considers the spiritual aspect the writers placed on their art. Mission analysis? Course of Action? Oldman wondered if the person was ex-army. He placed the small marker next to the books (someone had forgotten it), tucked the tell-all book under his arm, and went back upstairs.

Below, in the expansive day room, a group of four were discussing the new resident.

"The new chap seems nice. Wonder if he plays cards."

"We shall see."

At that, they resumed their game.

Later, as Oldman passed the day room and popped his mail in the post, his ears burned. He acknowledged the residents in the room with a discrete wave and examined as closely as possible the small group playing cribbage – his target group. He spoke to all, playing shy at the same time. He made an issue of learning names. Oldman had ditched games in favour of work. He recalled his desire to stab his younger brother when he, Oldman Senior, was winning hands-down at Monopoly. Young Oldman wouldn't stop the game. Holding a winning hand was a different matter. Oldman had continued to do that. He'd stabbed people along the way in a differing monopoly. Recalling the Monopoly game helped. Yet there was a sense of disappointment; one that told him he had been sidelined in the new intelligence in favour of a cloying political regime.

He studied the players. Their gestures and facial expressions gave away nothing. He knew they were assessing him, like the cards. He wished he'd learnt cribbage and bridge. He smiled broadly in their direction and passed on by.

One of the card school, a woman in her late fifties, spoke to the other three.

"Seems quite reserved. Where did he work?"

"Not entirely sure, Doc. A bit of a mystery, though his professorship is at an American university. He's an historian of sorts. He seems a decent enough chap."

Oldman indeed had a history of all sorts. Though settled in Canada he was of English extract; had worked with American Intelligence for years and then returned to Blighty, and to semi-retirement. Put out to grass was his outlook.

As they wound their game up and began to depart, one of the women spoke.

"Jack David, can you check him out, please?"

"Sure, Stead. Any particular reason?"

"No, nothing particular, everything in general."

"Is the room on our system?"

"No, it isn't. Check thoroughly, please." She looked concerned.

※

Oldman used the non-contract phone to call Griggs.

"What did Ms Smythe die of?"

Griggs was hesitant. "Death certificate says pneumonia. We will have to exhume the body if we are to check anything. It will create waves. She's well connected. Not a criminal mastermind or a thug, but an old dear who liked playing bowls and left a load of cash to an animal charity. Her GP's notes indicate all the signs of heart problems – breathlessness, and oedema – over a period of a year. I fear, Oldman, when we get to a certain age death is around the corner. Doctors are ageist." Griggs took a breath as if aiming to stop there, then the words tumbled out. "She may well have been our informer. We've had no more messages since passed."

"What were her connections?"

"I'll send you a breakdown via email."

"OK. In future I'll call you from a box. A rare sight these days but there's one down the road that hasn't been vandalised. I've got the feeling it's me who is under surveillance. There's always people loitering about. Introductions to all might have included something mixed in my welcome glass of wine. My place was checked over."

"Ah, Oldman, these people have been around longer than both of us."

Oldman wasn't sure what that was supposed to mean, but it sounded like a compliment – to them.

An ethical problem arose. The American intelligence agencies were, in Penny's estimation, shadowy. Prisoners had disappeared to countries where torture was possible. Waterboarding, wiretapping, and a serious failure around 9/11 were public, not to mention setting up the Taliban in Afghanistan. Penny wasn't sure whether his protagonist should be from the USA. And then there was Trump and someone call Ron, who sounded even more dangerous. Donald and Ronald? Oldman's background had to be sound. The sounding out of local intelligence in the pub in Loftus didn't help.

He needed to know more about opinions of the Taliban and Afghanistan. One man advised him never to go to any country ending in Stan. He, the pub oracle, knew six or seven countries that fitted such as he 'did the pub quiz'. Astounded by the breadth of knowledge of pub quiz teams, he pulled out his memo pad and scribbled: must find out about Stan.

Would Hart approve of Oldman? Oldman's background was perfect for the plot. Could he justify killing him off?

To his friends, his quietness was unsettling. Where were the theories, the lectures, the banter, the all-encompassing thesis, analysis, synthesis?

Penny mulled over the issue of Oldman's homeland. He so wanted his mole to be clean. He would be Canadian.

**Chapter 21**

Raed was checking iPad feedback from her team when 'Dr Death' called at the station without an appointment. How did he get in? She made a mental note to chat to the desk sergeant.

Regretting even more the admin load, and sorely missing pounding the streets – the real policing – she was more than happy to take a break, and curious to meet the notorious Penny. She was expecting him. The duty officer had called through to say a Dr Penny was there to see her. That he was in town she already knew. She wished Dove had told her. She would find out Dove was his own person, as was his friend, Periwinkle. In half an hour, she was off to talk to Muslim children at the school. Her scheduled appointments were usually stifling handshaking formalities, easily dispensed with. Meeting children would be enjoyable.

Penny knocked and, without observing protocol (which was waiting for a reply) entered the office, a bare room with a rug between the door and desk. Raed chose not to say anything about his manners and moved to greet him. He didn't appear too confident. Penny stopped suddenly. Raed paused. He wasn't what she expected. His face displayed an ear-to-ear grin. Rehearsed? It might open doors.

Raed reached to shake his hand. He wasn't there. His introduction was spectacular. The small mat, a prayer mat beneath his feet, and his ox-blood Doc Martens slid from under him on the highly polished wooden floor. Prone, he slid towards Raed who could scarcely hide her amusement, then concern. From his flat-out position, he reached up and shook her hand.

"*As salaam alaikum,* Chief Inspector Raed."

She withheld her comments about prayers being over as he leaned up from the mat to greet her.

On his feet, he noticed his little book on her desk. Later, being better acquainted with him, she wondered if he did it on purpose. Stagey suited Penny.

"*Alaikum salaam,* Dr Penny. I've got about twenty minutes only." Raed recognised a talker and hated being late for appointments. The fresh-faced man who confronted her had sandy hair, turning salt among the pepper, and faded freckles, like numerous locals in the area of mixed Scandinavian or Irish origin. His high colour suggested either fitness or drink. Later, she decided he ticked both boxes. He appeared humble (the fall may have helped) and candid; the opposite of the meanings connoted by media portrayals and shifty mugshots taken by shifty photographers.

She noticed the signs of carpal tunnel syndrome as the second finger of the left hand locked as he climbed to his feet. A flustered Penny unlocked it with his other hand. He was too embarrassed to make his usual quip about it happening only at the checkout in the store.

He was brief. He explained his reasons for being in Loftus and hoped he could help. On that, he turned to go. His directness was at once refreshing and disturbing. Was it disingenuous? His reputation told her to be cautious. Her father had forewarned her that conmen were always 'nice', part of their stock in trade. Her policing experience reaffirmed such.

She would hold onto her promise to keep him at arm's length.

He moved forward to help her with her coat.

"Thanks, I can manage. Can you give your details and address here and a contact number to the duty officer? You spoke to him on the way in. I'll be in touch."

Penny moved to her left and opened the door. How on earth had he got in?

Raed brushed past him into the corridor, leaving a hint of exotic perfume. Moreover was the sense of her strength and character.

"Take care, Dr Penny."

He gave his details and slipped out into the street, leaving a small package at the desk.

\\\\\

Hart was working around the clock. He had a gut feeling, like chronic diverticulosis, that Penny was on the horizon. Dove, Periwinkle and Penny were all there – the three stooges. This time he would be more careful. A small package in his pigeonhole confirmed his suspicions. He unwrapped *Dark Art* and, without opening it, slid it in a desk drawer. He was sure

Penny had tampered with evidence in the university fraud case and in the sickening Tableau murders. He couldn't prove it. Retrospectively, he'd asked himself if he would have done the same. His concern at the moment was to find the boy. He had a bad feeling about this one. Bad feelings rarely went away.

Hart recognised Penny's feedback loops and, in conversation with Raed, he highlighted his abstract nature.

"When Penny flaps his wings in Loftus a tornado hits the Home Office."

That was to occur in the future.

He was aware that neither he nor Penny were guilty of reminding the other of the charnel house at Carshalton. It lived in their everyday thoughts.

Penny spent his spare time listening to voices in the yard, the playground as he had called it as a child. These young adults called it the exercise yard. In contrast, the liberal nature of the school differed from his own experiences. Prison would have been easy after his senior school; aptly christened *Stalag 17* by former pupils.

He overheard hushed conversations that mentioned the castle. Kilton, he guessed. At times he questioned the voices and their existence. Voices had helped in his Tableau Case. The problem with overhearing snippets was stringing single words together in the hope they might convey a message. Kids weren't against setting up an old fart like him.

Overlooking Kilton Beck, the ruins of the once magnificent castle were quite extensive. It was years since he had tried to get down to it. It was on private land. Often in the countryside an irate farmer would prevent his rambles. Nature served in this instance. The dense undergrowth was virtually impenetrable. It was difficult to make out the size and shape of the buildings. Kids would find a way. Kids knew more about stuff like that.

Convinced that two of the boys – George and Kyle – were up to their necks in maleficence, he honed in on them. Other kids steered away from them or kept a wary distance. He must mention it to Liz.

In the limited windows the weather permitted, he walked along the tops to Skinningrove, stopping at Warsett Hill to take black and white photographs of The Guibal fan house with his ancient camera rescued from Skelton. The building resembled a church, yet the industrial concrete slabs contradicted that. The concrete once housed the huge fan. It was a cut above the church as it gave life and air to people and served them. A concrete cathedral! He stared down into the mesh-covered tiled tunnel.

Imagine an image on glass of that stolid building, and a verse... spectacular: *No bell calls us to praise, no choir sings a psalm, no one says a prayer for the concrete cathedral.* A page for his glass book. He stopped to take notes. His little brown book was a permanent feature now. Its faux leather appealed to him, so too did the band to mark the page.

On his way back he paused to take in the commanding cliff views of the North Sea. The polar easterly wind threatening the return of inclement weather curtailed his daydream. He detoured to look down at the castle and hurried on. He'd pass on his earwigging snippets to Dove and Periwinkle; they to Hart and Raed. The castle was creepy.

## Chapter 22

The wintry weather refused to let go. The east wind carried with it severe cold, early sleet and snow. Penny babbled about Eurus, its breath and spirit, its lack of import. He said something about Graupel.

"Soft hail," he explained.

Dove hovered, pint in hand. Nothing else followed. At least he wasn't talking about the mysterious Oldman.

The hope of finding Max alive was waning. Dove vowed not to partake in any suppositions from Penny. None came. They had searched the area together and when they had combed it all, they did it again. The kids in the yard were reluctant to speak about Max. Was he the innocent they believed?

Jack, forlorn and desperate, came back from the hunt along the clifftops and surrounding fields, shivering and shaking with cold; the beginnings of illness brought about by lack of food, and anguish. When not searching, Penny was listening – for news, the werewolf, Max, anything.

Jack stared at the sea as if waiting for it to give up his son's body. "It's the not knowing," he said repeatedly.

His friends offered no answers. Dove simply placed a firm hand on Jack's shoulder and led him home.

On one occasion, Periwinkle spotted Penny coming off the path about half a mile away, his familiar slouch recognisable and his yellow and black backpack. He was walking miles. Periwinkle understood both Jack and Penny's plight, the inability to sit still. Despite Periwinkle's affection for his comrades, he recognised their need to cut themselves off. Later, when they met in the pub around a blazing fire, Penny's arms and face were scratched by burrs or brambles.

Jack's bluish facial cast prompted Penny to buy whisky all round. Three glasses later they saw Jack home as the full strength of the Scandinavian weather hit the northeast coast and made reconnoitre hopeless. A listless fog ensued. Perhaps the werewolf rose from the sea seeking retribution. Or was that a film?

The station was busy. One police officer had seen the other two – the short bearded one and the tall one – along the cliffs, in the library, and on the bus to Middlesbrough.

Unable to search the surrounds, Penny focussed on the schoolyard. Who mixed with whom? At times, his heart rate would speed up and a shortness of breath would follow. He'd have to retreat to his cupboard, the bunker, and take deep breaths. An ECG had confirmed his heart was fine. It would have been difficult to persuade him so. Adopting Oldman as an imaginary friend helped. He had a friend in Oldman. Oldman had his work cut out for him.

The watchers were wasting time, a point he would convey to their boss Raed, who had nothing to do with his surveillance.

Raed was fed up with the references to his and his friend's whereabouts which, for her, built up a profile of the man who was inaccurate and misleading. She decided to resolve matters. He bedevilled and played on it. If his aim had been anything other than searching for the boy, she guessed he might have enjoyed the game of tag. A police officer reported her intel to Raed.

"Morning, ma'am. Saw your man Penny in The Alex in Saltburn on Tuesday."

(In the back bar of The Alex pub in Saltburn, Penny gained more information about the Batemans and the Bowers. He wrote the key personnel down.)

Later that day another officer called in on Raed.

She greeted Raed first. "Afternoon, ma'am. Saw what's-his-face – Penny – running along the back lane towards the old railway line."

Raed called the staff together. "No one, *no one*," she asserted, "is to concern themselves with Dove, Periwinkle or Penny – only with the job in hand. Find Max. Find the werewolf. They are searching, and so should you be. Forget Penny. Forget Dove and forget Periwinkle. That's an order! The cuts mean we can't afford to waste personnel. Do your job." Raed was doing her best, but one of them was on her mind.

She managed to get two extra staff drafted in. The severity of the weather hampered complete and on-going searches. The winds Dove estimated were around forty knots, gale force. They carried with them the sounds of waves crashing and moaning, and in the night from a farm nearby the restless Penny could hear, borne along by the howling banshee, the eerie caterwauling of peahens. Tiles on the roof lifted and banged, threatening to lift off altogether. Max was out there, and they feared the worst. He went to check his house in Skelton, bought provisions, and put the heating on for just a short spell. Prices were getting silly.

Reports from the school testified Penny was at the centre of everything. His philosophy class was fun; the study skills designed to amuse as well as enhance the planning of essays, time management and notetaking. He kept it straightforward and simple. A small group apart, the students rated him as cool and a geezer.

It was part of his avoidance, not a disorder, more a therapeutic tool, a buffer to the nightmares and his attempts to break down the trauma. Reading scholarly articles made it worse.

Kyle and George hadn't seen Spaz for days. They had heard enough tales about Dr Penny and his mates 'Ratchet and Clank'.

"Doctor my arse, George. Wonder what Spaz is up to. Is his dad back home?"

"Don't know. You know he doesn't like us calling on him."

"It's a wonder *they* don't call on him – the school people."

"Think they're shit-scared of 'im?"

"Can you blame 'em?"

They bumped fists and parted. If they only knew the target of their humour's background. Shooters they were.

93

'Ratchet and Clank' were in Middlesbrough scouring maps in the archives and talking to staff at Dorman Museum. Acting upon Penny's schoolyard observations, they were examining in detail the remains of Kilton Castle: old buildings, air raid shelters, remnants of industrial sites along the coastline, mostly linked to its mining past.

Jack was like the walking dead.

While they poured over maps, Penny spent his spare time chatting to Phibes in the exercise yard, snooping, and nattering to the kids. One thing only was obvious: they feared something. Their conversations often stopped dead on the appearance of certain individuals. Namely Kyle and George. Liz's sojourns in the exercise yard did bring about a certain quiet. Penny mentioned to Liz about the two boys.

"I'll follow it up. Thanks."

Old industrial sights, the brickworks, the catching bridge at Claphow Road, and the defences along the coast dating back to Roman times testified to a history yet unwritten. They examined the focus of Penny's attention – Kilton Castle – then finally Kilton Pit. The old photographs of the now dismantled Regent cinema, and rescue teams at Liverton Mines were secondary evidence of a past not long gone.

Where would one hide a body? The sea was the most obvious answer.

Once his comrades had studied archival material for long enough, a preliminary reconnaissance confirmed that the ruins were barely visible. In the dip, sheltered from storms, the dense undergrowth, the nettles and brambles, masked what must have been a dream of a building, and what was once a solarium. The fog was lifting.

Phibes understood Penny's proclaimed purpose to 'revolutionise the school' was secondary. His presence had more to do with Jack's mates, and the missing boy, Max, plus his apparent fascination with shifters.

"Hiya, Doc."

"Hey, me old mate Phibes. How ya doing?"

"Good, just patrolling the yard!"

"Cool. Anything on?"

"Keeping a weather eye on those two there – Kyle and George. Liz asked me to. They're Max's buddies and hang out with that kid Spaz, as they call him. The poor lad needs help. He's never at school. His dad works away; his mum died years ago. Dad never remarried. His gran is an oddball. You know of Gran Bowers, of course? Not seen her or the boy lately. He spends his days on a BMX bike his dad bought him with his first decent wage after leaving the mine to work away. He does visit her sometimes."

Penny hadn't met Gran. He wondered if she would let him interview her. "So, the woman who was attacked by the werewolf is the boy's gran?"

Phibes nodded. He found it difficult to talk openly about Gran Bowers.

"The bike – is it a black and yellow BMX?"

"Yep, that's the one. Poor kid lives on that bike. The kids here call him all sorts – Pale Rider or Spaz – behind his back. They're scared of him for childish reasons, mainly because he's bigger and different."

The apocalyptic reference jangled. That he was close to Gran struck a chord. "How is he different?"

Phibes's phone was ringing. He strode across the yard to his lookout post. As he went, George and Kyle fixed wary eyes on Penny and shuffled away to the perimeter fence.

## Chapter 23

*Oldman had infiltrated the games room. He was reading in a corner. The strange story of the twins had him hooked. Without appearing rude, he distanced himself from Ken, a gut instinct rather than a result of any informed intelligence. The bizarre nature of The Tableau was a fact. He wondered... did they want to get caught? He resisted turning a few pages.*

*Jack David had done his research and hit a brick wall. That made him more wary. They opted for 'friendship'. The group of four suspects introduced themselves personally. He feigned surprise as they reeled off their titles.*

*"Blimey," he said in his best mockney-English, "we have a doctor, a sea captain ex RN, a barrister QC, and last but not least a senior civil servant. I'm in good company. Never been a member of an elite club!"*

*He knew already each one's background in detail including their brothers, sisters and kin. The doctor, Stead, was still active with Primary Care Trust, though retired as a GP and known for her charitable works. Then there was much-decorated naval officer Commander Fielding; QC Florence Bingham, husband deceased and no children, only a brother who she hadn't seen in twenty years (she was the talker), and last but definitely not least, ex-chief* executive of 'something in the government' Jack David, whose pension pot was in excess of a million. He was up there with permanent secretaries and had stayed at the top for a long time. Mild-mannered on the face of things, Jack David was a tough nut. Oldman was careful.

Jack David began the task of sussing out Oldman's background. Initially coming up with a blank, he contacted an old colleague Lawson. When Lawson said Oldman was clean, he was even more suspicious. He passed it onto Bingham who had contacts in worlds he chose not to associate with.

Bingham was a tough cookie. Her expertise in the legalities of probate, death, dying, wills, and assisted suicide made her a prime suspect. It was rumoured she has strayed from the straight and narrow of her legal career. Nothing was proven.

As for Lawson, Oldman's old boss, he had moved on from the intelligence Oldman knew and trusted to a political intelligence working closer with government, a shift that made Oldman cautious.

Lawson, a complex self-seeker, didn't do anything straightforward. A telephone call to Oldman made him even more wary. All the psychological guff about self-seekers being vulnerable was crap. Lawson was covering his back for some reason personal to him.

None of them had signed anything. That was an enigma. The network wound its way into those services and above. The card players were at the centre of it.

He mingled with others and found most good company. Not sure of Ken, he steered clear whenever possible. Bingham was a bletherer. That made her a target, and he chatted to her whenever he could. What was he looking for? At times he wasn't sure. He had to wait. He wondered if others were involved too. He began to see Bingham's idle chatter as a smoke screen. What was concealed? He needed another tack.

Could he learn to play bridge? Cards against humanity was more familiar to him, and more appropriate.

His gut feeling, his inbuilt air raid siren, wailed a warning. He was beginning to believe the job was leading elsewhere for reasons he couldn't fathom, and that he might be in the wrong place. For other reasons (nothing to do with the case) he accepted his situation wholeheartedly.

Jack David was still digging for information on Oldman. He might be some use to them.

Oldman took stock. All of them looked fit and well. All of them were suspects in two very strange deaths – at least two that he knew of. Had they arranged them? Carried them out? Had they ensured that the complex system of certification was circumvented? What could they gain from those deaths? Was it money? Job satisfaction? Could he search their rooms? On one occasion he acknowledged Ken across the room. He caught a flicker of Bingham's eyes as she looked sideways at Jack David. Perhaps Reynold's Hall wasn't so cosy. He felt the tension in her unerring gaze.

He smiled at Ms Stead. She smiled back. Her smile was inviting. Stead was an attractive woman.

She wanted to find out more. Oldman's career was quite a successful one on paper, the money required for the hall not beyond him though stretching his resources. Who was paying? His furniture was a hodgepodge, and souvenirs of the eclectic traveller. It didn't seem like him.

He left his door unlocked. Oldman had unfinished business.

## Chapter 24

Penny left the school earlier than usual, though it was already getting dark. His study skills class had gone well. One of the students had set his mobile alarm off at the end of the timed exercise. He dismissed them with a smile and a 'wake-up' comment. He collected the papers and left.

The cold persisted. No sign of the werewolf. People were out and about in twos and threes, the brave, the foolish, the cavalier. They passed by wrapped up in hats, scarves and thick gloves.

With bare hands shoved in his overcoat pockets, his backpack carrying his classwork, he set off home. Impervious to the cold, the schoolkids hung out, the lads with hoodies pulled up, the lasses with short skirts and long hair. The lasses dominated. They swaggered along the pavement four abreast, one or two with e-cigarettes in hand. The boys tried hard to affect a strutting mad dog mean attitude that involved buttock clenching. Dove's summation was that the boys had something stuck up their arses. The girls were tougher.

Penny's own affectation at that age was a casual slouch that stayed with him, and which he regretted — his cool school phase. By then, Dove was already heading for the navy. Of Periwinkle, who knows.

Skeletons of trees, their leaves blown hither and thither, stood naked. The gathering wind that announced an early winter lifted the leaves again and took them away. The icy blasts erased one of the enjoyments of autumn: stepping through the variegated leafy pathways and sweeping them aside with one's feet. The wind was relentless. In the local, a weathercaster prognosticated that it was going to be a shite winter.

Penny wandered past Spaz's house. The school register gave his name as Michael Farrow. The house was in a small, neat, unassuming terrace. It offered no sign of life. No noise emitted from within, no lights shone. There was nothing to indicate anyone was at home. The small front garden was tidy and the property well maintained.

He wandered up and down. Before anyone would think he was up to no good, he headed slowly back to the digs. He bought chips in West Road, drowned them in vinegar and far too much salt. He ate them walking down the road. He felt the glow of old memories: the newspaper wrapping, the smell of beef dripping, the beautiful odour of excess, then the morning after, Redcar High Street and the stale smell of beer mingled with detergent as the cleaners mopped puddles out of the open doors of the dozen or so pubs and clubs into the high street.

Two boys from the school rode past.

One of them shouted, "Dining out, sir?"

Unable to respond due to a mouth full of deliciously greasy chips, he returned a smile and managed a quick thumbs up, dropping a chip as he flipped the thumb. Loftus was going to prove appealing. The beer was good and the chips excellent. He'd offered the use of the old cottage at Skelton to his pals. It was a no. They needed to be in situ. It might come in handy if things went awry. As he dipped the last chip in a pool of vinegar gathered in the bottom of the polystyrene carton, he pondered. Things usually did go awry. He tipped the remaining acidic pool out into the gutter and crumpled the packet and deposited it in the next litter bin. In a moment of self-doubt he thought of the school. Were things okay? His rebellious nature was a product more of a life outside of teaching than a desire to undermine the system. His life experiences coloured his teaching. The cautionary call Liz had received from the dean of faculty at Penny's university were symptomatic of a weak and peevish man. Liz was forthright – she told him.

She asked her new part-timer about the university. He told her about dean treachery. He talked a little about the Max affair.

He surmised that she knew his motives for being there, but he would aim to be effective while they had him.

She asked him round to meet her husband, Jim, one evening. "Jim is a plumber, working abroad in the Gulf. You will like him. We have our evening meal at the table together. When Jim is home it's a family ritual." For her, it was invaluable. Jim wasn't conversational, his trips abroad were work, or 'more of the same'. Plumbing was second nature to him. He never discussed it. "Thank God for that," she said. The presents he brought back and the mementos were enough. Jim was a quiet man.

Penny's skewed logic told him that Jim and Liz didn't fit together, somehow. He decided to use the invite to suss him out.

His grasp of schoolyard subcultural language was developing, his conversation spiced with youthful gems: 'how nice is that?' and of course, 'awesome!'. He stopped short of using 'bud' though, and 'sick' to mean good.

He felt more together, though small incidents panicked him. On one occasion he set off home and the twenty-minute walk lasted over an hour, most of which he couldn't recall. The teaching staff were 'sound'. Baron von Strucker had his good points and was a source of healthy satire. Penny's impressions made the staff forget their dislike for the maths teacher. The staff room became a warm place.

He spent time writing stuff down. Hints apart, he never spoke about his jottings. Now and then he mentioned the inscrutable Oldman.

*Oldman's Internet search on McKean landed on Hayley Banks's desk. Hayley was a boffin, and soon Oldman became familiar with the term 'redacted'. Huge chunks of McKean's work had gone, disappeared into the ether. Banks was aiming to bring it back from the other side, as she called it, back from the upper regions. Doubtful it was for security reasons; she found no evidence anyone else had tampered with the laptop. One cryptic reference remained regarding the cooperative surfaced, but it could've been anything.*

*Hayley concluded, "It's bigger and more complex than we thought... Plus McKean didn't fit the designated purpose of the group."*

Oldman agreed. The death wasn't quite the same.

"Keep searching, Hayley."

"McKean's laptop has been subject to data erasure – material purged, Oldman. I sense an expert. All we know from the notes is that she was researching the far-right National Action, and the like." She added, "We don't know much about them – highly secretive, homophobic, racist – you name it, Oldman. One aim is to reintroduce Thatcher's Section 28."

Back in the hall, he searched 'National Action' and 'Section 28'. He wondered what Ken thought of homosexuality. He started probing with the cleaning staff about general tittle-tattle. He was confident he had befriended Maggie. His conversations were innocuous enough, enquiring what people did in their spare time. Maggie inferred that they were not what they seemed. Interrupted, she withdrew sharpish. Loyal to their upper-class residents, someone reported back. He chose to be more discrete. There was an accompanying lull in the removals business, and he felt guilty, but not for long.

After a boozy evening with Ken, he made comments about a secret society in the hall. Satirical or not, he gossiped about the group around Stead. Ken encouraged him. He also mentioned Section 28. Ken dismissed it with a comment that implied he would welcome another Thatcher. Then he clammed up.

The residents of Reynold's Hall were disdainful of clucking magpies; gossip was beneath them. Maggie's confidant reported back. Maggie never turned up for work again. His enquiries as to her whereabouts were met with a stone wall. Oldman learnt fast. Leaks might be the way forward. He saw Maggie one day while shopping. She hurried away. At least she was alive. Oldman bit the bullet and paid one more visit to Ken's room for a tot – a nice

Highland Park (and a good measure too). Ken chattered about the problems of nosiness, a barely disguised warning, then the 'problem' of immigration and his perceived and somewhat bigoted notions of Islam.

Then without warning: "Have you ever killed anyone, Oldman?"

Oldman lied. "No, my students weren't that annoying." He thought he'd carried it off but couldn't account for his facial gestures. He changed the subject. He focussed on a large photo of a group of young men, Ken in the centre in uniform. "That you Ken?"

"Younger days, dear boy, good days too. I miss the action."

One of the faces looked familiar. He made to go. Ken insisted on one for the road. He seemed overly keen to keep him there. Oldman excused himself and left. Ken's politics were clearly close to Genghis Khan's. Oldman detested politics per se.

His host protested. "Just one more, dear boy."

Oldman refused. "It's past my bedtime." He nearly said, 'dear boy' (aagh). On his way across the ground floor lounge he saw a light in the dining room and heard voices. He paused. His curiosity got the better of him.

The door was ajar. He peered in. The tables were together. A heated debate was taking place. In his reckoning Ken and he were the only absentees. He caught a glimpse of the yellow beanie, heard Luna say something about him, something about Ken and mutual business. As she spoke, she stared at the gap in the door. She couldn't possibly see him. He moved back a tad. A noise across the lounge disturbed him. A shadow flitted away – Ken. Oldman scooted off to his room. That night he locked his door.

Cooperatives, mutual business, and the ethos of the cooperative movement, along with honesty, transparency and social responsibility were familiar to him, their values in this case inverted. Why was Ken not there? Why not him? Was this cooperative a burgeoning movement? Was it a closed shop?

Ken stopped meeting him; Luna shied away. The man was chary every time they met, never avoiding his glance, but rather looking right through him. He decided to phone Griggs and chase up what Ken's back catalogue contained.

Then Luna called on him. Oldman was reading. She tiptoed into the room like a child avoiding cracks in the flagstones. Her colourful attire, a dye works explosion, lit up the room. She looked him directly in the eye. Her attitude changed from child to parent.

"What exactly are you here for, Mr Oldman? If that is your name."

Oldman was prepared to spill the beans but that required one more call to Griggs. His boss had already informed him that Luna had been an investigative journalist, working on what Oldman called 'alternative media'. Like McKean.

"Luna, can we have a chat later?" He neither denied nor confirmed anything. "I'm free around suppertime if you want to call back."

"I will." She turned and, with the same cautious step as before, left the room. As she cleared the door she turned back. "Be careful what you say to Ken. Oh, and we have friends everywhere." She left the door open and walked away.

Point taken. It was clear the others were wary of him, including Stead. In fact, he decided to check out all the residents. That canny sense of an error, clerical or not, told him this wasn't straightforward. Ken must have informed the others of his snooping. He felt snubbed, especially by Stead; an emotional response he couldn't quite get the hang of. Luna may well have seen him. It hurt his feelings. Yet there was no place for sensitivity. That, and emotions lead to further errors. Stead was as sharp as a razor. Discretion was a natural part of these people's lives. Success was an add-on.

Luna never came back. She was not in her usual place for breakfast. Oldman searched her rooms. No signs of disturbance, nothing out of place; a vibrant coloured profusion, cerulean, Van Gogh yellows and rich throws. A splendid vibe, but no Luna. He needed to call in to Griggs.

Oldman borrowed a bicycle to ride the two miles to the village to phone Griggs. On his way to the box he spotted a silver-grey saloon on the road. The car picked him up shortly after leaving the hall, and near the phone box it sped on – amateurish. He took the number. Another task for Hayley. He dismounted and sent a message.

Hayley was mere seconds in answering. "It's one of ours."

"Can you find out who has signed it out?"

"The car isn't signed out."

Oldman felt alone – a new experience for him. He sat in his chair. Reflection had never been his thing. He thought of the dead: his colleagues, his enemies. His enemies? Whose enemies? He did what he had to; he did what he was told to. He fretted. The past was so limited and inexpedient.

Could his changed circumstances, which had changed for the better, have brought about loneliness, reflection? Unused to questioning himself, he hummed a Loudon Wainwright song: The sad thing is I'm so damn happy. As so many of us do at that *moment he wanted to give something back. Then he put the kettle on to make coffee, and read:*

'Peter is beginning to suffer. He bleeds easily. He is in pain. We've gained the recognition he desired. Our loss of anonymity is in one way a gain. We are but shadows of ourselves, yet the work gives us strength. We must look forward. There is more work to do before the end. Peter has an idea for a group "portrait"… We occupy the dark spaces and have forgotten the light, the play, human associations, touch and feel. There is no going back."

## Chapter 25

The narrow clifftop paths were treacherous after the heavy rainfall. The gale force winds refused to lessen. Squalling and whistling fiercely off the sea, any progress along the tops was painful. Notoriously uncertain even in pleasant weather, Penny had warned the kids about taking selfies on the edge, their backs to the North Sea.

Dove and Periwinkle moved at a snail's pace. Forewarned by local fisherman that 'some weather was coming in', they were kitted out with protective combat uniform, several layers, Periwinkle with his beloved beret glued to his head.

For no other reason than padding and warmth, they wore thick camouflage gear obtained in a shop in the Cleveland Centre, Middlesbrough. The man described it as their best seller. Periwinkle mulled over a list of reasons. He asked Penny. He wasn't prepared for the analysis of both style and function, or theories on urban terrorism.

Dove wore a tight mustard-coloured woollen beanie he'd found in an off-price retailer. He pulled it well over his ears. The small tents and sleeping bags fitted into an envelope. Basic rations were enough. Dove stowed a bottle of something warm in his pack. Neither of the men looked forward to their task. The severity of the weather was peripheral; the possible outcome of their search they dreaded.

Periwinkle understood that chaos governed Penny's random 'interdisciplinary' theorisations, his belief in the interconnectedness of things. Penny didn't understand fractals and was unaware of his nonlinear thought processes and their effect on others. They needed an effective translator, otherwise his perceptions appeared accidental. Periwinkle made the links between these arbitrary notions and moves. Penny's sense of reasoning, sixth or otherwise, and intelligence gleaned from the exercise yard had pinned down the castle as a place to visit.

"Okay, Periwinkle, let's visit the castle."

Dove and he did, without Penny, who was otherwise engaged. Why he used a casual term like 'visit' was unfathomable. Of late his suggestions were obscure. Periwinkle made the connections, joined the dots up.

Both men concentrated on staying on the path without slipping in the mud and slithering over the cliff. It helped to put to the back of their minds what might be waiting for them. They pushed on.

✼

The nightmares, which Penny described as premonitions, the snapshots of shocking pain imaged his worst fears. He dreamt. A torn body woke him and kept him awake. He was in part living in the dreams and elsewhere. Penny never met this boy. He felt for him and he felt for Jack. Yet an inmost misgiving about Max disturbed him and made him feel blameworthy. The dreams fucked with his mind, muddled his regimes of belief, a kind of fiction effect. Penny experienced his nightmares and regressed.

They agreed not to share their plans with anyone, not even Raed. It was, as Penny cautioned them, scraps of info only, things overheard, instinct.

At the mention of the castle, he heard one kid blurt out, "You won't find me hanging out at that freaking graveyard."

He avoided asking the kids directly. His situation was problematical. Penny's fragility meant he really wanted the staff and students to like him. Yet he was aware of the old adage 'don't smile until Easter'. He stayed as serious as he could. Dove had said just report back – anything, a crumb even! Morsels they got, and often unrelated.

In an esoteric vein, Penny said to Dove, "Trust is the postmodern problem, or lack of it."

Like Oldman, he felt he was up against a mutual organisation, a whole town in this case, and that change was coming.

*Oldman was aware that he was open to deception, though his paranoia was born of experience.*

Disintegration was imminent for both. The mutual organisation was in his case a culture of which he had once been a part. That too led to further feelings of disorientation.

Boundaries were everything. He would get his chance. His situation at the school needed to remain solid. He kept his Tableau dream to himself – the two indeterminate figures, alien to the area, horrid abuse. He read *Death's Door* by Blake.

Death's door was a castle with an ivy mantle. He flitted to and from Blake to Blair's poem reading aloud an excerpt of blank verse from The *Grave*:

> *By glimmering through thy low-brow'd misty vaults*
> *(Furr'd round with mouldy damps and ropy slime),*
> *Lets fall a supernumerary horror*
> *And only serves to make the night more irksome.*

In the sense that his dreams didn't make sense, he decided to go with it – his youthful dream of the dismembered body in the art college as the red light for further caution. Penny was seventeen and had recounted his dream at college. He recalled with trepidation the aftermath of recounting the dream to the students and the police interview.

The police officers deduced that seventeen-year-old Penny couldn't have chopped the body up and secreted parts in the lockers. He seemed incapable of anything apart from fantasising. He wasn't all there. The body parts were in the lockers, just as he said.

His story of the St Elmo's fire burning above the College tower was aimed at entertaining his mates. Instead it brought about an encounter with the police, and scorn from staff and students. Today, that fire burned over Kilton Castle, its damp and ropy slime.

\\\\\

The exterior of Liz and Jim's house was, in Penny's lofty estimation, eye-catching, with a definite oh-dear at one point.

Built in the 1960s and detached, it paid lip service to the 1930s. The distempered white exterior and balcony with its curved wrought iron balustrade on the first floor expressed European modernity, the wrought iron painted white. Penny couldn't settle as to whether he was falling foul of his own conservatism, or whether an innate sense of design told him it should be matte black. He scrutinised it with the eagle eye of the critic. Stylistically, it should be black. He pledged not to mention it to his hosts. He was to meet Jim, who was back from plumbing in the Gulf.

The bell was on the gatepost; the post box was on the gate; the gate was open. He had to walk back to find the bell. Liz told him that placing everything outside meant they could lock the main gates – security. He pressed it. Her voice told him to come on up.

On the ground floor was a spacious basement. Two bicycles leaned against the far wall. The rest was old-time childhood clutter: a wooden cot with peeling white paint in one corner, a vintage rusty tricycle close by.

Up one flight of stairs, the warm living room was at first sight a vibrant muddle of objects. Jim arose from his chair and shook Penny's hand vigorously. It didn't feel right.

Soul appeared lacking from the Catholic mix of *objets d'art*. Norman Rockwell's *Teacher's Pet* hung on one wall. The lithograph sat uneasily alongside African masks and carvings and a glass-topped faux Japanese coffee table with sinewy curved black lacquered wood supports. The plethora of objects, the arty posters and Picasso Cubist vase in the carved wooden cabinet relegated to a superficial collection of un-orchestrated possessions placed around the unused

(Penny wrongly presumed) shiny black piano. The masks spoke of colonial rule, the Turkmen mat of orientalism. Jim indicated the sofa and Penny sat down.

He so wished to find a paint brush and a tin of matte black paint. He scanned the room (a space he wanted to rearrange) and cautiously negotiated the polished wooden floor to look at a small table.

"Nice table." He scrutinised the rest of the room.

"Liz went to night class to study feng shui."

Jim's comment appeared pointed and unnecessary. It wasn't the content as much as his supercilious facial expression and matching tone.

Liz moved things on. "Thanks, Jim. The table's Japanese. Well, a copy."

"Gosh." Penny imagined another tier above with glass cupboards filled with tiny insects in trays with pins through them. He looked at Jim. "It's nice to meet you, Jim. Have you ever been to the Horniman Museum?"

"No, but I've heard of it. Is it good?"

"You'd love it – an arts and crafts building. They're negotiating the return of valuable artefacts to Nigeria."

The Trout's were working people who desired to capture elements of culture for their own pleasure and to evoke memories. The objects, mementos rather than possessions, acted not as a collection, but recollections, signs of happy times together, holidays, or gifts from abroad.

They proved to be amicable hosts. The food was great, the chat varied. A potato dish with Gruyère, garlic and flat leaf parsley accompanied by *haricots vert* and glazed julienne carrots was in Penny's estimation superb. Jim was eager to talk of his culinary expertise and went through his recipe of parboiled haricots thrown into iced water, sautéed with shallots, and finally lemon zest stirred in. Penny re-evaluated his first impression of the man. His handshake may have been insincere. His cooking was fine.

"It was lovely." Penny consigned the recipe to memory.

He needed to know about Max, Michael Farrow and Ms Bowers, the woman mauled by the werewolf. He didn't find the reports of her story credible. They were mixed and ranged from the banal and average to the surreal and incredulous.

Hart's involvement with the 'old dear' motivated him to find out more. Steering the conversation wasn't difficult. The werewolf issue snuck in. Jim didn't say much. Penny prodded him about his work abroad and threw in a plumbing anecdote or two from his days as a steel worker. He knew his pipe threads. Regrettably, Jim was reluctant to talk of his work.

Penny changed tack. "It must have been dreadful for poor old Granny Bowers to be confronted like that."

Liz's response showed that her feelings went out to Gran, with reservations. "If it hadn't been for her injuries, I expect no one would have believed her. She's a strange woman. Never know how to take her."

"Has she any close family?"

"A big and extended family, though disconnected. You asked me about her grandson, Mikey, recently."

"He's a Bowers?" He feigned ignorance.

"His mum was Gran's daughter, died of breast cancer, leaving poor Mikey with his dad who worked nightshifts in the potash mine prior to working away. He spends time on his own and needs help. Mikey falls within, or into, the broad spectrum of autism. It wasn't easily discernible when he was a young child. My assessment, one derived from my experience as an educator, is that he is on the periphery. He's a bright boy and requires more than we can give or afford. His mum was reflective, unconventional." She went on to clarify her statements, and then disposed of the list of red flags for autism one by one.

Penny speculated whether it was a mass syndrome and in us all, in the sense of 'autism-light'. He decided not to voice his slant as he was aware of the fact it was important how it affected a person's life. "Is he close to his gran?"

"Let's just say she cared for him while his mum was dying and for a short while after. His problems increased with close contact with her. Not her fault, of course. His dad is a good man at heart. He worked for a low wage and for long hours, leaving the kid at home. He left the mine and went contracting, which is better money. He works in South Yorkshire and comes home often. Mikey should be with an adult – even Gran! He does visit her."

Penny found that discomforting on several levels. Who kept an eye out for Mikey? Why didn't she say his dad's name? It was all very odd.

The dad with no name intrigued the sub-textual analyst. The absence of a name was also cultural – the blokes referred to the wife as the missus, the lasses to the old man, and some men used that old-fashioned term 'mother', a product Penny assumed of talking to the kids. Better than the ball and chain perhaps? The expression 'let's just say' nullified the act of caring. The caring took on inverted commas. Where was Liz in all this? They sounded very close.

Penny needed to say something, anything. "What a shame."

"He manages. His dad and Gran don't get on. Mikey's borne the brunt of family disunity, though it would be wrong to see Gran or his dad as persecutors."

Penny recognised her use of a transactional model and concurred. Who was the rescuer, the victim, the persecutor?

"Kate, his mum, was my best mate. Kate excelled at everything she chose to. Kate, bless her, could turn yoga into a competitive sport. Her son inherited her brains, and more, though not a need to win."

"Not competitive, then?"

"I asked him once why he slowed down at the end of the school cross-country run, and he said he didn't want to pass anyone at the end; it didn't seem fair. In a group activity, he would hand power to others, though he's perfectly capable of taking the lead."

While Lizzie, as Jim called her, was in the kitchen sorting out the pudding, Jim passed on the fact that Liz was really pleased to have him at the school.

Penny flushed. "I came cheap."

Jim's carefully chosen words smacked of an education of a different kind to Penny's. His control of language spoke of the public school.

"Have stilsons will travel eh, Jim? You could've been a member of parliament.... *carpe diem*."

"You might say that."

"Do you celebrate World Plumbing Day?"

"You're joking." Jim didn't look sure.

"It's in March. It's about societal health and plumbing's great role in such."

Jim changed the subject. Music filled the house and was as broad as the curios that Liz dotingly pointed at and then related each one's story. The artefacts turned, by affectionate sleight of hand, from possessions into narratives and fond memories. Jim, it turned out, was a good guitarist and played piano. They listened to Little Feat and sang along.

He raised his glass. The night went past quickly.

"Did you meet in Loftus, Jim?"

"We met in Durham. Lizzie was in Durham on a longish sabbatical. We swapped phone numbers after a coffee together. I missed her, took the plunge and phoned."

Liz nodded.

"Nice. I am nosy. Hope you don't mind?"

Liz shook her head in a not-at-all manner. Jim signalled the night was over.

"How well did you know Max, Jim?"

"Lizzie knew him well, of course. I spoke to him once. His disappearance is awful."

The bonhomie evaporated as he spoke. Jim moved to the door. Penny collected his coat and scarf. Jim saw him out. He gripped Penny's hand in farewell. His confident handshake and straightforward approach put Penny's senses on red alert. His own handshake felt uneasy. He wasn't sure why he was grasping this man's hand.

The hand was not that of worker – skilled or otherwise. The long slender fingers skipped along the keyboard; the sculpted nails on the right-hand played finger style; his fingertips were calloused at the tips only, a guitarist's fingers.

Jim didn't do the graft. He wished freckled-faced Liz had seen him out. As he walked towards the gate, he turned back and pointed to the wrought iron balustrade.

"It would be great in matte black."

Ten thirty p.m. and on the way home, feeling mellow and whistling *Paint it Black,* Penny saw Mikey cycling past, oblivious to his presence. The boy's extended wheelie was for his pleasure only. He may have taken satisfaction in Penny's modification from the tune to a shrill whistle of approval, which curtailed the next passage of the song. It reached a crescendo as the boy passed. The tune ended there on a high note and in a different key.

The ease with which Mikey lifted the front wheel and rode the length of the street was born of practice and natural ability.

As the boy sped away, Penny whistled again, this time through his teeth. He'd never ridden a BMX. Skateboards were in vogue when he was younger. He'd never tried one.

## Chapter 26

*The police were everywhere. Stead had called them. Luna was prone to wandering, and was absent-minded, but this was unusual: she hadn't signed out.*

*The inner circle of the cribbage and bridge games in Reynold's Hall now included a learner. Oldman was not entirely convinced by the invitation. They were keeping him close. He wondered about the security of his apartment. He often mulled over the meeting, the night he had a tot with Ken. He used his email with caution. He had his own take on e-trust.*

*Fielding sat out of the game at his side and helped the rookie. In his notebook, he wrote of his enjoyment, of his enthusiastic amateurism in the bridge rubbers and his liking of the participants, who appeared to put up with his blunders with the patience of Job. His role as west, his position at the bridge table opposite an exceptionally tolerant east, Stead that is, earned him the name Westy. West was under surveillance from all points of the compass.*

*The silver-grey saloon hadn't followed him for days. In his passion for the game he forgot his basic training. He decided to enter into a dialogue, not with God but with Stead. He also wanted to know more about Luna. The police had contacted relatives and drawn a blank. The law seemed particularly interested in him.*

*Stead was waiting for more information – a waiting bid. Her purpose was covert. Directed surveillance was her aim. If intrusive became necessary then she would deploy that too. The secretary of state was an acquaintance. Oldman had a history, which is all she knew. And he had been prying. She wanted to like him. She could see he enjoyed her company, and that could work for her.*

*For his part, he began to savour his time with Stead. It wasn't simply her amazing concentration as his opposite pole. She mesmerised him; she was clever. She was a handsome woman with a youthfulness that belied her sixty-plus years. His aim at that point was to keep his errors and mistakes to a minimum. He fancied her. That could help or hinder his cause.*

*She was probably plotting his demise. She clearly wanted to know his past. Oldman sensed it. He began to understand the term yarborough. She was ahead of the game.*

Penny's pencil hovered above his little red memo pad. He was reading his notes and deliberating on the gist of the conversation with Liz and Jim on the topic of Mikey Farrow. Jim's reaction to his question on Max was evasive, that he was certain of, though not much else.

The pencil never touched the paper. He closed the pad and smiled lovingly at its shiny redness. He now had two notebooks. On a whim he reopened it and wrote:'give power away!' Here was a mind prepared to break down ego and its accompanying discourses. It also meant other things for him.

How he could get to talk to Mikey was another matter. He was a key signifier that would open up a chain for him.

Somehow, carefully and casually they had to meet, build a bridge.

***

Dove and Periwinkle eyed the sodden jungle of weeds that encased the castle. Though dying back slowly with the encroaching winter, the briars and thorny brambles offered protection to remaining fruit in the sheltered dip, thriving in the cover offered by the remnants of the building that they held together as a thank you. In the torch-lit half-light Periwinkle discerned that fruit was still on the bushes.

The derelict buildings appeared completely inaccessible. Penny's rough map, his 'intel', was fairly accurate. Periwinkle wondered if he had consulted his friend, Oldman.

Max might be in the sea, though the sea was preternatural, and had an uncanny knack of giving up its dead. They climbed down through the brambles.

***

Raed's morning meeting with Hart concluded with the need for a chat with young Michael Farrow sooner rather than later. He didn't attend school; he didn't appear to have any parents at home, and he was a minor.

After the daily briefing, she called to speak with Jim. He was away on business. Another chat with Gran was pending. Fitting it in was an issue. Her diary included an appointment at the school in an official capacity to talk about drug-taking and the increasing evils of the legal high. Hart volunteered. It was his forte.

Raed feared Max was dead, though she didn't want to give up believing. The headteacher had been helpful in profiling the youngsters Max and Michael. The latter she confirmed showed no signs of depression, though was prone to fits of quietness, and may well be autistic. Raed's take on that was that it was all the more reason he *should* be in school. Max's profile did nothing to imply criminality. How reliable was the headteacher? Michael's profile implied much to Raed, but criminality was low on the list. Phibes was alert to any signs or difference in behaviour of the young adults and was, in her estimation, forthright and discriminating. How to approach the issue of the boy concerned her. Liz had given her an insightful résumé of him – his personal issues, and his sharp intelligence. Liz's story was well rehearsed. Phibes kept an eye out on George and Kyle. They were keeping their own company. She was sure the boy Max was party to mischief. Being party to something and imparting it around those parts was a problem. Charity apart and a comment on the weather, the locals gave nothing away to strangers.

**Chapter 27**

Max did not die easily. The very nature of torture meant no signs were apparent on his young frame; the intricacy, if such a word was appropriate for the methodical infliction of mental and physical pain and the terrible intimacy of torture, was evident in his young, frightened face. He had aged in those dreadful moments. Death had brought only relief. Dove and Periwinkle had witnessed the effects of grown men who had suffered torture. This was a child. Neither spoke. His tomb was a small annex on the side of the ruined castle.

Though hands may have held tight that young face, no marks showed – in the cold grey of his eyes only the torment, the primal terror and helplessness of the tortured. Periwinkle closed the boy's eyes, the eyes of an old man. In the corner lay a dead dog, blinded and burnt. Dove shattered the stillness.

"The rules of torture," he choked on the next bit, "are to keep the person alive. The rules had been broken."

He knew there were no rules. His experience of the absolute power of the torturer, and the subsequent helplessness of the tortured, brought about a small invocation. Then he unfastened the body of the boy laid out cruciform on a stout wooden beam and shrouded him completely in his sleeping bag. Crime scene or not, they were taking him home.

"Screw the police."

Periwinkle signalled his agreement.

Neither spoke after that. Touching nothing around them, they left, Dove carrying the boy wrapped in his quilted green shroud, Periwinkle leading. Neither of the men cast a single glance back at the small derelict outbuilding that had functioned as a torture chamber for a young man and a dog. Max had died alone on a rough wooden cross, cold and in stark fear while his father was nearby, walking the cliffs, searching for him, wandering, desperate, crying, calling for him against the gusting winds and rain, never knowing that his only remaining family was nearby.

On the way back along the cliffs, with Dove carrying the boy, they finally found a signal. Periwinkle called Raed. They waited. A police helicopter picked them up along the tops. Raed apologised for the delay. They now relied on air support from Leeds or Newcastle. She nodded curtly, but beyond the apology never spoke. Dove recognised what lay behind her brown eyes: despair. There was no reprimand for removing Max's body from the scene of the crime. Disbelief came first, then a consuming sadness. They detected in her a steely determination to apprehend the killer, or was it killers? A current of feeling passed between the three of them – anger.

On hearing the news, Penny felt no satisfaction in being right.

He muttered a few words from Blair's poem under his breath, "*To paint the gloomy horrors of the tomb,*" then forgot the next line as his eyes filled. He held Jack's arm tightly.

Jack, already worn out with searching, stood to attention for a minute when the news came. Jack had been in enough battles to realise his son Max was dead. The nature of that loss had not sunk in. The men did their best to comfort him. Hart arranged counselling. Dove drove him to identify the body.

Jack placed a hand on the boy's cold head. "Max... son."

He wheeled around stiffly and left, with Dove a pace behind him. They exited the cold clinical environs of the morgue together arm in arm. The coroner authorised an inquest.

Raed managed to draft in extra police. A second full-scale murder hunt began. Before the obligatory press release, talk circulated. Raed debated whether to publicise the torture and decided against it.

She explained, "The media's blend of fact, fantasy, fiction and prurience would not help our case." Her take on the pornography of violence for the hacks and public was a sad fact.

Hart agreed and asked that he might give the press release.

She agreed. "Regrettably, the English press and parliament collectivises everything. Islam, for example, is associated with terror, conflict — what they call Islamism. In other words, extremism. It's John Gaunt's, Jeremy Clarkson's and Julie Burchill's world, and it's sad. To put a cap on it, one has to weigh up the sense or merit of a press statement of this nature from a Muslim woman, its subsequent readings and interpretations." She was livid.

Penny supported the notion of a free press. He muttered something. Hart nodded his consent.

Raed's coldness was apparent. "This Dalek, as I was once described, would happily exterminate the perpetrators."

Unfortunately, they had nothing to go on.

Hart tried to offer a glimmer of hope. "The forensic boys and girls are there now."

"I doubt they will find much." Dove's comment wasn't meant to bring the mood downward, though it served that purpose. His aim was that they shouldn't fall for the high note to end the meeting syndrome, a managerial ploy in the meeting-as-therapy game. It fell short.

"Forensic analysis is notoriously inconsistent." Raed put a cap on it. Before Hart could reply, she brought the discussion to an end. "Our collective aim is to find the killer of a child, and a young woman, both too young to have the chance to experience life in the full! Let's go to work. Thanks to all of you for your input."

No one had a damn clue.

Hart was silent.

Penny wasn't. "It has occurred to me that there may be something else going on here that Max was party to." The words spilled out, "The werewolf is nothing to do with Max's murder, though the children will think it is. Nothing is straightforward, not even the blood-feuds." He steered away from academic jargon, though words like de-familiarise came to mind. "The werewolf is an immeasurable problem. Forget common sense. Work with the unquiet, the unspoken.

Move into the unmarked areas. Ask and dig out the Bowers-Bateman history. Start with Gran." He concentrated his gaze on Hart. "Can I ask you what you know about the headteacher's husband?" He noticed Hart was on his guard.

"We are following up Jim's and Michael's father's backgrounds."

Dove eyed Hart with a biting glare that recognised things hidden.

"Be nice to share what you come up with," Raed added politely.

"I'd better go and give my statement." Hart stood to leave.

❧

"This is a case of murder, the murder of a young man! That is all we have to say at the present time."

The baying stringers of the press howled for more.

Hart continued, "We will not stop until we apprehend the perpetrator. Max," he added tersely, "was barely sixteen. This is now a murder hunt!" He waved the press away as if shooing a fawning dog.

He walked back into the station as the three pals left. No one spoke. Penny raised a tentative thumb to support Hart.

They went to the pub for a bite to eat. A group of reporters, frustrated by Hart's minimal statement, surrounded Dove on the way, firing questions:

"Was it you who found the body?"

"Was it you who removed the body from the scene of the crime?"

"Was it you—"

Penny never heard Dove's comment. Whatever it was, it brought the snapping terriers to heel. They stepped back as one. He recognised Dove's mannerisms and the threat they carried. A perverse notion occurred: he wished that the reporters hadn't backed off.

In the pub, the three men sat alone, away from the locals. None of the drinking classes had anything to say. Once again silence came down on Loftus. Downward nods and sideways glances were it. The unspoken perception was that these three interlopers would find whoever did this. What might happen to the offender was a cause for speculation. In their minds this wasn't to be the usual local beating-the-shit-out-of-another-local, a Friday night closing time event. What had happened to young Max was terrible. No one finished their food.

Periwinkle prompted Penny. "What makes you uncertain about Jim?"

"Intuition, that's all. He might have been a plumber, but he isn't now, unless plumbing is a euphemism." Penny surmised that Jim's marriage to Liz was a charade. When it came to Liz his feelings were in conflict – he liked her.

Barely out the door, Dove turned to Periwinkle. "See what you can find out about Jim."

A break in the wintry weather followed. The warmer daylight was conducive to chatter and helped temper the warning blast of a fast-approaching severe winter. Alongside that a black veil of silence came down like the northern winter night. The town and its occupants descended into the grave.

An elderly man stopped Dove and said, "Waxwings are flocking the woods. There's chilly weather on the way."

Dove managed a feeble headshake.

In the schoolyard, an eerie hush prevailed. In the shops and the streets neighbours exchanged brusque greetings only. In the boy's neighbourhood, locals offered sympathetic stiff and downward nods towards Jack's house. Jack wasn't there. Jack was walking. He was up early. It wasn't actually clear if he had slept. He walked.

For the police it was a conspiratorial silence, though inwardly they knew that no one had any information. No one had seen strangers around. For Dove, it was replete with significance. The townsfolk knew jack shit. The trio set off on another avenue in their investigations, one they assumed the police had no inkling of.

"What have they got to hide around here? Silence, as you once said, speaks volumes." Periwinkle's poser brought about an unexpected response from Penny.

Initially, he raised his hands to say 'your guess is as good as mine'. He began to elaborate, joining up dots of conversations from the schoolyard, emails from Liz, and chats with Phibes. Theory, as one author said, would be flight. Although an incomplete picture emerged, it was nevertheless a sketch of family intrigue, family rivalry, envy and jealousy, leading to the killing of a young woman and the torture and murder of a young man.

He finished with the bold statement, "I have a notion that Max was linked into something nasty."

Jack's prime motive for calling Dove in the first place was to find out if his son was 'up to something'.

Dove reasoned that the werewolf attacks were the beginnings of an escalation of events.

Jack interrupted his thoughts. "Max was aware of… as you say, aware of, or involved in, something untoward." Jack guessed right. "My son's killers didn't take a chance. The torture was together punishment, as well as aimed at extracting information. Or was it perverse? Both? Why use torture if you're going to kill someone anyway?"

Dove paced the room. The evil that perpetrated such horror was out there. What was more alarming to him was that it was sadistic – and could be youthful. He so wanted to be wrong. The wellbeing of his old comrade worried him.

Jack had spoken little since the morgue. When he did, he mostly repeated, "Why?" then closed down again, and set off walking. There was a general feeling he might self-harm or harm an innocent. They chose the difficult path of allowing him to go and not follow him.

Periwinkle had other ideas. "I'm going away for a day or so. I'll check Jim out."

## Chapter 28

As a detour, and a way of working things through, Penny was scanning his latest chapter on Oldman. His cluttered notes specifying the most recent death required typing up before his spidery scrawl became unreadable. Reading it aloud helped.

*Bernie Catchpole, a well-known character (a thug and miscreant that meant) had shown no signs of illness according to his grieving family, who were about to inherit. It paid them to keep quiet. No traces of anything toxic showed in tests. Like the two before him, all legal aspects seemed above board. Other cases of the criminal classes expiring before their due date had come to light. Catchpole had lifted a glass in the pub, opened his mouth and passed on. Griggs ticked off another on the list. He called the police. Time to bring in the cavalry.*

*Bernie was well-known to the police, who had been trying to pin a raft of dodgy deals and killings on the man. He would have authorised crime rather than done the dirty work; his position required such. On the face of things he was a 'family' man.*

*It suited the relatives to have him removed or banged up. Bernie, bless him, had died peacefully. The certification was in* order: heart attack. Upstanding servants of the people signed it. Oldman suspected that the residents of the hall had links with 'upstairs' in his own department. That worried him. Could Griggs be playing him? How the hell was he to get anything from the card school?

What was Ken up to? He saw him chat to Roger, one of the older residents. In Oldman's book he was a slippery customer. Roger looked shifty. Oldman decided to take a chance and visit Roger after dark. Luna's disappearance had affected the school. The bridge players looked uneasy.

He also decided to call in. The bicycle was proving fun and the roads to the box and the village fairly empty. He left his helmet and, mounting the bike, set off at a steady pace. Hardly out on the road and the skies opened up. He made to turn around, then through the drizzle saw the phone box, a relic from a past he recalled with fondness, a red museum piece, not quite on a par with the Benin sculptures but a worthy relic. Quite fitting that K2, the original, should be outside the Royal Academy.

His call took a minute only. Hayley was going to do some more spadework. No one signed the car out. No one had responded to the request to register the vehicle with the 'company'. She was also gleaning through recent past sudden deaths. She transferred his call to Griggs. Oldman spoke first.

"Catchpole is on the list, as you know. His medical records indicate he was sound. I'm getting nowhere, in truth. Betrayal is alien to these folks. And the possible talkers have clammed up. One of them, Fielding, seems scared." He told Griggs about the meeting. "Anything on Ken?" He could only surmise. What were the bridge school fretting about?

Griggs didn't commit. "Keep chipping away. Use your charm."

Oldman laughed and put the phone down. The rain was heavier still. He mounted the bike and set off. No sign of the car. Straining his eyes through the downpour he checked left as he came to a T-junction. Despite the rain the engine revving was audible enough, and only at the final second did he blink to see the car speeding towards him head on. The driver hadn't seen him. With all his strength and agility he swung the bike to the right. The car swerved too, though not away from him, and side-swiped him. He went down with the bike, the right pedal piercing his leg, his head bouncing on the tarmac road. His coat had a thick collar turned up against the rain and helped break the fall. He laid there. Finally he moved a finger, then his head. It was splitting. He looked for the car – gone. He never saw the driver. The colour of the car was silver grey.

On his feet though dizzy and shocked he pushed the mangled bike back down the road. It was a sorry sight that staggered into the hall. The first person to see him sat him down.

"Let me get the doctor."

It was Stead who appeared. She asked him what happened. As he spoke, she checked him for concussion – okay. She placed her elbows in front of her and asked him to push. He did and she hit the wall two feet away.

"No problem there. A little anger perhaps? Can't find anything broken. Let's get you to your room."

May, the lady who met him and Stead, helped him upstairs.

"There's blood running from your trouser leg. Get them off!"

It was an order. He stripped and dried off. She dressed the wound. The bruises were beginning to show from his face, down his right side. His brain felt loose. That the bruising was on the opposite side seemed strange to him.

Not so, she explained everything would have shifted with the impact. "Your brain included."

He just wanted to lay down. He did. Stead disappeared and returned with a couple of hefty tablets and poured a glass of water.

"Take these. It will help you sleep. I'll call in later." As a mother would to a child she leaned over as he closed his eyes and pecked him on the forehead. "Sleep tight."

His whole body reacted; memories buried deep. He dozed off. His bruises subsided slowly over a couple of weeks, but a rattling headache would return now and then. He went outside to see a doctor. It was apparent the local GP thought he was neurotic, implying he imagined the headaches. Oldman pushed him.

"It's all in your head," was the sarcastic reply.

"Fucking headaches are you, jerk."

That was the end of his history as a patient in the village. He didn't mention the fact he was going to find the driver and kill them.

The writing didn't quite take Penny's mind off the unfathomable death of Max, or the werewolf. The key to unlocking this horrid bag of worms lay in the family enmities; rivalries that had festered and bred a sepsis in the blood of generations. Who was the link? Where did Jim fit in to this? He didn't. Granny Bowers featured in his deductions.

Dove, Penny and Periwinkle wanted to follow up the dragon slayer myth, and so they went in search of Scaw. It was to be a memorable day out. Periwinkle took sandwiches. The priory at Handale was gone, the naughty nuns history was recounted by Dove, the naughtier priests never mentioned. The small walled garden was pleasant, the replanting immature. The giant sword was not hanging on the wall of the cottage. Absence made the myth grow stronger.

Had they not gone to Handale that day they would never have seen the big cat. It appeared on the road twenty yards in front. Penny saw it but couldn't speak.

Dove spoke first. "Fuck me."

They stood transfixed, admiring its grace as it stalked a small roe deer. It slipped away in the long grass on the right side of the road. Penny knew it would help him at a future point. The sleek black beast had a symbolic value. Dove said a panther.

"It's a black leopard, Dove."

It crossed the road in front of them, turned, bared its teeth, and went into the field. Its length head to tail end was about four feet. Penny tried to change that to metric and couldn't. They watched every movement with awe until the lengthy curve of its tail disappeared into the field.

"What a sight!" Dove tried to follow its path; the deer stood unaware. He shouted and it bolted.

Periwinkle looked relieved. "What a beautiful beast."

Penny was quiet. The panther had pursued him for years in his daymares. At last, it was real.

# Chapter 29

In the sheltered accommodation of Reynold's Hall no silence ensued. Oldman speculated. Had his bridge companions command of the script, planned it, executed it, and written the eulogy? Who was next? The police had found nothing linked to Luna, though Oldman suspected they weren't telling all. He was going to find the driver of the silver-grey car and kill them. Stead didn't show her affection again but spent more time with him. She didn't trust him fully. That was mutual.

He knocked on Roger's door. No answer. Sensing the man was on the other side of the door he knocked again. He kept knocking. It was a frightened man who opened the door a fraction. Oldman pushed it open and walked in.

"Tell me about Ken."

Roger never answered. His body language and demeanour wisely spoke of fear.

"If I find you're up to something — you and Ken — I'll be back here with a message you won't forget... or won't remember." He left. Ken had asked him that first night at the bar to keep a weather eye on the card players. Why? He doubted Roger knew anything.

It was difficult for Oldman to see his comrades at the card table as cold-hearted killers. Was he making excuses for them? Griggs and Hayley were ploughing through profiles. Surely they would find stuff on Ken. Roger, he decided, was a waste of space and time, a sneak, lower than a snake's belly.

He read the Daily Telegraph for the news or was it commentary (reportage was old hat these days). It mentioned the death of Catchpole as a well-known citizen of the town and his charitable works, and his wife, once a local headteacher. Bullshit.

The bridge school attacked the games with a new fervour and a sharper focus that kept him on his toes and distracted. The fever was catching and Westy joined in with renewed vigour, with Fielding assisting.

The suspects had all been at home when the death occurred. The gang he played cribbage and bridge with if involved were, like Catchpole, acting as a 'consultancy'. They didn't sign documents. If anything, they authorised it, organised the complexities with the death industry and its certification. They were complicit. As he made his way to the gym, Oldman noticed the electricians around again, one of them conversing with Ken. Both turned away as he crossed the room.

What would they, the death industry, put on Max's death certificate? Torture resulting in death?

He held back from the writing. It occurred to him that, apart from a birth certificate, it was the only certificate that this intelligent young man was to have. Afterwards, he worked for hours on Tableau drafts, waking up in the chair around three in the morning. He crawled into bed stiff and weary.

Despite a new wariness, Oldman was enjoying his bogus retirement and the company of his newfound friends. That they were suspects in a string of murders caused him serious misgivings. Griggs was making noises about pulling him out. He had to stay put. That would allow him to be near Stead. He gave up the bike and stuck to his car.

He needed an informer. Without that, or bugging the whole place, his case was hopeless. Oldman didn't like bugging. He didn't particularly like a snitch. Roger that. In conversation with Stead (Stead and he were getting closer as partners in the game). Over a cuppa and biscuit (bourbons, his favourite), he had been highly critical of the 2011 News of the World hackings and Milly Dowler case, which he described as despicable and against the grain. He had in his own career in Intelligence been an unwilling party to it for a long time.

"You're such an idealist, Westy."

This ticking off caused a tingle of excitement, a memory of things past. He liked being Westy. Was she saying hacking was okay? More than likely she was probing.

She was still digging and her astute intuition taking control. She had an idea.

## Chapter 30

Against all his instincts, Penny followed Oldman's lead and, kept his mouth shut. It formed his main excuse to keep a social distance from people when feeling vulnerable. In his current mental state trust had no purchase.

Phibes had retreated into his hut. The yard was a lonely place without him. The familiar gangs of kids that hung out together had fragmented. Small units formed and broke like ants searching. Loners remained with their shyness, fantasies, or inability to mix. One girl of about thirteen came over, opened her mouth as if to speak, then went past him, the uncomfortable sniggers of troubled minds everywhere. Lost and alone, he was staring at the bike sheds when an idea came to him. Among the scooters and assorted bikes was an old BMX. He went over and examined it. If Oldman could play cards then Penny could ride a bike. He bought one.

The schoolkids admired his choice, to which he informed them he was expertly advised by Kyle and George.

The truth lay more in a sharp comment by George, "If you're going to ride a BMX, get Spaz to teach you on his Barracuda. He's the man!"

"Barracuda, you say?"

It helped open a dialogue with the boys. Their reactions were fifty-fifty between admiration and bemusement. Beneath their chilled, new openness, he could sense their barely disguised envy.

He kept the conversations to bikes. "Wethepeople's Envy LSD was top. I chose the Barracuda over the Redline." He could think of no other reason than the name was nifty and that Mikey had one.

Like Oldman, he too was about to join an elite club – his first. Raed had spotted him out on his new mode of transport.

She advised that he check out the Bradford Bandits on the Web. "Great meeting in Peel Park!"

On a biting cold Thursday evening, he wrapped up and cycled to the abandoned parking lot. He was attempting a wheelie when surrounded by five boys on bikes.

His miserable efforts annoyed him. He wanted to throw the bike away; blame the bike. Totally engrossed and appropriately clothed in his hoody, gloves and his favourite green scarf looped around his neck, he was at first unaware of the company. They appeared out of nowhere in a stylish and fluid way. They swerved their bikes in unison like starlings in a murmuration, seamlessly forming a weaving looping pattern around him.

As they spun around him to link up, his heart was in his mouth. His paranoia kicked in. A confrontation with kids was his worst nightmare.

One of them got off his bike, dropping it to the ground. The others followed suit. The bikes formed a barrier between him and the outside. He decided to bottle it out.

"Ah," he said boldly, "the infamous five."

Paying no heed, or not realising his reference, the first one to dismount spoke.

"You must be Dr Death."

Like Penny, he wore a hoody, but his light grey zip-up with sleeves extended over his hands. Penny spotted a tear in the left sleeve near the cuff. His face, cloaked as it was by the enormity of the hood, made Penny uneasy. He couldn't see his eyes. His greeting was friendly and demonstrated a canny nature. His enunciation of his nickname foisted on him by the press demonstrated admiration and awareness rather than sarcasm.

He couldn't identify any of them. He presumed they came from the Gulag, or Colditz, the local council estate. Penny was a council estate kid. Things had changed a bit since his day. What was it about this place that brought about names derived from internment or horror genres to colour darkly the schoolyard or a housing estate?

The voice from the hood spoke again. "Nice bike, Doc. What you trying to do?"

In a shameful voice that sounded thirty or so years younger, he said, "A wheelie. I was going to ride into school tomorrow doing a wheelie."

The grins were plain.

Hoody spoke. "You're doing it wrong. Here, let's show you."

Picking up Penny's bike, he explained the simple movement required. He showed him it. The others demonstrated effortless variations. It was the very lack of power that mattered. He gave him the bike back.

"Your turn, Doc!"

Penny mounted the bike, pushed off and, after a short run, tried. The front wheel lifted a bit and after a yard slumped down. The boys clapped. In half an hour or so, though not perfect, he could do a reasonable wheelie. To finish the training session the six of them rode across the lot, with Penny staying up just short of the boys who braked then skidded around one hundred and eighty in unison and fell off their bikes, rolling with laughter. Then they mounted up and rode off.

He shouted after them. "Gee thanks, guys!"

Hoody turned and called back, "See you tomorrow."

The wind was picking up. The noise from roof tiles and loose corrugated iron on the makeshift fences of Westfield allotments banged and screeched, threatening to lift off in the approaching storm. As he cycled into the wind, a token wheelie was out of the question. He was on a high. His breath more or less stopped; he laid all biking ambitions aside. He tucked his head down to allow air into his lungs and pushed on home. He was pleased with his new contacts, though uncomfortably aware that his mixing with these five young boys might not be a sensible strategy. At the digs he stored his bike away. Dove, who was just going out, gave him a peculiar stare. Periwinkle was away.

The morning brought a surprise. He mounted his bike and pushed off. Barely out on the road to school the infamous five joined him, riding shotgun, either to share his moment or have a laugh at his expense. Nearing the school gates, they sped ahead and formed a three-by-two channel which directed and waved him in. At the gates, Hoody nodded as if to say go for it.

Kids were hanging out outside the perimeter fence, some cupping a last fag, some nipping it for later, when he did a wheelie through the channel into the school gates the full length. He curtailed his instinct to do a celebratory yippee or a high five with the nearest schoolkid as he dismounted. When he turned to acknowledge his escort the five had gone. In a triumphal daze he locked the bike in the sheds. The yard was quieter than ever.

Phibes came out of his hut and then went back in again, smirked, and Penny heard him say, "Nutter!"

Passing staff turned a blind eye. Strucker, who was fastening up his rusty old sit-up-and-beg handlebar bike (as if anyone would nick it), came over to ask if he could show him how to do a wheelie. Strucker was in awe.

In the yard later that day, George walked across and spoke. "Excuse me."

"Yes?"

"How do you know The Five? Are they buddies of yours?" His tone implied false respect, malice, and more than a hint of envy.

Penny chose truthful expedience. "I met them out riding."

"They're seriously dodgy."

Penny, who was blissed out by his grand entrance, faltered. Before he could ask him about Kyle's recent absence, George stalked away. In time, that short ground-breaking encounter with The Five was to help turn the investigation around.

After school Penny knew exactly what Oldman had to do. Another chapter rolled off the pen... well, the laptop. The pen was mightier. He pondered. The pen was now for vaping. His encounter with George made him think.

"Have you got a family?"

Stead thought her question was fair enough. Jack David's search had found nothing. Oldman's letters to his daughter, Bridie, told another tale. The envelopes gave her address and it was noted. Wife, sister, daughter? It was, to use a non-bridge expression, shit-or-bust time.

"Yes."

She waited. If he was a mole he wasn't digging or hunting for food. He ate quite sparsely. He also didn't say much. "Yes, what?"

"I was married a long time back. I have a daughter – Bridie. My ex doesn't want to know me."

It was quite clear he didn't want to talk about it. Why had their search not revealed such? She would find out. "Bridie. Nice name. Irish?"

The conversation dried up.

Oldman's new cribbage and bridge acquaintances were beginning to throw invites out. Walks and social evenings filled in the time. In his thinking, strategy and skill at cards might help his case. In hers, it meant they kept an eye on him and they listened.

The wintry weather hardly touched Reynold's Hall. It was aglow with camaraderie. Stead nattered to Jack David; he with others, Bridie Oldman the focus.

"I'll try elsewhere. Strange that none of that came up in my search."

Oldman did, however, tell Stead that it was probably not since his early days with Helen and Bridie had he enjoyed life so much. Then things turned to shite, as they often do.

Six or seven of the residents had gone out walking. Before they wrapped up and set off, Oldman allowed the maintenance

145

team into his apartment. The three men, all in overalls, set to work on the electrics and plumbing. On that particularly blustery evening a short stroll along the Downs was in order. The little group separated out.

Fielding marched next to Oldman and passed him a small folded paper. "Read it later. Not now."

He stuck it in his pocket. Fielding issued orders. Oldman assumed that the navy years had eradicated the art of normal conversation. There was a sense of urgency underlying the directive. He tried to imagine giving orders in the same way. Institutionalisation, he concluded, was part of the training of the recipient, and necessary. As he walked, he fingered the note.

After school Penny cycled to the lot and practised. During the rest of the week he wrote. He felt alone yet watched. His wheelies got better and better. In a rash and heady moment he attempted a one hundred and eighty, then came off. His hearing, like his sense of smell, was good. His motor skills had degenerated. He heard faint laughter as he picked himself and the bike up from the grizzled tarmac. He decided the laughter was with him rather than derisory.

At school, a large part of the agenda of the staff meeting remained unsolved, lost to frippery. Liz, who saw around her a united workforce, was content to let it go. Staff talked about getting scooters, skateboards, and one promised to extract from the garage his now grown daughter's bouncy thing (which he couldn't recall the name of) and bounce into school.

Strucker offered the answer. "You mean a Space Hopper?" And to everyone's amazement said, "That's really retro!"

Oldman pushed his hand deep into his pocket and gripped the note. He strode out in front alongside Fielding, slowing on the hill above Portslade to allow the others to catch up. Back in the warmth of Reynold's Hall they drank cocoa and went their separate ways.

Written in an immaculate hand, Fielding's baroque looped links in pen and ink were a warning: 'Things are not what they seem, Westy'. And then, 'We need to talk about Ken'. He admired the efficient script, the calligraphy (his own was a scrawl). Besides, he recognised he was about to have a breakthrough in information. At last he was to be clued in. Another thought occurred: was it a trap? Ken was becoming a common denominator in the scheme of things. Fielding and Ken never mixed. As two ex-military men one would think they might want to swop spit, but no.

'I fear for my safety'.

Oldman was about to set off to phone Griggs. He needed to know about all the residents – their past, their income, and professions. Then an unwashed and unshaven Fielding turned up. Fielding didn't strike him as a man to be scared easily. Who was he afraid of? Oldman let him in.

He flopped in the chair. "They've been around."

"Who?"

"Them – the maintenance men." Fielding slumped in the chair.

"Fielding, make yourself at home. There's tea in the kitchen. Help yourself."

Fielding was looking over his shoulder.

"There's fresh linen towels on the bedside if you want to take a shower." A polite way of saying he was minging. A good Scots

147

word he imagined. "A pack of razors there too. Just stay here until I return. I'll not be long. Help yourself to whatever."

"I'll lock the door, Westy. Did you know we were the first to test out what became known as the Rainbow Herbicides?"

It was apparent he was addressing himself. Oldman chose to respond to his first statement. He knew about Agent Orange and its dreadful consequences. And he knew damn well it was the British that tested the herbicides out during the Malaysian Emergency. As for talking to oneself, that was another issue.

"Fine, won't be long." He set off at speed, calling Griggs as he walked. The phone box would have to wait.

Griggs was concerned. "Oldman," he complained, "I really don't know what is going on upstairs anymore, but sense a change is coming. The usual rats will leave. Performance is a central issue, and organisational planning is bereft. I think it's time to pull out. In plain old English I smell a rat. I will ask Hayley to check your list." He added, "Luna was a party-political agent on the left of centre and an investigative writer who resigned, accused of something not proven, as they say in Scotland. As for your man Ken he is proving elusive, that is apart from his army records. Nothing untoward there."

Oldman so wanted it to be the other way around.

# Chapter 31

The coroner's office report bore little testimony to the varying degrees of physical and mental torture Max had suffered. 'A psychological element was involved which is untraceable in physical terms'.

The objects removed from the castle – the black hood, the hammer-drill – denoted menace. The dark, the isolation, horrid abuse, the cold and damp this young boy had been subject to was beyond scientific analysis. Any deduction was speculation, an exercise in sheer horror. The dog was Gemma's. How it had got there was anyone's guess. What had happened to it was evident. Dove had confronted evil before, but cruelty of this kind left him seething and vengeful. Penny imagined Max had the dog for company. No trace evidence remained. The perp was a pro.

They walked the cliffs searching for a clue. Whoever brought Max to his dungeon must've walked him there or carried him unconscious. No traces were visible. Periwinkle detected a soldiery aspect. He also alleged that the digs were 'leaky'. The proprietor was prying. That was understandable. All further discussion was to be outside.

The three men took long walks along the cliffs and local sands. Penny was often quiet and introspective. Jack was absent. None of them could imagine what Max had known or done to lead to torture. If Penny had a theory, he chose to button his lip. Penny paused at one of his favourite spots to let the others walk on – the tooth rock. He stared at the North Sea. The storm had abated temporarily. The molar-like promontory loomed large in the bright light against the sea, biting at the sky. It broke into dots, bright pixels with an overall greyness. It was a landscape where painting melded with nature in the raw. The red memo pad came out of his pocket. The landscape was telling him something. He needed to do his sums.

Mathematics, algebra, calculus were mysterious things to him, though geometry was manageable for the dyscalculic art historian. He needed to plot a locus, a loci – or locate a plot. Every time he tried, the lines with people as locations converged on Liz, Jim, and Mikey. Then there was Gran. Dove and Periwinkle had vanished in the distance. No givens made it silly. He endured.

He stowed his memo pad away as the bright light on the horizon blurred a speck of a boat sitting on the pond-like sea. He allowed the stillness, the monumentality of the coast, to swamp his self for a while, and then returned to his geometry. The perspectives of Piero della Francesca or Seurat required here were not his. He moved on and turned to stare blankly at the fang-like rock. It was a painting: Seurat's Le *Bec du Hoc, Grandcamp*.

Dove's comment that a simple wrongdoing wouldn't lead to such retribution had credence. Could it be something sexual, something clandestine, something highly illegal, or something furtive? All of them?

He reflected on another angle, one not so obtuse. The torture may have been gratuitous, as Jack mentioned. Did the killer choose to do it for satisfaction? Did he exceed his brief? Was he briefed? Was there more than one? The main indicator of gratuity was the poor doodle's death. It spoke of perversion, needlessness. What would he do if he could get his hands on them? He decided there and then it was *they* rather than *he or she?* Were they hired? Money wasn't exactly obvious around Loftus. That narrowed the field, unless killing folk paid the National Living Wage, or if youngsters, a National Minimum Wage.

"What's it all about... Alfie?"

The dead doodle failed to reply.

The rest of the walk was in silence, an introspective hush. The three men allowed the beauty of the crumbling cliffs at Boulby to blanket their notions and still their thoughts. The towering, scarred cliffs that had remained undefeated by man, mines and quarries, were giving into the burrowing of birds along the seaside. Like ideas and the earth they would inevitably collapse into the sea. What man failed to complete; the birds would finish off.

Penny's soul and mind were at Etratat with Courbet. The wave that curled towards the shore and disappeared under them was the artful product of brush and palette knife rather than the moon. In a sneaked moment he was a feature in the painting and the painting was all around him. The jagged rock that fascinated him lay behind them. Five seagulls swirled and danced in the winds. The little fishing boat was a blurred impression on the horizon.

He turned to Dove. "The sea's voice is tremendous."

The sea hissed as the waves murmured to him... *Jim*. Jim had money. Could they find out how much?

The weather stayed clear for another day or so. The panoramic views offered by the clear skies brought the potash mine across the fields into full view. The severe geometry of the building provided authority for a while and then faded in comparison to the natural beauty of Cowbar. Penny spotted wild purple-sprouting broccoli and aimed to come back and collect a bunch for dinner. He chose to forgo the lecture on its history and its medical value.

In the early evening Penny rode his bike. Without The Five to show him tricks and skills he felt defeated. No textbook could help him. It had to be action-oriented, a term he picked up at a university meeting. They were watching, no laughter. On the way back Mikey cycled past. He paused to eye critically Penny's bike. He lifted both hands off the handlebars and put his thumbs up as he sailed past. Mikey understood Newtonian physics.

The saddle soreness had abated, the-over-the-shoulder glimpse before turning – a manoeuvre that had been easy as a flexible youngster was becoming easier. It required twisting the neck around, which generated a wobble. Penny felt empowered. He still kept his hands on the handlebars, two fingers on the brake.

Later still, he went to the pub and scanned the cartoons of him on the bike, pinned on the wall next to the dartboard. He liked the one of him riding the wall of death. It may not have been very skilful; it was obvious who it was. Everyone present had a good-natured laugh. To show his appreciation he bought a round, refused a drink back, and went for a short walk towards Easington. The old town of Loftus was so near to his birthplace of Guisborough, though it could have been a thousand miles away.

He was beginning to feel a part of the north again, a belonging that the jumbled for-profit mentality of higher education had never offered; a sense of comradeship; differing values, a different take on value itself. He fought back his exasperation with the education sector, their no-fail policy and then the forgotten families of the northeast. His own family ties were non-existent. His fondness for his daughter, Else, was strong. The mixed sense of relief and loss when she moved to Canada was profound, leaving her partner behind and a country sinking into a political cesspit of its own choice. It was safer. Her new chap sounded obsessive, interesting.

Family feuds severed the ties there in Loftus, as elsewhere. From his time in the Middle East his knowledge of Arabia was that Islam had united the warring families against the West. Nothing cemented the folk here; work had gone and, with it, pride. The cracks were barely visible, but the cunning agent could exploit them. He would draw on Oldman's expertise in the field. What divided them? What united them?

Penny had played bridge. His excursions into the world of bridge had resulted in firstly maddening his opponents, then his partner. No one could effectively read a permanent grin. His early years playing whist with Grandma Penny and Great-aunt Alice had been a tough training ground; Alice, with her huge chain-stitch cardigans (she appeared to wear two that hung around her thin frame in layers). The crowning glory of a hat had remained fixed on her head throughout. The hatpin that had held it to her grey locks was a weapon, one that Alice would bring into play at the drop of a hat In the game, Grandma's stern face would register dismay after an error of judgement. Would Alice draw the pin and pierce her partner if she or he erred?

BMX biking, he concluded, was more fun than bridge. The round in the pub was his seven of diamonds, the beer card. Penny felt he was getting nowhere. Oldman was getting nowhere. It was a waiting game.

Dove, Periwinkle and he exchanged information. Periwinkle passed on information to Raed. Dove's take on his liaison was crude. Periwinkle's response to such comments was as stern as Grandma Penny's reprisals. Whist! Five paintings came to mind, then a flood – Cézanne, Steen – Dutch genre. The baroque; cards and art; intimate spaces, cheating, the players keeping their cards close to their chests. Cézanne; the bridge school.

Information was building up in scraps only. Hart had checked up on Jim and reported that Jim was clear, but he intended to dig further.

Penny's opinion was blunt. "Clear means he's not clear."

And so they hung out in the cultural institutions of the north, anticipating an informer or a link. Dove was becoming a popular figure around town with his salty sea stories, unmatched, though bravely contested by local fishermen whose fables faded in comparison. Their stories of giant skates paled in contrast to Dove's skate stories of another kind. An eager crowd would gather when he was in residence. Their occasional slips on local rivalries were duly noted and fed back to Raed. The wall of silence was not one of misgiving; it was one of not knowing.

## Chapter 32

*Electrocution was a difficult one to suss, accident or design. The wet body acts as a conductor magnifying the effect: fatal arrhythmia, cardiac arrest. That it was in Oldman's apartment questioned the warm feelings he had towards his fellow residents and no doubt vice versa. Fielding's heart had stopped as a result of a shock. He had taken that shower. Luna was still a missing person. Reynold's Hall was filling with ghosts.*

*Oldman's experience in the field told him that the autopsy would show inflammation of the heart. He found Fielding crumpled in the shower. His shower. He switched off the power. Attempts to revive him were fruitless. He called Stead. They tried. Jack David rang 911. Fielding was declared dead.*

*The facts behind Fielding's note would remain undiscovered. From the back catalogue of his brain he lifted a file and dusted it down – a good few years back the electrocutions in Baghdad of a decorated US soldier as a result of wiring faults by a pump installed by a military contractor. Opening the file he saw the phrases 'natural causes' and 'negligible homicide'. Neither was suitable. Fielding died when it should have been him. He decided to check Fielding's room before the police. He took the lift up to the top floor. As he entered the corridor a noise caused him to* step back into the lift and hold the door. He peered along the corridor in time to see Ken with a bunch of files under his arm. Fielding's door was ajar. Inside, a brief search revealed nothing unusual. He slid a filing cabinet drawer open. There was a gap in the early alphabetical listing. He would confront Ken later. A mistake. Later was too late. Ken had been around at breakfast. He was noticeably absent when the police came.

Reynold's Hall was alive with police and engineers. The former questioned everyone once, and Oldman twice. The latter installed devices to throw switches out when problems occurred. The man with the grey overalls was missing. Spider senses kicked in, a professional anxiety that spoke of subterfuge, and a third-party involvement. A teary-eyed Stead hugged Oldman and held him close. He wrapped her in his arms.

She sobbed the words, "Fielding was a friend."

Uncertainty was a keyword in Intelligence. Uncertainty prevailed. Her apparent remorse at the loss of Fielding told another story.

"It could've been you, Westy."

He was the first responder. Survivor's guilt lasted days only, though a sense of social isolation continued. Trained as he was, this was now personal. His enquiries drew a blank. The electrician in the grey overalls disappeared; a man in his thirties, short fair cropped hair, nearly six feet. Time to question Ken. Kicking the door in at two thirty a.m. gave rise to repercussions, not all negative. Ken was gone. Oldman called the police. Bingham, who had taken over Luna's role on the resident's committee, had a quiet word and authorised the repairs to the door. She did so after placing her index finger over her mouth with a whisht. No one in the place seemed concerned. Maybe it was time to ask leading questions.

He notified Griggs. A thorough search occurred. Stead said nothing about his escapade. The young policeman appeared to know about the door. Bingham lied. Who reported it? Roger was his guess, but he didn't give a shit.

Griggs cajoled Oldman. "You're out."

Oldman put the phone down. It was his last order. In the department his bureaucratic peers were confused by the spate of incidents at Reynold's Hall. The move was proving to be controversial and expensive. Furthermore, the police were now totally involved – a sharp young detective, Millar. Bingham's explanation that they were concerned for Ken Briggs didn't go well with Millar. In Oldman's opinion they had a right to be. Millar was all over him like a rash. He didn't appear interested in Ken. Oldman lied to them and said I hope he's okay. Afterwards, he felt better. He slept well that night, his gun close by.

It was Millar who found Luna. Terror had a way of imprinting itself on the face. Luna in the dark, in a small dark cellar under the house, alive still, her beanie gone. Luna was bald. The police began a search for Ken in earnest which drew the attention away from Oldman. He was still high on the list.

"Don't go anywhere, Oldman!'"

He wasn't. Luna had been locked in one of the many cellars running under the hall. Oldman, aware of her pathological fear of the dark, formed his own conclusions. Ken really was the evil bastard he suspected. Was she investigating him?

He drew a spider chart that spun a web so intricate the interlacing became knotty and incomprehensible; the spider baffled by its own weave lost in the maze. He scrolled it up on his laptop, printed it, disposed of it, and wiped the original. Lost spiders. Griggs, Lawson, Ken, Roger, Luna, Smythe, and then the whole list of residents. The Electrician.

Shock turned to grief. For the posh residents, the process of mourning began. Resentment remained with Oldman, who had grown fond of his mentor and deeply sorry for Luna. He felt isolated in the hall; he felt responsible. His misgivings competed with his growing affection for his bridge partner. The nature of polite society hampered his case. No one asked what on earth Fielding was doing in his rooms, his shower. What could he say? Griggs tried to get him on his phone. Oldman didn't pick up.

Stead had been out for a stroll when the death occurred. She came back in time to help. Was it a coincidence? Later that day when she tapped on his door to ask if he wanted to go for a cuppa, he refused. He picked up his book and read.

'The process and artifice of our tableau was not a thrill kill, rather it was a serious work of art, a protest. The excitement was in the process and the final showing. It was our theatre of cruelty, aimed at disrupting the viewer. Our real feelings were untranslatable. We owed that to Artaud. Breaking down barriers like the great producer Peter Brook in his so-called Marat/Sade, we took on the binaries of good and evil and above all freewill.'

Oldman looked it up. Glenda Jackson as Charlotte Corday and Ian Richardson played Marat, Patrick Magee as De Sade. Set in an asylum it seemed appropriate, multi-layered, complex, funny at times, violent, mad. Like life itself. 'He who kills without passion, is a machine'. The words of the Marquis de Sade caused him to freeze his reading. He put the book down. Fielding's body had been taken away for examination, to him an autopsy, to the residents a post-mortem. Sewing up the body, the final step of an autopsy, he felt the stitches, he felt his brain removed and replaced, and revenge planted there.

The residents over seventy were accustomed to death. It joined you along life's way and accelerated as friends and relatives died; naturally or with 'the cancer' and its varying forms. One sensed death walked behind one. Violent death was familiar or installed in the memory banks of the two or three remaining senior residents as a result of 'the war' that took away as many as 'the cancer'. There was a wariness in his fellow residents' greetings. His isolation grew and with it his concentration.

Denial, fleeting numbness, then anger, and blame. In the wake of it all bargaining with life took place. Oldman heard the words, it could have been me, was the common response. Oldman agreed, though his was not a natural response to sudden death. He was out on a limb.

Acceptance came about quite soon. Grief was not a part of Oldman's makeup. The question did arise of why Fielding was in his shower. Millar, the astute young detective, and the police wanted to see him again. The questions touched on their relationship. Millar and a younger police officer, Pal Singh, were both switched on and didn't miss a trick. Singh got his turn and probed quite deeply into his past. Oldman avoided the signs of lying showing enough discomfort without being nervy. Open palms and eye contact. Millar gave him a card. Singh watched his every move.

Oldman asked if it was a common cause of death. He couldn't say check your sources and see if there were other cases in the southeast that matched. A hint was enough. He focussed on Pal Singh.

"The electricians were here recently. You should be able to trace them through maintenance."

*Another blank, but worth a try.*

*Millar took over. "Are you familiar with electric circuits, Mr Oldman?"*

*"Light bulbs and fuses only, sir."*

*He didn't look convinced.*

*Back in his role as Westy he occupied his seat opposite Stead. Bingham and Jack David were still partners. The grand slam was yet to come. The games were less friendly, the banter gone, the purpose altered. The walks ceased. To Stead, Oldman had lost a mate. He was determined to find out and dispose of those responsible. Accidental death my arse... Reynold's Hall lost its glow. Bingham seemed distracted and would often disappear from the table without excusing herself. On her return she had a steely look in her eyes that spoke of retribution. He was tempted to talk with her.*

*Millar came back. They checked Fielding's room for the umpteenth time – clear. Oldman highlighted Ken's absence. Millar didn't seem unduly bothered. His manner implied he suspected Oldman of creating a smokescreen.*

*"Did Mr Fielding use a laptop?"*

*"I don't know. Odd really, I've never been to his apartment."*

*"He only came to yours for a shower?" The sarcasm was obvious.*

*Then Singh called, off the record. "Mr Oldman, I checked and there has been four deaths of that nature along the south coast, none of which brought about any charges of negligence or otherwise."*

*Oldman was about to say thanks and ring off when Singh spoke again.*

"However, all the deceased (he avoided victims) were well-to-do and all connected with, shall we say, government."

"Does Millar know this?"

"I mentioned it to him. He merely said, 'Good job, Singh'. It's his standard response. Then he said I should focus on the perp."

"So Millar suspects murder, too?"

"We also checked out The Electrician. Contractor hired for the day only. I'm chasing that up but – and this is the strange thing – the credentials are false. No trace of him."

The grey overalls.

"If the electrical circuits had been tampered with it was meant for me."

Singh refused to engage with Oldman's suppositions. "I've spoken with the inspector. He has his own ideas. Must go, my other line is buzzing."

Nervously, he rang off.

## Chapter 33

As one carriage came up, the other, down. The water-balanced funicular at Saltburn stole away Periwinkle's attention.

"Energy efficient," he claimed.

Penny's thoughts were elsewhere.

The boy's funeral brought about a change in Dove. Jack and he were out and about, not probing, though by their very presence and Jack's mute silence, making the local imbibers uneasy.

Periwinkle reported back adding more issues to the case. "Raed believes there was some rather distasteful goings-on in the past that indicate our guesswork to be valid."

"Can you be more precise?" Dove's tone was tetchy.

They could sense the beginnings of a familial and complex jigsaw coming out of the box. Penny's personal encounters with such dalliances taught him there was always a piece missing. It would remain that way. Periwinkle was unfazed by Dove's shift in mood. Penny was edgy. Refuting pathology, he saw his own issues as discursive, the presence and weight of power all around him. He watched the funicular rise again.

"It's the absent father," Periwinkle stated. "A young lady, a juvenile, accused Mike Farrow's dad of molesting her. He is an outsider and not liked. His contracting away is no coincidence. The locals never speak about Farrow and Jim. Also, Raed thinks the boy was party to something within the school that wasn't nice."

Dove responded: "Raed mentioned a complaint against Farrow that never went to court."

Periwinkle's face showed sympathy for the man. "Saida says he was innocent and fell afoul of entrenched home-grown feuding networks. The accuser dropped the charges and it did not proceed to litigation. She changed her story. If I were to borrow a phrase from Penny, the accusation remained left open and in play, a rumour, and the readings of such were productive or, if you like, destructive."

"Fundamentally Farrow was fucked over." Dove summed it up.

Periwinkle's appropriated phrase caused a pang of withdrawal for Penny. A loud bang of a shotgun startled him; someone shooting in the woods. Quiet and noise were still issues for him, his mood veering between a desire to be in the thick of it and then to be outside of everything. At that moment the outside feeling dominated, and his thoughts were on the derealisation of others – Mikey and Gran – rather than himself.

"What does Hart think?" Dove's question sounded pointed.

"He's working round the clock. Raed is prepared to let him. He has an informer and will apparently sooner or later catch up with us."

"He'll need a fast bike." Dove's joke felt flat.

Periwinkle turned his attention to Farrow. "The little chatter and, moreover, the avoidance of his name, indicates a local chariness of the man. I reserve my judgement. I've never met him. Farrow senior returns next week for a month's leave. Jack knew nothing of it. He was at sea when whatever happened, happened."

Dove cut to the quick. "He must be a twat leaving a kid like that, whatever went down. Mind you. Young Farrow might be better off without him."

Just as compelling were Dove's snippets on the big cat. A farmer had found a pile of bones, most likely rabbits. In The Duke in Skelton, the remains grew from rabbit size to human. A local briefed him.

"The big cat confronted a lady walking her dog. The dog skedaddled; the woman close behind."

Then family matters took precedent – the Bowers, the Batemans. Who wronged whom?

Penny, whose dangerous romanticism and fantasies had brought about an obsessive desire to be an orphan from a very early age, would judge each case on its merit or demerits. What is more destructive than 'The Family'?

Periwinkle remained quiet on such issues. Penny expected Dove's take on the family would be novel. Dove never spoke.

Periwinkle summarised. "Mikey is a composite character, an autistic personality. He's different. Special, is a better word. He doesn't appear to belong yet he is no outcast. Rather, he chooses a form of action that Penny once termed outsiderism." Periwinkle liked the term. "Yes, and an active practice at that. Mikey is, or sounds like, a multifaceted human being."

165

Penny considered his own condition, his chronic art histrionic persecution complex. "I can sense information on the way, sniff it coming, and it isn't going to be nice, more a can of family worms. We need to talk to the Farrows, senior and junior."

Determined to have his point of view, Dove interrupted and drew things to a close. "Yep, I can feel we are near to a breakthrough. The meetings with Raed bring together an intelligence that would shame even a man of Oldman's experience."

Only Dove could do such, the bastard. He would hide his notes on their return to the digs. Would Dove spy on him? He held his left arm out across his body and pretended to write behind the arm with head down, a childhood gesture that left Dove wondering. Penny's trauma was acute. As for the meetings he dreaded them.

A week came and went. There was a shutdown on crime, on werewolves, big cat stories and, sadly, the final closure of the nearby steel plant. Mothballed by Tata in 2015 it meant more redundancy. A violent explosion with Michael Heseltine on the button removed the blast furnace in fourteen to fifteen seconds and waved goodbye to steel making.

The abyss was opening up once again. Talk of ideological warfare against the northern working class was the common opinion in the public houses. A sense of defeat hung over Loftus.

"Expect they'll stop the winter fuel payments before long."

"Aye, and the frigging bus pass."

Penny took it all back to the digs and opened his notebook. He began with Farrow and a conscious cliché. The plot, his own, in Loftus and elsewhere, was thickening. He spent a few minutes deliberating then moved on to proverbs, thicker being the link, blood the topic. Clan affiliations, family ties, and in a circular fashion back to cliché. He made a list and then negated them. He felt proud when he wrote: 'do not read between the lines'. Underneath, to add to the proverbial stew he wrote: 'blood is not thicker than water.'

Soon, the creaking family ties that bound people together or kept them apart in this northern town would give. The blood of the covenant. The bonds made by choice are more important. He closed his notebook and pondered.

His excursions on the bike were coming to nothing. He saw no sign of The Five. That evening he had a puncture. He'd long forgotten bike maintenance and wheeled his BMX back through the empty streets of the council estate.

When Michael Farrow shot past at a speed that Penny could only muster downhill, Penny's forlorn face must have had an effect. He who is happy to give power to others swung his bike round one hundred and eighty with ease and headed towards Penny.

"Puncture?"

"Yup."

"Got a set in my bag if you wanna do it now?"

"Cool. Thanks." Cold and fed up, the chance to pry was offered and warmed him.

In no time Mikey upended the bike and removed the tyre from one side of the frame. The puncture identified with spit, he had the inner tube mended and back in before Penny could think of what to say.

"Must be off, got a lesson. Stay cool. Try Magic Tyre Sealant or decent puncture-proof tyres." He vaulted onto the saddle and rode away at pace up the hill.

To give chase felt wrong. He knew who the lesson was with. To get information here, he needed to be forthright. He needed to be the local person he had once been. He needed to cast off the educational crap and the detective persona. Ask, and do it straightforwardly. Tell the truth and shame the devil. The worst thing that could happen was a 'go screw yourself' or a punch on the nose. He decided that the task in hand was more important even than his books.

Here was a conundrum involving children. If only the werewolf's first victims Matty and Sara could remember more. Hypnosis might work, but funding in the northeast was dire for police work. The incumbent police commissioner, a decent sort, was at his wit's end. If only...

Penny felt outside on a limb. Jack and Dove had become a double act in the boozer. Both were determined to track down who had tortured his boy and, in Jack's case, kill them and anyone associated with them. Penny discerned their need for payback in the subtext of the matelot's leading stories.

Farrow senior came back that weekend. The discourses that underlay all the problems began to rise like slag to the surface and then boil over. Dove reported an incident. It was the first manifestation of the underlying tensions breaking the surface and a clue to Penny about his earlier silly academic wandering on cliché.

Two mates in the pub had a go at each other. Dove heard one say, "Fucking bastard Farrow." There was no mistaking the heat generated between these two pals. "I'd like to stick one on him."

The landlady, not averse to throwing a punch herself, insisted on quiet, and it came about. The tension remained. One of the men left without the customary spiced goodbyes. Through the window, Dove watched him slouch off down the road hands in his pockets, head hung down in a posture that was nothing to do with the prevailing wind – a symptom of dejection as a result of a yawning division. Which side had he been on? It was still early and he was off to another pub to sit quietly with another pint and his anger. Those remaining supped their beer in silence.

"Interesting, eh?"

Penny agreed.

The divisions were beginning to show, the catalyst Farrow.

Penny's brief experience of therapy led him to discern that the solution to all problems lay in opening the cracks wide and focusing inward. He chose not to say it and to offer Dove an opening. He drifted.

Reynold's Hall still sounded like a cosy place to be at this moment in time.

"We know the local rivalries, but not the origins." Dove summarised, "Michael's mam was well-liked and local suitors were pissed off when she married a southerner." He briefed them on the families. "Sid Bowers, one of the eldest, held sway on the committee of the West Row Club. His younger brother, Danny, was a renowned darts player, arrows as the locals call it."

Penny had never been a club man. He listened to Jack's summary.

"Local lads tend to drink in the same pubs, sit in the same seats – The Golden Lion, The White Horse, The Mars, all have their resident drinkers. I tend to walkabout, and as a local don't get the frosty stares reserved for aliens."

Penny held back a remark about it not paying them to.

"The Mars has a karaoke to be avoided unless you want to hear The King killed off time and time again. The Angel has been turned into a residence." As if to counterbalance his statement on the Bowers's prowess and not take sides, he added, "The Bateman's are reputed to be shit-hot pool players, and both families are a mean hand at dominoes."

Games players – that was worth knowing. Was Jack a Libra? Signs were important. Rejected by scientists, the *perhaps* factor was important to him.

Farrow was from the Leeds area, the south. Such is relative. Dove would be from the Deep South, Periwinkle from Mars. He was to meet Farrow the next day. Penny was not surprised. So much was unplanned.

The call from Liz came next morning. She was out of breath and flustered, most unusual for The Destroyer. "Can you come round, Penny, immediately?"

That Liz was distraught was apparent. Nothing else was.

"Mikey and his dad are here."

Penny saved his notes and went for his bike. He stopped and thought of turning back.

Oldman was beginning to change as a result of the cosiness and fellowship which he feared was coming to an end. Should it go further from fellowship to fucking. He listened to everything and said little. He chided himself for his profanity.

Another murder was about to take place. Oldman was certain. Stead appeared withdrawn. The others distanced themselves. The games were intermittent, the bonhomie forced.

The warmth and chatter subsided. He thought about Fielding, the officer and gentleman whose composure at the bridge of a ship and at the card table was steadfast. His last look at the man alive with bags under his eyes and his normal ruddy complexion drawn and wan steadied his resolve.

The local police had questioned him at least three times. He had to lie. It couldn't last long. Accountability was a new sensation for him. It had crept into management speak of late. He ignored such as jargon. To find who was responsible was paramount. In Fielding's flat was a copy of Reinagle's painting A First-Rate Man-of-War Driven onto a Reef of Rocks, Floundering in a Gale. Fielding had survived the cruel sea, gale force winds, and the waves, only to die in a shower.

The post-mortem stated emphatically it was a heart attack caused by an electrical surge; unforeseeable, an accident. Oldman's sense of wellbeing dissolved. The police presence could seriously jeopardise his chances of any intelligence work. Life was about to get difficult… no problematical. His chance of a lead was gone. He sought refuge in a chancy romance.

*She, the lovely and secretive Stead, was his only hope of a break now. Pale and slender, she belonged to the woodlands, a woodland flower, she was protection, safe, she was love.*

*She, he suspected had sussed out his daughter and in turn him.*

*He hummed, "I put my hand into the bush, thinking the fairest flower to find…"*

Without putting his helmet on, Penny rode to Liz Trout's. As he turned the corner, The Five went past the other way. In sync, they looped around him in a figure of eight and then passed on by, a manoeuvre he considered amicable. In his mind they were trying to tell him something. If it was a message, Penny missed its meaning. He was going round in circles. Oldman's tricky situation was getting to him.

How consistent were people in real life? He knew when they wanted to speak The Five would. He'd imagined a misspelled note through the door offering the information he so wanted. It would never happen. Characters are never consistent. Penny pulled his bike up outside Liz's house. The drive was empty of the smart blue Mercedes – Jim Trout was away. He dismounted and pushed his bike up the drive. The balustrade was still white. Before he could walk back to the bell, the door opened. Liz ushered him in.

Inside, he hardly gave any time to the *objets d'art*. Michael Farrow sat next to a man who Penny assumed must be his father. In direct contrast to his shy, pale and skinny son he was suntanned and convivial. He was much younger than

Penny had imagined, and very fit. His slick-backed hairstyle suited him. He shook hands.

"Pleased to meet you, Dr Penny. I'm Caleb Farrow. Michael has mentioned you in despatches."

Mikey's face broke into a thin smile. "Hello, Dr Penny."

Farrow sat in a single comfy chair. Penny found a space on the couch and looked downwards. He was wavering.

"Can I get you something, Penny? Cuppa? Or something stronger?"

"A glass of water will be fine, thanks." He sat back and waited. He felt an inexplicable thirst, a product of what he speculated was going to be a let-down.

Liz's opening gambit countered that. "Okay, Penny, you need a couple of explanations."

Mikey stared at the floor, a red-faced juvenile. His dad remained unperturbed.

Liz continued. "I owe you an apology. I didn't think it was my business to confide in you about friendships and family ties, despite my faith in you as a person and a colleague, the latter being short-term, I guess." She waited a second.

He took it as a warning signal and didn't reply. She sounded as always: frank and transparent. Was she? He laid aside his doubts and listened.

"In a nutshell, Mikey's mam, Katie, and I were half-sisters. We were the best of friends. Grandad Bowers is long gone, bless him. He took me in when my parents died. Nana Bowers didn't care much, but he did. She was never cruel, just busy, forever changing things – furniture, whatever – manic. When Katie died, she left a hole in people's lives; a void reflecting her popularity and her optimism which she held onto until her dying day."

Caleb gave an affirmative nod.

Liz cast a fond schoolteacher's gaze over young Farrow. "I promised to take care of Mikey. It hasn't been easy." She sounded stern.

Put on the spot, Mikey gave what was a teenager's apology – a blend of annoyance, which underneath lay genuine regret.

"He is supposed to come for tea and then for lessons every day, though chooses not to. He does attend fairly regularly and often gets back late. My fear is that I may have to defend Mikey if his absence from school reaches the police. He is an adaptive learner. He is prone to spending hours on his computer playing games and riding his bike. In that respect Mikey is no different to any other adolescent."

Liz saw Penny's face redden. His own inner child was on the spot; his recent excursions into fictional bridge and online mah-jongg a daily fixation, not to mention his BMX. As a cop-out he put it down to free child.

"My difficulty is that I'm torn between friendship and duty. One: he should be at school. I can't make him. Two: if I do something about it, the authorities step in. To use one of your favourite expressions, Penny, which is the gap filling, only Caleb and Mikey can do it."

Penny listened. He checked his shoes. They looked odd. Caleb spoke first.

"When Katie died, I was working in the mine. The money wasn't great and I was reliant on childminders. Mikey was still a child – he still is. He could stay here with Liz. He is happy on his own. Neighbours keep an eye out for him. It was a difficult choice for me to work away. The events of the past promoted the move… Our childminder, Kylie, was good with Mikey and had to comply with my shift changes."

The regulated twenty-four-hour clock which defied the timepiece of the body was familiar to Penny, as was the strangeness of coming off nights into the light of the blinking morning. It still caused a moment's estrangement when he brought those memories back.

Caleb continued. "I returned home late after a back shift that had run over. I offered Kylie the back bedroom. Mikey was already asleep. I was barely into bed when Kylie tried to join me. She was seventeen. I said no and, leaving Mikey, drove her home. The next day the police pulled me to make a statement. The rest is history."

A phrase that meant everything and nothing. Penny failed to acknowledge he knew the case.

"In short, when the police asked her to write her statement down, she dropped the charges. A doctor never examined her to prove that anything had taken place, but she had already done the damage. Mud sticks."

Penny admired his openness in front of his son. Unperturbed, Mikey was waiting his turn.

"Err… well, thanks for being so honest with me, Caleb." Penny avoided the current expression 'sharing that'. Where was this going? Then, the gap-filling really began.

"Dr Penny."

"Call me Ronnie, please." With no change in the authority of that young voice, he initiated what was to be an insightful analysis of his neighbours, his friends, his enemies, and local issues. Mikey's intellect was one far beyond that of his years.

He made no apologies for his father, nor attempted to justify things. The critical gulf between them was apparent.

"I've always been a bit of a loner," Mikey said. "Dad being away doesn't worry me. The neighbours don't like him much and see me as my mother's boy. I was born here. So, they keep an eye out. Sometimes it is over-the-top. I do have issues helped with prescription drugs. And yes, I do spend far too much time on the games console." He eyed Liz. "However, I read endlessly. My condition means I keep odd hours. I don't know everything that goes on around here, but I do know who knows. My so-called mates at school call me Spaz, a derogatory term. It has stuck. I cycle around at night. I watch people. And they watch me, of course."

He looked at Penny, who was attentive yet uneasy.

"You've met The Five, from the estate. They too spend their time cycling around, skulking, if you like. Other kids see them as a threat. They are five harmless council estate kids who don't attend a regular school, a bit like me, though unfortunately they will never have an education. And they're bright. Gavin – Hoody to you – is one of the most fiercely intelligent guys I've met. The best therapist would envy his innate comprehension of people." After a pause, he added, "I have experience of the couch. He's a boy who knows people's needs and, without fuss, will help. If anyone knows anything, The Five will. They will not talk. They are the nuts you have to crack." He chuckled. "You have gone halfway to resolving that with your bike. And, before you ask, I can't tell you how to do it." He smiled a knowing smile, one of a soul beyond his years. "You have to be the dummy, take no part in the play of the hand. Let them lead you."

It was odd that he used an analogy to card games. Hacking occurred to him. Penny paid attention to every word. He couldn't hide an unsettled feeling. First Dove with his comments on Oldman, now the boy on cards. He tried to come to terms with his personal delusions. It was a coincidence. He listened.

"What I'm saying is that any local stuff including the werewolf attacks they will have knowledge of, and background on Max. There is no way they will go to the police even to talk to Raed, who they all fancy like mad. Those guys will, if you play your cards right, when it suits them, tell you what they know." He lapsed into a colloquial teenage speak, "They're not the divs the old gadjees around here suspect. The werewolf thing has something to do with Gran and Kylie's family. I'm too close for comfort. Start with her – Gran, me nana. She is doolally, but not as much as she makes out."

Penny grimaced. The expression 'me nana' grated.

Mikey ended abruptly, as if he'd had enough rather than completed his cryptic chat.

Penny accepted that. Kylie's family name was important. The burning issue was Max. "Thanks, Mikey."

Mikey sank in the chair. His dad turned to gesture a proud and silent thanks.

Mikey added, "I stopped knocking around with George and Kyle because of Max." He offered no explanation.

Liz stepped into the position of chair. "Time we had a glass of something."

"Good idea," Penny said. "A coldie for me, please."

Caleb and he had a chilled lager. Mikey took a soft drink. Introspective quiet fell on the room as they all sipped their drinks. Penny tipped his down nervously. Liz poured herself a reasonable sized whisky from the bottle next to her – Chichibu, single malt, a token from Japan.

She nudged the conversation back to life. "Mikey is telling you that local networks are as the mineshafts – deep and dark – so simply keep chipping away."

It was a succinct précis and analogy. The local ironstone mines closed in the 1940s and were filled in for safety reasons. The dense tunnels of parochial kinships and enmities also remained locked away in the past. Dig, or use dynamite.

Mikey had an afterthought. "Kyle and George know stuff. Kyle is Kylie's younger brother, a late surprise, and years younger. Naming kids round here is competitive, and new names appear constantly. The top ten is fascinating. Check the Web."

Penny prepared to leave; his determination to work on his inability to hide his feelings grew. Mikey could see right through him and his quick sideways glances were both a manifestation of his issues and a penetrating analytical focus. The jitters followed. They began to natter about work. Caleb's small talk revealed something of his person. He appeared a decent sort on the face of things. Penny left with the excuse of preparation to do. He finished his glass, said thanks, and left.

He glimpsed at the Rockwell poster, the boy with his satchel and his apple. "Interesting picture." The date, 1954 – the polio years.

Liz giggled, hugged him, and let him out.

As the Farrows waved him away, he turned back, only to see a tight-lipped expression on Liz's face.

Penny cycled back to the digs. On the way, his mind spiralled out of control, giving rise to surreal presumptions and notions. He wrestled with the differing points of view – Liz, Caleb and Mikey's – and tried to piece together the snippets.

Despite his mental whirl, he was aware that his dark angels, The Five, were keeping an eye out. They were better at it than the pros… and the cons? His list of issues on trust was growing. Conflicting interests? His inability to take things at face value came out of his academic self and a deeper mistrust grounded in his past. Safety was a thing of the past. He could picture Mikey's eyes boring into him, if only for a second at a time. Direct gaze was an issue yet his fleeting glimpses were enough. He hoped he had dealt with it sensitively. He didn't think so.

Afterwards, he couldn't grasp anything. There was time enough to find out what was going on in this deprived area, the target of every government, every budget and plan; this northern outpost stuck between signal stations; this 'Lofthouse'. Jim and Liz seemed personable on the face of things, but Jim distant, guarded even. Caleb and Mikey made the picture even more problematic. Mikey was something else. He detracted.

The Olympic torch passed through Loftus in 2012 after Middlesbrough (hell to Hart) and then onto Hull.

"They could do us all a favour and burn the bloody place to the ground!" Hart exclaimed to the group.

Dove knew people who could, and would, do it.

The cold was seeping into his bones. It was insidious frost-bitten weather. His reminiscences gleaned from parents concerning the pre-double-glazing era, chilblains, rime-frosted windows inside, slides on the ice, and washing in chilly water brought a shiver. In the museum in Leeds there is a picture of children in iron lungs. And there was polio. His dad would've been six or seven.

He knotted his scarf around his neck as tight as he could bear. The damp soaked through the layers and chilled him. It didn't encourage him to get on his bike. They had revealed nothing about Max. Mikey didn't associate with him. Association was another issue. Who did he associate with?

Snug under the covers with a lovely old faded green candlewick on top of the duvet, he recognised the need to bring all the investigators together, though not to involve The Five yet. They were his mates, and you don't sprag on yer mates.

※

He wasn't teaching the next day but chose to go in. If a clock had been present in his cupboard, he would have watched it tick the monotony of that day away. Liz was noticeably absent. Kyle was absent. George stood on his own. Penny waved him over. No response.

Penny wandered over casually. "Where's your mate?"

George shrugged his shoulders. "Gone missing." Then he wheeled away and stalked off.

Penny thought of Max. It was clear George didn't wish to make small talk.

He was becoming impatient. Undercover work was slow and he didn't have the patience. Why didn't things fall into place? Instinct told him George was up to something. The titbits of information he had obtained he shared with Raed and Hart, with minor omissions. He felt trapped. He was also concerned for Kyle.

Well wrapped up against the weather, he cycled and practised until he was sore with his wounds. He found a crude ramp and did jumps. He'd watched one of the local well-hooded local kids clear a five-foot fence from a ramp, spin, and land perfectly. He considered the move at length. The broken perimeter fence was less than five feet in parts. He weighed up the possibility. He saw himself as Steve McQueen hanging from the tangled wire in the Great Non-Escape. He duly left it out of his training programme. Dead sailors were not for him. He envisaged himself in the air. When he looked down he was staring at the ocean, and he froze. He should have mentioned Kyle to Phibes or Liz.

He left with a distinct sense of achievement. The last jump had been quite spectacular, by his standards. There was still time for a pint. He met Dove and they adjourned to a pub and found a quiet corner. The locals acknowledged Dove. Penny felt alien and yet enjoyed the anonymity. Whilst yearning for the spotlight, he felt better with obscurity. He promised that he would work on namelessness as a lifestyle choice. He was born with imposter syndrome and it wouldn't go away.

Dumb luck prevailed. He stopped and took out his phone. He called Liz. Dove stopped listening.

"To what do I owe this pleasure, Penny?"

"It's about Kyle. He hasn't been at school for a couple of days now."

"Work placement – a day or two with a local company. It's good for them. Back next week."

"Thanks. What a great idea. Nice to know there is work about." He stammered out the words. He was really pissed with George.

"Everything OK?"

"Yes, Liz. I was a mite concerned, that's all."

"No worries. He's back next week."

Penny said thank you and rang off. There was a word for people like George and it wasn't pleasant. Penny thought of adding to his mobile one or two words that could be conveyed at the push of a button. Next to 'Yay' and 'Cool' an 'Oh Shit' button topped the charts. 'Twat' came next.

Dove was at the bar buying a round.

What happened to the let's-chuck-it-all-in-the-pot-stir-it-around-see-what-comes-out Penny? The chef to a theoretical stew, molecular tasters, small bursts of academic flavour mingled with street food. Dove pondered and held back a sarcastic quip about Oldman chairing the meetings. Penny was wearing different shoes, both brown, but very different. Dove asked if it was a new thing. Penny looked flummoxed. Had anyone else noticed? Dove understood he would take an upward turn and reconstruct but, for now, he was struggling, Hart, too. Jokiness seemed to help though Penny wasn't laughing. Dove understood stress-related behaviour. What was Penny doing on those long walks? The hours he spent in his room were odd. He curtailed the small observations.

"Periwinkle is going to organise a meeting. Should we include Hart?"

"Yes."

Dove savoured his beer. "It's called Redcar Pier." His pronunciation included a punning, and a critique which Penny missed totally. "I'll suggest an early evening talk."

Penny nodded.

Dove, aware of his bike manoeuvres and his meetings with The Five, kept quiet. His own investigations unravelled a complex family tree, one that suffered a disease akin to Dutch elm. A beetle was burrowing away, the infection not easily identified. Peeling back the bark to reveal the disease in the branches could take years. A short-cut was needed.

The hours of the day leading up to the meeting were infernal. Country-miles were one thing but… Was there an expression for time in a similar vein? Penny was familiar with the flexible culture in the Arab world and the expression 'Gulf Time' came to mind.

It was like being at the rear of an endless fidgeting bus queue. In the northeast, where buses seem to arrive whenever, it was the norm. Locals referred to the missing buses as the non-arriva. It was a time of checking watches, circling without losing one's place, and discussing with others in terse voices the hopelessness of it all. Then two or three turned up at once, like ideas and chances.

Dove and Periwinkle had disappeared, leaving him in a netherworld. It was discomforting. He didn't know who to trust. Lying was predominant. More sinister and fleeting was a distrustful feeling of his mind hacked into, his novel stolen. A carrier bag full of wires was leaning against the couch. It didn't help his mood. He pushed them into the bag out of sight. His mind was jam-packed. Was he overdoing the writing? Writing can bring to the surface Hadean demons. And he was condemned to write. He mooched. He assessed his own logic repeatedly. Liz was central to *this* investigation, *his* investigation. His fondness for her was getting in the way. He wished he had suggested scheduling the meeting for the morning.

Jim was the key. Circling with his own snippets of information, shifting physically around the room and mentally in his head, he doubted his own rationale, his information and its validity. In that short chat with the Farrows, there was a hint from young Farrow that offered a way forward, to cut through the tangle of feuds and friendships. He had forgotten to quiz them on Gran's knowledge of werewolves. He must take notes.

He planned repeatedly how he would give his briefing and in which order. In what way should the facts come? Awake to his tendency to blurt it out, he wrote it down; bullet pointed it, rehearsed it, practised it, and threw it down. Its format resembled one of those Lib Dem local electoral leaflets which looked like a frozen food store handbill without the gaudy colour.

It was best to make the facts succinct without colouring them. Where were those study skills when you needed them, the erudition, performance, the theatre? He speculated as to what Oldman would do.

This was one factor only; collaborating with Hart was another. Hart didn't really work with anyone. He finished in a corner. Hart had plus points in his favour. Penny would work on Stead's relationship with Oldman, and his with Hart and Liz.

He rode around without purpose. Caleb and Mikey passed by in a car and beeped. Liz was a gem, broad-minded, tough and a great headteacher. Still, that sneaking feeling came back again that she was covering up. What had Jim said about plumbing? Jim had said nothing. One would think he might drop a hint about his job in the Middle East, or wherever. He'd forgotten to ask him where he was.

Katie had been special to them all. He'd been through emails to and from Liz over and over again. Nothing offered any clues to anything other than work, the school. It was her life. In the warrens of the estate where she had pinpointed those family rivalries, the bitterness may have led beyond punch-ups, satire, or slagging off to torture and murder. He could only hypothesise. That was his domain.

Katie had married an outsider, a blow-in. Liz, too. He recalled the term from his first trip to County Clare. The residents were either IBs or BIs. Katie was an inbred; Farrow and Jim blow-ins.

A pub companion made mention of Mikey's granddad, 'auld' Mikey. "He was a really nice bloke."

Inbred...

Penny circumnavigated the police station for three-quarters of an hour before the meeting. His notes were patchy. Everything he knew was in there. He hadn't been quite so nervous since his early days as a teacher. Resolving issues with Hart was going to be difficult, their mutual distrust ingrained, on a par with the Batemans and the Bowers.

Dove arrived exactly on time. Periwinkle was close behind. He was wearing his beret and one of his wardrobe's most magnificent waistcoats: a naval, blue moleskin. Penny speculated on how he transported the collection. They were an integral part of his closet. Scrounging through charity shops, he noticed that waistcoats were conspicuously absent these days and wondered if Periwinkle had cornered the market.

Hart was chairman. He sat at the head of the table. A young female constable, Evie, the secretary, sat next to him. Hart introduced her and asked the seated group if they were agreeable to that. Indicating her awareness of underlying local issues, he added that Evie was not local, though she had lived in Loftus since her teens. Polite smiles and pencils passed around the room.

Evie opened her notepad. Everyone turned to Hart. Raed and Periwinkle didn't bat an eyelid. Dove focussed on Penny. Evie surveyed the group. Raed's composure held the room and formed a contrast to the blonde Evie with her shy smile and smoky-brown eyes. Penny wrote 'smoky-brown eyes' in his book then closed it quickly, a schoolchild hiding a love note, a reductive male.

The qualities demanded of a chair were Raed's rather than Hart's. In that role he would have to show flexibility. He would have to keep order, move to adult. The role of secretary was powerful. Evie was good. Hart rose to the occasion. Above all, the progress and health of the meeting was his prime task and was essential. Other words came to mind, though Penny had deleted the word 'robust' from his dictionary as an overused buzzword. The aims and objectives were Hart's concern. He would have a casting vote.

Hart had drafted a simple agenda. At the top in bold was 'Chair's Briefing'. He began by welcoming the group, mentioning no one in particular.

He turned to Evie and said, "Make a note of all present. If everyone agrees, I'm prepared to run over the facts, allowing you to get your analytical heads on and make notes, if you wish. I – we – have decided that interruptions are welcome, especially where you discern that facts may be faulty or you may know more. I will guillotine the meeting after one hour. Please aim to be succinct." He squinted at Penny.

Penny fiddled with his pencil rolling it on the table, then wrapped a large elastic band around his fingers. Dropped in their hundreds by the postal service, he collected them. In front of him was a blank sheet of paper and a pencil. The void on the paper beseeched him to draw a circle then a line through the circle – a doodle. What was it about blankness that irked him so? The unknown? Doodles were now a breed of dog – Gemma's dog. He picked the pencil up and wrote at the top 'Doodle'. He added a question mark and an exclamation. He remembered the interrobang.

Hart summarised the attacks. He covered location, and no pattern emerged. He was thorough. He paused after his briefing, inviting comments. None came. Sara and Matty had recovered physically. Gemma's autopsy report was like the chill winter wind, and the temperature shifted downwards.

Forensic reconstructions illustrated that the attacker came from behind. Matty and Sara had said so also. The injuries to the throat and neck were committed by metallic claws. There were no traces of DNA material from the attacker. The blood smears showed Gemma had tried to crawl away. The attacker had severed a main artery. The haemorrhaging was extensive. Along with inter-cranial bleeding caused by the fall, loss of blood was massive. Forensics estimated that the time she lay there was between fifteen to twenty minutes. Transfusions were not enough. The brain bleed caused the oxygen supply to fall rapidly, along with blood pressure. Gemma's heart failed.

"The attack was swift, bloody and vindictive. Any questions?"

The room was silent. The interview reports with Sara and Matty confirmed such – they were both knocked sprawling from behind. Neither were lightweights.

"Sara thinks she fainted. Matty hit her head as she fell. They are still in shock and may gradually remember more. Matty's only memory is claws around her neck. She recalls trying to scream."

Hart proceeded to Max's torture and death. Touching on the coroner's report, he sensed the mutual rage in the room and paused. It was signalled not by screams but a silence. Hart felt his adrenalin pumping.

His briefing lasted no longer than six or seven minutes. Dove made a note.

Hart insisted on the need for confidentiality between the parties. "Especially those civilians present."

Dove informed Penny afterwards he had resisted a comment on collateral damage. On completion, Hart reiterated the purpose of the discussion: to bring together intelligence in order to apprehend the werewolf killers and those of Max.

He added, "The perp tortured and burned the poor dog before Max died. Who would do such a thing?"

Hart's voice broke and no one interrupted the anxious quiet.

The rundown was precise. Hart brought Dove into the frame with a warning shot, "Revenge is not the purpose here – though we appreciate that Jack, the boy's father, is angry."

Wrathful, or, totally bent on massacring the evil bastards, may have been more befitting.

Dove addressed the floor without notes and spoke in what Penny heard as bullet points – ordered, informative and succinct. He filled in the gaps concerning the boy's behaviour which had caused his father to ask them for help. Did the torture and burning of a dog indicate gratuitous violence? Penny ticked 'Doodle' and crossed out the question mark.

"The boy's behaviour had been noticeably different. Jack's first concern was bullying. Then he changed his mind. We mentioned drugs. None of that ticked any boxes. The boy kept a diary. Jack's code of ethics disallowed him taking a gander. The diary is missing." Dove added, "I do have crumbs of information about local rivalries. I will wait until Penny has spoken as he is far more knowledgeable on the matter. We don't want duplication."

At that juncture Hart chose to bring in Penny. "Would you like to comment?"

Running over his tête-à-tête with Liz and the Farrows caused uncomfortable movement in the room, shuffling chairs and glances. Evie gave a sympathetic smile. Raed listened with the air of one who knew the nature of loyalty and family values, yet one capable of stepping back and examining it clinically. She tried to fathom why these issues might lead to killing. She allowed herself a Penny moment.

Her own refusal to marry a cousin had caused a rift between members of the family. Not her father. That gave her strength. She glanced at Penny with a flicker of an eye that spoke of encouragement. He continued his breakdown on the families. Dove prompted him at one point. Dove's Ronnie-boy tag clearly amused her for a nanosecond.

Penny's mood lifted. His meeting persona gleaned from hours of university staff meetings started to kick in.

He eyed Hart and threw Hart's words back in his face. "I must stress that the information from the Farrows is private. I assume they realised I would not be able to hide it." It occurred that might be the very reason they told him. "It might be they too are on one side of the fence, as any local informant." He fixed an enquiring eye on Hart. "What I'm

190

saying here is that local information may well have to be taken with a pinch of salt." Part of the cure for poison...

He could see the formalities suited Hart. Penny had been chairman and secretary of the teachers' board – Stalin, the staff called him, though sometimes Mordor – and as such had access to all information right up to the Politburo. It allowed him to gather intelligence on past villains at work, Dean Treachery his favourite villain in his past life at university. He was Two-face to Penny's Batman. Unlike Stalin and the Dean, purging was not his thing. Hart looked comfortable.

Hart was lacking when it came to transparency yet advocated it of others. He would learn.

Hart replied. "I do have an informant. I can assure you that they have given me nothing to date that will benefit us here. They may be useful in the future."

"Thank you, Chairman." It did not roll off the tongue easily. "I have prospective informants who are juveniles. I will respect their privacy. We are in the realms of assessing potential here which, as an educator, I know means probabilities. Perish the thought that one day it might come about! I too will keep them out of it until the day that potential is realised."

Hart sought support from the impassive Raed. None came.

She spoke. "Chair, is there any other information you have that you might want to share on Jim?"

Hart twitched, somewhat flustered, then recovered. "Nothing concrete at this moment, ma'am."

Penny reported back snippets from the school, and asked Hart to check out with his informant the circumstances of Katie Farrow's marriage.

"The Farrows, who are related to Gran, think Granny Bowers knows more than she lets on. Everyone here seems related." Penny continued to let them know the gist, and hearsay, that the boy Farrow inferred Gran was the key.

"We will follow up on Gran Bowers, Penny." Raed made a note.

"Then I'm finished. Thank you."

Raed reciprocated. "Thanks, Ron – or is it Ronnie-boy?" she said with an elfish glance at Dove. "There is much to draw on from your statements. At this point, I'm quite happy to hear your ideas or guesses."

Hart took control and Raed's impishness was replaced by cold calculation. Penny detected in Hart a sense of him cornered by his own reticence.

"Thank you, Penny," Hart gagged. "What you say is extremely valuable. We get the sense that your juvenile informants need to remain confidential."

There was disparagement in his voice. So far Hart's umpiring was fine. His position as chair might just be convenient for him. Was he keeping schtum?

Periwinkle had his hand up. "The networks we need desperately are those that Penny has set up. Parents and teachers will judge more formal components as interference despite the gravity of the situation. Like it or not, we might have to do it anyway."

All agreed.

Penny stared at his notes. He crossed out 'stool pigeon' and 'grass'. Such common parlance was not acceptable in Reynold's Hall…

Periwinkle touched pithily on finding the body of the boy; information he had already shared with police and coroners. For good measure he added, "Our observations led us to conclude that the boy Max had suffered dreadfully. That Jack," he focussed on Dove, "wishes to kill the perpetrators seems justifiable. Revenge and redemption belong to fiction. The combined intelligence around this table will find them. With that aim alone, I propose that we meet regularly."

"I agree," Penny retorted, referring to revenge.

Dove never spoke. Raed signalled for Hart to continue.

Hart summarised. "We have shared information and ideas. In that sense, today has been a step forward. As you suggest, Penny, without local expertise we are high and dry." He didn't give his usual speech about time and money.

Evie was eyeing her copious notes and waving a hand around. Hart didn't see it. Raed signalled to Hart. He asked the young constable if she had anything to add.

She said, "Yes, sir."

Raed spoke for and through the chairman, who was studying his papers.

"Go ahead, Constable." Hart's tone moved from his role as referee to one of superiority.

"The two families, sir – the Bowers and Batemans – there are issues apart from Kylie between them that go back to Kate who was 'promised' to one of the Batemans. Kate was engaged to marry George, or 'Georgie' as he's known – Kyle's uncle. Family networks, as you say Mr Penny, are tightknit. I know that as an outsider here." Evie checked her notes. "When Kate, who was a real prospect, brainy as well, married Caleb Farrow from Leeds, a major fallout occurred

193

between the families. Rumour has it the enmity goes back further to abuse. I realise it's circumstantial. The men drink in differing pubs, the women might exchange pleasantries in the shops, but underneath there is a festering hatred for each other. If you befriend one you are then the enemy of the other. Gran was in what we might call no-woman's land, forbidden ground, isolated, alone."

Hart was writing furiously. Raed offered a smile of support to the young constable.

Evie faltered. "I'll have to take it away with me, ma'am. There may be more."

What side were The Five on? Penny twiddled his pencil between his fingers.

Hart thanked Evie for sharing this with them, failing to mention that her information was a breakthrough. What lay in the bowels of familial networks and the inverted values of the Loftus Mafiosi? Seeing through the mythic family values of such, Penny was applying more appropriate terms for the north-eastern dons: a patriarchal regime, father as God, (according to father, but don't tell your mother) and for inverted chivalric values, their inevitable crises and extinction. He was going to speed it up.

Raed signalled to Hart and tapped her watch. He brought things to a close. Raed thanked Evie woman to woman. Her pleasure at recognition was apparent. Hart was stony-faced. The meeting, she noted, lasted fifty-seven minutes.

Raed took over. "Before we go, I'd like to say thanks to the chair and to all present for attending. Dove, we appreciate your valuable intel and support for your friend Jack and know the difficulty he's going through. Ron, keep on at the

194

school and with the local kids. You're doing a fantastic job. A special thanks to Evie and Periwinkle for your insights. Today has indicated the need to liaise regularly, either formally or otherwise." Passing the last word to Hart and putting him on a spot, she said, "Wouldn't you agree?"

Picking up his files to go he said, "Most important, ma'am. I'll aim to organise it."

On leaving, Dove, Periwinkle and Penny wandered a while. Assuming Penny's given role in their relationship, Periwinkle was the first to speak. Never one to waste words, he spoke for all.

"The constable saved us time, don't you think?" Following Penny's habit of not waiting for a reply he said, "Raed's way of handling Hart is something to behold." He rounded off. "I'm still waiting information on Jim. It's not as clear as it first appeared. There are grey areas."

The very areas that Penny revelled in.

Loftus High Street was busy. Penny stared with no concentration in a few shop windows – a pot shop, a brown box shop – gifts and lifestyle. Loftus was really quite pretty. The sign on the roadside boasted the fact it was 'the home of the Saxon princess'. Dove remarked that she was at the bus stop waiting for the Whitby service.

"A stunning monarch with tats and a nose ring. The boots were something else – purple colour flames on the side and purple soles."

"Helios purple hologram probably." Penny's knowledge of subcultures came in handy. He could empathise with his admiration of the woman – the Loftus princess, and of Raed, though their own feelings were a tad more lustful, less well-balanced than Periwinkle's on the latter.

Dove spoke. "I have to focus on Jack. In the pub, he stated he was going to murder the perpetrator. I told him that I would assist him. When we do get a lead, I'm going to have to be quite two-faced."

Periwinkle corrected him. "Expedient rather than duplicitous. We don't want a blood bath."

They walked further until the inclement weather drove them indoors. Dove hoped the princess had her wet weather gear in her oversized black leather bag which matched her purple hologram boots. Periwinkle wanted to know more about the boots. Then he switched to something bothering him. Dove and he realised that the police's inclusion of the three of them had been quite extraordinary. Raed, he thought, was still sceptical of Penny. He came with the team. She had included him in the forum. Was it a way of keeping them close and under surveillance? Penny thought so.

For her part, she had warned them that if any mischief occurred, he was out. Her misgivings were multiple. He attracted bad press; he was a magnet for trouble. The list went on. A couple of positives arose along the way: he was willing to work (but easily distracted), and often his distractions led to openings.

Dove looked hard at Periwinkle. An afterthought came from his reading of detective stories. "Periwinkle, can you check out Jim's bank accounts? Is that doable in real life?"

"Best to pass that to Raed. The law is complex on criminal evidence, and a search warrant in an official capacity required by law. The identity of the officer is important. If it comes from us?"

"I guess you are referring to the Police and Criminal Evidence Act?

"Yes, PACE. I'll ask her."

## Chapter 34

*Without Stead, Oldman wasn't getting anywhere. The relationship had to intensify. In his present mood he wasn't sure he could do it.*

*The small package left outside his door was addressed to 'Prof' M. Oldman. It was precisely two weeks after Luna was found in the cellars. Oldman checked the date of posting. He smiled at the implications of the inverted commas ticked around Prof.*

*The envelope looked as if it had been trampled on, but not opened. He opened it in his room, sat in his favourite chair: an old brown leather affair that had seen better days. Lovely.*

*Where had the parcel been? Roger was his guess. Roger the slimeball was away. Perhaps that was unfair to slime, especially slime moulds — a most interesting fungus. Roger had gone away to visit relatives. Oldman pondered on the intelligence of slime mould; the ability to find a way through a labyrinth. His own confusion was growing with his sense of distrust. Was Reynold's Hall hell or redemption?*

*He felt a sense of the uncanny, a journey, a spiritual awakening. Death. Stead's comment that the hall had changed of late reverberated noisily as he opened it with shaking hands.*

*Inside was a file, the sort bought in high street retailers, handy, plastic and containing thirty-something pages of articles. In the* front was tucked a brown envelope. He opened it with his index finger sliding along the seam. The writing was neat and not a hand he recognised. He turned it over.

'Oldman. I checked my sources. I still have some out there and that is your name. I also checked who you work for, so some of the names I mention will be familiar to you. In my career outside I spent years following right-wing groups in England. I was the Le Carré of the left, spying on university colleagues with right-wing sympathies. From then on, I worked for leftish journals. I covered The National Front, The Racial Preservation Society in the 1960s. You name it I chased it up. To cut this shorter, I had retired when I met Ken and Generation Identity. You can check them out online – pan-European and white supremacist. It resurrected a burning passion. I decided to check him out.

'To the point: Ken helps train them, these new right-wing volunteers. I have no evidence he is a member; he bumps up their military skills in the field, they do hand-to-hand combat with others. Check out their conspiracy ideas – the Great Replacement. A bit like Scottish Dawn. You can do your own research. Exposing people like Ken is important to me. He is, in plain speaking, an unsavoury bit of work. There are other issues in the hall too, but not so relevant to me. He knows I'm onto him… I hope you get this. He's capable of violence.

'My notes are included. I fear for my own life here in what I thought was a sanctuary, away from anti-Islamists and misogynistic terrorism, extremists, fashy femmes and trad wives.'

Oldman reached for his phone to check the terms. The alt Right was not simply a manosphere. He read on.

'I did my share of undercover work, expecting it would end here in Reynold's Hall. It has. Page one has a list of names, not prominent public members but those who hide behind their desks in Whitehall and elsewhere. My research is thorough Oldman, my list honest. The articles are unpublished material. Do what you want with them. Luna.'

Oldman scanned the list first and sat down to read. Several names stood out: Eames, and Campbell. A footnote implied the links may go higher up the food chain; under investigation, not proven. To Oldman it sounded as if Luna had been intending to leave the hallowed hall, yet never got the chance. Had she instructed someone to post it if anything went wrong? He pictured her that day, the day they stretchered her from her tiny cellar, her skin a bluish cast, her comatose state baffling doctors. By that, Oldman assumed she was lucky to be alive. Lucky?

What had appeared as a cushy number was building. The adrenalin flowed. He checked his gun; he did some exercises; he made coffee and sat with the file on his knee. It read like Weird Weekends.

He put the file down at two thirty in the morning. The pictures of men drilling in blue t-shirts, the blurred picture of Ken in France, the references to the Great Replacement and a book of the same name, finally a declaration of war; a movement without an umbrella. This was not Oldman's territory. He tried to separate Luna out from the politics and his seething hatred for Ken and conspiracy theories. Both contradicted his Broad-Church ideas, his inbred Canadian liberalism.

The anti-Islamist aspect; the winning back of the Iberian Peninsula – madness. The xenophobia appalled him. The alterophobia sent him checking the Internet dictionary. The job was just beginning for him and for Luna. He must visit her. He imagined her, unresponsive, eyes closed, everything she wasn't. He couldn't. The passages on the supremacy of whiteness horrified him yet he knew their accuracy and felt uncomfortable.

What to do with it? This was not young men playing soldiers or silly buggers. This was serious shit. Luna's notes warned him not to pass it to the British police. Pal Singh perhaps? He parcelled it back up and sent it to Griggs.

Bullying seemed to be at the core of alterophobia and bullying was hateful, cyber and otherwise. Alternative subcultures and the impaired were targets. Griggs would know what to do.

His desire to pay back, however, played havoc with his politics and job spec. He posted it the next morning from the village, and posted it signed for. He suffered some guilt, a strong feeling he was copping out. He felt regret too. Perhaps the cases would intertwine. They often did. Luna survived.

He visited her in St. George's trauma ward. He held her hand. He told her of the goings on in the hall and that he was following up the file. He sang a little tune. Luna never blinked. It was three weeks now and the signs were the diagnosis of a vegetative state might ensue. He hoped for her, he hoped she would either die or wake up. He rose, looked around the trauma room once, then left.

## Chapter 35

The unwise physical attack on Dove came as he walked home from the pub. Lacking the intelligence networks of the police, the perpetrators struck as Dove sauntered along the High Street. Passers-by witnessed 'the rumble', close to the store, a reference to a greater fight in the jungle. They testified the man Dove had not 'at first' responded.

The dismal prospect of all-out war that Penny had feared loomed large. It was not to be as he imagined. As a result of their assault, the would-be assailants were residing temporarily in James Cook Hospital under observation.

Dove informed Raed in his statement that their injuries were not substantial. "I was extremely careful."

In keeping with his personal code of ethics, Dove had warned them in the first seconds of their assault that they were going to come off worse. They laughed it off. To the onlookers it was funnier.

To Penny, Dove proclaimed, "I've adopted a more postmodern approach – broke away from health and safety towards risk assessment strategies. I warned them of the risk. I did not say to what extent I would injure them. There were no broken bones this time; unbelievably bad bruising for which Periwinkle advocated leeches."

No one filed a complaint. The baseball bat was handed in by Dove. The man who wielded it, inexpertly Dove told Penny on the side, had extensive bruising to his legs and would suffer an ongoing knee problem as the result of a kick; the memory of that scrap evoked by a constant nagging pain and profound limp.

"I kicked a little harder than intended. It will act as a stern reminder of his folly."

The other was more fortunate. He couldn't recall what happened. His injuries resembled a collision with a bus. He was the lucky one.

Dove continued to drink in The Arlington. The punters were friendlier than before.

The bartender, who had an eye for Dove said, "No one here would dare even to take on the Bateman gang like that, never mind hospitalise them."

Dove's take on that was that they were fortunate to be in one piece. The free pint of the guest bitter 'from Skegness' was just reward. He supped his pint without comment.

Penny muttered about the theatre of beers. His mumbles were audible enough to the drinkers close enough to hear him. He opted to stop reminiscing and decided to recount his excursion to the Lincolnshire Victorian Brewery another time.

What of the other side – the Bowers? Dove wondered if the police had got to the 'godmother,' Gran Bowers.

"She is a crafty old git."

Penny talked to Oldman. At night he pointed at the moon and stars when visible and showed his imagination as one would a child. Struggling against forces of darkness himself, he felt alone as the stars faded. A single light gleamed, a satellite. Was it watching?

Hart was talking to Gran on a regular basis. As a result, his waistline was gradually disappearing. His current addiction – to fruit cake and Yorkshire Parkin was to blame. A devotee of cakes and scones, he was convinced they were a weapon in her extensive armoury. Whenever a breakthrough was close, she would change characters. It was both fascinating and frustrating.

Guile, deception, disingenuousness, and Gran's different voices, along with awesome currant cake, made her a formidable opponent. In a rare moment of humour, he decided Penny could only achieve three out of four.

## Chapter 36

*A watchful Oldman was wooing Stead. She took his mood swings to be part of the grieving process. He had developed an aversion to showering and used the bath. He had also unearthed plans of the hall and was intrigued by the network of cellars underneath. 'Used for storage I guess – and torture'. Ken had mentioned them once with a sly laugh.*

*For her part, Stead threw herself into the relationship with a new fervour. The affiliation (as he referred to it in his reports to Griggs) was close to consummated, not in his apartment, or hers, but just off a permissive bridleway on a windy day on The Downs where they began to wrench one another's clothes off.*

*He reminded himself it was like riding a bicycle, although bicycles had gears and brakes. It never happened.*

*She placed her hand over his mouth and said, "Not now."*

*Stead was going to be the breakthrough, though not as he imagined. Her sources were a step ahead. She knew his background.*

Penny was becoming a part of the story, or was the story becoming him? It was a double-edged therapy which alleviated the symptoms of his trauma and drove him back to drafting his big book. He returned to the USB sticks and the images and text of The Tableau murders and drafts began to take shape. It was not a happy relationship. The cyclic loop of highs and lows drained him. Escape, the motives for his writing, was impossible. He began to separate parts of his mind from the world of fact. When coping became problematic, he spoke to Oldman.

Liz never mentioned again any of the events discussed. Did it really happen? Mikey often waved or stopped to say hello. He didn't appear to be with Kyle or George anymore.

Penny daydreamed of his old track bike, the predecessor of the modern mountain bike with multiple and low gears and suspension, which he claimed to have invented, though they were around before he was born. He couldn't afford a mountain bike, so he made the bike from spare parts. He fitted a twenty-eight-cog secured from a rubbish tip allowing the three speed gears to drop down a cog, then added studded tyres. His finishing touch was a sweeping pair of cow horn handlebars that gave it fashionable class.

It caught the eye of other teenagers and differenced the mountain bikes, and the older sit-up-and-begs coming back into fashion for the sedate. Not satisfied with the end product entirely he worked on a suspension system but didn't have the know-how to achieve this. Painted matte black, of course, it had part-mudguards to stop the clart flying up his back, and front and back bars to bolster the shock. Sometimes he'd put a piece of card from the forks through the spokes to emit a powerful whirring warning noise.

The Five watched. He practised. His heart was no longer in it.

206

If other kids were beginning to find this man funny, Kyle and George steered clear. Dove's encounter didn't help. They were uncles, or whatever. They were out of hospital and keeping a low profile. The burly chap who hobbled passed Penny with an antagonistic glare was the Bateman who had made the silly mistake of wielding a baseball bat at Dove.

In truth, they, the families, were as one brave local who spoke out in the pub, shit-scared of Dove and Jack.

Fired up with beer, the pub orator then proclaimed, "If he could do what he did with minimum effort on his own, what the hell would he do to them in an all-out brawl? Kill them?" Then for good measure, "His funny mate Perry-whatever, the one who doesn't drink, might be worse. Bad ass both of them, if you ask me. You've got one chance only. Not even that bunch of thickos are daft enough to have another go."

In private, Raed thought the Bateman's encounter with Dove amusing. Her public statements signified she was disdainful of any violence. Hart, already aware of Dove's expertise in unarmed combat and the outcomes of such had nothing to say. They had indeed got off lightly.

Without the aid of a BMX, it was Hart who made the next breakthrough. His informant had mentioned to him to ask Gran Bowers about the Batemans.

"I…" he had stuttered nervously, "I mean, if you're not convinced by what I say about the sheer hatred for each other, mention them to her – see what happens. Oh, and stand well back!"

Hart did. Gran's volcanic self, erupted. Trained as he was, Hart got the hell out of it, and fast. Gran's violence was a mixed blessing. It signalled the end of the Parkin and currant cake washed down by gallons of Yorkshire tea. It brought Gran into custody. Hart suffered withdrawal and gradually with exercise, the return of his waistline.

Gran had flown off the handle at the very mention of the name Bateman. The trigger effect, deployed artfully by a salesperson using stories, authority, specifics, and scarcity as a ploy, meant zero to her. The name Bateman was enough to activate what Hart painfully described as a psychotic episode.

Her mood swing was instant, switching from her motherly "have another piece of cake, Richard," to "get the fuck out of it!"

She scanned the room for a suitable weapon to enforce her threat. She then ran into the kitchen – for a knife was Hart's guess. He didn't wait. The hatred was pathological. He would miss the current cake.

Raed took over. Gran Bowers, Hart warned her, was remarkably strong for an elderly woman. She showed an extreme aggressive streak. She was capable of excessive viciousness.

"Locals are scared of her for more reasons than her witchery, or should that be craft?" Hart said.

In their follow-up discussion, Dove offered to go in and sort her out if he could have the baseball bat.

Raed hid a smile. "That's not going to happen, but it does have some cred." Raed asked two constables to bring her in.

Kyle's parents had taken him out of school. He was staying with relatives. Left on his own, George still commanded the yard with his arrogant swagger.

"How about your informants, Penny?" Hart asked.

"They've revealed nothing of import so far. Will let you know when that happens."

Hart's face implied he'd heard that before.

Raed intervened. "The attack on Dove suggests that the Batemans believe you are on the side of the Bowers. Can we get that to work for us?"

"I doubt any information will come from either side as a result. It's all part of something closeted, personal, or should we say it *was* until the werewolf attacks, which I now think were symptomatic of the feud." Dove as usual was succinct and accurate.

As the trio walked home, the evening light changed from overcast to a luminous orange glow that lasted ten or fifteen minutes and pre-empted a storm.

Mimicking the local fishers Dove said, "Weather's coming in."

On a redundant chimney top, the strange glow in the sky spotlighted a big old woodpigeon. His white neck patch and pink chest shone brilliantly in the eerie evening light, his tiny head in bas-relief.

Periwinkle paused, pointed up at the pigeon and spoke. "Information is on the way."

As he spoke, the light altered to a dull green and the pigeon lifted from the chimney with an ungainly clatter, then after a short glide downwards disappeared out of sight. *A Cloudy Sky* by Joseph Wright; Turner's painting *Fishermen at Sea*: a message. The power of nature, the colours of Wright and Turner. In the greenish light Penny saw the bird and its brilliant colours as a symbol of the faithful in the tree of life, a symbol of air, guileless, unlike— He never concluded. The storm broke. Battering down, the rain had the appearance of hailstones as it bounced back up from the kerb and ran down again into floods of swirling water that gushed into the gutters. In no time, the drains gave up and water washed into the street.

"That will clear the air," stated Dove, a remark Penny connected to Periwinkle's comment about information on the way.

It gave Penny a sense of strength. He tried to put it down to negative ions. Then he opted for a more mystical concept that a bird that comes to hand would deliver a message. As they walked the rain slowed, running like woven threads before them and then petered out.

All five-foot and one and a half inches of Gran 'The Godmother' resisted arrest. She broke a constable's arm. Despite the handcuffs she attempted to smash the car up on the way to the station. The police officers, in fear of their lives, left the old dear cuffed and restrained in a cell. Hart was correct, she was crazy as a loon and unpleasant.

In the cell, she switched from the devil's double to dear old lady, smiling sweetly at those who called in 'to visit her' and sang to them. Then she started humming to herself. The staff drew lots. Raed volunteered.

"Can I have a cup of tea, please?" Gran whined. "Milk and two sugars."

"You may. But first, I want some straight answers from you. I'll give you the time to explain why you inflicted bodily harm on two constables when they simply wanted to bring you in to ask you a few things."

Gran smiled. "Did I?"

"Ms Bowers, are you sorry you broke a Constable's arm? Or are you saying you can't recall what happened? Which?"

Gran started to sing, a cracked voice with a crescendo to the last words of the lines dragging out the final syllables. "*Two lovely black eyes … oh what a surprise.*"

Raed shuddered at the outlandish lyrics and incorrect language of the song. It was at once alien and awful. Penny, with his penchant for trivia, offered to explain it to her when she brought it up later. What did it mean for Gran Bowers?

"Charles Coborn wrote it in 1886 parodying an American song by Ida Morris—"

Impressed or not, Raed stopped him there. "Thanks, that's really helpful. The central issue is whether Gran would be aware of that."

Her ability to shush Penny was an art very few could boast of. Her interpretive know-how was at work. Gran couldn't recall her assault on the police officers, though there was the possibility she was faking it. The identity she inhabited at that moment was the currant-cake lady. It was clear that she disassociated herself from what had happened, or from that identity.

Raed's experience of such matters, and of astute policing, warned her against making medical judgements. That was for a forensic psychologist. Nevertheless, she had read of Dissociative Identity which might stem from long-term severe abuse or persecution. Hart would know more about it. On leaving, she made sure Gran got a cup of tea with two sugars and milk. She was still singing that silly song. The tune was catchy. It recalled an operatic piece.

Gran smiled knowingly as Raed left the cell.

※

Hart confirmed from his studies in psychology that each identity (he was careful not to use personality) had its own memory. Diagnosis was difficult. The common term, split personality, is probably not appropriate, schizophrenia, redundant. Though what psychiatry terms as the 'alters' – sub-personalities – might be relevant in this case."

He was thankful he hadn't had to go in and empirically test out his theory. At last his studies came to use; his knowledge helped refine the case! Raed decided to have Gran assessed professionally.

Hart's common or garden-self saw Gran as barking mad. Could Gran have committed the werewolf attacks and then faked her own attack? Or, as Penny had hinted at, was she covering up? It was possible. Her condition might block any memory of this alter. Anything was possible in this godforsaken hole, was his opinion.

Hart turned back to his books and studied. Gran's image hovered and bothered him then split into two, then three, a mental aberration with no voice.

※

Raed clocked Gran in on arrival. She informed her of her rights in detention. If she wanted a solicitor, she could name one, or they could provide one. Gran laughed. Raed followed the book. She wanted to hold this woman as long as necessary. They had sufficient evidence to charge her with grievous and actual bodily harm. She made sure no loopholes existed that might contravene the Police and Criminal Evidence Act.

Before the day was out she had applied to a magistrate's court for permission to extend detention pending interviews. Gran's apparent lack of memory of the events meant a psychiatric evaluation was forthcoming. She was comfortable, unaware of her detention. Raed put it to her in writing. She had scrawled on the paper a signature and smiled sweetly. It was illegible and indecipherable.

"Dissociative Identity Disorder is often pleaded in court," Hart pre-warned Raed. "The passive identity that smiled upon the world and sang may cloak one or two other identities, each separate."

Confirming his worse fears Raed asked him to go in and take a statement if he could.

Gran's welcoming as Richard came home convinced him she was mad. "Have a slice of currant cake, Richard."

The pangs of abdication caused him to look around for the goodies. He took a statement that was utter balderdash. For one, it was clear that Gran couldn't really write, and two, her childish block script was worth passing to a handwriting pathologist.

As a student, his detailed reading of the chapter 'On the Writing of the Insane' in *Mad Humanity: It's Forms, Apparent and Obscure* appealed to his academic nature. It was old, published in 1898, and its precursor, Bacon's earlier book published 1870 *On the Writing of the Insane* was still in the shops. Bacon had been a medical superintendent at Cambridgeshire County Asylum. The problem of building bridges between research and practice was ongoing for him and the comfort of research beckoning. Gran's writing was unintelligible, somewhere between sanity and madness, but closer to the latter.

She was uneducated, deranged. Was Gran wily? Yes. Was Gran cunning? Yes. Was she insane? The alarming increase of insanity that led Forbes Winslow to write his book on this 'terrible complaint' was on his bookshelf. Was the Ripper a Woman? Hart digressed.

In a friendly moment, one of empathy, he mentioned it to Penny who had read Winslow's *Anatomy of Suicide*. He tried to recall the gist. These writings from the Victorian period had once fascinated Hart's scholastic nature. He took it from the shelf with some trepidation. Things had changed in the mental world of Detective Hart. He remembered Penny's retort.

"What did we learn from it, Hart? It is easy to find reasons to justify our preconceived notions and carry out our opinions."

"Something we both need to bear in mind?" He left it at that.

Hart had a niggling suspicion Gran may have had an accomplice. He asked her to tell him about Fenris. She knew the bare bones. She was reciting the little she knew by rote. While on a roll, he decided to question her further, not formally, but to eke out what he could about the family. Addressing her as Gran, which brought about an endearing if not frightening opened-mouthed smile, she nattered on.

214

"Gran, tell me about young Mikey.

Most of it was prattle: the boy was the light of her life; he came to see her regularly and always brought something for her. "Yes, he comes here regularly!"

"He comes here?"

"Yes, every day."

Gran had had no visitors, though both Batemans and Bowers had sent her a card, both stating 'thinking of you, Gran' – a strange occurrence to Hart.

He chatted for a while and she offered him tea. He declined and said, "I've got work to do, Gran. It's really good to see you."

With a goodbye, he left. She was oblivious to the fact she was in a cell in the Loftus police station, closed to the public. Her rambling incoherence apart, he felt he was getting somewhere. Dare he broach the subject of Liz or Jim?

## Chapter 37

Oldman was fighting the demons of lust and love, his professional instincts wavering. Since the walk on the Downs, he wondered if she was as bad a person as he supposed, and then, if the relationship was bogus. He studied himself in the critical mirror in order to reflect. Guilt and self-doubt invaded his mind for the first time in his career. A sense of being alone increased. It felt wrong. The only thing to do was break all the rules and ask Stead directly what was going on. The very idea of such amateurism kept him awake. It spoke of defeat.

He mulled over the deaths and wondered who was involved on the outside and how important they were. It had never occurred before, but was Ken involved? Time was running out. Griggs had hit a stone wall. He had poked around but no one had any information on The Electrician. He was being protected. Oldman warned Griggs to be careful.

In the hall he enquired after Ken. "What do you know about Ken? Where do you think he is?"

Stead's reply was cautious and not fully formed. "Ken was a strange man. What his role was in the army I shudder to think." Then she relaxed. "I don't think we'll miss him."

*Oldman never responded. He took that to mean Ken wasn't coming back. The past tense implied something else. Oldman disliked Ken intensely but felt empathy. He too felt his card was marked.*

Suffering from writer's block and a BMX learning plateau, Oldman's creator and mentee cycled to the lot. He sat down on the cold tarmac which suggested the aftermath of a minor earthquake. Cracks spread out and ran along the width and breadth; tarmac clints and grikes – fissures – fractured the surface of the once pristine car park. The discoloured and acned surface testified to years of neglect and austerity.

The flow of detection drifted in and out in a tide of meanings and guesswork, none of which came to anything. Wrapped up in his thoughts and woollies, he neither noticed the cold creeping in, nor the boys who had dismounted from their bikes and were sitting in a ragged circle, with him as part of the circumference.

"What's up, Doc?"

The impression was good and served to stir him from his mental flight. In fact he jumped. He was a swallow seeking solitude in the desert. Like a hawk they had swooped in silence and settled. There was no solitude.

"Hi, guys. What's new?"

"We heard they got Gran. 'Bout time. You have something to do with that?" The voice from the hood.

"Partly, but I can't claim it as a victory. Hart, the copper, did it. She's an old woman who's not well."

One of the others spoke. Hoody's predominance was apparent; his body language denoting a chairing of the proceedings. He removed his hood. The fresh scrubbed freckled face startled Penny. The boy grinned from ear to ear. The sandy tousled hair and freckly face were him as a kid. Short trousers and flannel shirts had long gone out of fashion even then; the functional and cheap replaced by the hip (mostly cheap).

Hoody laughed his words out in response to Penny's facial expression of surprise. "What were you expecting – a teenage werewolf?"

Penny gathered his savvy. "1957!"

"We're talking movies aren't we, Doc?"

"Yep, sure are." With more than a suggestion of self-reflective innuendo he told them about the cycle of regression of the central character Tony Rivers. He was played by Michael Landon. The teenage Rivers is experimented on by a mad scientist, Brandon, played by Whit Bissell. He replayed scene after scene till his shooting by the police.

Hoody spoke first, his face betraying their joint disappointment at the ending. "Was he like James Dean?"

"Exactly like James Dean. Good thinking. I think *Teen Wolf* made in 1985 was another version with Michael J Fox."

They sat bolt upright around the ragged circle. The other boy spoke again, making eye contact with Hoody before doing so. "We know that Gran was the werewolf. We saw her. Me dad talked about her. He felt sorry for her. Her dad did stuff to her. Dad said she tried to do it to Spaz. He told his dad and they fell out. We won't tell the police. We don't shop anyone. Not even Gran."

A form of respect echoed around the lot. Penny was thinking at high speed in spite of his relaxed manner. If they wouldn't tell the police, how could he present the evidence? Would it be admissible? One of the lads held out a carrier bag. Penny held it with gloved hands and peered into the bag. He didn't touch the contents. A small metallic glove of sorts with claws rested in the bag. It resembled the fore claws of a badger, no longer than an inch and a half. Who could have crafted such a vile weapon?

"Gee. Where did you find this? Have you handled it?"

The chairman took over the proceedings. "Gran Bowers left it hidden after she slashed her own throat. She's loopy. She did it when the law were scouting around." Then to answer his question and add to it: "We wore gloves. Don't want our dabs on it. We don't need to look for trouble! We watch things from above."

The boy with the bag spoke again. "She hid it, then went back for it. We'd already taken it. We didn't touch the contents, got Gran's mark on it. We hid it in a secret place."

Penny chose not to ask about Gran's mark. Forensics would find Gran's prints or DNA on the teeth and claws. Gran had gone back the night they were out searching for Max. Disturbed by police activity, she had injured herself. It might have been a mistake. Depends which Gran did it...

"Doc, we aren't going to talk to the police even if Gran is in the clink. You might know what to do?"

Triumphantly, Penny raised his fists and put two gloved thumbs up. "I know exactly what to do. No one will know where this evidence came from." What was bothering him was how she obtained the vile stuff in the bag. Was she some sort of zoanthropic? That she was aggressive was a given.

It was apparent that the boys feared her. Then came the clincher.

"Doc, Gran Bowers is rich, stinking rich. We guess she won a smacker on the Lotto. They're all after her money."

"They?"

"All of them. She's from both families!"

"Bowers and Batemans?"

"Spot on, Doc. Cool dude."

"Bejasus," he whistled between his teeth. What was behind all this? Had this pairing led to the torture and death of a young boy? Buried in the local enmities and what he feared was cruelty or ill-treatment, abuse of some form, a sore that had rankled and turned to poison between two families had led to war. Throats slashed open; injuries so bad that a young woman died of her wounds. Two young women suffering trauma. Max?

Gran was never going to talk. And, if she did, it would be prattle. For the police it was a bad dream. Penny had a plan. It was dominoes-related rather than bridge. It might necessitate some brutality. He owed The Five, and Oldman.

He got to his feet, stretching up to ease the cramp and said, "Thanks, guys. You don't know how important this is to me!"

Hoody concluded. "They won't let her out, will they?"

"No," he promised, full of good feeling and self-belief.

"Sound." Hoody spoke for all. He pulled his hood back up.

Penny mounted up in a cavalier fashion. On the way out of the lot he turned to wave. The bike wobbled. The Five were still sitting there unmindful of the freezing wind coming from the North Sea and chilling the moonlike craters. The empty space on the circle where he had sat was conspicuous. It told him that was the end of his sojourns at the lot. The hawk had delivered.

His gloves on, the carrier bag stuffed inside his backpack, he rode towards the police station. On the way he picked up two blowing carrier bags. With great care he tipped the badger claws into one bag and disposed of the original bag in a convenient bin, holding the first bag with the second. He was unaware of what the lab could achieve and thus could afford no chances. His gloves added another measure of safety. One set of claws resembled a cockerel or turkey's spur, able to tear eyes out or rip flesh apart. They threatened to tear the bag. The sight of Gran with claws and her missing teeth made him shiver. It conjoined with the cold that began to leach into his bones. He pedalled faster.

A police car went past, light flashing, then a second as he came near to the station. The second car passed him, turned into a side street, and parked up. It was not more than a hundred yards from the yard and another two or three hundred to the pub. Two officers got out and rushed down a side street. Dark was coming down early.

There was no desk. Was there CCTV? It hadn't been apparent. His mood dipped. He started walking back his words to The Five. This was a job for Periwinkle. He didn't want to involve anyone else. He didn't want to hang around too long either.

He stood closeted by the gathering dark on the opposite side of the road to the yard. "Dark matters," he whispered.

The car park was to the side of the station and CCTV evident. He had a clear view of the street. Not a soul around.

He was about to give up when he saw Hart pulling up just short of the station, and rush to the door, hit the entry code and dive in out of the cold. He ran from the car at pace.

Thanking Hart inwardly, he locked his bike outside the pub away from the parked police car. Inside, he threw his coat down and settled. At the bar he asked the time, twice. There was barely a customer in. Two lads nattered to the bar staff. After ten minutes or so he went to the toilet, leaving his coat and pint but lugging his backpack. The lads were totally engaged in discussing the police chase and placing bets on which local ne'er-do-well was scarpering from the fuzz.

"I hope it's that—"

He removed the carrier and shot out the back into the street like a bullet. Never a sprinter, he showed the cleanest pair of heels. Breathing heavily, he ran towards the parked police car. He could hear the sounds of the chase. He threw the bag onto the bonnet, then paused to tuck a corner under the wipers. His heart was threatening to burst from his chest. He was back in the toilet in a flash, removed his gloves, and then took his place in the bar, supped his beer, and bought another. Dove would've timed it. That he was red in the face and gasping escaped the attention of the three chattering occupants. No doubt it would've raised a comment about what he was doing in the toilet.

Operation Carrier Bag wasn't exactly stylish, wasn't exactly Oldman or Periwinkle, and he wasn't sure if the street was on camera. He heard the police car go past. The lads were still debating the identity of the scally who might now be in the car with the police.

A strategy was emerging, for him and for Oldman, one that would bring change.

The bartender smiled over and supplied the reason for the lack of clientele. "Football match on telly! Not watching it?"

"No, can't stand to see the Boro lose. They forget it's a game of two halves." He finished his beer, made a fuss about leaving, and checked the time again. Placing his empty glass on the bar, he said goodnight and walked out into the windy street.

Penny's assailant that night was a Bowers man. It proved Raed's theory wrong. That they had sent one-person enraged Penny. What was it about him that led people to underestimate his skills and competencies in the field? Dove had mentored him. He was relieved.

Outside the pub, about to unlock his bike, a man in his thirties confronted him. He was stocky and, unlike Dove's attackers, talkative.

"Right, ye fucker. Keep out of our fucking business."

Penny didn't follow Dove's risk assessment strategies with assailants. "Sorry, who is fucking who here?"

As he spoke, he weighed the man up the way Dove did. That one sentence allowed him time. The legs were the point of weakness. While the man was working out the import of his statement, Penny kicked him just below the right knee with the toe of a boot. Walking boots weren't as effective as steel-toed working boots, though the satisfying smack as he contacted with the man's shinbone was spot on. As he lurched and fell, Penny moved in close, then taking a leaf from Dove's book stamped on the other crooked leg, to make

223

sure he stayed down rather than to break it. The man was in some pain.

Leaning down, he spoke directly into the man's face. "Guess you're not a Boro supporter?" He unlocked his bike to ride away. Both tyres flat. He pumped them up and then rode home. He watched the man on the pavement while inflating his tyres.

With some difficulty, the man got to his feet, cursing, and limped sorely away. Hobbling was becoming a family trait for both the Bowers and Batemans. Had it been two, Penny might have had to run. He now had four alibis: three to say he'd been in the pub for the duration and one outside who wouldn't support his statement. No one asked.

Slowly, but very surely, snippets of information came in; the beginning of a complex jigsaw that went back sixty-odd years to the 1950s. It was a tale Hollywood could never tell. They might try. Who could play Gran Bowers? Who could play Dove, a hardy tough, or Periwinkle, a tall public schoolboy.

It was as if the town was now protecting Penny and his mates from two warring families who were increasingly isolated and had lost all credibility. Retaliation was possible. Relief was obvious. For the two warring factions resignation was the order of the day. People began to talk. No one knew where the evidence for the werewolf came from. Penny did have qualms about Operation Carrier Bag. He needn't have bothered. As far as the failed assailant went, local gossip confirmed that the bloody schoolteacher flattened the bastard. That opened the door to more local gossip.

Penny didn't call the police after the scrap. He went home. Despite the schism, the local grapevine saw to it that the news swept across town: the dopey teacher, the one with the BMX, had floored Bowers.

"Bugger me," was the standard response. There was more to come from the dopey teacher.

Dove listened to the story several times – each version. It mattered little that small embellishments occurred. Penny had done the job. Several days later, while seeking a quiet moment, Penny burst in through the door. He was talking before entering the room. Dove heard to his joy and relief.

"Dove, I have a theory!"

Dove groaned. Simultaneously, he endorsed Penny's appointment with the real world, *his* world. It was, he hoped, a permanent return. It wasn't. He'd been impressed by his handling of the Bowers attack. He resisted a 'taught him all I know' remark. The lame and limping Bowers and Batemans had been neutralised in a way that they couldn't comprehend, nor cope with. The fear of them was beginning to melt away. With a simple kick they had lost it. And, as Penny remarked, the Boro actually won that night, then pausing before adding the clincher:

"A goal from a free kick, a set piece, Dove!"

In truth, the game was scrappy, not unlike his carrier bag strategy.

The Bowers and Batemans retreated into their separate homes with their tinnies and cigarettes and stayed there to lick their wounds. The pubs lightened up. Information wasn't flooding in, but channels were opening.

Dove was prepared to accept one theory at a time and before Penny could flood the conversation, chose to offer his take. "The history between these families tells of intermarriage years back which turned to ill-treatment or, more aptly, maltreatment. Gran may have been on the receiving end. She is related to both families. Some of the present generation don't know what the roots of this feud are. It's lodged in a memory passed on without sense... unspoken. Each generation knows only that the others are guilty... of some misdemeanour or crime against the other."

Periwinkle filled a gap or two. "Saida tracked the families, and Gran was the daughter of Kevin Bowers and Margaret Bateman. Saida thinks that something horrid happened. Hart's informant told him that her parents divorced at a time when such was stigmatic. If asked, Margaret would say that her husband died. That isn't uncommon."

Dove eyed Penny who was staring at a piece of paper. He noted the use of Raed's first name by his pal.

## Chapter 38

*Desperation was a new sensation for Oldman. Griggs drew a blank with The Electrician. Ken was gone. Griggs suspected he was 'a protected species'.*

*"Lawson laughed me out of the office. Said I'd been reading too much fiction. He mentioned Elmore Leonard."*

*"It sounds like he's rewriting the script."*

*Taking liberties with wiring came to mind. Could Stead and the others have tinkered with the shower? Nothing was positive. Romance was getting in the way of his judgement. He began to wonder about the credibility of the information he was being fed from above. What was he doing there? Gaping holes existed in intelligence, holes that suggested a problem of synergy. He thought of a common saying: too much information. Most of it bullshit.*

*The undertakers removed the body of Fielding. He still looked the same (the current hadn't burned him). The forensic bods seemed confused by the shower. Had someone tampered with the shower circuits? They weren't sure. Insurance took over and accidental death was the verdict. Oldman's gut told him that The Electrician had tinkered with the shower circuits. But who authorised it? He wanted to believe Stead was innocent. He wanted her to tell him everything. They walked; they talked. At*

227

times the intensity of his own dilemma got the better of him. On those occasions he would pull away from her. She never asked why.

Pal Singh had closed shop, his superiors giving him a hard time. Social esteem didn't hamper Oldman's character, yet he felt isolated one moment, then part of something the next, swings and roundabouts. He was having difficulty connecting. A looping chain of love, suspicion, anxiety, and plain old desire bound him; that this woman might be complicit in the murder of a friend revolted him. His leading questions came to nothing. He felt that even the bridge school operated on a surface level. His reports revealed his doubts to Griggs and his failings. Griggs too was under surveillance. A sense of foreboding arose as he went to the phone box.

He contemplated. He was there to fail. In an office referred to as 'upstairs' in central London, the faceless ones, bastard bureaucrats he called them, suggested he should reveal his identity to Stead, his cover blown. Upstairs was in the middle of change, an inconstant bureaucracy. The pretenders to the throne and their lackeys were conducting their own purging. That much Griggs had clarified.

He reflected on his own changing persona. His professional dedication was breaking down in an unplanned retirement plan. Love and companionship hadn't been a part of it, and neither had bridge. Isolation or fulfilment-which was it to be? Hell or redemption? The maze.

Walking in the Downs hand in hand as horses trotted past and cyclists pedalled the trail between Winchester and Eastbourne wasn't enough. They talked excitedly of doing the whole Downs trek, stopping along the way at differing hostelries. It was best when it was quiet. He hummed a pop song from the last millennium, though he didn't know who sang it. What did it mean to him. Were they so connected they didn't need to speak. Or were they both so wary of each other they didn't want to slip up. On one of their longer rambles they came across an old churchyard, headstones leaning against the crumbling flint wall, the church demolished, rubble. Oldman felt he'd been there before in some undefined past. They read the stones and a plaque.

Stead recited:

"'The living come with grassy tread, to read the gravestones on the hill,

The graveyard draws the living still,

But never any more the dead.'"

He listened. The sense of being there before would not lift.

"'So sure of death the marbles rhyme,

You can't help marking all the time.'"

Stead broke off her ominous recital. Oldman was eyeing the stones. They walked away down a grassy lane in silence holding hands. No one to be seen. He didn't ask who wrote the verse.

Time to assert oneself; claim back his probity, prove his worth; risk his life at the hands of his new love and the co-operative killers.

The death certificates of the now five dead criminals were all in order, each buried or cremated with all requirements in place. McKean didn't fit. He was less concerned with how than who. Perish the thought it might happen to him. The idea of dying in unsuspicious circumstances appalled him. He turned away from the grave.

Griggs's last memo had read: 'Sorry, others have stepped in. The only way forward is to use you as bait.'

Griggs subtle use of stepped was clearly ironic. It was most likely a cavalry charge. His superiors were bloody smart and he smelled a rat: Lawson. He consigned it to the ethernet along with all other messages. Oldman wasn't ready to be side-lined by his company, ensnared, buried, or burnt. He hatched his own counterplan. It didn't include the lovely Stead.

Their idea was simple. Mail evidencing his involvement was to fall into the wrong hands. His idea was to use his networks to buy a place in Bermuda, a place he'd fallen in love with years since. He was planning his disappearance and retirement proper. It would be his last job, unfinished or not. False passports were abundant, a change of identity was a simple matter. The hardest part was Stead. He upped his time in the gym. His new regime of fitness was difficult. He knew it would stand him in good... stead? Jogging for miles was hard and lonely work. He laid off bread. He lost weight. He cut back on all dairy products. He felt ten years younger. Stead loved the new Oldman and encouraged him in the belief it was for her benefit. So she thought...

She was busy too. She had tracked Bridie down. Bridie was about to get a visitor.

The most difficult part was how he would cope with the change in her manner when the leak occurred. He wasn't to know. He wasn't party to the process of the leak; he was merely the foil. The years in the field had left him with the instincts of an alley cat. He set a date for his departure. Then he had his first breakthrough, too late. It was south, – Bingham, playing opposite north, Jack David. A slip of the tongue.

The newspapers digested and a good breakfast, Stead, Jack David, Bingham and he fancied a hand of bridge. Oldman, leading the conversation, highlighted a scammer in the paper.

Bingham eyed Jack David and said, "Another deep-cleaning job for us perhaps?" Realising her error, she clammed up.

Stead showed no signs of surprise, a puzzled look only. She studied Oldman. Jack David stared across at Bingham.

Bingham pushed the table back and made an excuse. "Just remembered I have a call to make. Silly me."

The next day she was gone. To her sister's, was the party line. No one knew where that was. Stead seemed unconcerned. Jack David seemed troubled. Oldman knew their background. Bingham didn't have a sister. His search of Bingham's room revealed nothing. It had been thoroughly cleansed. No laptop, not a thing. Hard to tell anyone had lived there. In his own parlance they had him stymied, shafted; the bridge was gone, the compass shattered.

He rang Griggs from the box. "Can you do a search, without the police knowing? Find Bingham."

"No, I can't. I can contact international resources, Interpol. A Yellow notice? I'm not sure the mutual commitment to our future security is a value we hold dear anymore."

"Do it. Keep me posted." He had to find her.

Griggs never mentioned pulling out.

Oldman had sussed that Ken too had had an aversion to Bingham. She scared him. For that reason and others he liked the woman. The last time he spoke to Ken, Oldman had quizzed him about Bingham and the school. He knew nothing. Oldman's built-in polygraph told him he was lying. It was clear that 'Major' Ken had friends of his own; the residents were all connected in some weird compact. He asked himself. Was it a class thing? Oldman rang around. He had his suspicions that the whole of the hall was complicit in some way, though Roger and Ken were traitors. He was wrong and maybe he was right. Trepidation followed. What would he do if he was right in his assumptions? Stead, Jack David and co would no doubt have to act upon it.

Griggs found out snippets about the major and his past. He was indeed a major, and had a good record, though one that hinted at a man capable of breaking the rules and getting away with it. Ken wasn't a man to mess with. What was he doing at the hall? He didn't mix much. He was, as Oldman assumed, from a lowly background, and had jumped up, as Griggs described it, without any sign of condescension.

The wind on the Downs was picking up, switching and swirling side to side whichever way they turned, catching their faces with the sharpness of a clip around the earhole. They climbed above Portslade to the South Downs.

Stead grasped his hand. "I'm thinking of leaving Reynold's Hall."

He heard the word leaving. He missed completely her intonation which lost its former warmth. Affectionately, he squeezed her hand. He concentrated his hearing.

As the wind buffeted them, she spoke again. "I have a place in mind in Suffolk – a two-bedroomed cottage."

Again he squeezed her hand. His bulky coat that kept off the winds hid a slimmer figure. He was concentrating on other things. He was under active surveillance. They were being watched. Stead didn't appear aware. Did she know?

His walk and sense of wellbeing felt to him more like his younger self. He thought of her kiss, his very own golden period. He had to get knocked off his bike to achieve something. Bikes were useful. He trembled. His disgust and mindfulness of his so-called colleagues out there tracking him and more than likely listening to a mate was bubbling up, turning from disgust to anger.

He turned and eyed Stead. "Not enough room for an ageing teammate, then?"

Bugging was an issue. Her room wasn't safe, his definitely not. There was nowhere to go. The clock was running down. He simply had to go along with it. In a crazy moment he wanted to say will you marry me? It never came. Did she know what his fate was to be? His only hope was that his alternative retirement plan remained undiscovered. His experience told him that was so. It was watertight – a flight booked with several changes of plane before he would reach his island, alone. He let go of her hand and, demonstrating his new fitness, in a boyish way ran up the hill for fifty yards and then fell over laughing. It allowed him just a glimpse of a car and two men. Stead caught him up and laid on the ground in fits. She seemed unaware of the surveillance team.

The two watchers spoke to each other. "Oldman seems unaware of his pending removal, don't you think?"

"Let's check around his old haunts. In fact, let's do a search of his contacts and informants, his family, and increase our surveillance at the hall."

Back home he forgot his fears, had a shower, and flopped in his chair in his dressing gown. Bridge ceased.

Another murder occurred. This one shocked him to the core. He received mixed messages. It was Hayley who contacted him and passed on an order to drop everything and report in, then within an hour told him to hold his position. U-turns were a feature of current politics. Griggs was dead, murdered; his office ransacked.

Griggs had been seeking The Electrician and was 'following a lead'. Everything related to Oldman was missing. The Luna file was gone.

Oldman had a great deal of respect for Griggs. Over the last few months it had waned. Griggs had been aware of what was going on in all corners of The Agency's work. Seventy-odd or not, he was in charge. Or was he? His last move was to break his own rules and send an email to Oldman on The Electrician. Griggs's laptop was missing. Oldman called Hayley. No answer. He rang reception.

"Not turned up for work and not answering calls," was the brusque reply. The receptionist refused to give Hayley's contact address.

Could Stead and co be complicit, guilty of organising the beating of an old man to death with a claw hammer? Their ways were more subtle. Such a ham-fisted job might well detract an investigator. Who or what was on the Luna file that was so important? Question after question. No bloody answers.

Fielding and Griggs's deaths didn't carry the hallmark of the co-operative. It was sudden yes, but brutal. Oldman was getting nowhere. His undercover work had been fruitless. His time was short. Fielding wanted to spill the beans. He'd had enough. His loyalties got in the way and destroyed him. He died instead of Oldman. That was something Oldman could never forgive. In his mind the person out there was an assassin, hired… a mercenary. He had an idea who it was that was doing the hiring, and in the hall who the leak was, the prime conspirator.

An incident on a train convinced him other hands were at work, and further up in the company, something shitty was going on. With no one to consult with, Oldman began to move forward his exit plan. Trust created its own problem patterns in this case. Trust was on the way out, and group sanctions were taking over. For the lone individual this was the end. His judgement and consistency wavered and his relationships took on a negative.

He met his surveillance team of three on a wet day on a train between Portslade and Chichester. He was going to meet Stead and take in the cathedral carvings of humans and half-humans dancing, its mixture of modern and mediaeval. No one else was in the carriage (the weather was stay-at-home). Two of them joined him on the train, one sat opposite, and the other next to him. His well-honed senses told him there was a third. He disliked the man next to him immediately. It was him who spoke.

"You've heard about Griggs?"

"Yes, a sad loss. He was a close colleague. And my boss for years. We had little contact. What happened?"

"You might tell us."

"This conversation is over!" He thought again. Any moves he contemplated would be subject to a search and scrutiny by that lovable wily old man. He wanted to find his killers. He relented. "Why kill a defenceless old man like Griggs?"

The men pushed him back in his seat, one with an elbow, the other with both hands. He allowed them to. He held back a desire to fettle them both.

"I know he was an old bastard. That's no reason to get rid of him." Whatever he said would be suspect, and silence complicit. "How did it happen?"

"We thought you might know what happened? Griggs, who should have retired years ago, bludgeoned to death with a hammer. It was amateurish. Your records disappeared. How strange is that?" The man relished his telling of the murder. He smacked his lips as he spoke.

Oldman liked him even less. To him the thorough and systematic removal of old records implied a professional element. "Two things: first, why would I want rid of Griggs? We knew each other well. We've had our differences. Second, why would I want my records? Light reading? A tell-all autobiography?"

The conversation played out hand by hand. Declarer, the nasty one next to him, spoke first.

"You appear to be especially close to the suspect, Ms Stead."

The man's leer didn't provoke him. Oldman studied their faces. He revealed the palms of his hands as he spoke. "I am. It hasn't detracted me from my work." Self-doubt blended with personal revulsion for the man. He was well-informed. By whom was the question.

The man opposite, the dummy, showed his hand. "Did you do it?"

The play proceeded clockwise. He weighed up them and their game. They had no evidence of his plans or an inkling of the scope of his relationship. That was clear. Bluff wasn't even a part of it. Pure intelligence was at work here versus amateur sleuthing. He was at the helm. These new guys were calculating and ambitious. Experience was lacking. The two men departed suddenly at Barnham.

As they left, the talkative one turned and said, "Loser!"

Oldman replied with a question. "You don't drive a borrowed silver-grey saloon by any chance, do you?"

Nasty's shoulders froze, then he stepped off the train.

Oldman shouted yet another retort. "How about electrical work?"

He watched them walk out the station. He moved slightly to allow a view of the third man shuffling along, head down briefcase

236

*in hand. He walked past the other two who stopped and were talking.*

*"Bodgers," he muttered under his breath. Who had killed Griggs? He had just spoken with them, or one of them.*

*He went to meet Stead. The faceless ones had materialised. There was no one to trust. After meeting Stead, he felt like the bait in a trap.*

*"You look like you've met a ghost, Westy."*

*"Not quite a ghost… yet. Just seen the spectres of the future." And the past, he thought to himself.*

*Stead never replied.*

"What is real and what is not real? That is the question."

Thrashing out and debating say-sos, Penny stopped writing. He was Oldman, and Oldman was precious to him. He'd learnt much from the ageing agent who guided him. In the pub, a pint in hand, he blathered to all present, a stage-whisper that came easily to him. No one sat next to him. Three or four men sat separately around the small bar. They listened. He eyed Ray, the bartender, and beamed.

Penny winked and spoke loudly. "Makes you wonder what these guys had against each other. History, I guess? Something ingrained in memory banks way beyond it happening. It may be anything. An Irish mate told me his gran hated the Black and Tans vigorously because they ran over and killed her cow in Donegal. If it had been the IRA, the result would have been identical."

Penny had an audience. His credence had altered in the days since his bundle with Bowers.

He put his pint down square on the beer mat, oblivious to the snickers. He picked up another mat and flipped it over. It was the same on the other side.

He drained his glass, placed it back on the mat. "Which family ran over which one's cow?"

Others had drifted in and were earwigging. Several pairs of eyes were scanning the others for support. The parable of the cow had not gone unnoticed. Some of the regulars looked uncomfortable.

*Mary Grigg's few words on old Griggsy were moving and intelligent. In defiance of the circumstances and her sixty-odd years on the planet as Griggs's wife, she stood up and spoke of him with tenderness and of his garden, which he loved. He was always old, and she was always there for him. Mary was just as Oldman remembered her when he had met her thirty years before. He also recognised a veiled threat to the perpetrators. The ultimate judge would decide. Right now Oldman was doing the judging.*

*A grey suit with multiple cloth-covered buttons down the jacket and a simple white blouse and black shoes denoted the occasion. He witnessed no signs of mourning in her. The two men from the train escorted her from the long black car parked on the periphery of the crematorium. Mary walked the few hundred yards to the small group outside the crematorium building. He recognised no one else. No one spoke to him. It was as if the warmth had gone out of his life.*

*The hearse came separately. The pallbearers included the two men on the train, and two others who smacked of The Agency. They cast him a sidelong glance.*

On the way in, Mary shook hands. "Oldman, so pleased you could come. Robin and I missed your company when you moved away."

"So sorry for your loss, Mary. Griggsy was a pal. He was special to me."

"Thank you." She hugged him.

The funeral was short. The Humanist minister surprised him with his opening words. "Robin Griggs was never a religious man."

Oldman saw Griggs as a churchgoer. It went with his manner and beliefs, a man who prayed; a man who feared God. Not so. Griggs was an atheist. To Woody Guthrie's This Land is Your Land, his battered body went into the fire.

He couldn't leave without finding out who killed a dear friend. He sang under his breath, manoeuvring the lyrics into a threat for those who threatened him and had killed a pal. The pallbearers didn't join in.

As Griggs's body was committed to the flames, Oldman thought of the appropriateness of the song, the possible origins in a Baptist hymn. That was a part of his family background which he left behind. He was keen to prevent it from being his future. Griggs was a closet Christian. Oldman wasn't prepared to give up an opinion. Despite his misgivings on organised religion it felt good singing The Carter Family tune.

The arranged killings that came from Reynold's Hall, with help elsewhere, were clever. His brutal killing, battered to death with a claw hammer, an at-hand weapon workers left behind, was problematised by the missing documents. Griggs must have had evidence regarding Reynold's Hall.

Outside the crematorium was a donation box for Amnesty International. The guests donated generously, the two escorts and their fellow pallbearers standing back. Oldman tried hard not to dislike them. He was changing. Dislikes or likes had mattered not in the past. The job was all-important.

Mary Griggs came over to him and said, "Can you walk me to the car, Oldman?"

"Of course, Mary." He linked her arm.

The two men fell in beside them.

Mary stopped. "Please allow me this moment to walk with a true family friend." Her voice was commanding, her tone assertive, usually deployed when she told him and Griggs off for being silly.

Annoyance showed on the two men's faces.

Instead of a straight walk to the car, Mary led him around the flowerbeds, stopping to point at the sturdy still flowering luminous orange montbretia and fragile-looking multi-coloured patterned pansies. Some were beginning to fade, a reminder of life's passing.

She spoke quietly. "Oldman, Griggsy was on to something to do with this case. Please be careful. The two pallbearers, Campbell and Eames, have followed you for some time. A third man, Griffin, is involved. He's not as bad as the others, but keen to get on." She paused and turned around to point at the last remaining blazing red petals of the montbretia's posh cousin crocosmia and cast an authoritative back-off glare towards the hesitant and uncomfortable Campbell, and a conceited Eames.

"I've met them," he whispered. His inner self confirmed they were going to meet him again, and soon – and they wouldn't like it.

The car loomed as they spoke. Warning words spilled out.

"The people in Reynold's Hall are involved, but it goes much higher. They act only as a consultancy, though it is as you and Robin surmised: a murder co-operative. The man Fielding was like you, a plant, not a beautiful crocosmia." She said the last three words loudly for the prying duo who had moved in closer, then her voice fell again. "Fielding was a lovable old rogue," she hesitated, "Griggs's words not mine. It wasn't your acquaintances that did it – an outsider. It's all quite grubby. Eames is a killer. Ken is a mystery and his files are partial only. You know what that suggests?"

They reached the car as Oldman saw a third figure in the trees. The go-getting young Griffin? Red in the face, Campbell and Eames were there in no time. Both tried to usher Mary into the car, mumbling about security. Her look was one of condescension.

Mary turned aside once more and spoke loudly. "The flowers are still lovely at this time of the year. Thank you. They offer so much. Griggs would talk to them when he was in a corner or short on ideas. Trust them, he would say. Trust the flowers!" With that personal eulogy, she wrapped her arms around him, hugged him, then took his hand. Lowering her specs she allowed her sharp blue eyes to focus on him.

Oldman knew why Griggs loved this woman. He reflected on another flower and a kiss. It was time to go to war. Griffin was to be first, the one who hid in the trees. The flowers also meant vanity. The vain were his target.

He walked to the station. On the way back his mixed emotions meant a brain chock full with ambiguities. Mary knew something and had tried to impart it. Eames and company were nervous when she was with him. The flowers were important.

"Jesus bloody wept," he said. Griggs would have ticked him off for such profanity.

Who did Griggs talk with? Griggs's closest friend and ally, the now retired Colin, a loyal man so full of knowledge and information

241

he left others speechless? Colin 'the brain' was retired. But Colin still had thorns. Colin Flowers.

Back in the hall he took off his suit. Checking the pockets, he felt something in the pocket – a slip of paper. Unfolded, it read:

'Oldman, I don't know the full content in detail of the files you sent, but they have names and evidence of right-wing, clandestine activities. I don't know any more but I fear for my own life. Don't try to get in touch. Hayley.'

It was worded as Hayley would speak. He hoped she was safe. Mary must have slipped the note in his pocket. This was not men playing silly buggers, toy soldiers, but those who belonged to the belief-before-reality brigade, Britain as a great nation. Did they learn from Suez? He doubted it. The file was missing. Something in it was troublesome. He couldn't put his finger on it.

# Chapter 39

Everything pointed to Gran. She was saying nowt. She was happy with her stay in a secure wing of what she thought was the old St. Luke's hospital where her shrill rendition of *Two Lovely Black Eyes* simultaneously amused and horrified politically correct nursing staff. The hospital had been knocked down years before but there was always a lobby to bring back the asylums. Some Roseberry patients had moved to Sandwell in Hartlepool. Gran stayed.

*Silver Threads among the Gold* was OK. If asked anything she obliged with a song. The voice wavered and had that tendency to snap off the last word – a result of years of listening to female pub singers. It was clear that she could hold a tune. Everything else about Gran was guesswork.

"Dove, fancy a stroll?" Penny needed to get out.

Dove was already up and heading for the coat rack to pull down a hooded fleece. The mutual feeling was that everywhere was unsafe, a postulation that fed Penny's delusional self.

Hardly out in the street, had Penny said, "Dove it's time to rattle some cages!"

Dove's face lit up. This was his territory. He asked for more.

"In the pub I talked somewhat cryptically about the feuding families."

Dove listened. Explicit clues avoided Penny who was hiding from the world at large. He seemed excited.

"We have bent the fear element in town, but it's not entirely broken. We can't assume that they're not going to regroup and reassert their bullying ways."

Dove was all ears.

Penny continued. "It's time we went into battle. The police are getting nowhere. No one is going to shop anyone around here," he rounded off.

An hour later they returned to the digs. Periwinkle was out. Events over the next few days brought the plan forward, then put it on hold. Dove reconsidered. That surprised Penny.

"Ronnie-boy, better to use your head than aggression."

He couldn't believe what he had heard. He so wanted to have a go at both families – physically.

Dove continued. He was more than up for a scrap, but it was a no-go. "Putting your brain to work on the issue might alleviate other issues and dispose of irritants. You've done it before."

Penny sensed that one of the irritants was nearby. He had helped Lance on his way to prison during The Tableau Case. Lance detested him and he felt sorry for Lance. Was Lance out of Oakwood? He wasn't, but his 'eye' was out there searching for Penny and his enemies. The Internet was all he needed. That, and a burning desire to hurt Penny.

Another meeting followed. Hart held his head high; a lip curl signalled his haughtiness. Penny felt deflated after his euphoric mood of the day before. His affective presence caused Penny to bristle. What had Hart done to him? Why had Dove backed off on the proposed assault on the families? Surely it was his reason for living. Why the inconsistency? It shouldn't happen, even in a novel. Someone always ended up dead.

Raed opened the proceedings. "Certain members of the Bowers and Bateman families have suffered what resembles a severe attack of gout, actually, a good kicking. One isn't contagious, more to do with diet, though aggression can be. I don't want any further attacks." Raed eyed Penny and Dove.

Dove blanked it; Penny feigned the posture of a schoolchild ticked off. Hart's self-righteous face vexed him. Dove and Jack had ideas that went beyond contagion. Things would happen as a result of whatever they were up to. He wished his own ingenuity could come into play.

The next day he received a letter terminating his contract at the school. Liz, never one to hide behind a script, called round and gave him it in his hand. He offered to continue his tutorials.

"That's good of you. It can't be, Penny. There are no excuses about funding or contract. Your prime task here isn't helping the school. Sorry." As she spoke, her eyes, usually so focussed, veered away. Then she touched his arm in a gesture of affection and held it.

He shook her hand formally. "'Bye, and thanks."

Liz spoke hurriedly. "It doesn't mean we can't be friends. You're always welcome at the house, anytime."

He saw it differently. He wanted to believe that Liz had been honest with him. Was she being honest with herself? He recognised a mental downward spiral and fought it. His BMX career had taken a dive; career and dive being the operative words. He'd crashed trying a manoeuvre the spectators at the Olympia Stadium would have marvelled at. The fact that he swerved and fell off ruined it. His grazing was healing, his ego dinted. The termination of his days at the school placed him outside again, a situation from which he could benefit. Liz was no longer his boss. She was one of a crowd and dubious. His loss, perceived and otherwise, took control. He took out his notebook and wrote 'stroke a dog'. Then he went looking for a dog.

Rather than wait for the gout-ridden to rise again he would go for them. It was time to act. Once again the townsfolk were reluctant to engage.

A coincidental meeting helped his case. Passing him by at considerable speed, Mikey executed an admirable turn with brakes on – a perfect one hundred and eighty.

Turning to face him he said, "Hi, Mr Penny."

"Hi."

"No bike?"

"Not at the moment, Mike." It mattered not that Mikey clocked the grazing on his cheek.

"I've moved in with Aunt Lizzie. She's really cool. Dad's working away more or less permanently. I guess he's had enough of being in the middle of two warring sections. I advised him to try games. I have a great collection and it does help." He grinned. "The only thing, I guess, is to exterminate them. I'm joking, Mr Penny. The Bowers and Batemans will never meet." Changing tack, he said with a contentment never apparent before, "It means I'm back at school."

About to ride off, he turned and showed that obscure wisdom that Penny had seen in the young man before.

"Whatever the causes, they lie deep in the lower levels of the game, though one or two of the older ones will know. Need to move up a level or two I guess." He rode off.

The spiral began to move. Subterfuge was the way forward and Penny knew what to do. He came across a dog, a small thing, and he went to stroke it. It growled at him and he decided to give that a miss.

**Chapter 40**

Finding Colin Flowers was easy. Colin, a man of tradition, was still in the phone book. Oldman felt refreshed calling in on a retired colleague. The train ride into London Victoria and tubes to Tooting Bec was busy with no watchdogs apparent. He told Stead he was seeing an old friend. No names…

He felt fit. The miles of running, old-fashioned exercise, press-ups, the skipping – which all at Reynold's Hall had found comical and so wanted to join in with was becoming easier by the day. He sang skipping rhymes as he worked out. The residents joined in with **The Big Ship Sails. Cinderella Dressed in Yellow** was most popular.

Colin welcomed in a friend. Before closing the door, he stepped out and peered up and down the street. Colin, a man in his seventies, appeared concerned at his presence.

"No fears, Colin, no one has tracked me here – Campbell, Eames or otherwise."

Colin's face told him he was aware of the three stooges. He ushered him into the living room of his humble terrace. The room had the pleasant smell of lavender polish. The wood furniture belonged to an era of solidity and capital, though a small utility table sat in the corner evoking days of genuine austerity. A lovely

248

old couch with sagging springs, and curved mahogany legs beckoned and Oldman sank into it.

"Fancy some char?"

"Yes, please. No milk or sugar, thanks."

The tea, served up in an old metallic pot, was Darjeeling. A small tin plate with four digestives joined forces with the pot. "Get a package of decent tea now and then from old friends abroad. It makes a subtle change from the bleached tea bag." The smiles of greeting ended there. "Guess you're not here to discuss tea. Awful about old Griggsy, wasn't it? I didn't go to the funeral. Not so mobile these days."

Oldman didn't waste time. "What do you know about this case at Reynold's Hall?" And before Colin could answer, "And what do you know of Eames, Campbell and Griffin?"

"You realise I've been retired for years." He supped his tea and dunked a biscuit in the cup, enjoying the soggy digestive while avoiding it turning into sludge in the cup.

Oldman resisted.

"Tea is from the Giddapahar Gardens Tea Estate." Colin always kept posh tea for special guests. He had friends everywhere that supplied him with small luxuries, and information.

"Griggsy and you go back a long way. He trusted you. I spoke with Mary at the funeral. In her own quiet way she pointed me to you." It was subtle and went well with the tea, another form of dunking, a baseball term to Oldman.

"How was she?"

"Mary expected him to die in the field. When he moved behind a desk, she joked that he would end up in a fight in the office. The fight, however, has something to do with me, and with my work at Reynold's Hall. Mary lost a husband whom she loved dearly. His death was a shock to all of us. The manner of it was barbaric." Colin stirred. The mention of his friend's demise brought a tear. The old man wiped his face with the baggy bottom of his worn cream cardigan. Oldman allowed him the moment. He knew a different Colin, one to whom tears were alien.

Then Colin moved up a gear. "Eames, Campbell and Griffin are the new boys, the up-and-coming heroes of the agency. All are power hungry. Griffin would sell his soul to the devil. Unfortunately for him he's a family-oriented person with a young child. A dodgy move for one so keen to get on in a job where family isn't always helpful."

"I know."

He paused. "Griffin isn't a killer like his associates. Eames does the dirty work and appears to enjoy it. There's always one, eh? Campbell is an oaf."

Oldman listened.

"Griffin lives not so far away in one of those posh period homes which for me are soulless. He has been around here several times probing. When he said he wasn't far away, I did some checking myself. We – Griggs and I – talked about music – our mutual passion."

Olman eyed the shelves of immaculate vinyl – classical and jazz.

"We played them while we talked – very loudly – and I guess over the years we became increasingly open. The music encouraged us to discuss subjects when Griggs was troubled. We checked to see if they had bugged my place, tapped my phone – negative. They see me as a doddery fool. We did take precautions. Griggs had the place checked and my assumptions were correct. Never underestimate an old fool." He supped his tea and dunked a second biscuit. It too did not fragment and fall into the tea. "If you don't want one, I'll finish them." He helped himself to another. "Your first poser: the Reynold's Hall reconnaissance wasn't aimed as a set-up for you. It may seem like that now." He laughed, embarrassed. "We underestimated the hierarchy involved. I don't know all the names. It goes up to government level. It involves hacking, both of phones and emails, in a nutshell, the removal of bad elements in a decaying society, cleansing. Just the beginning."

Oldman considered the notion of bad elements. Bad was everywhere. At times he felt his own company to be bad. Colin rubbed his hands together as he said it and crumbs of biscuit fell away. And, to prove Oldman's supposition that he knew more...

"Your significant other is but a link in the chain. Fielding, the old man, the linkman, wanted out. His death was nothing to do with your residential companions, not their style, but linked to young Eames, Campbell and Griffin."

'Young' sounded regretful.

"Griffin isn't the hard man. Before you jump in feet first, the issue here is that the people who collaborate with you, or you think work with you, are involved. Games play, Oldman... They estimated that Griggs and you wouldn't produce anything. Then case closed. Stead is a part of the setup." He hesitated. "I don't know how involved you are or in what capacity. It was unfortunate – or fortunate, depending on your position – that your relationship," he peered over his teacup as he spoke, "appears to be more than a professional ploy. It was causing concern." Colin's eyes wandered to his records and he detracted. "It's a money jungle now."

Oldman nodded. He saw in the neat catalogued racks of vinyl a symbol of this man with a brain like a computer. Colin was doing the algorithms, the output invaluable. His stored records and files he could bring out whenever he wished. His scruffy cardigan, battered slippers and old brown cord trousers were effectively a camouflage. He would always be in the field. Nevertheless, he could discern a weariness in the older man. He changed the topic.

"What you listening to these days?"

"Less and less jazz, more Mozart. I love it. It appeals to my autism, my neurotic sense of detail. I do still play my Monk collection. It's hard to believe the Monk recordings are as old as I am!" He joked about his high-functioning autism, then moved on.

Oldman thought about his own symbolic life. What was driving his inner senses? Foremost was killing. He put two and two together.

Two and two together make three: Eames, Griffin and Campbell. Get to Griffin, Olman thought. He's the weak link.

He thanked Colin. "Your memory banks are still as fantastic as ever. If I come again, we can listen to The Magic Flute together and drink more tea." He knew that wouldn't happen. "You say Griffin lives near here?"

"About five miles away in a dreadful walled estate with security. Nothing we can't get around, eh?" He put his empty cup down and eyed the few tealeaves in the bottom as if reading them for inspiration.

Oldman wondered if his posh tea was better for the reading. What did the pattern of the leaves say?

Colin put the cup down with a smile that said 'silly me' and interrupted his drift. "It's called the Holmes Estate. For me it's a bad pun – not home in the sense I would see a home… or something to do with a fictional detective. Who knows?"

"Colin, thanks. Do you still have a key to the lock-up?"

At the door, Colin unhooked a rusty key from a rack and gave it to him.

He gripped Colin's hand firmly, "Mind how you go, Colin. One more thing: did Griggs mention an assassin, The Electrician?"

"A new one on me." Colin leaned in his open doorway as he spoke, his Daily Telegraph under his arm. He waved with the paper. "Oh dear, I forgot. There is a bad element in the hall. We don't know who, but someone in there has a hold over our co-operative." Smiling a goodbye, Colin waved again. "Time for the crossword!"

"Take care, Colin. And thanks!" Oldman was already researching the Holmes Estate on his mobile. Online it referred to it as a gated community. He doubted it. As for the bad element, he knew who that was. Turning round the corner and out of the street the smile disappeared. He was going to meet Griffin and he wasn't going to say hello with flowers. Crosswords came to mind. First, he needed to 'borrow' a car.

Griffin didn't know what hit him, more precisely, who stuck a needle in his arm. He was at the gates of the Holmes Estate closed settlement. Oldman found it as dreary as Colin implied.

First, Griffin's automatic key hadn't worked. Second, the intercom failed. Third, he had only a vague memory of going to the gates. His wooziness informed him that whatever was coursing through his bloodstream wasn't nice and the persons that did it was serious. Not a dating ploy. He tried to delve into the rule book of his professional training. Nothing came back, only nausea and fear. Vaguely, he remembered being rough-handled and bundled into the back of a car. Blackness followed.

Oldman's huge coat hid Griffin as well as what Eames and company had suspected quite wrongly was his swelling gut, a product of his easy life in the hall. More fatal for them was their choice to bluff and cajole. On coming round Griffin chose to deploy threats and bullying tactics. Foolish move.

"Fuck you, Oldman, and you are an old man. Either you let me go or all the shit in the world is going to come down on you."

Oldman broke off for a moment. It wasn't the kind of parlance he appreciated. He missed the old days.

Griffin had read it all wrongly. He continued to threaten. "You're done for. Untie me, you moron."

Ignoring the insult though wanting to commit vandalism (mainly to Holmes Estate) he reached down and picked up an old petrol can, loosening the screw cap a turn or two. He considered the can for a moment. Next, he swung round on Griffin.

"Sorry I couldn't find you orange overalls. I'd hate to ruin your clothes with gasoline." His American accent, in truth Canadian, a source of entertainment to his English co-workers, carried a sense of icy menace. He reached for Griffin's belt and undid it, pulling his trousers down to his knees.

Strapped up as he was, there was nothing he could do apart from a limited wriggle and writhe.

Oldman smiled tersely, picked up and then placed the can nearer. The woody smell of petrol lost its appeal. Oldman held Griffin's mobile to his face. It was a classy thing which made Oldman's phone a museum piece.

"You have voicemail."

Griffin's puzzlement turned to horror. He heard his wife, Rebekah. On loudspeaker she screamed at him. He required no in-depth analysis to understand her anguish.

"Maisy has gone missing. Where the fuck are you? The police are here. For God's sake, call."

There was more, but Oldman cut the phone and pocketed it. He walked to the door.

Griffin was convinced Oldman's tactics were old-fashioned movie bullshit. No way was he going to take this.

Oldman gave him time for second thoughts and curtailed his speculations. "Bye, Griffin. You can shout all you want – no need to gag you – and if by chance anyone hears you it won't help Maisy's case. The lock-up is secure, though I'm not sure about humane. There is a rat's nest somewhere."

Griffin's chest pounded. Where had all his training gone? He tried to concentrate. He eyed the tarnished can positioned next to him, the lid open. He would kill the fucker. His trousers were down by his knees, his legs firmly tied round the ankles, his arms trussed behind him. As the metal door creaked to a close and a padlock snapped, nausea overcame him. A picture of his curly-headed four-year-old Maisy hovered in sickening waves. He vomited on his trousers. A lean rat scurried across with something in its mouth. His training deserted him.

In desperation he called, "What do you want?"

Oldman mouthed, "Answers." He thought of revenge and how popular it was among the voting classes back in the USA – and in Britain. This was not revenge, it was a job. It was a deterrent.

A car started up. Griffin heard it drive away. Consumed by his own thoughts, he fainted.

Oldman was aware of the limited time allowed him. Nevertheless, he needed his prisoner to have time to stew. He drove to a nearby café to eat an all-day breakfast. He called Stead from Griffin's phone. She didn't pick up.

"Love you. Work to do. Catch up soon."

He left the car with the keys and walked back the mile or so. He thought about Griggs. Griggs's obituary was in the papers, his death was public. Stead would have known he was at the funeral, either through informers and or her connections upstairs. The newspaper coverage was small but national.

# Chapter 41

Gran shifted into victim mode. Dove recollected. One of Penny's many homilies taught him that the victim can become the persecutor, or rescuer can become the victim. A transaction? He didn't require analysis to see that Penny had done something untoward. Dove read it on his face, inwardly enjoying the pending results of his schemes, a satisfaction he was unable to hide. He looked more like the old Ronnie-boy.

Dove's practical bent told him that if Jim was involved with dodgy dealings, it was highly placed. Periwinkle hit a cul-de-sac with his enquiries. That said a lot. He thought of letting the aggrieved Jack know Liz was involved, or responsible in some way. That could be plan B. In truth, there was no other. It was A.

The absence of the boy Kyle and the offer of shelter to Mikey, not to mention her willingness to accommodate Penny in the school, lost its welcoming innocence. Surveillance was a two-way thing, power pervasive.

Dove and he went to the pub and drank two or three pints. They clinked glasses. Behind Dove's cheers a worrying cloud hovered.

"Is Liz really involved?"

Penny didn't want to talk about it. Bigger question: was Jim connected? And of course the constant nagging about the source of Gran's knowledge. Did she watch American series on television? Where did she get the information from? What of the badger's front claws, five in all? Tested by forensics, the copies were reputed to be as strong as the originals, lethal.

Penny checked the web. Badger claws for sale, both real and manufactured. Easily available. He looked up badgers. Their bite was stronger than a black bear. Hart had mentioned a bit force quotient. He feared social media would be swamped with badger scare stories.

After the badger research, Penny was working through a scholarly article on the Internet about the problems of war and how one breaks down old antipathies without inciting new ones. Empathy? A scheme was emerging, his ill-feelings ebbing away. The next meeting was to be his final liaison with Hart and Raed. He closed his eyes. He called up that vision of her in traditional costume. He recalled his first encounter with Hart and Freeman at the university and his mixed feelings. He liked Freeman; he didn't dislike Hart.

"Hart remains the same old... nothing has changed. It's such a pity. He has so much going for him. To resolve the Bowers-Bateman conflict is outside his remit if that makes sense?"

His unattached statement was inexplicable to Periwinkle, not so to Dove. Whatever he was going to do was clandestine and required local cunning. Dove hoped it wouldn't go awry – and that it wasn't illegal. As if…

\\\\\

The last scheduled roundtable convened in Raed's simple rented apartment in Loftus. Penny did an uninvited survey of the few books and films in the living room. A small television and DVD player sat on top of an old oak chest. A *Koran* and some wooden beads were on a carved table alongside the phone. He tried to count them: thirty-three.

The few films signified a political mind, though not current in movie terms, current in other terms. *In the Name of God* caught his eye. The cover for *My Name is Khan* laid open on the side. A book, *The Reluctant Fundamentalist*, lay open with a marker. Before he could pick it up, Raed signalled him to take a chair. Penny, the smart surveyor, was himself surveyed.

Raed knew of his politics. She sanctioned them. She had read his files with endorsements, not completely approving of his actions. Her reading of his file brought about some admiration mixed with suspicion, and a dash of circumspection. She watched him peruse. He would be analysing her through her choice of film and literature. That analysis would form his profile. There is no way of predicting human behaviour. She was happy to let him make his educated guesses. His political activities on the streets were on record, his verbal attacks on the police of interest. Their retribution had been silly. His and Hart's warring nature puzzled her. She put it down to masculine stuff.

Hart opened the agenda. It involved some basic psychology which Penny consigned to the dustbin. "Penny, could you brief the group on the Bowers-Bateman situation?"

Penny touched his nose three times with his right index finger. Keep it out. Hart was irritable.

Raed moved Hart on. "We can come back to that. In the light of Penny's change in circumstance we need to have a head-to-head with Liz. We'll do it circuitously." Before Hart could volunteer, she said, "I'll do it."

Penny breathed an audible sigh of relief.

Hart clicked his tongue. He interjected, insisting that "Penny must stay away from the school."

Penny refused to bite. He wasn't going near the place. He acknowledged Hart by raising his head and swung it side to side in a supercilious manner. "It's a no-brainer, Hart."

"The warring factions seem unusually quiet." Raed broke the deadlock.

Lowering his face initially, then focussing on all, Penny spoke in terms that his friends were familiar with, and welcomed, terms that made Hart wince. "The said Bowers and Batemans did not face any enhanced interrogation techniques; rather a subtle conversion."

Hart reddened. There was a dramatic change in the air. To Dove a good hiding was a good hiding and key members of the families had received such. He was clueless what Penny was up to.

Hart overrode his annoyance and soldiered on. "Liz is much tougher than these men, the Bowers and Batemans." He eyed Penny. "I sensed a certain caginess of her in the locale, one not entirely due to respect for her position."

Following on, Periwinkle did an excellent précis of their findings. In an act of brevity, he offered a way forward that might enable the deadly enemies to work together. His next statement aimed to cement the team — empathy versus antipathy.

Penny wondered if he had been reading the same articles.

"Penny and Hart have helped a great deal. Let us keep working together to resolve Max's case, then we can all go home," Periwinkle advised.

Hart bit his lip to hear his name conjoined with Penny's. Through clenched jaw, he couldn't hide his admiration for Periwinkle. His research into the man had revealed nothing. Periwinkle did not exist outside the armed forces. His naval records were confidential — a conundrum with the name Periwinkle. Not so Jim.

Dove's face showed that he was wondering what to do next. As for Liz, Raed would peel a few layers off her and her husband. Mikey would be safe with Liz. There was a tie that bound them.

Periwinkle hadn't taken off his beret. Dove hadn't told him to either. Raed had expected it.

She spoke for all. "Between us, we will find the perpetrators of those crimes. That the reasons came from the local populous is bothersome. Inbred vendettas and discourses have confused matters. We are beginning to separate them out. The rivalries hamper investigation, but the clue to the killing of Max lies outside these blood feuds. I strongly believe the death of Max didn't come from among the good working folk here. A morally evil, more discriminating mind is at work, one that has manipulated local discourses and hidden behind them. It has only made things worse in the town, though like many an ill wind, it may lead to a solution to other issues."

Penny relished the discursive reference. To everyone's surprise, he then stood and said, "Goodbye." He needed to write it down.

His farewell was an affirmative one that caused Raed to cock her head on one side and place her hands together, linking her fingers, thumbs touching. Hart threw an oblique warning gesture at his boss. That was the group's last joint meeting. Foremost in Hart's mind was what the fuck Penny was up to now.

Penny wanted to hug Raed and so did everyone else in the room, for varying reasons. A hug would help Hart. He had the forensic mind of a good lawyer and lacked the stomach for his task in homicide. His own fears were running rampant.

Penny managed to exit the room without stumbling, though he felt lightheaded. There was the sense of having lost something. Nailing the destroyers would be difficult. First, he must find the persons who hired them. He would be working on his own now. He would cope with the loss. Such was a permanent feature of his ongoing dreams: missing suitcases, missing tickets, missing clothes, lost friends, lost lovers, and absent children, fictional and real. The dreams were gaining in strength. His little book kept notes of key factors, and repeatedly he returned to the dark dreams and attempted an analysis. The dreams were a worst-case scenario. The disasters pending.

No one from the school got in touch for a week or so. Subsequently, a note dropped through the door from Strucker. It read quite simply:

'I will miss your cheery nature. Good luck, Ron, with whatever path you choose. Hubert (The Baron).'

# Chapter 42

*When the lock snapped and the door creaked up and open Griffin was desperate. It was dull outside. A pinpoint of light filtered in to alleviate the gloom. His watch was gone. Oldman must've removed it with his phone. Time had been important but was on hold. Then the door closed. His dignity had suffered. His sick-covered trousers had remained around his knees for a brief time. Then they slipped further down as he wriggled. His expertly tied bonds below them stopped them falling to his ankles. He was cold; he wanted to pee. The light went on, dim but enough to see his tormenter. He had called out. Oldman was right: no one was listening. He was hoarse.*

*That this man was prepared to use his daughter indicated his determination. Use whatever is available, his own training implied. This man didn't give one iota for his training, or his daughter. The man was out of control.*

*Oldman saw it differently. He'd pre-empted all that sloppy nonsense. If necessary, he'd kill Griffin. Then there was Stead. He must stay at the wheel. Without speaking, he eyed Griffin directly. The coldness in Griffin increased.*

*Oldman stared for a while then spoke. "You have five minutes to talk and explain what's going on." Setting the countdown timer* on Griffin's mobile he placed it on the petrol can. He placed a small cigarette lighter next to it. He hit the timer. "Five minutes. Timer's running. A word of warning: I may decide to kill you whatever you say. I don't like you, Griffin, or your kind." He removed his revolver from his bag and tapped it on his left hand.

Despite feeling he was in a bad movie and needed only to act his part out, Griffin chose intelligently. He talked. He'd fathomed out that Oldman knew something of their machinations. How much he knew wasn't clear. Oldman wasn't playing games. Griggs's old lady couldn't have told him anything. What about the old duffer, Colin Flowers? He was past it.

Oldman countered his timewasting and ideas of vengeance. "If you live beyond this day and anything happens to anyone associated with me, anyone," he asserted, "The Griffin family – mother, father and daughter – will be consigned to paperwork, and, young Griffin, it does seem we both know the people who can do that, legally or otherwise."

Griffin's position at the tree of life (or was it road to salvation?) ran counter to the signs and symbols he played along with; the griffin, saviour or antichrist. As a trainee, he had seen his role as the guardian of salvation. Training deserted him. He had failed to realise the ambivalence of his personal symbol. He resented the 'young Griffin' tag. This was not the time to dispute anything.

Oldman eyed the phone, the petrol can and then Griffin's soiled underwear. It mattered not to Oldman that they were designer – and at this moment to Griffin either. What was he going to do with the petrol which the irksome man had referred to as gasoline? The cigarette lighter.

"Three minutes... talk, young Griffin. First, tell me about Griggs. Who did it?"

"We did." He struggled to get the two words out. "Griggs was about to blow the whole scheme out of the water and coin in. He knew you were there to fail."

Oldman moved forward then let it run. His deadline was important. As for coining in, it was insulting. "Who's we? What scheme?"

"Eames and Campbell. I was elsewhere."

"Go on."

"We surveyed Griggs and you as a team. He was well past his sell-by date." He wished he hadn't said the last sentence.

"Who authorised it?" Oldman checked the timer. "Under two minutes." He tapped the gun again, pointing it towards Griffin's groin.

In the dank cold of the lock-up Griffin sweated. He had access to much information. To spill it out was going to cause him some grief. He wrestled between his sense of survival and his professional ethics. "The name you want is a top-ranking civil servant, close to the premier: Lawson, James Lawson."

Oldman knew Lawson. Top he was. This was getting shittier by the minute. Dark sweat patches discoloured Griffin's grey suit jacket, his visage a sickly pallor. He looked down at his soiled pants. He was a picture of self-pity, his professional training wasted, his hatred for Oldman mingled with shame and self-disgust.

Oldman knew he'd recover in the future, if it were to happen, and would think carefully in times to come. Now he was utterly defenceless.

Griffin remained staring down at his trousers; his vulnerability consumed him. This man was going to kill him. The next sentence came out as fast as Oldman stopped tapping the gun and pointed it at his soiled underpants. The seconds ticked away.

"It was Eames killed Griggs. Meant to have the appearance of a break-in and a savage random attack. Taking the records was a mistake. The killing was a mistake." He tried to bite his lip, but the words flowed. "Eames was linked in with some political stuff, right wing faction. Griggs had evidence... in a file."

"Who leaked it?"

Griffin didn't know. That was apparent from the sheer terror on his face. Oldman theorised. Had Griggs talked to anyone?

The alarm beeped. Oldman allowed it to run for a short while before hitting the pause. He holstered the gun. Griffin peed. Piss mingled with dried spew.

Colin had proven to be an astute and dependable colleague. Oldman was faced by his worse fears. Stead was part of a network that involved figures way up the ladder.

Luna had nailed Ken in her files. The links were becoming clearer. Griggs's death was linked, Ken the common denominator. Lawson?

He wasn't sure he was able to do what he had to do. Killing Griffin wouldn't help. It might offer some satisfaction, catharsis. Killing Stead and Lawson might help. Killing anyone might help. He had another idea. There had to be another link. Who was it? The job was knottier than he imagined. He had been what his colleagues from across the water called 'the patsy'. That wasn't worth mulling over. Time for action. There would be time later to theorise. In fact, theory wasn't worth it. Do the job and get out alive.

"Okay, Griffin, I'm going back to finish the job in my way. A final word of warning: all the security in the world won't protect you, gated and otherwise. If anything happens to me, or my friends, I've instructed a pal to see to things."

267

"My daughter, Maisy? Please Oldman."

"You have one more task to do before your daughter returns to your charming home, which, like the furniture, shows taste, especially the antique dresser. And your wife is very pretty."

Griffin balked at the reference to an old male-oriented joke.

Oldman dialled and held the phone to his face. "Tell Eames to meet you here, a lock-up off the main road to Holmes Estate, third along. Tell him it's important and to get here as soon as. There's a St George's flag flying which is visible from the road."

Griffin detested himself even more. The phone was on speaker. Griffin spoke with Eames. Eames asked if everything was okay.

"Yes, of course. It's important." He told him the location. "Get here as soon as!"

Oldman cut the phone. He stowed it in his pocket. Griffin was close to tears.

The lock-up was so close to his lovely home. That hurt. It made no damn difference. He could be a mile away or next door. He was still alive. He said nothing though snide comments came to mind.

Oldman went outside. He carried the petrol can and disappeared. He left the door of the lock-up ajar. Then he returned, gun in hand.

"I want a name. The Electrician – the man who killed my friend Fielding."

Griffin slumped in the chair as much as his well-constructed ties would allow; his damp underwear and spattered trousers felt less problematic. He was alive. Oldman trained the gun from his face downwards.

"I don't know a name, honest. He's a new boy, a fixer, an assassin. Eames calls him 'the wire for hire'." Griffin got a modicum of satisfaction from that despite his situation.

"How about Ken Briggs?" With his free hand Oldman backslapped Griffin across the mouth.

Blood spurted. Oldman left. It was apparent Griffin didn't know anything about the latter. Griffin was terrified. Oldman reflected: romantic shit about assassins being cool; people without a creed.

"Don't yawn or laugh, Griffin, it'll make the bleeding worse."

Existential shite, Oldman thought. Assassins were more likely to be paranoid, and bloody aggressive. He was there to do a job – a jobbing assassin. It did lead him to question himself. He had killed before and would do again. Conspiracy was becoming a truth. Disinformation abounded. He dropped the philosophy and concentrated on the job in hand.

He muttered to himself, "Fucking vigilantes. I prefer a jobbing assassin…"

Eames couldn't fucking change a lightbulb never mind wire a shower. The man who did for Fielding was a skilled spark.

Griffin was finished.

\\\\

Griffin wasn't aware of the time that passed. He was heedless of the disgust on Campbell's face when he arrived. "Thank God. Where's Eames?"

Campbell untied him.

The combined odour of stale urine and vomit caused Campbell to wrinkle his nose and turn away. "Whoever trussed you up like this knew what they were doing."

269

Griffin ignored his soreness, matted underwear, and fastened his trousers up. The ads were right: sitting is the new smoking. He felt like shit.

Campbell, a man who usually managed to get by with two to three words, spoke at length. He found amusement in the sight of Griffin trussed up with his trousers down. A short-sighted man. "Eames is close by and armed. He's a handy fellow, as you know. He didn't like the sound of your call, so he contacted me. Shit happens. You're alive and well, so pull yourself together." And with a thin smile, "And pull your pants up." He surveyed the interior of the lock-up. The sound of scurrying caused him to wheel around startle. Rats did that.

In his mind, Griffin could see the petrol can. He said, "Gasoline."

"What?" Campbell followed his anxious glimpse at the empty space. Then he shrugged. "Let's get you home. You are obviously in shock."

Eames was not by the car. The car was gone. Griffin didn't ask. There was nothing to say. The walk to Holmes Estate was onerous. Griffin felt hollow, his soiled trousers uncomfortable.

Campbell tried to get his head around things. "What the fuck happened to Eames?" As they walked, he called Eames. No answer. He called in to report Eames's disappearance from the scene. Conveniently, he left out the description of the car.

At Holmes Estate, Rebekah let them in. Her fury was at boiling point. "Maisy's home. Says she went for a drive to a playground... with a nice old man. A doctor examined her – she's fine."

Her tone was not one of relief. It carried with it an accusatory harshness, a threatening element that Griffin came to realise was to bring sudden and unwanted change into his snug life.

Campbell phoned for a taxi. He called in to the office and reported all well at Holmes Estate.

"Any word from Eames?"

He called in again. He pocketed the phone and addressed his colleague. "They want a full report in the morning face to face. I hope you can talk by then. No word from Eames."

The cab arrived and he left Griffin to his endless misery. The emptiness he felt would stay for a long time, its lesson forever.

At that moment, Maisy rushed in shouting, "Daddy."

He started to cry.

"Mummy, Daddy's crying. Silly Daddy."

Rebekah left the room. Loneliness seeped into the cosy space they proudly called home. The handmade furniture lost all its value, the beautiful rug its splendour and its colour. The dresser Oldman referred to would have to go. Everything was tunnel grey. He undressed, and showered, threw the soiled clothes in the bin.

Griffin's briefing was short. For the record, he didn't know who attacked him, or how many there were. He explained that they had taken his phone. He changed the story accordingly. He remembered the phone call to Eames who was still missing. One of the operatives in attendance mentioned later that his expedience merited promotion.

The medical team suspected benzodiazepine or a date-rape drug, not easily detected after twenty-four hours. The urine sample showed nothing. They took a hair sample. He didn't recall talking to anyone. Then he did. His story didn't gel. There was no one to contradict it.

Maisy had been at the swings with a nice old man who brought her home and left her at the gate.

Griffin cursed inwardly. The spare room beckoned. In just over a day life had changed for the ambitious young 'counterspy' and happily married man. Oldman wasn't far from his mind as he slunk into the spare bedroom. The images of Oldman tapping his gun were brief but powerful.

Oldman was back at the hall. It felt strange, but still a refuge. Stead and three others were playing a friendly hand of cards. He paused at the door and made to go upstairs. She caught his eye. He nodded. No response. In his room he showered, donned a pair of old shorts, and laid on the bed. He had read that James Brindley, the great canal engineer, slept on ideas and woke up with new ones. He desperately needed ideas. He slept.

The cleaner knocked early. No answer. She knocked again. Then she opened the door with her skeleton key. Oldman was gone.

On the early train to London Victoria, he felt a spasm of regret. He was a dead man. In career terms he was knackered. Without proof of Lawson's misdeed there was little he could do. Lawson wasn't the man to give in or to mess with. He was tough, bloody-minded and cunning. He didn't care for family. If Griffin was telling the truth, Lawson was head of a co-operative involved in murder, and not just of low life. In Oldman's mind he was also responsible for Griggs's death and the electrocution of Fielding. Ken's role was less clear. There was still an issue. If he discovered anything, what was he to do? Who were the fixers in between?

Lawson would know he was on to him. Brindley was right on one thing: sleep worked a treat. He simply had to get to Lawson, then, get the hell out of it.

Eames and his burnt-out car found a last resting place in a flooded quarry, his cremains never found. The gasoline came in handy. Oldman pocketed the phone. That too might be useful. He skipped through Eames's phone while staring into his last resting place. No recognisable names, though coded: 'Boss', 'Mate' (Oldman wondered if he had any) and calls to 'Her'. There was several calls to a mobile listed under 'General'. A rank or what?

Oldman decided to throw it, then as an afterthought took his own phone out and checked to see if any of the numbers tallied. Bingo. Scrolling down he came to Ken's number. General – a general busybody, nuisance, a little Napoleon. Perhaps Ken was more than that? At that moment Ken moved up a notch in the list of possible suspects. What was Eames and Ken calling each other about? There was no messages in voicemail. The politics – they linked up. Luna's Nightlight's file was a pointer.

By now Stead would have read his last will and testament. It was in her post box in a sealed Manila envelope. Men would be moving his furniture out. In the envelope was a note written in pen. It read:

'You know what to do, partner. Much love, Westy.'

He'd talked about leaving everything to his daughter. He had left something out that Stead, would be aware of. Stead was reading through as he travelled into London.

She placed the note in her briefcase with a wry smile. "Partner West. Thine will, will be done."

A dilemma resolved. By the time she called Lawson, Oldman was sitting in the outer office, waiting. Sir James was in conference.

Oldman spent the few minutes conjuring up the catalogue of artefacts on his boss's massive oak desk laden with mementos, each dusted daily. The gallery of photos; the globe he inherited from his father dating from the cold war period standing proud and polished on the extreme left of his desk, a reminder of a different Europe. Oldman grinned inwardly at its symbolism and wondered what it meant for the old man.

His secretary answered. Despite the hushed tone of her reply Oldman heard.

"Yes, Ms Stead. I'll tell him right away. Urgent, you say? He's in conference. I can go in within a few minutes."

Oldman sat tight. No point in trying to surmise what the conversation was.

He saw no one leave. The buzzer had implied conference over. An administrator went in with her message. She was seconds only.

"You can go in now, Mr Oldman. Sir James is expecting you."

On entering, Lawson's greeting hid the very devil. Sir James, 'Jimbo' as he had been known in the field, was halfway across the room to welcome him. "A glass of something, Oldman?"

He shook his head. He shook it again, this time to clear it. He wasn't sure why he was there. The globe was in place. Should he kill him for wiping out some low life? Was he responsible for Griggs? Fielding?

Sir James gave nothing away. Then, as adroit as ever, he placed Oldman in the position of telling him what he wanted him to know. Oldman hated lip-biting. He felt guilty. Between the lies a change was coming and things were happening fast.

He blundered into a series of educated guesses, dressed up as deductions which Lawson smiled at.

Sir James told him to go away and do his homework, then call back. "Do give my best wishes to Stead – a fine woman."

That signalled the end of their chat.

West wasn't sure he would see East again. Why had she called Lawson?

He eyed Lawson and spoke. "I wouldn't mind a name... The Electrician?"

"No idea what you're talking about." Lawson looked bewildered.

He left and picked up a cab. After a block or two, he stopped it and got out. Using bogus credentials, he then hired a car. Lawson was a tricky old rogue. It went with the territory. Other forces were at work also. As he left the room with its gallery of memorabilia, he stared at a photograph of a group of men on the wall. There in the middle in uniform stood Ken Briggs. Fuck. Tricky or not, Lawson did look genuinely confused at the mention of The Electrician. No doubt he would follow it up. As for Ken, Ken was an old comrade, dear boy.

As he left the office he turned. Lawson was reaching for the phone.

## Chapter 43

Following the eerie silence Raed referred to, a new pitched battle between the feuding Bowers and Batemans broke out. To witness the Bateman and Bowers in the arena of the dartboard and the pool table was too much for the locals. Custom in the pubs fell. Seeing them locked in corporeal combat was like watching a ticking time-bomb, though deepening recession and ideological austerity might have caused notable absences in the ale houses. They, the Bowers and Batemans, were oblivious of the empty rooms. Armed to the teeth with dominoes, pool cues, darts (arrows, as they called them), and a cribbage board, the battle commenced.

The Batemans cursed the Bowers and vice versa from the toe line, the oche; across the pool tables and the domino table. The Bowers, so the gossip had it, were ahead at that moment. The Batemans were in training.

One of the older members of the family, Fred Bateman, went on record as saying: "No Bowers is going to beat us at arrows!"

They, the Batemans, were ahead on the dominoes, a greater game. As for pool, the Bowers led by a margin. The cribbage games score was even.

Business picked up again and improved as it became clear that past enmities had turned into something more positive than brawling. The slagging off remained, though it was sporty rather than abusive.

One good citizen put it more succinctly: "They were pissing against the wind, anyhow, daft fuckers against real hard men."

No one could fathom out what had happened though one or two wondered.

"I'll swear the funny geezer who was sacked from the school has something to do with it."

No one dared to ask the families as they drank not quite together under one roof. As yet, they were buying their own beer. Time would tell. Penny was in Skelton. Dove had his suspicions.

Penny handed his notice to the property owner, paid rent in advance to cover things and left no forwarding address. He so wanted to inculcate a version of the scam he had perpetrated into his own plot to save Oldman. In the house in Skelton he fell into his worn easy chair. He noted that people lived longer there than in Loftus. In Guisborough, the place of his birth, another ten years' life expectancy over Loftus was the norm. To be sure, Skelton could be light years from Loftus when in fact, it was down the road.

The heating fired up and in no time it was cosy. Everything was in place, just as he had left it when he worked out his solution that led to the removal of the underhand perpetrator in the fraud case. He lifted the old computer screen from his desk and replaced it with a new laptop, the old hard drive conveniently smashed up and disposed of a year ago.

Oldman was in trouble. Lawson was untouchable. How was he to resolve the issue with Stead and Oldman? Where did Ken come in? He met Dove and Periwinkle in Skelton later that day.

"Hart called," Dove informed him, "He was sorely troubled by your recent disappearance. Do give him a call."

His thoughts turned to others: Lance, who was still residing in HMP Oakwood as a result of his 'aptitude'. He reminded Periwinkle and Dove of the phone call in Otley, that Lance had called him a cunt and threatened him.

"Can you imagine that guys? He called me a cunt!"

Periwinkle looked at Dove. Dove looked at Periwinkle. Neither spoke. Neither smiled, nor gave away anything.

In retrospect, for an unrehearsed piece of theatre and a statement, Penny admitted it was brilliant. "C'mon, guys, cut me some slack here," he pleaded.

Back home, the place was toast-warm and the work to do surreptitious. The room brought back other memories. Lance would be due for release soon. Grudge was Lance's middle name.

Penny switched on the laptop and spoke. "Fish to fry!" Then he leaned back. "Let's begin with Gran or Nana as the locals call her." Despite his affection for local parlance the word *nana* made his skin creep. Gran was good enough. He went down and locked the front door.

"I wouldn't have left the cat with her while we were away if I'd known." Gran's next-door neighbour's statement said it all.

Gran, 'The Loftus Werewolf' was in a safe place. For the time being Roseberry Park would suffice. She would remain there, or in a similar hospital, for the rest of her natural life, the evidence stacked up against her. A court case was inevitable. The forensic psychologist thought it was doubtful Gran was mentally fit to testify in court. Why waste money? Others wondered if she would escape. There was still dangerous others out there who were culpable of torture and killing, and still free. How about Liz? Liz with the guile of a serpent, no, energetic, multi-faceted, clever, sinuous, and, if necessary, perilous, freckle-faced and bonny. She was still out there too. Liz was a damn good-looking woman. And Liz had given him a job then taken it away.

His list of adjectives grew along with pronouns, the latter aiming to reduce gender assumptions and functioning as a side-track. He and Heo.

For Liz, there was positive, there was negative, and most important, those that might slip either side of the marker and designated good and bad. They were connotative. She was shrewd, energetic, adaptable, strong, duplicitous, and hard to pin down. He opened a new file. He wrote a title: 'Myths and Legends'. He wrote alongside his notes:'everyone has pronouns'.

Liz was to be Lilith, then he thought that unfair. Was she a she-demon or a victim? A 'dem' maybe? He envisaged the painting *Lilith* by John Collier and the image hovered for a while, but Liz with a coiled serpent entwined around her seemed inappropriate. Or was it? It was certainly sexy, and she a symbol of independence, liberation. She was uncontrollable. Liz was all things to all men; powerful. Anyone reading his file would assume it was fiction. Was it? He didn't understand encryption. This would do. The cast: Gran, Naamah, his own magical reality, a bible for now.

How does one trap a snake or snare some trout? Oldman and he were on similar paths.

*Oldman booked in at a B&B near to Reynold's Hall under another name.*

*Lawson belonged to a new intelligence, one that collaborated with politicians rather than working for them. He might well be on the sharp end of that, bearing in mind the close relationship with the press and police, a marriage of convenience, that formed a triumvirate; one that could make or break whom it wanted. Lawson fed the press spoonful's of what he wanted.*

*In an out-of-character spiteful mood, Oldman wished he'd killed Griffin and Lawson; Griffin the spawn of an intelligence agency to which he no longer related, Lawson at its head. His short chat with Lawson may have driven the whole co-operative thing underground. That was a result. Lawson had offset his every move. He could rely on Griffin being quiet for a while longer. Lawson clearly knew of him. Lawson had shown genuine surprise at the mention of The Electrician, denoting either lack of knowledge, or the opposite? He made a list of priorities. His 2B pencil chewed at the end resembled one of those sticks he bought as a child from the chemist: liquorice root. The chewed pencil, a schoolchild habit,* returned when he was anxious. It tasted better than the root. *Remove Stead…* was at the top.

Killing her would be difficult. *Damn it.* The pencil flew across the room and landed in a corner pointing back at him. All he had to go on was the word of a failed agent. He should have killed Griffin. By now Stead would have his will. Would she read below the surface of the text? He'd booked a flight for three days later in the name of Brendan McLeish with an Irish passport. In his bag a change of clothes and his HK 45 pistol. He chose it over the standard issue M9 which he disliked because it was standard. He fondled the grip. The back straps meant it nestled low in his hand. He liked the physical control it offered and the smaller degree of recoil. He loaded the magazine. Ten rounds would be more than enough. Then he would have to part with it. No excess baggage. He took his books down and left them in the exchange. He packed the pistol in his case and locked it. He turned back and took one book back, the marker at page ninety-three. He picked up his other borrowed book and placed it in his bag. The *Tableau Twins*:

'We invited the art historian, Penny, over. Peter and I found his talks inspiring and we followed his path. He would be our biographer. Meanwhile, to pass the time, we sketched out several ideas for the man and his colleagues, should he refuse.'

In Oldman's opinion, the author was a troubled soul.

Penny fiddled with his pen, rolling it around his left palm until it fell on the floor as his fingers lost their grip. He left it where it landed and stared blankly at the laptop. He could think no more about dark feminine and dark masculine, the shadow aspect. He made a list of pronouns and decided to honour, no, embrace his dark masculine. He practised by checking out to see if he had a shadow. About to write another few pages on The Tableau, he flitted between Oldman's fate and his own. They became intertwined. They doubled.

What was Jim about? How to get Oldman out?

"He had to die. He shall die! He shall die!" His rendition of an old comic song, one of Gran's, died on him. Amid that lapse he had a brainwave. No one was going to blight his life.

He reached out to Oldman. The next few days were a flurry of activity: running, and writing, calling people, emailing contacts, and chatting to Dove on Dove's secure line. He thought of skipping.

"Did Periwinkle find out if Jim is on record anywhere? If your sources are still good."

Dove ignored the provocative nudge. "Periwinkle will find out where he's from," he assured Penny. "He's also to check Jack out and see if there's anything in his past that might impact on local stuff." For a moment Dove was quiet. Jack was his friend.

Penny added to the mix and changed the direction. "I would follow up the absent boy – Kyle. He knew something. Max's murder runs far deeper than Bateman-Bowers territory."

Dove's chuckle, a low throaty sound, meant he was thinking. Then he spoke. "The families are getting on like a house on fire – perhaps that's too chancy an expression. The whole town is in shock and may need treatment for PTSD. The police are baffled by the new 'special relationship'. I guess it may have come out of intelligence-sharing rather than intelligence per se. It's anyone's guess." Then, after a pregnant pause, "The downside is that it hasn't led to any leakages from the community which might imply that they have nothing to do with the boy's killing."

"Precisely what I'm thinking, Dove. Has anyone talked to Gran about the united families? Naamah, the ancestral singer – I mean Gran – has an extra-special place in that 'special relationship'."

Ignoring Penny's mythical, and to him barmy, allusions, Dove gave his profound medical diagnosis. "The old biddy seems out of it, raving loony – a fruitcake." Then, "That depends whether she is a passenger in that body. Are Gran's alters genuine? If that is the case, the switches are a psychological trait. Gran is capable of extremes of violence to others and to herself. Mikey has a similar condition – dissociative – though his is milder. He's more a dreamer than an aggressive loony. But there are similarities."

"Have they attempted hypnosis on Gran?" Penny had read up on hypnotism and was advocating it for everyone, bar himself. Forbes-Winslow again. He imagined hypnotising Winslow's suspects in the Ripper case. Disassociating the disassociate, came to mind.

Dove agreed it was worth a try. "I'll pass it on."

"Okay. Catch up soon."

Penny stared out of the window. A faint sound, a reflection worried him. He was being watched. He peered into the street. No one there. The street was deserted. No lockdown in force, no apocalyptic reason, just empty and unsettling.

## Chapter 44

The voice of winter was quiet in Loftus; the calm before...
mackerel clouds rippled above. Light began to fade and
darken. Native lore predicted a change in the weather.
Penny in his light tracksuit and top placed the redundant
computer screen where the totters could see it from the
street. As light faded, a thin glow of white lay across the tops
of the Cleveland Hills then retreated by the minute. The
starlings flocked and circled above Saltburn Woods. Those
argumentative clever birds fascinated him. He had meant to
check on the story that Mozart had a starling.

He went back indoors for his rain top and as he pushed
the door shut, spots drizzled on the windows. Back in the
street, he blinked as a light from the hill caught his eyes, then
locking the door and placing the key in his pocket, he set off
for his run. It was a year since he'd been down through the
woods along the beach and back through Upleatham and
past the tiny church. He made his ritual stop on the seashore
to wave, as his hero Courbet had at the fishing village of
Palavas – a final farewell.

The year previous, alongside the autumn woodland
path, helleborine orchids had established themselves in the

thickest part of the wood leading up to Skelton. The whitish ones were ghost orchids, a sign of spectres on the horizon, and conversely, artistic endeavour. A cloth marker signalled where they were. He wondered if it was for orienteers playing their outdoor games. Or was it a more sensitive sign? He plodded through the mud and past the ragged marker.

He was beginning to think like Oldman. Small signs elicited infinite meanings. He focussed on them and brought sense to them. The dynamic marker on the tree was a sign. He had his concluding chapter tied up. A broken tree; splintered, scaly, resembling a pineapple.

The winter air was moist, the ground viscous, causing him to raise his feet to separate them from the clart. "A good northern word." As he spoke, he turned his head to the right where his imaginary audience sat, while executing a gesture of self-congratulation.

The rain abated within fifteen minutes or so and mixed blue and cloudy skies followed. In Skelton, he passed the Royal George and the refurbished, once dismal Duke William, was alive, given a new lease of life, lit up, quirky and inviting. On the little green outside was a carriage from the old mines. Opposite stood a robust sculpture celebrating the ironstone miners – *The Spirit of East Cleveland* – the gaffer with his waistcoat and fob, and a long bar checking the roof; two others, one grafting with a Blackett Hutton Rotary Drill, the other with a large piece of ironstone, the stuff that made us the engine room of the industrial boom and an honorary place in Asa Briggs's *Victorian Cities*.

It promoted pride first, then regret for his hometown of Redcar, the endless recession, redundancy, and closure.

How big business recovered its supremacy after the 1930s he could never fathom out. Where was the opposition? It would come, and when it did, in a youthful form. Out of austerity it would come from the right. How did trust break down the way it had?

He warmed down, and, in doing so, expelled negative reflections of the past and current politics. His deductions on Jim were that if there was nothing, then there was something. Periwinkle had gone back to London, taking Jack with him. Before he left, Penny asked him to check out his laptop. He feared his email account hacked. It was. Periwinkle did not take long to source the hacker. The location: Oakwood. The perpetrator: Lance. Wedjet was Lance's nom de plume; the single eye his laptop. He could track people from anywhere. His decision to leave it surprised Periwinkle.

In the shower, Penny allowed his mind to empty. When he switched his laptop on to begin his contemporary Lilith fiction, he was short on a fictional plot. It was either that or clean the house, a diversion he deployed to avoid doing what he should be doing. After eyeballing the vacuum cleaner, he opened a document. The vacuum remained where it was. He thought of nothing and nothingness.

*Oldman pulled Griffin's phone. About to throw it as far as the duck-less duck pond outside the B&B, he changed his mind. He dialled Reynold's Hall. That the mobile was active may well be deliberate. He would be out of there in no time.*

*"May I speak with Primrose Stead, please?" His Irish brogue wasn't perfect. He didn't recognise the switchboard lady's voice. A second or two went past.*

The new switchboard lady said, "Who's calling?"

"Brendan O'Siar, that's O' S.I.A.R." He waited.

"Ms Stead isn't in her room, sir. Would you like to leave a message?"

His brogue improved. "Thank you. Could you tell Ms Stead that I called?" He rang off. If a trace were on the call, his location would be known by now.

As a secondary measure, he texted Stead from the phone and arranged to meet her at one of their favourite spots: 'I'll be there late morning, say eleven o'clock. Best wishes, Brendan.'

Stead did not reply. Within twenty minutes he was several miles away, had changed cars and was about to change names.

He skirted the wood where Stead and he loved to stroll; the backpack, the shopping bag of older men, slung over his right shoulder, a bottle of water in the side pocket, his beloved pistol tucked below his shirt. The wood was more tangled than he had imagined. Where the trees were most dense, he paused to spot a fungal growth at the foot of a mature beech, close to the buttress of the tree. As a child in Canada, he had seen beechnut woodland destroyed by fungi. He took a photograph with Griffin's phone. He studied the crisp brown leaves from the previous fall. Reflecting purple in the light through the branches it was difficult to make out if the fungi had spread. Ustulina, the raven of the woods and slain, ate the heart out of the tree. Back home it was called brittle cinder. He sent the photo and details to the Woodland Trust. He signed it 'Griffin' and gave his address. He cleaned the phone and left it at the foot of the tree. No Stead. Not that daft.

Usually busy with walkers, the woodland was quiet due to inclement weather. He walked back to the car, circling the muddy pathways. He checked exit routes on his sat nav. Two exits existed:

a back road which lead to a string of villages, and a side road to the A3. There was still time to kill Lawson. That would jeopardise his chances of the job in hand. Lawson had given him one clue that, at top level, he was the only one involved. That the small team at Reynold's Hall was it, was questionable. He was convinced Ken was it. Ken had a hold somehow. Stead was pivotal. Lawson wasn't against using them as pawns in his career game. She was important in another way. Oldman's will said so. He was now far enough away to watch without discovery. A distant hilltop was good enough. He did not need to spot faces, just figures.

Half an hour passed, and two cars pulled up from differing routes. Two men left their vehicles and went into the wood. One other stayed, leaning on the car. The hawkish figure of Campbell was distinguishable. His stalking gait was that of the predator seeking a victim. Campbell, and colleague. No Griffin.

Stead had received both messages. So had Lawson's people. Lawson disregarded the Griffin connection. He had plans for him.

Oldman's family solicitor now had his will. He was of the opinion that the Griffins and Lawsons of this world were no longer his people. He had thus downgraded them below humankind. He considered the fact that they had lowered themselves. Dumbing-down was taking place in intelligence generally – counterintelligence specifically. What was for sure was that they were inventing strategies to suit the politics and ideologies of the government, and this was different. Where were the morals? Where was trust? It didn't have to get personal. Killing was a part of the job. What he had done at Reynold's Hall was exactly what they had assessed he couldn't do, and for that he must pay. He had unearthed the rot at the heart of the tree; Lawson and one other, yet to be proven.

*Aware of his fragile position in the scheme of things, he didn't wait for them to reappear from the wood. The next B & B was five miles down the road. He passed it by and found another some twenty miles away. This time he was Smith, James Smith. His passport stated that he was born in Hampshire.*

*The man at the desk guessed his accent. "You sound American." The man chattered.*

*Allowing the man to natter, he humoured him. "Well spotted. I've travelled a lot and worked abroad. I'm returning to my ancestral home, as we yanks call it. Oh, can I leave my passport in the safe?"*

*"No worries, Mr Smith. I'll give you chitty. Do you need anything?"*

*"I'm good. I'm also tired. Flying gets harder in old age. I'll rest."*

*"Again, sir, no probs."*

*In the room he tucked his bag under the bed. Half-dressed, he lay out across the top of the covers and fell asleep. This was a cat nap. It extended into a deeper sleep. His most testing role was imminent. He woke early in the morning. The day would bring other problems. He chose another passport for his travels: Barrymore. He liked the actors that owned that name, and the great roles they played. He had used them all barring Drew and Ethel. He tucked it in his inside pocket.*

*He favoured a light breakfast before a day's killing. He was going to meet Lawson again, to beat information out of him if necessary. And in the process find out more on dear boy Ken, then Stead. Cereal and toast did the job with strong black coffee. Coffee mug to his mouth, he glimpsed around the room. There was only one other in the breakfast room, a young lady, who*

289

smiled across and then focussed her attention on a worn Hello magazine.

Oldman rubbed his eyes. The cover image was blurred. Was that Prince Harry on a motorbike?

"Celebrity culture," he grumbled with some acidity. The bloody royals were getting bad press lately.

Leaving a substantial tip on the table befitting an American returning home, he went upstairs, checked his pistol, collected the soon to be redundant passport and paid up.

"Thanks, a wonderful place. I may call in on the way back."

The man at the desk was different, though equally polite, and obviously pleased at the size of the tip. The room was empty and the tables cleared ready for lunchtime. The young lady was gone.

"Bye, sir. Have a good day!"

As a farewell, 'have a good day' never quite worked for the English, even those well-travelled. It sounded rehearsed. His instincts moved up a gear. He was aware of another person in the room. It felt wrong. As he turned to see who it was, his vision blurred. He raised his hands to his eyes, then tried to slide the bag off his shoulder as the floor came up to greet him.

## Chapter 45

Liz's morning emails included messages from an unknown source.

The first read: 'Brussels. Where's Jim?'

The next three highlighted County Cork, Tokyo, and Taranaki. Two were blank apart from location.

The other stated: 'Check his bank accounts'.

Jim had travelled to all those places for work. Jim had always been a tradesman, a plumber (or master plumber as he would boast), first trained as a shipwright.

The fifth, Bahrain, simply read, 'Jim, a Plumber?'

Seven arrived. The one naming Indian Rocks, Florida, the longest by two sentences, included a bastardised word in the last sentence: 'I will finalize the details of his visit later.' The z grated on Liz. She reached for her pen.

Jim was there on a high-rise plumbing job and staying at The Don CeSar, the pink palace. Jim contacted her daily, sometimes for a few seconds only to say, "Love you, Lizzie." His favourite quip was, "Keep busy, Lizzie."

Police officer Evie had become a regular and unwelcome caller at the house. She was a pain. Not the sweetie she appeared, Evie was persistent in her task, dogged, bothersome and bright. The school regretted losing Penny. Liz hoped Penny would realise the difficulty of her situation.

Difficulty was a cause for concern for Evie. What difficulty? No reply. Who placed her in difficulty? No reply. Liz fobbed her off.

Over a cup of tea, Liz convinced herself there was nothing to worry about. She was overreacting. A bloody student? If it was they would pay dearly.

Reporting to Raed, Evie made her assessment. "There are gaping holes in Liz's statements. The removal of Penny from the school suggests a rear-guard action if that's the right phrase?"

Raed agreed it was, yet the fact that Liz may well have been party to partial information only, like Hart. Evie was raw but Raed saw her as a future detective.

Liz saw her as a threat.

Dove went to see Gran, with Raed's 'permission.' As he entered the Ridgeway section he was told to wait. They phoned through and he was told to leave his belongings in a locker. He handed the bottle of gin over, paid a pound for the locker and was escorted to the ward. Gran was in fine fettle.

He had to book twenty-four hours in advance and reported back that Roseberry was low secure. Each time he took a small bottle of gin. There are no drugs to combat dissociative disorders, and he hoped the staff were happy to turn a blind eye to the alternative medication. They sat singing, or as one nurse described it screeching old songs.

Their burlesque lampoons, though close to the reality of the audience's waxing of the songs in their music hall settings, nearly drove the staff insane.

To Dove, the staff blended well with the patients. Insanity, Dove recalled, had something to do with who is locked in by whom. Giving into the noise, several joined in. Gin or not, Gran never dropped her guard.

On one occasion, the nurse who showed him out thanked him for the entertainment, asking, "And are you a relative?"

Gran had shouted 'goodbye son'.

The implications were clear. He was in danger of being committed. Not again.

He put two thumbs to his temples, waggled his fingers and tongue and said, "You think Gran's mad. I've got the certificates to prove it."

The nurse decided not to pursue the matter. The huge doors clanged shut and the locks turned behind him.

Personal wisdom was a highly complex thing, personal safety a guiding principle. The nurses left them together. Dove listened to Gran's rambling. Gran didn't make a slip-up; her throwaway remarks raised issues to consider.

In Loftus, Hart thought about Penny, who was acting stranger than usual.

Penny was busy sending emails. On his well wrapped-up wanderings he began to sniff a tail. He was on edge, aware of the watcher's gaze. Outside his field of vision was a lurking presence. Would Oldman protect him?

Liz was edgy and decided she should talk to Jim before reporting it to the police. No, the present was it. She would talk to the Hart chap rather than Raed. The morning after a message, 'Nigeria', she called in. The operator finally directed her from a national centre to Loftus.

An appointment with Hart followed. He wasted no time. He opened the laptop and Liz directed him to her email. Hart was authoritative and scrupulous. He scrutinised the mail. He then turned to the headteacher and held his focus a moment.

"Have you any suspicions?"

"About what?"

"About who could have sent them?"

"Jim has always worked away. If he gets up to a bit of mischief when away I guess I can live with that. I don't like digging dirt, DI Hart. As for who sent them, I have no idea in the slightest." Then, as a gushing tailpiece she slipped up, "The only person I've upset recently is Dr Penny who I had to pay off due to instructions from above. It's doubtful he would stoop this low." Unaware of the precarious relationship with Penny, she then added fuel to the flames by trying to right the wrong and give Penny a compliment. "We miss him at the school."

Hart's face flushed. "Yes, he is a minefield, though as you say, he's not spiteful."

Liz was beginning to regret taking the laptop into Hart. The laptop should reveal the truth.

"Have you spoken to Jim about it?"

"No, I came to you first."

"Ms Trout, do you mind if I take your laptop for the technical staff to examine?"

"No worries, I have a spare."

"That will be great." Hart placed the laptop in his briefcase. "I'll be in touch. Thanks for your cooperation." He gave her a receipt.

Liz did not like the way he took the laptop. It smacked of guile.

Hart knew more about Jim's plumbing career than his wife. He was eager to see what Penny was up to. If he was, as he imagined, up to his old tricks, then this time he'd nail him... good and proper.

After a day or so, he handed the printouts of the mail to Raed. "What do you think, ma'am?"

"Leave them here."

"The head thinks Penny may be involved. I'm not sure."

Raed refused to involve herself in what was clearly a petty male quarrel. "Does Jim know about these?"

"No, ma'am. The team are still checking the hard drive. Doubt they'll find anything." He was painfully aware he had given yet another clue to his aversion to Penny.

Raed chose not to show her deeper understanding of the situation. "Good work. Have you any ideas?"

Hart seemed unaware of the fact that Liz could be in danger.

Hart hid a smile. "Not a clue. It all seems a bit crazy, though clever and orchestrated. Liz Trout informs me that Jim has worked in all those places."

"I see."

Information on Jim was drizzling in, enough to warn her he was a ticking time bomb. Penny wasn't a fool, nor did he appear malicious. He played the former. Underneath Hart's investigation other agendas ticked away.

Hart wished her goodnight and left. Pinning down Penny would be unachievable. Against Raed's instructions he decided to check him out briefly and set a female constable on him.

After three days in Skelton she had nothing to report. He gave up. Raed would be asking about deployment. If the police officer had been better trained, she would have noticed there was another watching.

Two more emails came in while the police held the laptop: one from Borneo, where Jim had worked voluntarily at an animal sanctuary for two weeks, and a further from Iceland looking at caves.

The latter merely read: 'make sure they check the grammar or should that be grandma?'

It must be Penny. He was playing a peevish game; one he was going to lose. The gist was similar in all, as were the innuendos.

"What's Jim up to today?"

Liz was a rational person. This was nonsense. It was still getting to her. Penny would have to breach her laptops to have access to some of the information. Nothing he had done in terms of computing told her he was capable of that. The very idea that Penny might be able to hack a computer was laughable. She missed him.

## Chapter 46

Raed's business-like invasion of his place put a cap on the teamwork. Her manner was formal.

"Dr Penny. May I come in?"

"*Ahlan wa sahlan!*" He wished he'd simply said welcome. It sounded snippy, forced rather than welcoming.

Raed entered the small front room. She refused a seat and launched in. "This is business. We need to examine your laptop. You can allow us to take it, or we can use our authority to do so. You shall have it back in no time."

"Am I allowed to ask why? And who is *we*?"

"At this point it's a no to both." She avoided sorry.

He went upstairs, Raed close behind. He reached across the desk, unplugged the laptop from the mains and removed the printer and speaker cables. He handed it over. She eyed his desk. Immaculate.

"Thank you." She put it under her arm and went downstairs.

He opened the door for her and said goodbye before she turned to go. As she walked away, he saw Hart in the driving seat. He was barely covering a smirk. As she approached the car, he stepped out. Posing heroically, he held the door open for her. His stance, one leg slightly in front, one arm raised, was a well-worn pose borrowed from antiquity and reserved for portraits of the moneyed classes, or in the here and now, the pompous celebrity. At least Hart had talent and had achieved a lot in his short time. In his favour, he was no friend to the media and wisely not bothered by celebrity status.

On the doorstep she gave him the once over for any tell-tale signs of his feelings. She clocked a half-smile on his face, lips tight and eyes that showed amusement. More transparent were signs of disillusionment. Suspects usually tried to manipulate her, but this gave her no comfort. She didn't want to find that he was the culprit. Liz's laptop had revealed nothing. The emails, she concluded, were below Penny's code of ethics, and the skills above him. He was more likely to do whatever he felt was appropriate in the open. Yet Penny did not do everything openly.

Penny's parting statement was confusing. As she walked away, he said, "The vase was broken!"

She chose not to parry with him and left.

Innocent emails apart, to Periwinkle and friends his laptop contained a curious version of a story about Lilith, and a cast of three angels – Semangelof, Senoy and Sansenoy – and their efforts to resolve a conflict between Lilith and Adam. They would combat the other side and the banished Lilith. Penny wondered how Hart would take to the idea of him and his comrades as angelic. He would of course remember his last musings on country music.

It was with mixed feelings that Raed handed the laptop over. The resultant feedback from the boffins lasted ten minutes. For the first time in her career she felt dirty.

Reading mail to and from Periwinkle put the cap on it. Hart was finding it difficult to hide his delight at the chance of catching Penny at anything. It didn't feel right. She did a fly check herself. The Rabbinic stories amused her. Who, she wondered, were Lilith and Adam? Who was banished from this garden of Eden? Why? Was it Gran? Liz?

The backroom boffins returned the laptop and found nothing that would indicate him as a source of the emails.

Hart ordered, "Make sure you check everything again more thoroughly."

"We have, sir. There is no evidence that those emails came from that laptop. None whatsoever."

Raed had broken a personal rule behind his back and countermanded his orders. She ordered the backroom boys and girls to focus only on the emails. "All we need to know at this point is did the emails emanate from that source? Leave his personal writing alone."

Forensics obeyed, but not so Hart. "I want feedback as soon as – to me first."

The backroom boys suspected a further cover-up between their boss and Periwinkle, and made some mileage of it behind her back.

Periwinkle's intelligence pointed the finger at Lance. Following Penny's requests, he chose not to inform. The precision of Lance's knowledge and skills were unquestionable, the content a product of his puddled mind. That Penny should protect him was his problem.

Raed's opinion of Periwinkle and his unrestricted access to files that were confidential to her was a source of aggravation and wonder. Who did he know? She spoke to Hart. He smiled, a cryptic smile. What did he know?

Lance could have authored the book on website design. Instead he was using his skills for bad. The information gained from Penny's communications with Periwinkle and others allowed him access to Liz. What a brain. What a waste.

"I could be a lawyer," Penny sang, and thought of Hart. Hart had seen a chance to nail him. He was on Penny's trail like a wrathful dog.

Lance provided him with a new driving motivation, one born of disappointment. Rather than see it as a setback, he saw it as a new avenue to explore. Assumptions led to further ideas and that led to a scheme. He forgot his writing as he walked down into the woods toward Saltburn. He paused under the Victorian viaduct. Turning away, he noticed a new cutting in the weir, a rough-hewn job. He sat down to analyse the situation. He tried to picture Lance, but somehow his physical self-escaped him. Lance was a virtual presence. He stared at the cutting. He took his notebook out.

It would allow fish upstream to spawn. He had often pondered about the weir and its role as a dam. The beck below the weir had cut quite low over the years and a passage upriver was near impassable for fish. The job was rough, but effective. Nature would prevail and the beds of spawning fish would bring life to Skelton Beck again. With a new awareness, one that always brought satisfaction, he walked up the steps and through the woods back to Skelton.

Near the underpass the cold east wind caught him and burned his face. He hurried to get to the house for shelter.

He stopped writing. He'd submitted several chapters of The Tableau manuscript. Oldman was in limbo. His faith in the law, transitory as it was, was gone. Raed, was a copper. He trusted Dove, Periwinkle and Oldman. He muttered, "The vase had been broken." How active was Liz in all this? There would be no more sharing for him; information had dried up. It was going to flow one way only. It was not peevishness, more a sense that he could resolve things alone. His panic attacks had lessened with the inclusion of Oldman in his life. The moment he climbed the steps away from the new cutting in the concrete of the weir, he considered the scene with satisfaction. He saw no fish. They were there still; upstream, and downstream. He saw no one watching him.

Lance Peirce paused over his laptop. HMP Oakwood offered a platform to change one's life. Lance was brainy enough to realise that, yet his emotional attachment to Penny, one of hatred, a loathing he himself couldn't understand, drove him on. Penny was a threat to him. His pain lay deep, and the object of his hatred and his reasons for his malaise were unfathomable. Penny's optimism and positive nature pissed him off. He reflected. His own emotional intelligence was lacking, and he realised it. Whenever Penny was mentioned his objectivity evaporated and he was back in the loop. At times, he hated himself.

Some years before, the prison had been referred to as 'Jokewood'. Lance couldn't see it. He was there because of Penny. His academic nature knew he was projecting – it was inside outside. Resentment was his first emotion, then anger and loathing. He tried to convince himself his blame was unwarranted then a vision of Penny grinning at the front of the classroom loomed. He tried to blank it. He felt helpless. He opened his emails and began to type.

## Chapter 47

Raed returned the laptop in person. Penny blocked the door. There was no greeting. His acknowledgement was curt. She tried not to grin. (She did so inwardly.) Hart's comments to her evidenced the fact he had circumvented her orders. He had stormed into her office with the laptop and, as ordered, had given her it back.

"Gibberish, more gibberish and advanced gibberish."

More important for her was the fact that none of the emails had come from Penny. "Stick to your remit, Hart," she barked.

The all-too innocent Penny held his laptop under one arm and began to close the door with his other.

Raed stopped him. "I can offer you an explanation."

Tongue behind his teeth, he shook his head.

She chose as a substitute for her apology a hurried Parthian shot before walking away. "I'm sorry, Penny, we had to investigate. Elizabeth Trout has been getting unexplained emails. We had to eliminate you." Leaving the issue with Penny seemed a suitable ploy.

The vase broke. Penny showed no signs of emotion, only dull acceptance. She turned out past the churchyard into the high street and left.

She heard him say, "Screw Hart."

Should he mention Lance? It was difficult to accept he couldn't get on with folk. His feelings were mixed. He wanted to know the content of the emails. She had blocked that by her formality, and he by his stubbornness. What is it about the working class and the police? The emails emanated from Lance, and his silly notions of Wedjet, the eye of Ra. It was yet another ill wind that might blow some good. He too had eyes everywhere. Back upstairs, he plugged the laptop in. The photograph taken in Chicago standing below the elevated train tracks came into view, an image which, in his mind's eye, he resembled Clint Eastwood. His mobile gave its familiar chime.

"Dove, you okay?"

"Yep. Has Raed been round?"

"She has."

"Did you understand the purpose for the laptop examination?"

Penny surmised Dove wasn't sure he did. Either that or he was aiming to justify the invasion of his privacy. He answered with a positive that could mean anything. "Yes."

Dove ditched his intentions to say she had acted honourably and in doing so had put Hart on a spot. "Periwinkle is following things up on Jim. That will remain apart from the police. It's a slow process. He has reason to believe Jim may have had a say in your removal from the school. He's connected."

Dove and Periwinkle had been working overtime. Periwinkle's liaison with Raed was also helpful.

Calculating the planning of the messages from 'inside', Penny decided to get on to Periwinkle right away. He was going to use it to their benefit. Lance was going to be the facilitator.

He switched to Max, a different scenario. "I can't get it out of my head that Jim and he met briefly. Why has no one questioned Jim?" The development of events leading up to Max's killing begged such. He hesitated to use scenario – common parlance in the pub. He began to list words that had found their way into the great dictionary of public discourse of late. He got no further than skitter. Skitter and Scenario. He kept fishing.

Dove's frustration was apparent in the edge to his voice. "Are you implying Jim killed Max?"

"What I am saying is that the investigations should focus on Jim, Max, and his cronies."

Dove was clear on one thing, well two: first, that Penny had a premise he wasn't going to impart, and two, he wasn't to be a part of it. Dove's beliefs were that the culprits were professionals and based elsewhere. "Can you say any more?"

To Penny, Dove sounded uncertain. It was out of character. "Max was not the innocent child we considered him to be. He was hiding something." The latter was a Penny hunch based on nothing but pure theory, instinct.

Dove had to respect his cloaking; the cloak was fine. It was the impending dagger that concerned him. "Okay if I pass that on to Raed as a speculative notion from myself?"

"Of course."

It entered Dove's mind, as a further issue, that Penny might be setting Raed up... then it passed. He wasn't a vengeful man, more byzantine. He wasn't sure what it meant. Periwinkle had said it. "Will you be coming to the meeting next week?"

"I doubt it." Penny was reading his manuscript. How had he managed to lead his imaginary friend Oldman to this point? Oldman was trapped.

*In the corridors of power... A hackneyed phrase to Oldman. corridors were everywhere and led to wrong doors. Sir James Lawson's retirement had gone to press as a disaster. Lawson oversaw the burning of multiple files himself. It was for government, the press and politicians a sea change. Oldman would've applauded.*

*For the agency, a change was taking place. One that heralded a different intelligence was imminent, one not so bound up with politics. Still, in the new regime removing bad elements might well be politic. Oldman's native slant on the agency was that it was a clusterfuck. His disappearance had rattled a few cages. (More clichés.) Stead and company were about to vanish from the hall. Oldman felt strongly that he was to be the co-operative's last removal. What would his death certificate say? He wondered what Bingham's fate had been.*

Penny broke from writing. He tried to think of other words rather than *cliché* that might suit – chestnuts, platitudes even. Did they resonate as much? He was about to research them, then welcomed back his old *Roget's Thesaurus*. Its cover was torn, and a sticky label on the back read: 'school library copy'. He lent them it.

*The coincidence of the absence of Oldman, Bingham, West, then Stead and Jack David from Reynold's Hall was a riddle for years to come. Fielding's death took on another life. Was that coincidence? Luna lived on in the unaware. Luna lost the thing that drove her on: her consciousness. In her sleep she aged. Oldman visited and wanted to visit again, but that wasn't to be. No nightlight accompanied her sleep.*

*The caretaker's statement said there were no farewells at the hall. The first sign was their vacant rooms, and then, a once busy card table without players. The gardener put his own spin on the mystery. It involved conspiracy first, then alien abduction.*

*A member of the dominoes school paused her game. "First that nice lady Bingham went, then that man Oldman, then his partners in crime. Stole away in the night, I reckon."*

*"Very strange, I remember seeing a programme on television about people who disappear. A man went shopping and never came back."*

*"It's those left behind that suffer."*

*"I think I saw that programme," a third added.*

*"In black and white," another chimed in.*

*Time only exaggerated the story. Witty residents began to reference* The Flying Dutchman *or* The Marie Celeste. *The legends would live on. Whodunnit? The ghosts had landed.*

*Lawson never let it worry him. Stead and company would be far away. Bingham was another story. They would not get in touch. The conclusion of their work disallowed it. He would sleep well in his retirement. He picked his globe up from the desk, held it for a* moment, spun it, then dropped it in a bin bag and left. It stopped on the North Atlantic Islands. He wasn't party to Oldman's removal. Indeed, Lawson was as much in the dark about the situation as Griffin. Griffin didn't want to know. Lawson, a pragmatic man, wasn't going to lose sleep. Not his concern anymore.

The remaining duo of Campbell and Griffin were employed to seek out stuff on their colleague, Eames. Griffin trembled at the thought of it. Eames was missing presumed dead. No one really missed him at all except Campbell, who appeared wanting. Eames was a cold case. His last known action was to call Ken.

Griffin had his own ideas on that. The company wanted to close the books on him. Griffin's stomach for the job had changed, his ambitions diluted. He despised Oldman and his aptitude. Simultaneously, he was in awe of him.

Spirited away or not, Oldman was like a shadow, a shade that dogged him everywhere, the Oldman in his head. In his home, he looked over his shoulder. At his desk, he fidgeted with things and frequently inspected them. In the street he would turn suddenly as if expecting him to be there. Oldman gazed down from a panoptic tower. Oldman was everywhere, his power and influence constant. Griffin fiddled with his pen. The ridiculous nature of his obsessions was bothering him. On the wall a framed certificate from the Woodland Trust hung, another riddle which kept him alert. It read: Thanks, well done, and a few words about fungus.

His peers expected he would get over his trauma. For him, the corridor was dark and long. Rebekah had asked for space to think things over, take time out, and taking Maisy had gone to stay with her sister. His posh house lost its materialistic glow. She never came back. At Christmas he tried to light the place up for their first and only visit; so much so, Rebekah made a wisecrack about that appalling film, The Griswold's. The lights still hung there three months on. No thanks arrived for the lavish presents. Had they opened them? Presents did not make up and carry messages. The meaning of the gift is complex.

He sat on the couch and turned. Oldman was sitting in Rebekah's chair, the one he'd bought at a posh London store made up of scraps of recycled furniture, and rough painted. He wanted to punch him, throw him out of the chair, kick him, and beat him to pulp. Then in a turn of mood, he wanted to thank him. Then he was gone. Where was he? Where were the so-called co-operative? Lawson was gone. The new regime was healthier.

Campbell was getting on his nerves, raw as they were. His continuous repetition of the hope that they would find Eames and Oldman was bollocks. Griffin resisted drink, though the bottle was close to him and opened frequently. Neither he nor Campbell had any notion of what was going on. They lost sight of Oldman. The bridge players too had gone without trace. Lawson was unavailable for comment. Then there was Eames, or rather, then there wasn't Eames. What had Oldman done to him? He pictured his day or so at the lock-up and the gasoline. Fuck. The ballpoint pen snapped as he twisted it. It could have been him.

Their last briefing was a disaster. He and Campbell had disagreed completely in their assessments of the progress they had made. Their new boss's perplexed glances as she moved her head from one to the other to listen to the contradictions spoke volumes.

She resisted shouting, "Advantage, Campbell," and after a couple more moves, "Match point, Griffin!"

Campbell reported at length their exhaustive interrogation of the residents of the hall and its staff, and at the hotel where

Oldman was last seen. Both proved to be a blank end. Luna was in what he understood was a state of hypoxia. The hospital hadn't yet classified her as in a persistent vegetative state. No answers there either. The woman in the restaurant remained untraced. Stan, the man at reception, had gone for a cuppa and done his rounds. On his return Oldman and the woman had gone. If someone had been at the desk, it wasn't him. A large tip remained on the desk. Campbell turned to Griffin for back-up. Griffin's new position required him to be enigmatic.

"We've found nothing that will lead us anywhere."

Their new boss thanked him for his integrity. She asked Campbell to put it all in writing in future and, in a foul temper, he left. Outside the room Campbell called his former comrade a treacherous bastard. One of those words irked him.

Inside, their new gaffer, Sarah Theakston, picked up her Royalist Weekly magazine and buried her head in frippery. The tabloids high and low, the broadsheets already digested. Sarah checked out the celebs.

For his part, Griffin went back to the hotel and cross-examined Stan, the desk manager. "Tell me what you can about the lady."

"I told you before," Stan reported charily, "she had her head behind a magazine. I then went walkabout. I assumed she was waiting for someone."

Following this, and a further stopover at Reynold's Hall without the accompanying arsehole Campbell, his written request for a move away from active service came as no surprise to Theakston. He interviewed a creep of a man — Roger — who had a lot to say about Oldman that he wanted to agree with but refused to give him the pleasure.

He was aware Theakston had earmarked him for early promotion in a job she judged he would be particularly good at, behind a desk consulting with those in the field and in charge of the back office. He was to be her link to the field, her Delphic oracle she said, but open all hours. The gender shift was ignored. He was happy to play high priestess to Theakston. His advice wasn't ignored and he felt valued.

Griffin viewed his promotion with mixed feelings. It did at least remove him from the field of action for which he had no stomach. When he settled in behind his posh old desk, he realised a way forward. He wrote to Rebekah. He wasn't expecting a reply but felt satisfaction in doing so. Before sealing the envelope, he dropped a small token in for Maisy — a lucky charm in the shape of a tiny magnet. He tried it out first and it picked up pins. That night he swore Oldman was smiling at him from his chair. A few weeks later Oldman began to fade. He didn't miss the spectre, though in a perverse way felt he owed him. Where was he? He was missing believed dead. He didn't believe it. The wily sod was out there. Eames faded totally from view.

Campbell needed watching. That would be part of his new post, not a priority, merely keeping an eye on the man. Had Theakston considered that? The chances of Campbell finding anyone were slight. That was a comfort. Where were the bridge school now, that lovely lady, Stead, and the shrewd Jack David who he knew of through despatches? A note reminded him to keep an eye on Luna's progress in case she awoke. Ken was still on the run, possibly aided and abetted by someone inside. With Lawson gone, would he survive? He'd concluded that Ken was a nasty fucker.

Lawson had retired to the country. The card from his old boss congratulating him on the move was on his desk. The message stated quite simply: *Congratulations, old man.* His new ability to constantly interrogate things critically, and if necessary keep quiet, helped his promotions. The lessons learnt stayed with him throughout his career, unspectacular as it was, but full of small rewards.

Rebekah moved on. He saw Maisy regularly. She wore her little magnet. He often pictured her that day and her sad little face when she had said, 'Daddy's crying'. Maisy's tears were worth it. As she grew and graduated and onto a professional career, he noted with some joy that she had his ambitions, though tempered by a wisdom that he had not possessed. She wasn't as greedy. He never took a tipple from the bottle.

Where were they all? Where were the old guard? Dead, sick, locked away. The office beckoned as a safe haven. Then he remembered Griggs.

✎

Florence Bingham's addiction to bridge meant the few weeks of upheaval caused by her being spirited away, brought about a temporary bout of the shakes. She started a new school in her Spanish home, one that did not include that lethal opponent Stead and her partner, West. Her self-titled addictive criminal syndrome also needed feeding. She battled with that, and her withdrawal ebbed and became a case for disavowal. All four knew it could never last. West's real name would come to her. She was on a winning streak though moving was always a tedious upheaval. This time it was organised by Stead and had been a smooth transition.

Getting rid of the married name was a relief. A new life, another passport. It had been her late husband's name and she had gone back to her birth name of MacDonald. Where was Jack David? They had never used first names at the hall barring his case, an honorary title perhaps, an exceptional man. None of them had time to say their goodbyes. The orders came to abandon ship. Each one did so in the spirit and fashion they had maintained throughout their professional lives. It was a shame about Fielding though. He clearly hadn't realised that above them her friend Lawson was pulling strings, Eames, Campbell and Griffin lobbying. Ken, who she despised, would no longer hold her to ransom. One error in a long successful career. How the hell had he known all the stuff he used to coerce them into the so-called bloody co-op. Yet, she enjoyed the work, and that worried Ken. The best thing she ever did was drop that note into the man Griggs. Oldman brought it all to a head. In a sense he'd help dispose of Ken.

She was pleased it had ended. Ken had his own personal vendettas against 'the list', as they called it. And he wanted to see it continue. It was him, no doubt, who'd organised the attempts on Oldman's life. He was vile in the extreme. As for poor Luna.

The commitment to their task had stayed with them. Moral aspects were an issue, depending on how one defines moral duties. She smiled. She spread a winning hand.

Getting rid of a few scumbags was the commonplace description but Bingham preferred cleansing, revenge it wasn't. Then there was Luna. In that case she demurred. Revenge was good. She wasn't going to invade Poland but she was going to wait until the time was right to pay back. She wouldn't miss Ken but would miss the work as it stretched the imagination and offered an interesting challenge.

On a personal level, people moved in and out of her life continuously, as with the others. None of them would ever contemplate the whereabouts of their once resident bridge school after a few weeks. Then there was the troubling thoughts of Ken, the man who wanted to cleanse politics too, a dangerous little man, the man whose list would include anyone from what he deemed the left, that included liberals. Removing his files before the police stepped in was a good move and an eye-opener. Her own made interesting reading. Luna had him sussed. She called a meeting. Unfortunately Ken was informed. Roger.

Florence MacDonald eyed her cards with satisfaction. She was proud of her role, working the legal aspects of death and dying. The attendant physician signed the death certificate with evidence of the underlying cause, and not the actual reason for death. Her own father lasted a day on a morphine pump. The death certificate said cancer, not a day on morphine, or an overdose. Was it not the medical profession that was unethical? How could that be?

The difference here was that the underlying cause of death in those cases was criminal, yet she hated the fact she was cajoled, initially, then blackmailed, by Ken. The death certificates were ethical and honest, in contrast to the codes practised by doctors. Left unmentioned was vaccination as a cause and puerperal fever as a result. Stead had advised only. They, her comrades in arms, existed as signatures only. There were no official complaints. They, the co-operative, were loyal to an oath that she would hold until she herself died (sort of hold to). She checked her hand. The cards were falling her way.

The investigation that had taken place emanated from the very same office the orders came from and were part of an upheaval. Why should anyone grumble? The fact that the past-his-sell-by-date Oldman (ah, yes that was his name) had come up trumps had made things difficult. The widow of the vaccination victim was now a very rich woman. The three incompetents — Campbell, Eames, and Griffin — were supposed to resolve Oldman's unexpected success. They failed. One died along the way.

Stead was a brilliant organiser. She masterminded the removals with the aplomb of a top-class player, one of psychic proportions, one able to fool even her partner. They made a super partnership. Always a softie for relationships, matchmaking, and newspaper astrology, she saw them as starred natural partners. MacDonald laid another hand down. It did not contain the best possible cards though it was close, yet ace-less. A cognitive moment occurred and she saw West and Stead together.

Then came a warm glow as she mulled over her very own final job. The network she had nurtured outside the hall meant the occasional snifter with the criminal underclasses. She couldn't wait for Oldman to get Ken. Just as poor Luna feared the dark, Ken feared heights. National Geographic informed her that the Atlantic Ocean off the US had the most sharks. (If he survived the drop.) Nice touch, dear boy. Hateful man. As a parting gesture, he would have a yellow beanie placed over his head which would be stapled to his skull to prevent it flying off on the way down. Why, Florence thought, did these guys — guys like Ken — keep mementoes, fetishist souvenirs of their crimes? Power to the beanie. Power to Luna. Not resting in peace. The fantasy of the airplane drop waned. The alternative was cheaper and very satisfactory. She pondered.

Major Ken was in France, resting after one of his camps. After strutting his stuff with the boys, they would be partying the next day. No doubt there would be the usual boyish pranks. He loved all of it and had a few ideas up his sleeve. He couldn't wait. He put aside his thoughts about Bingham. He gloated about McKean. Would Oldman pin that on the co-op.

Bingham had guessed he hadn't finished with the residents of Reynold's Hall. He'd track them down. Bingham knew she was a done deal.

The boys would help. That bloody lefty nuisance, Luna, was out of the way — a fucking vegetable. He had only to transfer the money and Bingham's bridge-playing days were over. He savoured it. After tomorrow's celebrations he'd get down to the task of erasing the co-operative altogether. History. Stead, he suspected, was with the late Oldman. He bathed in his success.

A simple phone call would suffice. The next morning, early, he was in the process of transferring money when two men collared him. Neither spoke. He never finished the transaction. They cuffed him and put a bag over his head. He didn't laugh — best not take the fun out of a practical joke by a couple of his paramilitary trainees. Good old boys. They tied him and carried him gently outside. He never saw them and neither spoke. That's training for you. He was aware of the fact he was in the back of a van. The journey took approximately twenty minutes which meant they would be at the camp. His excitement grew.

The hard-on melted away when the bag was removed and he found himself perched on France's harp-cable bridge, the Viaduc de Millau. (It appealed to Bingham and was inexpensive. Furthermore, it was a bridge). The windbreak barriers didn't deter the two burly left-party volunteers who launched a yelping Ken into space.

Bingham had checked the height and statistics: a three hundred and forty-three-metres drop. That was revenge! It was another assisted suicide. They followed instructions to the letter. No words were spoken and the job done at dusk. Crepuscular stuff. No confirmation needed. The newspapers would do that. Thirteen cards of the same suit is a perfect bridge hand. That day she felt she'd held that hand.

Articles revealed some of his movements in the shadowy paramilitary world of right-wing populism. He was wearing the ultras blue t-shirt too, not one worn for paint balling. Guns – the Great Replacement. The yellow beanie was found. Replace that, you fucker. To the police it seemed anomalous, to her friends full of meaning. Luna was a friend, the moon, intuitive, magical and for Ken dangerous.

Jack David cleaned out Ken's files on them. Knowledge might be power, and Ken's files were there to do the dirty. Power was diffuse and not always negative. He chose not to read them. Jack David would enjoy disappearance. His new faceless status would amuse him no end. He was a bureaucratic genius, a man who knew the positives of bureaucracy and avoided the small-minded red-tape brigade who made the possible impossible. He worked the other way around. His grasp and knowledge of bureaucracy meant the paperwork was in order. He didn't want to know what Bingham had planned for Ken. He tracked him down; he told her his whereabouts; no paperwork required. Dear me. Bingham was something else. The obituary filled in the details of this dreadful suicide. The yellow beanie filled in a few more for some others.

*In his office Griffin pinned a note to the Ken Briggs file that read 'missing in action' and filed it away.*

## Chapter 48

Four emails sailed from Penny's laptop, two on his unsafe account to the university. The first was to Brigid agreeing the terms of his retirement. He thanked her for her support in the past. The second, a blanket mail, went to all the catering and support staff, thanking them. The third, on his safe account, went to his friend Periwinkle, asking whether there was any news. The fourth went to Phibes at the school. It wished him good luck and invited him to call him and arrange for a dram sometime before he left. He wasn't sure if Phibes took a drink. He'd been an important contact.

He deleted dram and wrote shandy. 'I miss the yard and the craic. I trust that Liz is okay? You take care. Please give my best wishes to all. Penny.'

He speculated what Hart had made of his coded stories. Raed was more honourable. A wedge between the two was inevitable. He'd no wish to speed that process up.

Liz had some earnest questions to ask Jim. The police had testified to Penny's innocence. The emails had petered out, then another arrived that implicated Mikey. Liz was beginning to hear alarm bells.

The email read: 'What's it like having a shifter in the house? A canine pet, or is he more than that?'

Her staff were unaware of her predicament. She was beginning to distrust those around her. In return for her inexplicable silence, she received stares and whispers. Mikey was doing well at school which was a plus. The man Hart had been sympathetic. Raed had been business-like. The malicious emails were untraceable. The yard wasn't yet a glass box under the ground though to Liz it felt like it. The monster mansion. She retreated to her office and closed the door.

Penny wrapped his favourite green scarf in a double-wrapped noose, donned a pair of thick woollen gloves (which were meant to prevent his lifelong habit of sticking his hands in his pockets) and set off walking. Periwinkle called. He dug his phone out, removed the gloves, and swiped the screen.

"I'll get right to the point. The hacking came from inside – literally!"

Penny interjected. "HMP Oakwood, I presume?"

"You knew?"

"No-brainer, but I'm grateful. I needed it confirmed! He must have intercepted emails from me to Liz in the first instance, and vice versa, our mail too and Mikey and Jim's. Getting holiday information is one thing, but how he sussed anything out on Jim or Mikey I don't know. He did better than us. You should take to hacking or hacking the hacker. Prisons tend to be informative places, his ability wasted. A

320

black hat with a small mind, a weak ego, and malice as his driving force. Jim is it I assume?"

"He is it, as you say, and quite a handy man. Like salt, sugar and fat, a hidden menace; an undercover eliminator."

"Or sitting down?" Slime ball seemed more appropriate for Jim and sitting down the new smoking. He learnt that from Griffin.

"When I spoke to Saida I left Lance out."

Penny thought of Liz.

Periwinkle pursued the topic of Lance. "Lance seems determined to make life miserable for you and all around you. We will come back to that. He is talented in the extreme, though a silly man. There is no reasonable doubt: he sent them. One word from you would see him languishing in prison for quite some time. What do you want to do?"

"Nothing at the moment, and thanks. You're a pal." Did Periwinkle really use the expression 'cover is blown'? No.

Penny turned up at the meeting. He desired information. He had something up his sleeve. He was more his old self. His smiling entrance took Hart by surprise. He shifted uncomfortably on his seat as Penny beamed around the room. Penny removed a pair of black woollen gloves and dropped them on the table. He had worn them while running and wiped his nose on them. Hart eyed them disdainfully.

With an obscure comment about east, west, and another about poles apart, Penny sat close to Hart. He took a sheet of paper from his backpack and placed it on the table alongside a cheap ballpoint, which he dug out of his pocket before Evie could supply the pencils and paper.

The proximity of the devil incarnate unsettled Hart. He kept glancing sideways, then moved his chair to afford some distance.

Hart's briefing on Liz was succinct. He didn't have much to go on. "We have no idea why she is receiving these troubling messages!"

Hart was holding a handful of treys and deuces. His position opposite Dove meant he really didn't have a partner in the game. Penny had all the cards. Hart was being expedient.

Penny led with no trump. "Are we saying here that 'we' haven't a clue?"

Mindful of Penny's angle, Dove responded quickly; not to support Hart rather to avoid a clash at this point. "The messages began only with the boy Mikey moving in. Has anyone spoken to him at length? Checked his laptop?"

Hart said, "Noted," thanked Dove and turned to Raed.

She put her pencil down and said, "I did, though not at length. The boy is clever, that's for sure, and he may have been lying. He claimed to know nothing about our werewolf. He is truly knowledgeable about the shifters, howlers he called them. A reference to a film, I believe. There is one lingering issue: who procured the badger's claws and other vile accessories Gran used? Forensics revealed her and the victim's DNA traces. No one else's. No way did she obtain them."

Penny nodded. "The guest was invited in, in this case."

Hart led. "I'm aware of the film and biblical reference, Penny. Raed and Dove have a point."

322

Penny did not wish for a sticker for his comment. He had to protect his mates, Hoody and Oldman and, for the time being, Lance.

Raed managed a smile towards him on Hart's blind side. Hart turned quickly and missed it.

Raed was convinced Mikey was involved. "It's back to square one. DI Hart can talk to the boy. I want another word with Liz who we now know is living a lie – that's all we need to say about Jim's role abroad. His government connections won't give him protection here. It is best he doesn't know we are aware of them."

She'd already put out a Red Notice through Interpol on Jim.

After a short silence which Penny failed to fill, she spoke again. "Periwinkle suggested we might find out more about the family – Liz, Jim, Mikey and his pop."

Penny smiled at the use of pop.

She finished by saying, "We need to shift our attention onto the school."

Hart was unaware of the origins of Periwinkle's reasoning. Penny's face revealed nothing. What had happened to Penny, the man who displayed all his feelings with the transparent innocence of a child? Well, some children. He sat next to Hart poker-faced, wanting to be loved, learn and contribute. For once, he wasn't twiddling with pens, pencils or elastic bands. The sheet of A4 stayed where it was, the ballpoint on top. The sheet remained blank. Bridge time.

Penny spoke. "Yes, we've got to get back to the beginnings. Gran is very fond of the boy. Her condition apart, she is cunning enough to feign her forgetfulness. Or she is quite poorly." Eyeing the baleful Hart he then misquoted a phrase from The Five adding, "We watch and we listen to the silence, Hart. Yours included."

Hart appealed to Raed again, his manner suggesting he hit this man.

Dove offered a safety valve. "Silence can mean that no one knows anything. Here we suspect *they* do, the family."

Penny addressed Hart face to face. "Look here. Yours isn't a conspiracy of silence. It's a lack of joined-up thinking, your unwillingness to share." He enjoyed using such a chestnut, one drawn from an old lexicography relating to his late university life-wank words bingo. He'd forgotten that there was some fun in university life. His not-yet-official retirement was beckoning. "The family ties don't concern Jim though they may affect his standing in the community. People here don't blab. We are your only chance, Hart, and if you choose to alienate us where will you be then?"

"Ma'am," Hart protested.

Read's left hand signalled, showing her palm in a gesture that prompted quiet from all.

Penny wasn't going to let go. As far as he was concerned, if they didn't act on his advice, they could go and fuck themselves. His tone implied such. "You have been examining the wrong hard drives. Have you checked Liz's more closely, both of them, the work one and the home one? What about Jim? Has anyone asked for his laptop? Don't bother. It will be heavily encrypted. You won't find anything. Has anyone spoken with him? Have you checked Mikey and Max's laptops?" He didn't stop. "Grill Mikey. Grill George and Kyle. Check their computers."

Raed sat tight. Hart deserved his dressing down. He had access to information on Jim and had held it back. Some dubious link to the secret services was Periwinkle's message. He wouldn't divulge any more on the phone. She went along with Penny's scathing attack yet didn't endorse it openly. Hart's policing was intelligent, informed yet unshared. It wasn't so much the taking of Penny's laptop, and betrayal of trust that held her back from supporting a colleague, it was the fact she felt Hart had manipulated her. It was to get at Penny rather than the truth.

Penny drifted as the room descended into a speculative gloom. He needed to go back to, and reconsider, Oldman's dilemma. Then Liz. The relationship between Liz and the boy was rumoured to be more than one of teacher and pupil. Suspension would be automatic pending an enquiry. Not the first time such had occurred in those circles. The Cleveland child abuse case had left an indelible stain on the area.

Cautiously Penny added, "Liz is a good headteacher, a decent person, who may well have strayed from the truth due to circumstances which involve her plumber husband, who is but a hired gun." He hadn't finished his admonishment of Hart. "You do have many good points. Ask more of Max to Jack, his father, who despite grieving is a clear-sighted man. I would assess he is on the edge, though he must know more about his son. Who were his friends? His enemies? Who did he relate to at school? Who did he call on? Ask about money, pocket money."

Afterwards, Raed issued orders to grill the boys, the whole school if necessary, and for Hart to bring in the said laptops using discretion.

Hart was downcast. "Yes, ma'am. What of Gran?"

"I will see to Gran. I will see to Liz. I will bring them in here if necessary, to where it won't be so cosy. Bring Kyle and George in together and then separate them. Wherever Kyle is, bring him here. They will need an adult with them."

The next few days saw a flurry of activity: knocking on doors, collecting laptops, bringing people in, juveniles escorted by adults, adults complaining, and Gran in a cell faced by Raed. Raed had had her fill of untruths and bullshit. That was her opening statement. Without tea and rich tea biscuits Gran attempted her singing routine then dried up. Her voice became a broken cackle.

Raed sat tight. "You are going to prison shortly and I'll make sure it isn't a rest home. If you want a drink there's water.

"I don't drink water," she whined.

"Your choice. It's there for you. We're bringing Mikey in and Liz later. You may have to share the cell with Liz."

Gran didn't like that. She didn't seem as upbeat either. Thereafter, she was still, and gave up crooning. She ignored the question about access to free legal advice, laughed at the suggestion she might want to contact someone. The medical advice was pending.

Liz informed them Jim had arrived at night and almost immediately left on an urgent job. No one present was surprised. Would he return? His links made life difficult for Hart. It was duly noted that she had waited until he departed before contacting them.

Periwinkle had sussed out Jim's extra-curricular activities, and they weren't pleasant. He gave his findings to Raed. Jim wasn't exactly the government man working on confidential matters – he was a cold-blooded fixer. He spared them details at the meeting but shared with Dove and Penny. His thinking was that Jim would not have any cover. Liz was an unsuspecting alibi.

"He will have to drop out of sight," said Periwinkle.

Penny had another slant.

## Chapter 49

Penny's academic senses, honed in the field of detective-cum-spy thrillers, told him that following recrimination, retribution would occur. Jim would be spitting blood. Penny felt sorry for Hart. The headteacher thing about having a spouse on her arm for functions was relevant. Liz had an old-fashioned nature. Was her natural inclination to punish?

Pending enquiries Liz was suspended from all duties and a deputy put in place. The slightest sniff of a scandal was enough to remove her from her position. Penny felt responsible, though he held his tongue, he had said enough. Raed was ahead. She must have heard the rumours. Dad was right.

Raed despatched Hart to Billingham to follow up some information on twins who were dealing in crack and drone. Hart liked his new role. He wasn't comfortable with the twin aspect. Twins were out there to fuck him over. Those lads were identical and shrewd. He wasn't going to allow them to outwit him – this time.

For an hour or more after the meeting a semblance of normality returned. Reality was not appropriate a word. Dove and Penny made songs up, as they had done in the past when together. Goodbye Hart was a chart buster. The number of songs that offered the chance for crude satire kept them going for quite some time. Then normality fizzled out. They both had sympathy for the man.

For Liz, the precious objects took on other meanings. With time on her hands she saw them as camouflage, a cover-up for Jim's activities. She wasn't quite sure of the details. Her take was that the police officer covered his back. What had this loving man she married been up to? Her own guilt consumed her. She began to fill the spaces with worried speculations.

Penny cared for Liz. He knew she would act on her misgivings. Liz was not a bystander. The shattered pieces of the Cubist vase lay where they fell next to the now silent piano in non-geometric shards. It was when Liz would act that made him nervous. He needed to do a few things first. He stopped going to the pub. He purposefully built up on his obsessions, and thus refined his authorial instincts by imagining differing scenarios of how and when an attack would ensue. One thing he concluded: it would be full-on. He considered skipping but never got a rope. He sent an email through his unsafe account to Periwinkle and onto Lance:

'I don't know what's going on here, Periwinkle. Liz is angry. I suspect she is on the edge over the emails and her suspension and will act without using her head now that Jim has gone. I hope it resolves itself. Jim is another story... I wish we knew more about Jim. The police are checking emails from Mike and Max... looking into Jim's bank accounts. They will probably find the hacker too and he or she will go down. Best, Ronnie.'

Aware that Lance was intercepting emails Periwinkle left out key details. What lay behind Penny's warning Lance? Or was he goading him? Lance might hack Jim's laptop or phone. Liz had had a clean sheet until her suspected fling with Mikey. For him, it was a tragedy. The reply:

'I'm sure it will resolve itself. P.'

Periwinkle checked. Lance had but a month left of his sentence. That would depend on forces he wasn't aware of. The venom in Lance would one day destroy him. Of that, Penny was certain. The cause of his malice was indiscernible. Did he assume he had not got what he felt were his just rewards? Did he prioritise with 'Lance' at the top? No abuse came to light. Profiling was a farce. He was vindictive, clever in the extreme, and warped. Try as he might, Lance's actual physical self – his looks and demeanour – escaped Penny. The thought of him brought on an attack of aphantasia, at least that's what he thought it was. He tried counting sheep and failed. It was, he thought, a combination of his dyscalculia and a touch of aphantasia. Visual images escaped him.

Penny felt lost. Twice he made to call round to Liz's and twice he returned home. Once, about to press the bell outside the closed gates, he turned and slouched away. Things were coming to a head. Raed was getting somewhere. Gran burbled on about Liz to Raed and her interfering with the boy. She clammed up afterwards refusing to define the nature of the so-called interference. The very word interfere took Raed to Liz's house. Gran's reliability was suspect, but she couldn't ignore the information. Denying her prosocial self, Liz told the truth. Some risk assessment and a lie would've been appropriate.

Max and George had terrified Kyle and were in awe of Mikey. Max's computer told other stories. Max was up to his neck in things clandestine, pornographic, and Mikey and he were regular communicators. That was worrying. Badger's claws.

*Was Oldman dead? Some wished it so. Others believed so. The absence of any news of him plagued Griffin. His vow to silence on what happened that day in the lock-up remained strong. It was strengthened further when Campbell died suddenly. The fearful sweats returned. The news sent disconcerting messages up and down his spine, a black-framed telegram with his name on it, one that brought back the uneasy spectre of Oldman.*

*Satisfied that if he stayed put behind his desk and said nothing all would be well, he pulled his chair into his desk and did just that. He was sure that Oldman was abroad, in the old-fashioned sense. Campbell died in his sleep. A death certificate was issued. He wondered if it was 'pseudocide' and, like Oldman, he was still abroad. He remembered the tale of the man who staged his death, faked a certificate and misspelled registry. That cheered him somewhat but didn't detract from his gloomy thoughts. He fought his beliefs and rationalised. Belief over reason was popular in the press and in politics. He wasn't going to fall for it.*

*Griffin decided not to go to the funeral. Sarah, his new boss, never queried his decision. She left the office in a smart black suit. On her way to the funeral, she stuck her head in and complimented him on his excellent work. However old, or experienced, a compliment served the recipient well. In the office on his own he sensed the presence of the late Oldman. He went to the filing cabinet and pulled the folder on Stead. She had* disappeared like a puff of smoke. A file accessible to a few only, located Jack David. Stead was brainy, a cunning sod. It crept into his mind that she was party to Campbell's death. Not only had Campbell been guilty of harassing the old navy man, but obsessive in his search for Oldman. Campbell's desire to find his colleague Eames and curry favour with his new boss drove it along. Had he uncovered a lead? He left no evidence to imply a breakthrough. He considered Bingham too, a woman not to be messed with; disappeared. So many loose ends.

A long-winded draft email concerning Eames dated three days before he died remained unsent. It implied he was following up networks to find Eames and Oldman, dead or alive. Griffin, having little faith in his old team and a pathological fear of Oldman, chose to move on. He filed the hard copies away in a dark corner. He took out a file that was burgeoning: the Ken Briggs file. He looked at the documents. Griggs had received it from an anonymous source inside Reynold's Hall.

Anonymous, my arse. It was Oldman. Everything was Oldman.

On this occasion he was wrong. He returned to his desk.

Penny found the characters he created coming alive. They found a life of their own and were making their own way through the intrigue. Oldman lived. Griffin represented his own deep misgivings.

Griffin had suffered loss, something he would dream about for ever. He knew the import of the small dreams of a lost train ticket, a piece of baggage missing, returning to his locker and his coat missing, a wrong turning, a bus missed, missing trousers, a stolen bicycle. Rebekah featured in those dreams and things went wrong, or more crudely turned to shit. In the day he dreamed of dreams. Odd shoes. They weren't frightening in the sense of a nightmare, and they were always short. The moment of waking left him drained and on edge. He decided to suffer them rather than seek professional help. He dubbed those strange dreams 'mindings'. His optimistic side believed his sense of loss was down to anxiety and was temporary. Forfeit, even in fantasy, taught him to be careful.

Liz emailed Penny to apologise for her poor guesses and assumptions and asked to meet up, offering an open invitation to the house and in bold wrote: 'any time, Ron!'. His reply was discrete. He realised Liz's brief encounter meant her career was over. Gran had seen to that. The werewolf's last victim. No claws required, well not a badger's.

'I'm so pleased, Liz. It was difficult for me as we worked well together. Will be in touch. Best Wishes. Ron'.

He never mentioned Jim. Liz, he felt for. Jim had used her. Beware the rescuer.

## Chapter 50

Raed and Hart concentrated their investigation on Kyle and George. Together they interviewed the pair. In a change of heart she brought them in together. Hart chose the quiet role. It allowed him to listen and make judgements on their speech patterns and body language. Raed did the questioning. A parent had to attend. Both boys insisted on being alone. Raed countermanded that and insisted one parent accompanied them. Their mothers drew the short straw. Raed thought it a desirable choice. George's mum had worked as a juvenile officer in a past life. Introductions were formal, the fact made clear that it was an interview, not an interrogation. Raed emphasised the need to record it for all parties' benefit. The questioning began informally. Evie was at hand to work the recording. (A copy to be given to each parent on Raed's instructions).

Both women were working mothers. Raed had done her prepping and had discovered that their fathers were part-time workers and guessed that like so many local men felt on the scrap heap.

She began. "Tell us a bit about Max."

Kyle eyed George.

George responded. "He was our mate, a member of our gang."

"Yes, I understand. I was in a gang at your age." She smiled as if reminiscing. "There was only four of us, but we were cool." Whether the gang defined them, whether Max actively recruited them or they joined through peer pressure was worth finding out. "What made you start the gang?"

Not answering the question he said, "Max and I started it."

Kyle's discomfort was beginning to show.

Raed focussed on him. "Must be nice to be in a gang."

Kyle eyed his mother. "I guess so."

She eyed both. "Could anyone join?"

George puffed himself up, offended. "No, only special friends."

His mother interrupted. "They all hung out together, the three of them. Gary and I often worried about what they were doing. Sometimes he would come home with a new t-shirt, which he claimed to have earned through a favour."

A silence ensued. Kyle's eyes shifted side to side. Raed turned away from him.

She addressed George's mother. "Thanks, it's really important we find out about Max. Any small thing might help us."

George was unrepentant.

Kyle chipped in, "Max put pressure on us to join."

Raed kept her focus on George. Kyle was growing more desperate by the minute.

She took it in her stride. "Joining a gang is common. It depends on what the gang does. It might start as a peer group, it might end up as a street gang, or worse, a criminal organisation." She let it sink in.

Hart was observing. Kyle was sweating. His mother, a tall handsome woman, was staring sideways at her son. Raed highlighted the problem of gangs and high-risk behaviour, sexual and drug oriented. That did it. Kyle was at breaking point. Kyle's mother mentioned some dope she'd confiscated. Kyle blabbed that Max got it from someone.

George was unmoved. He cast a sidelong shut-the-fuck-up glance at Kyle and remained haughty. Raed signalled with clasped and unclasped hands and an oblique smile at Hart, which signalled him to take over. She thanked them for being open and honest so far.

As Kyle looked relieved, she turned on him. "Why did you want to belong to the gang, Kyle?" She deferred to press on the actions of the gang, to eke out more about the joining. George, she imagined, was in it for outlaw status, Kyle for protection. The economic environment and the area was ripe for such, though Max's role was central.

"Why did Max ask you to join, Kyle?" Kyle's mother nudged him.

"I was hard up and fed up and he said I could get pocket money."

George was flexing his knuckles and bunching a fist. Both mothers cast accusing looks at their sons. Kyle snapped. George was furious. His vehement capacity showed. His mother was stronger and restrained him. George was like a coiled spring. His mother's facial expressions told him enough was enough. George shut up. The rest poured out.

Kyle ended by saying, "I was made to do it."

Hart checked the recorder. "Made to do what?"

From ten years old Max and George practised their shitty goings-on, bullying of the extreme kind and hazing. Sexual threats, violence and protection were the core. This was not the low-level stuff she and her young cronies had got into in the street, this was serious shit. Choice is a peculiar thing. Raed felt sorry for the parents, their hopeless situation, the dreams and desires for the future of their progeny, the lack of work and alternative activities in the area.

Kyle made a full statement. George's mother marched out the station, her son in tow. Raed let them go. Detaining them for twenty-four hours seemed pointless. Hart's observations were insightful. The malevolent streak in George was one to watch out for. The element of defiance, the hubris, and the lack of guilt made Hart feel sorry for his parents. What could they do? He consulted the probation service and sought effective probation pathways.

They had yet to establish a link between Jim and Max. Max led a group that initiated kids in extreme ways. The initiations bordered on the sick, the violent, and included sexual favours. Recriminations were carnal and wrong-headed. Their parents would have a lot to say. George was a co-partner, Kyle a lackey, but a willing one. Their mothers left, sick with worry and disappointment. The naughty step hadn't resolved anything. It never would. Kids don't hate steps. And steps don't resolve unwanted behaviour, rather they create resentment.

The naughty step apart, this was hazardous stuff according to the textbooks on child abuse. Hart was coming to grips with the underlying unpleasantness. No avenues pointed towards who might have killed the boy. Kyle and George, part of the admission's team, as they called themselves, were panicky on the issue of Max's death, and weren't sure if other kids had done for him.

Bullying was hateful, and it was rife in all levels of society, and in all classes. Torture and death as rebuttal was the realm of the sick. Raed needed to talk with Liz. The hunt was on for Jim. And Jim was out hunting.

Hart moved to Middlesbrough temporarily and arrested a man for stealing his own car. Left at the garage, then charged an enormous bill, one that did not reflect the original estimates or problems, the customer had taken his spare keys and driven it away. Hart could see the comical side of it.

The terrible twins had been nicked, caught with the goods. To cap it all there was the sad death of a young woman which occurred outside a pub late at night. The autopsy revealed a cocktail of drink and drugs, including a lab made high. He issued the statement. The twins were going down. A result! His radio appeal concerning county lines and the recruitment of youngsters groomed to move and supply drugs opened up channels. Penny listened on his phone as he walked. It was very good.

Scarf, huge gloves, fleece under his denim jacket, and an old warm overcoat, Penny wandered into the Duke William and sat alone in a corner with a lime and soda. The place had been tastefully refurbished. Two old men sat in a corner. One wore a flat cap and had an empty pipe in his mouth, a sad, defiant gesture. The scene recalled a Cézanne painting. He wrestled for a while with Oldman's plight. What of his own battles? Where was his searching gaze?

"Shite," he exclaimed loudly as his mind gave birth to an idea.

The two men turned and nodded as if in agreement. There was a fault in the plot. It needed resolving. Placing his empty glass on the bar, he left. At home, he locked and bolted the door. He usually left it unlocked – a symbol of trust. He opened his laptop.

In the morning, still alive, he ate a light breakfast, wrapped up and caught a bus into Loftus, and walked. Eyes turned away as he strolled. He wanted to say hiya in his best local accent: how do; now then; good morning; hey-up. He thought about the women in the Bowers and Batemans families. Did they share a chat on the weather, lean into a new baby's pram and make a comment? What did they think? He stared in the gift shop window, the brown box and the eco-friendly stuff.

A nor'easter, as the matelots dubbed it, was coming in. Heavy rain was to follow.

He called Liz. He left a cheery voicemail. "Pleased you got in touch. I'm in Loftus. Be good to catch up."

He felt some relief that she hadn't picked up. He wanted to meet her but feared the outcome. The emptiness in his gut countermanded the ideas in his head, a mixture of things past, present, future. He walked to the lot. The temperature had lifted though the wind persisted. Hoody was there alone sitting next to his bike.

"Given up on the bike, Doc?"

"Police took me laptop."

"Got any pervy pictures hidden?"

"Thanks, pal, but no, work only. I have a query for you."

"Fire away."

"Tell me what you know about Liz the Destroyer and Mikey."

The weir came back as an analogy as the information flowed. It was a shock. Hoody was exceedingly well informed. The police certainly had their potential whistle-blowers though someone in Loftus had stolen the pea. Max and his protection racket was old hat. Liz and Mikey's brief encounter too. It helped confirm things.

"You really are something, you guys! Respect!" He put his palms forward and Hoody slapped both.

Intelligence had come from within the community to an honorary member from those who didn't betray confidences. Furthermore, it didn't seem value laden. He strode away. Respect he had. He didn't look back. He never saw Hoody again. He often wondered how they were, all five of them, and what they might be doing. He never knew the others' names. He exchanged his Barracuda BMX for a new ride, a more sedate ride with a pannier on the back to hold a bit of shopping.

Unable to sort out the differences in the plot in his novel and native intrigue, Penny began to doubt his geometric assessments, the lines drawn back to the root. Juggling with his ideas, he walked across the fields toward the coastal path. It was as if the world had deserted him. The wind was blowing stronger. The strings of rain petered out. In his bag he carried his blue waterproof trousers and a fish knife. Oldman owned such a knife. He made for the tooth rock and, once there, sat staring at the shoreline, studying the outgoing tide, the in between, the all-important grey areas between high tide and low. As it receded, piles of seaweed remained. Gulls and crows flocked. He took a jazz apple from his bag and bit into it. Hybrids were interesting and he promised to look up jazz apple. Water followed from the side pocket. Engrossed in replotting his loci, he saw Liz only at the last minute.

"Hello, Ronnie. May I join a fellow outcast for lunch?"

"Hiya, Liz. Please do." She had a plastic food container under her arm.

"I see you've brought your bait box!"

"Yep, in west Yorkshire, Caleb's home area, it's a snap box."

"Must be nice to be travelled."

Liz opened the box and chose a sandwich. She offered him one. He refused, showing her his own sandwiches wrapped in greaseproof and held by a discarded post office elastic band. Taking a last bite of his apple, he threw the core towards the cliff edge for the birds. He turned to Liz. She perched next to him on the rock, her long legs stretched out, jeans rolled up, her bare feet resting on the grass, her socks and walking boots discarded next to her. Her girlish sensuality matched her giggle. Her youthful face showed no sign of the years of teaching nor her recent situation; her fair skin with the freckles barely below the surface, her youthfulness a product of being with kids.

Liz opened the conversation. "Mikey is all I have at the moment. I don't want to discuss Jim. He's not even a part

341

of this place. He never will be. My name is not Trout. Worse still, I don't know if Jim's his real name... or Trout. He," her words fractured as she spoke, "has lived a lie. I can't say I'm any better."

"Tell me about Mikey."

Liz was never one to waste words. "We slept together and then regretted it. Guilty as charged. Where Raed got her information from is debatable, but Gran is my bet. As you know, even a whisper of such means suspension and that is usually of a permanent nature. Mikey is old for his age, mature, the reason the other boys were in awe of him. Since that night we made a vow to stay apart. I do love him. And in his boyish way, he has a crush on me."

"What did you know of Max's gang?" He needed to change the subject.

"I feel stupid. I never saw it. What started out as childish games turned to criminality. They were running a protection racket. It involved bullying and sexual deviance. That doesn't lead us to the culprits who abducted and tortured a youth – police didn't publicise the torture aspect – but this is Loftus, a small town in the north. People don't talk to the police. But they listen. And I am from Loftus. I hope to God Jim wasn't party to it!" She looked at Penny for support.

None came.

He stretched the rubber band that held his sandwiches around his fingers, expanding the fingers as if exercising them. "My guess is that Max was going to tell."

"Tell what?"

Penny digressed inwardly. What did Jim think of his wife? He wasn't sure he wanted to go there. Mikey might be in danger. He switched tack. "Raed will rope in the whole school – gang members, victims, swots, geeks, the maligned and mistreated."

"I keep an eye on my nerds and geeks and protect them. There is often something resilient about the geek, anyhow. I first came across the werewolf thing when one kid made a joke."

"Go on."

"A slanted reference to the full moon. A fifteen-year-old who was being cocky warned me to stay at home as there was a full moon that night. Until the first attack, I made nothing of it. When murder occurred, I did."

"Why didn't you go to the police?" He answered for her. "You're from Loftus." It could be the whole of the northeast.

"Not that simple." She stared out at a boat fishing the coastline.

Penny watched the blue and white coble and the swelling sea and was pleased he was on shore.

Liz was heedless to the bout of severe weather coming in. "To think that my children were party to this made me disgusted with myself. That was horrid in itself. The ghastly truth is worse." Her face told him she knew Jim was party to it. "I was in denial." A tear trickled, then she wiped it away.

"You knew Jim was party to something?"

"I couldn't get my head around it. Every time I was with him, the man I loved, I put it on the back burner. My whole married life a falsehood. Gran, bless the old cow, puddled as she is, sussed it out. As for the werewolf scenario, how she got hold of the claws is anyone's guess. Mikey said you can get them on the Internet."

That Mikey wasn't a part of the protection racket was emphatic in emails. Who bought the claws? Who told Gran about Fenris? He needed to say something about Jim.

Her next statement shifted the conversation. "Raed is clever. And so is that annoying man Hart. Raed is different. She's more open, more approachable."

"Raed is police, Liz. She may be smart, yet no different to Hart. She lives for her work." The coble began to roll uncomfortably in the rising swell.

"Sexy Saida, as my schoolboys nicknamed her, deduced that kids had something to do with it, or knew stuff."

"Liz," he put his arm round her shoulder as he spoke, "Max's laptop is beginning to reveal his secrets. The missing diary is no coincidence. Raed knows how to hold her tongue until she gets what she wants, and she will. Hart is another kettle of fish. We have a history." Avoiding an explanation of the origins of the phrase 'kettle of fish', and momentarily seeing Watteau's *Fête Champêtre,* and a wild Scottish salmon boiling in the pot, enticed him to make a pun on Hart's capacity for pique. He stayed focussed.

Liz's alarm was apparent. "Are you saying Raed knows who did what? She can't arrest a whole school!"

"She knows who gave the orders. She also knows who is responsible for my sacking."

Liz looked uncomfortable. "Dear God. How the kids know of torture and pain and its indelibility is from lord knows where. Not from school, I trust."

He begged to differ, but kept his gob shut. He squeezed her in a hug of encouragement. "Collective suffering is common to the area, and common to torture."

She deviated. "I don't know how you guys resolved the Bateman/Bowers dispute. It was the beginning of a breakdown of one particular enclave and may well have repercussions on the case. I hope so."

He offered no explanation.

She continued. "Mikey will stay with me until I can arrange better for him. Locals will not forget our brief sexual encounter. I will have to live with the guilt and ridicule. Gran sussed out our dalliance by wit and native cunning. She will dance rings around the police, singing all the while. Something tells me Raed knows all that too."

He took his arm from around her shoulder. In a gesture of closure, she placed the lid back on her sandwich box having eaten one sandwich only and put her socks and boots back on. She clambered to her feet as if to go. Placing the box down, she held his hands in hers and kissed him lightly on the cheek, then stepped back. The kiss was a peck only, fresh and friendly. He wanted to take that pace forward.

"Thanks." Liz's torment was apparent.

"Liz, you are a great headteacher. You display a canny knack of knowing, combined with an uncanny intuition, informed by investigation and topped with foresight." He stopped at that. It wasn't quite the truth.

She pointed at the sea and an incoming wave. "It's a beautiful painting. Thanks for the reference. Just as God creates out of nothing, your Mr Courbet does so too."

Penny understood her reference to Courbet's *The Wave* as a goodbye. He watched her long legs stride away across the fields towards what he was not sure. Her home had changed. The sandwich box remained on the ground. The soul had gone out of her home. He resisted the desire to go after her with the box. He sat back down and gaped at the North Sea. The wind had fallen into calm. The sea was a palette of three colours, blue, green, and an ominous purple, painted with a palette knife. Courbet sharpened his palette knives along both edges. A double-edged tool.

As a small wave broke, a spectrum of light interrupted the three colours and mixed them on the sea's canvas. How did she know of his love for Courbet's works? He guessed he'd told her. The boat had gone. The sea began to show some turbulence.

So many minds were involved, and each unquiet. He never got round to telling Liz the whole truth about Jim. Jim had another family. Jim was not just a killer, but a bigamist. Liz would never know. He turned from the huge expanse of sea, aware of its power to frighten and to calm. He walked back to Loftus as the sun disappeared behind a bank of cloud. Deepdale pathway felt lonely and he breathed a sigh of relief as The Mars Inn came into view.

## Chapter 51

Outside Raed's office his memories of their first encounter caused a brief gaucheness, an awkward happy feeling. She called him in, left her desk and as was her custom, moved towards him hand outstretched.

"Sit down, Ronnie."

The familiar use of his name felt nice. He eased into the chair opposite her and beamed. The spilling of the beans was not inopportune. Raed listened to every word intently.

She made no notes. When a young police officer knocked, she insisted with a polite hand movement not to disturb them. He told her everything he knew about Gran, the intermarriage and the Lotto win.

He imagined she knew a bit of the story already. "Gran, addled or not, is very crafty and rich."

"I can only hazard a guess at your sources. I admire your wish to protect certain people. I think I could fill the gaps. The final thread, the reason for Max's death, escapes me. I'd have to delve into fiction for an answer. Max knew something about Jim."

"The headteacher has been really helpful." He had to wheedle out a reply. "I'd like to know what you think."

"Our files are growing by the minute, Ronnie. Max suffered the fate that spy systems, bullies, and dictators suffer when things go wrong, a bit like Stalin's purges... maybe." She paused for thought. "Gran has suffered, a particular type of torture, abuse, and her condition is evidence of it. She can't talk about it. She did the werewolf attacks. We will keep her locked away with those other poor unquiet minds. You unearthed much of what has gone on. To use current idiom; a lot of people won't go there. It says a lot for you. You'd make a good police officer."

She faced him directly. "Hart speaks highly of you to others. I can see why. He is in truth an upright police officer and his knowledge of the law is without question. If I pull in everyone for questioning that will indicate equality at least. If that is what I have to do, then I'll do it. Spies, torture, secrets hold places together. The world itself is an unsettled place." She breathed deeply. "The horror of Max's punishment and death is sinking in. I'll bring the perpetrators in. They are not locals. I have not forgotten the terror young Sara and Matty suffered, nor what Gemma went through. Both cases have unearthed a minefield."

Penny listened.

"Off the record, Jim's governmental connections has caused great difficulty, but Periwinkle is helping. Jim's crimes will not go unpunished. Gran's ungodly acts will bring punishment of a different sort."

Penny owed Raed for the notion of the unquiet, be it in life or the grave. He explained he had come to say thanks and goodbye.

"Thanks for staying around. We appreciate your skills," she laughed, "and competencies. Dove is staying around for a bit to help Jack, and of course Peri."

Her eyes and her use of the short form of Periwinkle's name spoke of her affection for a man Penny considered a dear friend. His originality, and ingenuity, contradicted his boyish good looks and unassuming manner. There was more to come from Peri.

"Dove's aptitude was apparent when I first met him. He is loyal and highly intelligent. You make an effective team." She smiled again, this time an introspective grin. "That some ignored the signs that you guys emit was their loss." She cocked her head to one side. "We do want to know what happened to the feuding families out of curiosity. Perhaps when Peri and I meet you elsewhere?"

He turned to go. Twice that day women had reached out to him. It felt good. First, the slender freckle-faced Liz, her bare legs stretched out near the tooth rock, then this sensual woman with a brain the size of the planet. He left in a daze. In his head were two unavailable women and, as always, an issue, and a burning fire in his momentarily frazzled brain. This time no theory came apart from the fact that life was complex, and when one thing turned up so did another that was comparable. A choice ensued.

He pictured Tammy, a fellow academic, and wondered if *fellow* was gender neutral. To him it was. Where was she? What was she doing? His awareness of a lifelong ability to miss out remained. It was his perception. Tammy, who was bright and bonny; Liz was his kind, crafted in the mould of the north – a northern lass – part of his northern renaissance, fashioned by a Holbein; Saida the other, an exotic, *The Grand Odalisque*, a work of art crafted by the hand of Ingres; one a teacher, the other a copper, and both spoken for. The latter spoke.

"What holds this place together?"

Outdoing Penny at his own game of hypophora, she answered. "I'm tempted to say disillusionment with politics, politicians and Westminster, with God, religion, with economics, family. A sense of defeat – even to the peculiar extent of a sense of pride in defeat." She signalled with her hands for inspiration.

None came.

"The cement that binds people together here is oppositional."

He mulled over the idea, then moved back. Reason was the problem. Up to date they, the so-called team, had all been reasoning. The answers lay in unreason with which he was familiar.

"Truth," she declared, "is a difficult one. It can be absolute and yet generally falls short." Raed looked away. "Gran is never coming back home, not even temporarily. The woman needs care. She says a lot, though it will need psychologists to sort out the accuracy of her statements. To her or hers it's all accurate." Gritting her teeth, she spoke to the air. "She had her coat on last time I saw her. She was ready to go out, a new leather handbag on her lap the size of a large black bin bag. She was as pleased as punch. She's going nowhere in the real world."

They said goodbye.

On the way home Penny saw Liz. She waved across the road. Mikey was alongside her. He waved and they walked on, Liz, a nodding acquaintances rather than a close colleague and Mikey who was unfathomable.

Dove had heard quite a bit from Gran. He learnt some songs that made the blood curdle. He had had a chat to Saida. Max had realised the path was narrowing and had tried to get out. He had set the parameters. There was no getting out. He was the casualty of his own rules. Subsequent searches of the house never found his diary. It would no doubt tell the story, the boyish delight in horror, scaring others by being strong; being a part of something that was nothing. His laptop did.

Penny had been in 'The Life Boys' and he liked that. Joining anything these days met with derision. Where were the youth clubs, the Scouts and the Boys' Brigade, the controlled hangouts? Max must have confided in somebody. Penny's guess was Liz.

Caught in a circle of regret, he put the kettle on at Dove's and Periwinkle's digs. "Let's have tea and biscuits."

Oldman offered a way forward, along with Stead and Saida.

\\\

Raed commandeered a suitable building in the school. The objective: to close the files on Max's wrongdoings. Parents brought kids in day in and day out. The files grew. Raed brought Kyle and George in again. Raed got tough.

Penny, she heard, was up to stuff, a phrase concomitant with his name. He wasn't around to hear the parental abuse. Dove was. He called Penny.

"They think she's a nutter."

Penny added to that, "A brave woman."

Hart came back from hell and confessed to liking his time in the Boro. He'd been to a football match. The evidence showed in his use of the barbed insults he'd gathered from the fans, mostly aimed at their own team, and 'most suitable' for his repertoire.

Dove queried, "Was that the match they lost against ten oil drums after injury time?"

Hart managed a faint smile.

In the Boro, scallies abounded and were visible. He was having the time of his life. Visions of a new *Robocop* soon disappeared, subsumed by comforting paperwork. The amount of police work and the detail was considerable. The never-ending trail of school kids to grill kept him busier than ever. At the end of the day he was happy. One of them would slip up. It was a matter of time. His new status as a Boro fan, be it a token one, and temporary, would never affect his real support for Wolves.

Raed interviewed Mikey. Liz came with him. Raed observed the affection between them. The focus was to be on what they knew of Max. Mikey knew Max a little, and swopped emails, though not his furtive nature and surreptitious activities. Mikey was an innocent in her eyes, though not free of guilt. Mikey was back at home. She still suspected he might have bought the claws for Gran. Max and Mikey were in the frame.

One of them had supplied the claws. Liz's apprehension with the situation was apparent.

Day five, Hart struck lucky.

Hart interviewed a girl called Ella. Hart was a model of correct behaviour. On his desk a well-thumbed copy of Wescott and Davies's *Interviewing Children Witnesses* bore testament to his academic and correct self. No room for errors. He avoided yes/no questions, passive, negative, and multiple questions. He was fully aware of the culture of silence in the place, and that lies came naturally as a defence mechanism. Fabrications required a good memory.

At the close of each day, tired though buzzing, the team reported many cases of speech disturbance and non-verbal behaviour. In a clever twist, Raed turned it into a learning experience for staff that were tired and at the end of their tether. They discovered anew the thrill of learning and found intriguing the linguistic techniques involved and the basics of gesture and body language.

Hart shared a sceptical joke with Raed about good practice. "I had the pleasure of cross-questioning Penny once. It was no use asking for a yes or a no."

Raed let it go. She had succeeded in keeping Penny at arm's length. Hart couldn't.

It was the aspect of non-verbal behaviour that gave Ella away. Bound as the others would be by some childish oath, Ella's nerve gave way. She kept glimpsing over her shoulder. Hart asked her if she was okay. She began to pour out the true character of Max and his gang. As a victim, the results of which had affected her health, she told her tale, close to tears. Oral evidence of the sexual favours followed.

Hart went by the book. The criterion for truthfulness, he informed a young constable, is difficult, though it must be stuck with. He had a handout prepared detailing such. There were to be no mistakes. Neither Hart nor Raed expected honesty from these children. It wasn't on offer. The timespan meant serious problems of memory which accounted for discrepancies. The absence of inconsistency in the statements revealed a bond that went beyond schoolyard comradeship: a fear of recrimination. He recalled George's hubris.

They compared notes; they contrasted findings. They learned the difference, and the differences were marginal. Raed set to the task an independent to go through statements. Penny and Hart would have been her dream team. He and Hart would've had a field day in reading below the surface.

Mr Popular had written another chapter of his novel. He detailed the changes that occurred within intelligence after rigorous research. Periwinkle clued him in. A footnote for Peri. His closing chapter of the abridged version almost completed, he returned to *The Tableau* and the field of battle with renewed vigour.

In the pub with Dove he said, "I feel more like my old self."

Dove wasn't sure. Was it subjective or objective this self to which he referred?

## Chapter 52

*Oldman awoke to hear his favourite song by The Platters, his daughter Bridie's shrill soprano torturing the lyrics. He tried to grimace. His face wouldn't complete the necessary movements. He couldn't speak. The coffin was spacious, yet he couldn't move. John and Yoko's Imagine, and the Cantata Herz und Mund und Tat und Leben played at his wedding, and which he adored, succeeded it. Was it the Westminster choir? Finally, Cat Stevens's Morning has Broken trilled around the crematorium which he could not see. Heart and mouth ceased to work together; a passage came to mind from The Tableau Twins book depicting Penny's return to the mausoleum that was the twin's gallery, handcuffed, the trauma of the operating theatre, the demons that refused to be exorcised, the writer a troubled soul.*

*Disembodied voices joined in, a spectral choir. Some sounded familiar. The eulogy was touching. His daughter Bridie's words steered a fine line between gravity, wit and grace, and highlighted things he'd quite forgotten about his time as a dad before he split up and became a non-person. He would never see them again. He'd lost everything. He passed out.*

*His journey into Hades (his ex-wife often said he should go) was not a straightforward one. He felt the coffin was still with him* on the trip. Hell, Heaven, purgatory. What the hell. It was crap. He could hear the singing afterwards and then announcements, though couldn't quite discern their content. His last images were of Primrose Stead. He'd loved her for what she was but blinded by his affection for her and tricked into distrust by his training he'd paid the price. Her abilities to thwart the law had come into play. The agency deserved the discredit. His very own employers had aided and abetted the bridge school. Someone else too: Ken. Damn the man.

He wasn't to know that recent changes wrought in the upper echelons of The Agency had come about partly as a result of his work. And they were for the better. Politics would never be divorced from the new regime but they weren't central. The woman in charge was grateful to him and to Stead. So grateful was she that Stead undertook one last job without her comrades. It was a task she undertook with a fervour that hadn't been present before.

Ah, the flight into Hades. It was comfortable and it was lengthy. An unbeliever, he wondered if there was a waiting room there for him – a purgatorial place.

"Primrose," he heard his voice say, and then he closed his eyes to sleep. The final sleep.

Penny had one or two more aces up his sleeve. He wrote with a new intensity. Oldman had a job to do.

Hell wasn't what Oldman expected. The beaches and sea were idyllic, the trees that curtseyed towards the ocean, the golden sands of Cheung Sha. Mr and Ms Westerman booked into their suite in Hong Kong. Mary Griggs received a postcard that read: 'Keep talking to the flowers. Sleep tight.' No name.

356

The next flight would take them elsewhere. It was several months before the newlyweds would move into their small accommodation in Bermuda. Hopping country to country was a necessary precaution. As a honeymoon it was perfect.

"Tell me about Fielding."

The new Ms Westerman took a deep breath. "Frank Fielding was a dear friend, and I was closer to him than the others. A witty and erudite soul, with a conscience. I can only surmise what went on in his head. He wasn't sleeping, the whole clandestine thing worried him. Just when we had agreed to pull out, he decided to spill the beans on Ken to an undercover agent who everyone in Reynold's Hall liked and knew was a mole. When Ken absconded we felt safe again."

"The late Mr Oldman a mole?" Oldman grinned foolishly.

"We too had our sources and Ken was our mole. Actually he was more than that: a mole, a rodent, and a predator, a grasshopper-mouse, nasty little fucker, a weasel. Shall we say he had a hold on us and leave it at that? His connections upstairs helped him until Lawson retired. Scratch the surface and lurking below was a white supremacist, a man whose army records indicated a vicious nature; a man who understood that knowledge is power and abused it. The removal business came to fruition under him. However, it was Bingham who masterminded it."

Oldman looked surprised.

"It was also Bingham who helped bring it to a close. She passed on the names — our names — to Griggs, knowing that upstairs was involved. A complicated woman Florence Bingham. You were wrong-footed. In fantasy football you get your chance to be a manager. We had a taste of working for the other side. Fantasy cleansing. Each of us had erred in our professions and

357

Ken knew it. How, is anybody's guess. Fielding was going to blow it. He was determined to expunge his past. If he'd lived a wee bit longer it would have been okay. What was unfathomable at that point was that it was your room that The Electrician wired. What did you do?"

He answered with a question. "Ken organised that?"

"Most likely – and The Electrician. Bingham sussed him out for what he was."

He suspected they let him win at bridge too. Ken, the bastard. He wanted to ask about Luna. He left it.

Primrose interrupted his thoughts. "I'm going to find out for definite who fixed your shower. It won't be you who sorts it out however, but I now know people who will. Luna was a darling and what he did to her was inhuman." Then her look changed. "No more questions, Mr Westerman."

There was so much he wanted to know. He clammed up. He let out a comic book, "Eeek".

She wasn't joking. She thought of those she would miss including her niece, Sarah Theakston.

In England, the new head of intelligence felt smug. The last death, Oldman's, was a pièce de résistance. Whereabouts the deceased and his bride were was their concern. She would miss Aunt Primrose. Her aunt was a star.

The dazed Mr Westerman had awoken to find her smiling down at him in his coffin. The fixer, her role in the gang of four, had all the documents in order as usual. He laid there for a while and then began to howl; laugh like a drain. As he stared in disbelief from the open coffin, Primrose touched his lips with her index finger.

"Later, Mr Westerman."

*He didn't argue. If this was purgatory, then he was up for it.*

*Her new name was Janet Westerman (that's what the passport said). Lecturer, retired. As the lid went back on he scanned his coffin for scorch marks. The lid closed, he sniggered and went to sleep. He didn't like his new first name Myles. Westerman was okay, but the y irked him. It was suitable payback, and he appreciated the sardonic nature of it. He decided to go with it. Best not to mess with Janet Westerman nee Stead. Death had been forever present in his job. It stopped worrying him. He'd already experienced it.*

Penny felt empty. He started writing again, bits in his memo book. What meanings do we impute to our dreams – Griffin's lost clothes, dreams in which we walk naked, lost bus tickets? The uncomfortable fantasies of the night, lost in locations unknown, the missing passport, friends, lovers, and family led him to feel sorry for Griffin. They were Griffin's dreams and the reality of the outsider. Penny realised he'd missed his daughter Else's birthday. He wondered how she was. How old was she now? She would be better off without him. He was about to shut the laptop. Instead he sent a message to Liz. He speculated as to what Lance might read into his simple message. Bearing such in mind, he sprinkled in a smidgen of guile:

'Hi, Liz. Nice to see you and Mikey. I heard about Gran's new handbag. What does she carry in that handbag? It must contain a lifetime's secrets and mementos. We should meet up again. I enjoyed seeing you outside school. Whenever I see Mikey so happy, I think of Jack's son Max who I never met. I have a picture of the boy in my head. It's so sad. He must have spoken to you. So much we say and do is under surveillance or passed on either to those we trust or unwittingly to those we don't. Ironic too that those malicious emails should bring us together. Keep your chin up. Ronnie'.

Satisfied with his slyness, he closed the laptop with an emphatic gesture. His pal Oldman now inhabited 'Hell' (in the North Atlantic), and he felt Oldman inhabited him. Alterity was the key. He sat back and basked in the completion of his novel. The Batemans and Bowers were having a match that night – darts, and dominoes. He would have loved to have been a fly on the wall.

"Normalcy is the issue here." His address was unexpected, the abstruse nature welcome. "Trauma is usually an effect of the unexpected."

"Like listening to you," Dove said cheerily.

Penny chatted regardless. "We can do nothing to prevent it happening." He spoke with Shakespearean aplomb. "What was I saying? Ah yes, normalcy is a hindrance." He paused as if digging for an alternative phrase. "It might include an exaggerated sense of emotion."

Dove realised he might not be talking to him. It was as if he was addressing another audience. He suspended trying to fathom out if it were leading anywhere or had any relevancy.

"It might even involve what the therapist calls delusional. Is that clear?"

"Not yet."

"What I have experienced of late may be paranoiac, an aberration. Someone is stalking me. I smell death."

Dove knew better than to interrupt at this point.

"He is going to kill me. My growing world, my childhood, was one inhabited by psychosis and paranoia. I understand it."

His odd choice of language apart, Dove's experience in the arena of killing told him that this was serious. A heightened sense of smell goes with survival in the field and detects the predators. What wasn't clear was whether Penny was critically examining his own self and his delusions. The smell was a product of anxiety in the receiver.

"Who is it?" Dove asked.

"Not sure. I get the sense the hunter is cold-blooded. I feel he or she has a back-up team which are nearby. And if one fails, the other is going to finish the job. The silly thing is I don't know why they want me dead." Penny paused and, with a skewed smile, threw a switch. "I failed one of their children's term papers or essays? Thank God I'm not a linesman or a referee for children's football games." Penny was overwrought. He was doing his best to self-analyse. "Blowing the whistle is important. If the ref gets it wrong, may the Lord have mercy on him."

"How do you know you're being tracked?"

"I don't know."

"You haven't really been yourself lately. I'm more than happy to track the tracker."

"I haven't been well. The writing throws up the past. It works both ways. At times it's therapeutic, it offloads baggage. At other times it brings baggage to the surface to remain there like spume on the top of the waves, froth trying to reach the beach, washing back and forward with each wave.

Now and then the wind catches it and deposits it on the sand, held momentarily, then picked up by the wind once more again and blown hither and thither. I am sleeping fitfully, running miles, checking the locks on the front and back doors during the night, and I keep humming a Cliff Richard song."

Dove didn't ask what song. He sussed he was not saying everything. He waved his hand around in a circular motion to encourage him to continue.

"On the way back from the shop, I caught a flicker of light on the hill there." Penny pointed up to the tops where he loved to see kids sledging in winter. "It was a pair of binoculars. He's waiting, making me suffer first."

"Have you spoken with Raed?"

"I'm not bothered. That's what's bothering me. Guilt can trigger things."

Dove didn't prod.

On the hill, the high-powered lens of a pair of binoculars surveyed the scene. The hunter liked the name of the binoculars, and on the strength of their name alone, he bought the glasses for the hunt. The prey, human in this instance, popped out of the scenery. The predator could see all. The glasses were good. The prey was talking to his mate who had cast a cursory glance up the hill.

The hunter wished he'd bugged the infernal man's place as a precaution. He was wary of Dove. Not wanting to err like the Batemans, he had done his own enquiries. He was dangerous. The small, stocky, bearded man was reputed to be fit as a butcher's dog, battle-scarred, hard as bloody nails, lethal. He had been in the forces, the Special Boat Services. Since coming out, the police files on him had been busy. A man had died from a heart attack after aiming a car at him. Keep focussed on the quarry.

The glasses were handheld and light. He could do the job now and remove both men. They were now inside. Better to leave Dove behind.

"I'll nose around," Dove assured him. He took a left into the high street, then right again and circled. The man on the hill was gone. On the hilltop the minimal signs of a presence were clear. The watcher was tidy. Whoever it was, they were a seasoned hunter. Dove called Periwinkle.

Penny locked up. He checked the front and back doors twice before opening the laptop gingerly. He went downstairs and sat it on the couch on top of one of his tapestry-style cushions he found in a magazine for replica museum pieces.

Periwinkle's call to catch up with Hart's sidekick, the detective Lucy Freeman lasted minutes. He was packing as he spoke. No time for his waistcoats. He put a change of clothes in a brown leather suitcase, put on a warm coat, his beret, and a huge black knitted scarf. There was a train from King's Cross in an hour. Barring theft of cables, delays, and the usual nonsense (leaves on lines, the wrong kind of snow) he should be in the northeast in three to four hours. Time was at a premium.

In transit, he kept his case close by. He didn't want his homework stolen. Having to blow the thief to smithereens by detonating part of the contents raised a moral issue. The crook might be in a crowded public place. He placed the case next to the window and rested his right arm across it, put his head on the top of the seat back and dozed. He dreamed of blowing up Kilton Castle.

**One day.**

## Chapter 53

"These are kids. Be careful Hart!" was Raed's opening dictate.

Hart bore it in mind. Her recent collegiate warmth towards him was beneficial. Bearing in mind the detail of her brief, he sat in an interview room and smiled cheerfully at young Ella.

"Thank you, Ella, for being honest. You can go now."

Hart's final statement of thanks to thirteen-year-old Ella Hopkins after a day of hearing lies and more lies caused the girl to squirm. She had said enough. They had a dependable witness.

She reddened and then stuttered, "Thank you, sir." Ella was close to tears.

Hart let her go. As she stumbled to her feet in a rush to go to her mam, he brought the interview to an end with a cautionary, though cheerful, conclusion. "You've been helpful and honest, Ella. We may need to talk with you again."

The girl avoided all eye contact. "That horrid boy Max and the old biddy were friends." She ran.

Hart was in no doubt who the old biddy was.

Raed was talking with parents and wasn't aware of the plight of the child. She had missed this non-verbal display of a troubled conscience and a frightened mind.

"Did you not see that, chief?"

"That's a negative question, Hart. I told you no negative questions. Just joking! Was it a result?"

Hart stifled his intended tit-for-tat reply likening her to Penny. She was the 'guv' (or the gaffer, as the locals referred to her). He told her the gist of Ella's whistleblowing. He felt they were going somewhere at last. He was sick of fabrications, glib lies, torture, and death.

"We could keep a watchful eye on young Ella, but I doubt any recriminations will occur now."

When he found Penny waiting for him outside the station, he looked shocked.

"Hi, Hart. Got five minutes?"

"Five only, Penny. What is it?" Hart was chary.

Penny cut to the quick. There was no way Hart was going to engage him in small talk. "Two things: first, a piece of information; second, I have a request."

"Go on."

"What do you know of Mikey?"

"That's a question."

"Okay, Hart. Check his paternity."

"That's it?"

"Do it."

"And the information, Penny?"

"That's it, Hart. Not every question merits a mark. Let's call it a request." Penny walked away.

The watcher laid his binoculars down. He was an expert, one used to covert work; callous and precise. What was going on?

Hart was thinking, why should we check the paternity of this young man? Curiosity would inevitably drive him to do just that. It would require samples.

On the way back to Skelton, Penny felt dizzy, then nauseous and disorientated. He went inside, drank water, and fell asleep. On waking, he wasn't aware what time it was, or what day. He opened the laptop. The time on the bottom right-hand corner read eight thirteen p.m., the date November sixth.

He didn't believe it but his mobile confirmed that it was the same date. He checked it twice. Outside the weather had settled. Everything was out of sync, the insecurity a blessing and a curse. He needed to get out. He stepped outside. It was cold. The relentless winds had calmed. The sky was empty. It was going to fill, then it would bucket down or snow. Then they could go sledging. He went back indoors and locked up.

Periwinkle was changing trains at Darlington when his phone whistled. The original request from Dove was history. Periwinkle knew all about Jim's past, far more than Penny, Raed or Hart. The email was from Penny. Jim was toxic. Dove had said that. He, or an accomplice, was after their friend. Periwinkle clutched the case under his arm and set off along the platform and out of Saltburn station to the bus stop.

Penny was writing an addendum to his last chapter.

*Janet Westerman was up early but her husband had pipped her to the post. He must be in the ocean already or jogging along* the beach. She put the kettle on. He was doing neither. He was sitting on the veranda watching the North Atlantic Ocean as the turquoise waves curled in on the shore. It was barely dawn. A yellow streak caught the soft coral pink sand and turned it rose-gold. Jane traced a line towards the water. She loved the ocean and all its vibrant life.

A travel bag was sitting alongside him. She knew the outcome. She decided not to make it easy for him. She eyed the bag and her new husband. He spoke first.

"One more job to do, sweetheart." The sweetheart didn't sound sweet.

"You didn't disappear in the night this time."

"You spoke to Bridie?"

"Yes – at your funeral." The tone was brusque. She smiled. "Nice woman."

"I want to do this. In my cowardice I got up and left in the night. I couldn't do it again." He pushed himself up, gave her a gentle hug, picked up the case and turned to leave.

She didn't respond.

As he began to walk away, she spoke. "You look good for a dead man." Then, "Am I allowed to know who, Mr Westerman?" She suspected it was Griffin or Ken.

"All I can say is that it's to protect a good friend in danger. He's an author." He walked to the car. If the press were anything to go by, he was going to meet the devil himself. Bugger the press. Bugger the devil too.

The dossier that Griffin placed on his boss's desk contained one name running throughout – Jim Trout – an international operative and assassin gone AWOL, rogue, and vengeful. For Jim, the leaving of his family home was a constant.

368

*How her new husband got the message was a riddle for Stead. She had her own message to impart. She went into her study and came out with an envelope. Placing it in his pocket, she insisted he read it only when he arrived at his destination.*

*Westerman became Oldman. Penny became Oldman. Oldman conjured up an image of Bridie. He pictured her playing in the sand with her flaxen-coloured tangled hair, hair almost matching the sand, her pointed face dotted with fernitickles.*

*"Bring me something back, Daddy. Please." Bridie always sensed when he was going away.*

*The two cats sensed it and would mooch around his legs. When he returned, they showed only contempt – a manner that spoke of his desertion. How could such animals feel like that? Bridie never bothered.*

*As he walked away Stead waved once, then turned and went into her private study and made a phone call.*

\\\

*Oldman walked to the harbour, picked up the boat from the moorings and sailed to the mainland. From there he flew to Greece, then on to France. The final leg was by the Eurostar to St Pancras. In London, he stopped to pick up a sealed parcel from a small shop near the station. The man said nothing until Oldman was leaving.*

*Then he said, "I've included a gift."*

*Stead had disposed of everything he had. One thing he missed: his gun. In the parcel was a pistol and a stun-gun. Handy. Handale Woods sounded an intriguing place, Jim Trout a nasty bit of work. The next leg was risky. He didn't want to hire a car. He chose public transport. It occurred to him that it may be a trap to bring him out in the open. Who would do that? Griffin? Ken?*

*He'd skirted the truth when he said it was a friend. He'd never met this man Penny and didn't know him from Adam. Jim was an expert and out of kilter. Penny must be something else if he could unhinge an operative of that calibre.*

Penny stared at his laptop. He recalled the golden sands back home and his own sandy hair full of golden grains; building castles and digging a channel towards the incoming tide to flood a moat and watch the castle slowly collapse in the cold waves of the North Sea. He sailed a little blue boat along the channel.

He sang a made-up tune, "I built a sandcastle with a moat and on it sailed my little blue boat, a lollipop stick, a sweet-wrapper flag, and collected shells in a carrier bag."

He pictured the beach. The groynes grew from the sand oak barriers with strange leering tree trunks without branches in between the sturdy lathes. Granddad explained they were there to stop the sand from eroding, leaving clay only. How could the sand wash away? Sand was forever. How did they, these strange tree stumps, one with a triangular thing on top, stop it? He recalled a voice shouting him 'Ronnie, where are you?'. He was prone to wandering away. He was about to again. The laptop was open and on when he left.

Periwinkle found it on the floor. He read the first few lines only. He closed it and tucked it in his bag. It was already night-time. On the doormat was a note: 'Look out, Mr Penny, there's a man following you. He has a gun. Five.'

He pocketed the note.

No one saw Periwinkle enter the house, nor the town. He checked the time. It was eleven thirty p.m., pitch black, and a rheumatic dampness hung over the place. The pavements glistened despite the moonless dark. Periwinkle left unseen. The writing was part of the story of Oldman. He scanned Penny's script. Why Handale Woods?

'The file that Oldman received on Penny detailed something of the man and his involvement in The Tableau Case, a case that had offered the press a field day and earned him the name Dr Death. He gave the impression of being harmless, an academic. He was not from the cloistered world of academe, rather a man of the streets (the back streets in Oldman's estimate). Penny's profile drew his attention, especially the notes that illustrated he was physically capable of self-defence, though not by nature an aggressive man. Was he aware of the extensive material on him on file?

As a young man he had marched against the National Front. and engaged with them head-on. As an older man, he was still out there campaigning against the ultra-right, men like Ken.

Oldman read up on the area of Loftus. Its history and legacy of the old alum trade, the fossils, the mining, the strange people with their Viking heritage, their fishing, farming, their stubborn resistance to change, appeared like a part of his own history, a different and remote place. Tourism, history, nor archaeology was the purpose of his trip. Jim was going to kill Penny. He was going to circumvent that and kill Jim.'

Periwinkle paused and scrolled down.

'Oldman couldn't help thinking that he owed this man… Reading into the file, Penny was a man on the edge. Jim was one of the agency's flyboys, a mercenary obliged by his trade to live a *duplicitous life for which he was highly paid. A mercenary in his dictionary, though he, Oldman reflected, was no better. This job was payback, giving something back.*

*He wouldn't get time to see the Saxon princesses' jewellery at Kirkleatham and there would be no other time when this could be satisfied. He would have to give in to an online viewing.*

*The thought arose that it was a set up.'*

Dove abandoned the notion of calling Penny to say it was kids messing about that were causing the reflections. He was never prone to anxious moments, yet the hunter's very presence made him uneasy for his friend. As for Periwinkle, his part required anonymity. They were not to get in touch with each other. Dove's guess was Jim.

What had brought about Jim's return and his aim to kill Penny was baffling. He would be at risk himself. Dove's take was that it was easier to kill Penny than extract information from him.

Periwinkle should have read on. There was no time.

## Chapter 54

Arriving in St Pancras, Oldman walked to King's Cross and booked a single train ticket to Saltburn. He stared at the board and recalled Stead's envelope. He sat down in the newish waiting area and dug it out of his pocket. He sliced it open with his finger and peered in. Up above on a veranda a man had a falcon which he let free. Pigeons fled from the station.

A business card. He placed it in his palm and studied it. The board indicated a cancellation. He had an hour at least to wait. For a second the card confounded him. He didn't need an electrician. He flipped it over. Written in Stead's hand in miniature on the reverse: 'Fielding was a friend. This man is responsible. Trust me. Love you.' No name...

"What the fuck?"

How could this woman get this kind of information, and who from? Insider stuff. He flipped it back and the address and a mobile number were on the card. He was already tapping in on his mobile... then stopped. The address was on the way to Camden Lock – The Gasholders – barely ten minutes' walk along the canal. On the towpath, he picked up a short length of rope. Barring cancellations trains north were every hour. He reached his destination: The Gasholders. He called the number on the card. A man answered.

"Have a job for you."

"How did you get my number?" His reply was acidic.

"You are The Electrician, according to my colleagues Lawson and Major Briggs."

"Sorry. Wrong number."

"I worked with Eames and Griffin!"

The phone was already cut.

Oldman waited. He admired the set-up, the conjoined triplets attached at the spine, the old Pancras gasworks. There was hope for architecture. He was outside the apartment, lingering, when the man left in a hurry. Electricians must be on a hell of a whack – the apartments weren't cheap. He was wearing a blue t-shirt and had a tool bag with him. In his hurry he didn't notice Oldman tucked in behind him. It was the man in grey overalls who first 'checked' his electricity. No room for error here. Written in pen on the back of the card was 'The Wire for Hire'. He could ask later if he came out of this just where in the hell she got her information. Hell was becoming an interesting location.

He wanted to make this man suffer, but time forbad. Oldman skirted around him and blocked his path. The man recognised him.

"What the fuck? Old—" The Electrician pushed him aside.

Oldman collared him, held tight, and moved close to avoid him kneeing him in the balls.

"Who the fuck do you think you are?" Griffin's words.

"A friend of Fielding. You got the wrong man."

The man's hand shot into his leather workbag. Oldman didn't wait. A taser full-on could kill, cause cardiac arrest or leave the victim with an impaired memory. The Electrician went down, pole-

374

axed, with the gun in his hand. A Glock 26, a baby Glock, compact with carry ability; deadly. Oldman's gloved hands fondled it for a moment. He removed the taser barbs and tightened his grip.

No one emerged from the moored barges, though a barking dog further along the canal towards Camden Lock warned of a presence. Oldman pocketed the taser (a free gift and a fitting implement indeed), wound the rope around The Electrician's neck and bundled the man into the water. He held onto the gun. The cold revived The Electrician and he began to struggle.

As he broke the surface Oldman yelled at him, "Who authorised the job on my shower?"

"Fuck you, Oldman!"

The dog was getting closer, a yelping spaniel, it's owner still in the distance. He tightened the rope and held. He tightened further and pushed him under. Unconsciousness would follow vascular neck restraint though it could be four or five minutes before death. The dog came running up, its owner still a way back standing along the canal side in the distance. Oldman shooed it and it fled. He held the gun in his left, the rope in his right. The dog walker seemed unaware, though he called his dog and hurried back the way he came.

The Electrician surfaced, still alive, thrashing the dark water of the canal. He gasped and opened his mouth wide to scream. "Major Ken, it was. He's dead!"

Oldman thought he might savour the moment, but he needed to finish his task. He spoke one word: "Fielding."

Forcing the gun into The Electrician's mouth he pushed him under, letting go of the rope. He pulled the trigger. The noise underwater must have been deafening. The Electrician never heard it. The links were joining up: Luna, Fielding, and Ken.

Despite the gloves, he wiped The Electrician's gun, placed it back in the bag and ditched it in the murky water. It sank immediately. Bodies float, bodies sink. He didn't wait to see. He walked back to King's Cross and caught a train. No sirens yet, no police presence. The Regent's Canal – a final resting place for art thieves, a dumping ground for murderers, and an infamous location for suicides, claimed another soul – The Electrician.

Welcome to the Murder Mile. Here endeth The Wire for Hire. He tossed the card in a litter bin. Pieces of the jigsaw began to link. As he walked back to the station a past life experience flickered. Was it a memory, or had he read it somewhere?

He dropped the gun and taser back to the shop. "Needs cleaning, though I didn't use it. Keep the taser, too. It came in very handy."

The man took both and disappeared into the back. Oldman left.

In his office, Griffin was shredding a file.

\\\

The train was empty. It passed the National Railway Museum at York. A Pullman went by the other way. Under normal circumstances it would have drawn his full attention. He glimpsed in appreciation then began to focus on the task ahead. There was an hour delay due to trackside problems. Copper cables were a popular target for thieves. Darlington station was quite the coldest place on earth. For a man of Canadian extraction that was something. The cold appeared trapped and held in the historic terminus. He was late and time was running out. The short train journey to Saltburn was aggravatingly slow. He arrived around ten thirty in the evening, the last train. His interest in the industrial archaeology had waned. He had to get to Jim and silence him. Jim was a loose cannon and would show his hand.

Was Griffin around? Was Ken really dead? Was it a frame? It would have given him faith to know that what was left and unclaimed of Ken was in La Morgue en france.

Griffin was safely ensconced behind a desk. His incoming boss had great plans for the man. He was an excellent administrator. Once, that would have aggravated the self-seeking Griffin. The death of The Electrician filtered in and silenced him further. It would also indicate 'his' return, a bloody revenant.

Jim would be close to his wife Liz. His other wife lived far away in the USA, and though he saw her regularly (well, as much as one can as a travelling plumber), he wasn't going back to either.

Jim was a slippery geezer. Inside Oldman's bag rested a pistol – a HK45 – and a filleting knife. His status as a dead man with a certificate to prove it meant he felt secure in one respect. Yet, there was a persistent feeling all was not well. He would need transport.

## Chapter 55

The email from Dove came through. Penny dropped everything; stuffed one or two things in a bag, leaving a printout of his last chapter scattered around and his laptop open.

He replied: 'Thanks, Dove. I'm going to buy a paper at the store before it closes. See you at Handale Woods in an hour or so.'

He sent it then deleted the original message.

With no idea what he was doing, he set off.

Dove watched him leave the house from his position on the hill. Penny had his backpack on. It was bulging. If he was anxious about a pending assassination, his cavalier attitude and casual stroll didn't reveal such. Dove started down the hill. His phone beeped as he ran.

Penny walked slowly to the store. He came out minutes later with a folded newspaper, heading back in the direction of All Saints Church, stopping occasionally to browse shop windows while slapping the paper on his thigh.

What was he doing? If Jim was going to strike, now was good. Then, Penny did a complete turn, and strolled back towards the store, crossed the road sharply (ignoring the zebra) and vanished.

Dove was sure of one thing: Jim was going to kill him. Dove read Penny's message.

The frightening aspect was Penny's sentence: 'See you at Handale Woods.'

More worrying was what Penny was going to do at Handale.

Dove wondered if he had underestimated Jim's desire for revenge. Would Jim make Penny suffer, like Max? His guesswork was close, but it wasn't Jim who had done the dirty work on Max.

Dove stowed his specs away and hurtled down the hill. The X bus to Loftus went past as he reached the church. It stopped at the Co-op.

Jim started the car. He spotted Dove getting into his battered banger. Dove dodged the traffic until the bus terminated at Loftus. Penny wasn't on it. Despite a nip of anxiety, Dove had to laugh. Penny was getting better.

The laugh choked and meshed into a description of his friend, "Bloody maniac!"

Inky darkness had descended and the temperature plummeted. Rain was forecast.

Jim hadn't even bothered chasing the bus. For his part, he was laughing down his nose at the fact that Penny's dumb colleague had fallen for an amateur ruse. Or so he concluded. Jim pulled over and called into the store.

He engaged the ladies at the desk. "Just spotted my mate, Ronnie. Did he say where he was going?"

"He's a nice bloke, but a funny geezer, if you ask me. He said something about big cat spotting. Why on earth anyone would go to Handale as night comes down, and in this weather, beggars belief. Don't think I'd like to be around those parts with that beast roaming around."

She hadn't finished when Jim was out the door, leaving the newspaper on the counter. In the end one bullet from his beautiful Ruger 77 was going to finish the job. The elegant rifle lay next to him covered by a sleeping bag in the hired green Ford car. A great hunting rifle, it eliminated the need to hold over. He might have to take that shot at a moving target; that was no problem. It would be entertaining to see the oaf run before he pulled the trigger. He might get time to kill the boy Mikey, too.

"Two funny geezers in one day." The shop assistant picked up the paper and placed it on the side.

The lane to Handale Woods was pitch-black when Jim parked up and found the path. Where the other funny geezer was, was not clear. Strange place to visit. How did Penny get there?

Dove could not suss Penny's latest move at all.

Penny tried to call him as he wandered the uphill road. His head was in a whirl. No signal. The area was dead. Dead was a key factor here. The best alibi he ever had. No one could get hold of him. Periwinkle had now skip-read the full addendum to his manuscript.

Penny's light-headedness returned and he wobbled. Following this was a focussed clarity like nothing he had ever experienced before. It was time to meet Oldman.

*Oldman's mobile bleeped before he lost the signal altogether. He needed to be careful. It was really a matter of who got there first and set up camp. Stealing a car was second nature and the big old Volvo he chose was perfect. He needed it for a night. Would the owner miss it? He removed the filleting knife from his bag, an unused blade. It was sharp as a razor and just the job. He imagined slotting the blade in below the head of a fish before taking the first fillet. He had tried it, but it wasn't a success and the ling fillets were definitely ragged. Filleting this Trout was a different matter. He opened his phone. No signal.*

Penny had made only a token attempt to avoid his pursuer. His bus ruse convinced Jim he was either an idiot or had something up his sleeve. Penny thought Dove must have something up his sleeve too. It did seem peculiar to go to Handale at nightfall.

Dove too had dropped into the store, and, describing Penny to the letter, asked directly if his friend had been in.

"Gone to Handale Woods big cat spotting." She didn't say 'nutter'. "Another man was asking after him just now."

He was out the shop in a flash and, breaking their agreement, he called Periwinkle.

Lost for words, the woman in the store managed four: "Three in one day!"

Things were moving fast. Dove filled Periwinkle in on details. "I followed the bus, and then turned back. I doubt Jim fell for it."

"What do you think he has in the backpack?"

"No idea."

"Did he keep one of the guns from the pub raid?"

"It would be comforting if he had."

"Any ideas? He has written one or two peculiar things in his manuscript. Novels are strange things to me, per se. The big cat features frequently in his script. His hero-protagonist is Oldman! He's going to resolve the conflict with Jim."

"I can't see why he would go to Handale. Hope he's gone away somewhere else instead. He's prone to wandering off. My mobile will cut soon. I'm now on the south road from Loftus. He knows that the signal fluctuates in strength. Stick around, Periwinkle. I'm going hunting."

"No, you're not. They don't know I'm here. I'll go."

Dove picked up Periwinkle and he laid low in the car, a feat that was difficult with his long legs. No traffic passed either way in the streets or backroad to Handale. Dove dropped him and returned to Loftus to the police station. He popped a note through the door along with his mobile number: 'Please call me as soon as. Urgent. Dove.'

\\\\\

Oldman parked the car as close as was wise to Handale Woods, out of sight under the trees. The pine trees were abundant and thick, the area empty of humankind. There was no bosky walking path through the woods. It was thick, dense, and musty. No one was likely to pass that way. He took no chances; he was in black and moved with the stealth of a cat.

The black leopard, a beautiful feline creature in Penny's book, had kept evening dog walking to a minimum, despite clement intervals in the weather. Still in a thrall, he scouted the area around Handale Woods. No Dove. Parked under the trees at the edge of the wood was a green Ford. He heard another car and hid until it passed. He couldn't see Dove.

*Oldman noted the green car and parked further along. He walked back onto a path across a cattle grid. Barely visible in the faded light, a huge black bull stirred. He backtracked and found the path that ran from the road. He generally avoided trekking across muddy fields; his respect for large black bulls came first. He checked the green car before setting off. A large sleeping bag snaked along the back seat. The keys were in the lock. Jim or Penny had beaten him to it. The track was just as muddy. It clung to his shoes and made lifting his feet difficult. He ploughed on single-mindedly, slipping occasionally in the slithery pools lying on top of the sodden track. The grass path was dim, though a waist-high barbed wire fence to the left helped as a guide. His gloved hands touched it lightly now and then as a prop. He entered the wood to his left.*

*At first, he saw nothing. He was aware of movement ahead and briefly two shadowy figures. Damn it. Either the figure had moved fast, or another was present. Both disappeared and he couldn't be sure. Both melted away into the gloom. Vision was difficult. The darkness shifted to a dense charcoal as he moved stealthily into the thickness of the wood.*

## Chapter 56

Periwinkle merged into the dense growth of trees, ignoring the bull and taking the shorter route. The bull stirred slowly. As he skirted past, the huge beast lay down heavily and passed into sleep. He thought about the list on Penny's desk. Words: spectres, illnesses, or afflictions were listed, and an old thesaurus opened. The word 'phobia' was highlighted. The list included words like hypoxia and words beginning hypo, then aphasia followed by Luna in brackets. No time to ponder Penny's current mental state. What on earth did the divine personification of the moon mean to him? Who was Luna? Best not to ponder.

He recalled Penny saying the black leopard was a phantasmagorical creature that pursued him while running. He would turn when he felt it closing in. It was never there when he turned. Only a shivery feeling remained. It was a ghost, one only of the many spectres that haunted him. No therapist could remove this cat until it was dead in his mind. Penny had said that it was very much alive. It was something he couldn't shake off, or someone close; at once related to him and alien to him — family. It went away now and then, only to return, signalled by the tremor that ran the length of his back and an unfriendly sweat. He could never run towards it; it was a shade. He could never befriend it; it would trick him if he got close; it would deceive him. Periwinkle wasn't afraid. It was a beast and would do him no harm. Hopefully he wouldn't have to do anything to the cat.

Penny skirted the wood. The big cat was close. He walked on. There was no shake or shudder – no cold sweat. He loosened the backpack and removed a small package, unwrapping the paper with gloved hands. Then, stuffing the brown paper in his anorak, he carefully placed the contents in his side pocket.

*Oldman chose a spot, settled in as comfortable as was possible on the ground, and waited. Slowly his eyes adjusted to the speckled darkness of the pine wood and his mind began to function along with the wild. He could sense the cat which was visually undetectable in the dark. He hoped it had dined well that day. He stayed prone. He discerned a slight movement to his left, twenty metres away. He saw nothing, then heard another rustle. This wasn't a cat. It was too big. Regardless of the lowness of sound, he knew it was another human being. The quiet tension exaggerated it. It had come from someone staying put, a pro.*

*The knife was in his left hand and though he wanted to transfer it to his right, he remained still. In his head a tune formed. It was the one of the songs they played at his funeral: Cat Stevens's* Morning has Broken. *A movement left, ahead. A barely audible swish caused him to hold his breath. It could have been an animal. His time in the field told him this was his adversary. Where was the intended mark? Waiting was going to cramp him more so than the younger man. Waiting it would have to be. His eyes remained* fixed on the spot. If he was wrong, or it was a decoy, then Jim was better than he imagined. A sound closer to his right side caused him to stir. Something was moving through the trees low down. Flat on the damp dead bracken in the cold of the pines, his left hand felt clammy inside the black glove that clutched the knife.

A knife was practical and silent. Sweat blurred his eyes. Lying face down he knew he'd made an error. The thick undergrowth might protect him. His only hope was that Jim had done likewise and left himself open. The scurry about twenty yards away implied he was right about one thing. To his left total silence descended. There was the strong smell of cat pee. He rolled a yard or so as the noise ceased. He was under thicker cover. The odour of cat pee was stronger. The cat was marking its trail with urine. He was satisfied that it wouldn't attack a grown human. In the darkness of that wood laid prone on the ground his conviction faltered.

A thick splintered tree stump, spars jutting from it. It felt like a giant pineapple. It leaned left in a curve, offering minimal cover. This was the tree of life or death. He crawled to it for better cover. Its thickness offered more shelter than the slim choked pines. He touched it with his right hand then traced its stem. The wood was clean. It was no higher than four feet, enough to crouch behind. He smelled the wood. No charring or burning. Huge splinters projected from the trunk; the bark was gone. This wasn't lightning. He wished he could see it. He could see nothing. The cat could see all.

## Chapter 57

Jim intended to enjoy the hunt. His quarry, a man he detested, had interrupted his cosy lifestyle, screwed up his job for him, and, he suspected, his wife fancied the man. That bit was hard to get his head around.

"World Plumbing Day indeed." He cursed. Society would be healthier without Penny or the like.

The kill promised a small degree of compensation before leaving to a new home and another family. He would soon forget them. The boy Max, the devious little fucker, had listened to his conversation the day he popped into the school and made a call from Liz's office. That he hadn't noticed him was a cock-up on his part. Going into school was a rarity. He was sure he'd passed on the news to Mikey, another thorn. Liz wasn't looking so good at that point.

He had done his homework on Max. Max was a scheming bully. Unable to reflect on those characteristics as prowess in his own field, he saw them for what they were. Jim reported to his superiors and waited for further instructions. He heard every word of the conversation. Killing kids wasn't his forte. Jim's superiors ordered him to do it. Make it look like an accident. He employed the outside help of two contractors.

He never met them. They came highly recommended, and they came from Leeds.

His instructions were to dispose of him, and remove the body, not torture him, or practise vile and devilish rituals ending in his demise. Contractors had never let him down before. Their professional standing was high. Colleagues recommended them close to government. No one knew anything personal about them. They didn't know him. But they had ways and means of checking things out. Jim Trout came to the surface.

He should have done the job alone. His idea that he should be away when it happened was a prime mover. What did they do to him? He should have hired them to remove Penny. He took a cautionary measure. He left his contractors instructions to finish the job on the off chance he might fail. If they opted to crucify him or rip his limbs from his sockets on the rack that would do nicely. Not required. He now had him pinned down behind a tree.

Jim was important to his superiors, a man who killed or contracted out jobs. They chose to leak false information to Hart which might stall things. Jim, they reported, was an important government representative. He required anonymity. Hart was a dependable man to them; Raed, his boss, not so... and not a man. Wrong school.

How Penny had sussed him out was a puzzle. He wished to take a little time to find out before he killed him. No time. There was an alert out for him. Make the kill and go. That would be gratifying. No point in any form of interrogation as the man spoke in riddles.

Penny hoped Jim's ability in the field might be as faulty as his knowledge of modern plumbing. Penny had competencies he could bring to bear of which Jim was unaware.

*Numbing cold hung around the pines. They dripped condensation. Oldman was soggy with sweat and oblivious to the wet.*

*Jim was not going to waste time. This was going to be a straight kill and then out. No excuses, conservation, culling, population management. It was for enjoyment, with just a smidgen of retribution thrown into the mix.*

*Oldman couldn't work out where the quarry was. He shuffled slightly to relieve an ache. The first shot went past the splintered tree. The thick rib-like spars saved his life. The wood fell on him. He didn't move. The next bullet hit the 'pineapple'. He tried to guess what rifle it was, a hunting job for sure. Was he using glasses and could see him?*

*Jim's ego disallowed such. He wanted to hunt and kill with his instincts. Oldman clawed his way further under the thinner clustered trees, digging into the safety of the muddy terrain and pine needles. Jim was going to rush him. He was wrong. Jim wanted his quarry to feel fear first. He wanted to coax him out.*

*Oldman took a chance. He rolled a yard or more further and dug in behind a choked clump of young saplings fighting for survival.*

*Where was Penny?*

*The pitch darkness of the wood offered a slight advantage. The wood hadn't been coppiced for years. He felt something brittle* next to him. He ran his free hand over it. In the pitch-black of the wood he couldn't see it. It was the bones of a human. How long had it laid in this wood? The corpse gave off no odour. It was old. He edged around it slowly. The boneyard was about to expand. He gained another yard. Still there was no light, only oily darkness. Ahead there was no sound or movement. He veered away from where the shot had come. The cat's presence was less, though the smell of piss still hung in his nostrils. It wasn't far away. He remained focussed on the shooter.

"Supper's on the way, sweetie!"

It was barely audible. He laughed inside at his stupidity. He made a lunge forward as a second bullet smashed into the tree behind him.

Jim had given up on the idea of persecuting his prey but hoped he might maim him before he put a final bullet through his addled brain. Penny was demonstrating skill in the field.

Oldman crawled on his belly as fast as he could as the ricochet echoed and whined through the wood. As the sound died away, he lay very still in what he judged to be was ten metres and a short run from the shooter – if his fitness proved up to it. The damp was beginning to stiffen his joints. He breathed circularly and wriggled his toes. Four or five minutes passed in still silence. He would have to make his move soon.

Jim was motionless. He was good. Oldman lay thinking, unmoving. A branch thrown to the side would not fool this man. Indeed, there was no room to chuck anything. In his favour was the fact Jim was not aware of his proximity. The branch trick would give his position away. Procrastination had never been a part of his make-up. He lay there, stalling the inevitable.

Slowly, the last quarter moon began to peek through the pines, illuminating small sections of the wood, signalling the need for closing action. The dark straight trees stood in cameo against the orb-like yellow background. Pine branches criss-crossed in patterns like a huge printed curtain. The cat was discernible first. Jim hadn't seen it. Another figure flitted away. Penny? Jim was intent on the dead tree, Oldman on Jim. The beast was to Oldman's right and closer to Jim. The cat stretched, head raised, sniffing the night air and humans which Oldman hoped were too big for bitesize.

He wondered what it was thinking. He saw another figure but the cat seemed unaware of such a presence. He edged forward on his belly with equal feline stealth. The moon began to light up nearby patches of the wood. Jim would see the cat soon – and him. Yet Jim's focus was on one thing only: he was going to kill Penny. He didn't see the cat.

Oldman didn't believe in providence. His funeral and experiences with Stead had left him with a healthy cynicism and enlightened him. The light crept towards him across the woodland floor as the moon emerged fully from thick cloud. That it would spotlight Jim first was too good to be true. It did.

For a second or two Jim was clear. He dug in. The light flickered and moved across to highlight, in all its splendour, the cat, its sleek blackness fully illuminated for a split second. It bared its teeth. It was hungry. He moved forward. It would take him seconds to get there. He was so close. Jim had the rifle ready. Instinctively, the big cat moved suddenly, disturbed by a movement behind it. It turned. Jim heard it and swung towards the noise, aimed the rifle and fired. The dark figure that disturbed the animal moved away into the trees and vanished. Oldman surged forward. The ache disappeared. Dodging trees, he covered the ground in no time.

Whether Jim ever saw the cat wasn't clear. In the spot-lit space between two trees his mouth open and eyes wide, he half turned and tried to shoot. One cut was enough. The filleting knife was ideal. If there was a third person, he was as quiet as a mouse and had evaporated away. The big cat heard something and turned. Cat and mouse. The shock on Jim's face before his carotid was sliced and spurted implied a complete misunderstanding of what was going on. The big cat had done Oldman a favour. Penny he assumed was hidden in the trees. Without warning it started to tipple down. Jim's last view of the world was one of disbelief.

Oldman kicked the rifle aside and manoeuvred his way out of the wood as fast as he could, skittering on the mud. The rain was beginning to thicken and pour. Not a sound came from behind him after the gurgle of warm blood. In the moonlight offered in the clearing Oldman was unrecognisable as a human. He slipped. Mud covered his whole body and stuck to him. He aimed for the car. A spray of blood remained on his left side, dark patches among the sludge. He wasted no time. Stripping off all his clothes, he double bagged them in thick black bin bags, poked holes in the bag with the knife and dropped them into the back of the boot. Normally he would burn them. The downpour stopped that.

In the car, he towelled himself down as best he could, put on a warm vest, a pair of dark blue overalls and woolly hat, and then drove unhurriedly towards Loftus. He wanted away from there fast but he couldn't risk the police pulling him over. If the cat was really famished it would nibble at the late Jim's bloody throat. A starter. The rain came down in sheets as he drove. The windscreen wipers barely did the job. The roads ran awash with *surplus water; the woodland returned to quag, footprints erased and the skittering marks on the sweet-smelling pine-needled floor washed clean. He needed to dispose of his things and the knife. He drove through Loftus, then further on turned along the Guisborough road humming a tune. Well before daylight he was in Middlesbrough. He drove to the water's edge to see The Tees Transporter Bridge. The skeletal beauty of the bridge shone blue above the murky water of the Tees. He weighted the bags with a brick or two.*

*From his backpack he took a packet of crystals and carefully emptied them with gloved hands into the bin bag. On contact with the wet clothes the crystals reacted violently. He tied the bag quickly and threw it into the Tees. It took forever to sink. Were the crystals producing hydrogen? Finally, the bag disappeared below the murk. The knife followed. Oldman melted into what little remained of the cold, wet wintry northern night. As daylight broke, he was on the A1 heading south. He sang on the way, a song by Lindisfarne. Now, it was home to the wife – if she would have him back.*

*First time he'd partnered a big cat. For him it was a novel ending to his career. He thought about the other presence. Was he imagining it? Was it Penny? Then he realised his mistake: the green Ford. He'd left it by the roadside. The police would follow it up. It was too late to do anything.*

## Chapter 58

"The children have spoken." Raed's words had a liturgical ring to them. "Max ran a protection outfit matching that of the Mafia."

Ella's trickle of tears turned to a flood of information. What started with, "he stole my pocket money," resulted in a catalogue of vindictiveness, bullying and sexual threats, threats a young girl would find frightening to excess. And they were prepared to carry them out and did so.

Penny had little sleep but felt elated. He was in the chair when Dove brayed on the door.

"Get in the car."

Penny grabbed his coat and followed. They covered the five and a half miles to Loftus in ten minutes, left the car and, at pace, headed for the cliffs. Irradiated by an eerie green light after the downpour, the gnarled and crumbling edges of the sandstone cliffs took on a surreal quality; a Daliesque shimmer. Further along, a small and static group stood on the high point near the tooth rock. It consisted of Raed, Liz and Mikey, with Jack standing to the side, a statue, a lone stolid figure, unmoving.

Raed was sheltering her eyes with her hand and staring at the water. It was wild and a high tide pounded the cliff face. Mikey cuddled close to Liz, their backs to the sea. Penny was unsure what was taking place. His mood dipped. He felt frozen in time, a fossil among the rocks. Dove eyed Jack whose physical distance from the others denoted a man apart, separate from reality. The news of his wayward and cruel son finished him. Bearlike and passive, he stood, his arms held by his sides, a broken man.

Everyone appeared distant to Dove. Periwinkle was absent. The ragged group avoided each other's gaze and focussed on the sloping wet clifftop and the sheer drop to the sea. The others began to converse in this strangest of conference places. Who chose such a venue?

The tooth rock broke up in the bright northern light. He studied the ragged group. The geometry of the plot had become clear, the locus he had not wanted to find intersected with Liz. Liz stood on the cliff edge just feet from where they had sat that day. She knew about Max. How could she have lied? Was it to protect her reputation, the school, or Jim? The claws issue still nagged him. Mikey? Max? Take a guess. The rock continued to pixilate in the glare of light and then merged with the dominant grey aura of the sky. Small lines of colour traced their way through the grey. Penny was white-faced, his former elation gone. He stumbled as he reached the splintered group.

"You all right, Ronnie-boy?"

"The clifftops are awesome on a day like this." He stopped to gaze.

Dove choked at Penny's choice of the descriptor, the 'A' word. Since school, along with 'sound' and 'no-brainer', he used it frequently. He had to admit it was fitting. In a Penny moment, Dove made a list of alternatives – breath-taking, overwhelming – then decided awesome wasn't bad. As for 'I'm good', that grated. Sick was just that, sick.

"Yes, I'm good." Penny never started his next sentence.

Jack was extraordinarily strong. He was also fast. His agility and speed caught the group off guard. Mikey was holding onto Liz, his arms wrapped around her waist as if to protect her. Stooped as he was in the act of leaning into Liz, Penny judged him to be as tall as Liz and uncannily similar in bearing and build. Jack broke the circle and seized Liz and the boy who hung on to his love. No one managed to stop him. He launched into the air and vanished over the cliff edge holding both tight and clearing the jutting rocks. Dove never moved. Nor did he show shock or emotion. No sound came from Liz. Mikey went with her as Jack cleared the edge.

Raed had her phone out, no sound but the sea could be head in that moment. Her urgent message to coastal rescue forces and lifeboat done Penny heard the sea lashing the cliff. The wind howled as they trooped back to the station in silence, Penny with the air of a man in a trance. Death was familiar to him and to those hard northerners. It was not death that occupied Penny.

\\\

Raed had insisted on seeing Liz and Mikey. She called her. Liz had laughed, a jittery laugh, not her usual giggle. She cut

Raed off. She had accepted her fate, and the loss of her job, yet couldn't face any more news of Jim. Mikey and Liz were to be separated. Caleb was conspicuous by his absence. Raed drove round to the house. A neighbour said they, her and the boy had gone out in a hurry and were heading for the coast.

"The big man, Jack, was following them from a distance."

Alarm bells rang. Raed contacted Dove who contacted Penny. Hart was busy, Periwinkle out of town, the rest of the staff occupied.

Raed had an urgent need to talk to Liz after Jim's disappearance. Liz, she guessed, had made an error of judgement and assumed she wanted to pry further about Mikey. Neighbours confirmed she had hurried him out of the gate.

Jack confided in Dove. He had heard the gossip about the headteacher, and her knowledge of what was going on at the school. As for Jim, Jack longed to strangle him. His eyes were empty of life. Dove had seen it before in men unravelled by battle, by death, by grief. Lost.

Periwinkle's research was painstaking. Jim was working on the fringes of government.

"Plumbing the depths of a murky world of subterfuge and unpleasantness, a world I have no time for." Periwinkle felt disappointment with humanity as he read his findings out on the phone.

Raed was going to make waves when she got the next bit over with. How could Periwinkle get information that she couldn't? She felt like throwing in the towel.

She filled in gaps. "Liz was aware he wasn't what he made out to be, though never asked. She lived the lie, got on with her job, and never once raised the issue. It led to an unsettled and troubled mind. Along the way she took Mikey to bed. That caused her endless guilt. We don't intend to broadcast it."

Too late. Had she spoken with Penny he would have offered another damning theory. The coroner might find other connections between Liz and Mikey if the sea gave them up. The sea didn't always give up the dead.

Periwinkle's information went further. "Jim is rather good at his job, has two families which he keeps…"

Dove stifled a backhanded compliment.

"… and uses two rather odious 'chaps' to do dirty work when he needs to stay clear."

"Two chaps? Any names?" Dove had his pencil ready.

"I have yet to discover who they are. It may be that Jim didn't know them. I'm not going to stop until I find them."

Penny recalled the recurring dream: two figures which were incongruous, two unrecognisable figures, the torture vivid in his nightmares. Disturbed by his behaviour Periwinkle had asked him what was on his mind. He couldn't put it into words.

Periwinkle eyed his notes. "We don't have names. We do know that they do others' dirty work and one of them at least seems well versed with methods of abuse. It's hard to believe that the torture was part of their filthy contract."

Penny felt his insides turn over as his dream surfaced. The room had the atmosphere of a séance gone wrong, the glass flying from the Ouija board and breaking. Penny had witnessed it.

Raed replied to Periwinkle's intel. "Kyle has disclosed information that Max overheard a phone conversation. Max walked on the dark side, drawn towards criminality and evil, and we know that has a way of taking over. It's addictive."

Hart had joined them. "The rest is a gap-filling exercise."

Hart asked Penny if he was okay. He was unaware that he had used one of Penny's favoured expressions. What he said next recalled something Raed had said.

"The attraction to wickedness gains strength, so does the confidence and ability to manipulate. Criminality or extreme malevolence ensues."

"So Max blackmailed Jim?" Penny blurted out.

"We don't know," Raed answered. "There is no evidence whatsoever to confirm such. No evidence of money changing hands. Jim ordered the killing, we are sure. It is horrid. It occurred to me that the killers have connections that hinder our case. Liz was aware of something. The school will be in shock. I think Jack might have found out a detail or two. Liz was well-liked by the community."

Dove gave Penny a dissuasive glare.

"Oh, one more thing: Jim has gone underground. His whereabouts is a mystery. Cleverly relocated no doubt, or simply absconded. That's not based on concrete facts." Raed finished there and then.

Dove peered left, then right and down. Penny was doing his infernal twiddling, this time with a toggle on his hoody, winding and unwinding it from around his fingers. Oldman wasn't there to help. Penny felt futile and tired. Oldman had filled him with purpose.

Later that day the three men talked.

Dove posed a question: "How much of Jim's background do you think Raed and Hart really know?" He threw the conversational switch, aimed as much at Periwinkle as about finding out what had gone on behind closed doors. He wanted to know about Penny's reasons for being at Handale.

"I think Raed knew very little. As for Hart, he has more contacts out there than Raed. Shamefully, it's gendered. A woman will be less likely to find informers, especially an intelligent and ambitious woman. Hart was more involved with the national scenario. Hart was gullible and used by his superiors." Periwinkle spread his long arms in a gesture that said that is it, not concisely, but 'that is it'.

Dove picked up the story. He had never quite worked out how Penny had resolved the feud. He left that until last. It might offer a humorous diversion. His warm-up began with the werewolf. His parody was apparent. The growl remained.

"My excursions into music hall with Gran Bowers enriched my vocabulary and catalogue of songs. Overall, I had an insight into the effects of long-term abuse, the family, and differencing and its manifestations."

Penny eyed Dove with more than a tad of asking where this was going.

"Gran's court case is pending. There's no way she's fit to plead. She's not capable of making an adequate defence. It's doubtful she would understand the proceedings. Forensic tests had established that the claws were hers though, the origins are an enigma." He continued. "Gran wanted to protect Mikey from something that was in her mind and was a product of her infinite loneliness and inability to reach out to others, or open up and talk about those family skeletons,

401

the ones that created the warring factions. Incest was a part of this, a child not born to the mother who acted the role. Was there another? A child that died, a child adopted, a child aborted? We don't need to know. It's all surmise, anyhow. Gran is quite well-to-do. The difficulty of facing up to this refracted on the small community and its' fragmented, guarded, and hidden self, its inability to speak; its personal privacy and tragedy... as in all communities. It was a frigging mess."

Both listeners smiled with relief when his erudite summary finished with an expletive.

Dove threw a second lever. "Secondly, Gran shows an intuitive, catlike grip of the world. She is guileful. She is able to fool the police, the neighbourhood and herself. It depends on who she is at the time. Alterity is a peculiar complaint." He hesitated. "It doesn't detract from the fact that she murdered a young lady who had not yet experienced life in its fullness, and damaged two others. That people can inhabit other bodies is not so mysterious. We'll never know how she obtained those vile claws. I hate this bit, but the suspects fall into a group of two. Both my choices are dead. No one checked to see how well Max knew the old lady. Mikey did, and he visited her." He lingered, weighing the merit of his last statement, then left it. "In her case the sub-personalities came to the surface and then either vanished or were once again submerged in among other alters." In the course of the next sentence he demonstrated a growing pity for the old lady. "The courts, if it goes that far, will no doubt bang Gran up for life in a place suited to her issues. I think she'll enjoy it and find appropriate alters that will accommodate. She taught me quite a good few songs." On that note, he stopped.

Penny had been awaiting the inclusion of Hart and vitriol. It never came. Hart had taken too much on board. No expletive rounded off. Penny gave a nod of appreciation.

## Chapter 59

Hart was on his way back to his beloved south. Raed had recommended him for a post in Winchester for reasons he never sussed, nor wanted to, just when he was beginning to appreciate the Northeast. None of the trio had anything to say about him. The refusal to criticise was a result of their experiences. Temporarily they were searching for social, cultural, or pathological reasons for him being such a dickhead. They admired his work ethic. Penny thought of one or two young Boro players he might use as a comparison – hardworking, though frustrating.

Raed stayed on to wind things up. The case for Max's killers would take place elsewhere. Intel suggested Leeds. She would be back in Bradford and would link up with Lucy Freeman on the torturers. Back home, Penny called Raed once. She fobbed him off.

She was polite and firm. "I'm busy. I'll call you when I can."

The call came six months later. It was a bright Friday in late May. Penny was close to putting that final full stop on *The Tableau* writing. Proofing and editing was yet to follow. He was listening to music, the living room window open wide, revelling in the blossom and scents of the coming summer.

He made one last trip to the in Leeds to thank Betty and Rita. They'd gone. The store was 'under new management'. The place buzzed with fresh-faced trainees, the aisles blocked with them and metal trolleys. Some things never change (they had not yet realised ergonomics). He manoeuvred his way around the trainees and bought liquorice in memory of his epiphany. His phone rang. The number unrecognised, he left it.

The young man at the checkout said, "Cheers," and asked if he wanted a bag for it.

Penny shook his head. Did he need help to pack? Was his card a pin or swipe?

At home he put the liquorice on the hall stand next to an unopened letter from his agent. He flopped in the chair. The call had been from Raed.

A stern voice message stated, "We need to speak face to face."

He texted: 'Call you back later. I'm busy.'

In the chair, the day's work over, he felt a satisfaction never gained in higher education. He called Raed.

She was curt. "We want you here in Loftus as soon as. I've contacted the others. Loose ends need tying up."

"Will it take long? I have editing to do." He hoped she would ask what it was.

"We can have you brought in."

"I'll sort things out tomorrow and be there the day after. Will Dove be there?"

"Already here. Periwinkle is on his way." At that she hung up.

"A wanderer found Jim's remains in Handale Woods. DNA is positive." Hart spoke.

Both statement and inquiry, it fell on indifferent ears.

The trio avoided eye contact with each other. Hart was unmoved. He had difficulty sounding sincere about Jim's demise.

He continued. "The corpse had liquefied, though scratches on the bone implied a big cat had been to work. It was impossible to ascertain the cause of death." He gave his forensic line. "Forensic date the death around the time of the final weekend of our case here, approximately six months ago."

Raed was angry. "Jim may have been prepared or diced in preparation for the cat's supper."

Her piercing interruption rattled Penny, and her sarcasm brought about a hush from the three men.

Hart read on. "The heavy rainfall washed away potential evidence. The samples obtainable hint at massive bleeding, a main vein such as the carotid, jugular, or both, sliced through. It's possible a hungry animal would eat the soft tissue." Forensic report over, he turned to Penny. "What he was doing there is anyone's guess, a high-powered rifle near him to boot. It defies logic."

Raed took over the formalities. "We have to ask you all to make a statement. Where you were you on the weekend Jim went AWOL to begin with. The hunting rifle was fired three times. Forensic dug three bullets out of two spots including a broken tree. He was firing at something. The cat perhaps?" she said sardonically. She eyed the three men. "The woods around Handale are dense and hardly ever walked. Do you know them?"

"I don't know them well. I went over there with Dove and Periwinkle a while ago. The whole place is isolated and has a spooky feel to it. We saw the black cat. It bared its teeth, showing no fear. A stunning, and from what you imply, a lethal creature. We didn't go into the woods as it was getting dark."

Hart moved on. "We found another skeleton in the woods."

No response.

Dove, Periwinkle and Penny closed ranks. Hart just wanted to close the books on Jim.

Penny tried to ease the situation. "Was it the cat that killed the other chap or woman?"

"No," Hart said. "Forensic claim the first body was an old man. He may have died from a heart attack. He must have been there for years. No identification yet. Make sure we have a reliable contact address. Our formal inquiries aren't over."

Raed shared her recent findings. "The files on Jim are gathering thick and fast. And out there," she gestured towards the window, "are two men who were employed to do his dirty work."

Hart chipped in. "Jim went to the wood armed, and therefore had a purpose. So did someone else. I would surmise that the cat merely did a clean-up job, the upper part of his body gnawed and the neck area stripped of flesh before liquefaction. His car, a hired Ford, was rough parked in Skelton. No one saw it parked up; no one claims to have stolen it though we've questioned the local 'likely' lads. We dusted it and found no familiar prints, not even Jim's." Hart raised his hands in surrender. He was regretful. His face said so. The meeting was at an impasse. He had wanted to disclose his information on Jim from above. Raed forbad it. Raed was not sure just what Penny knew.

For his part, Penny held back information, and his tears for the dead. The parental theory would die with him. Liz was a casualty. The sea had kept them. Their secrets were safe with him and the uncompromising North Sea.

He managed to say, "Thanks, Hart."

Hart responded. "Welcome. Oh, and thanks for the little book and a footnote."

Statements made; they left the police station. One of the Batemans was calling across the road to a Bowers. None of the trio were sure who was who, until they addressed each other by surname.

"See you tonight, Bowers, in the Golden Lion for darts and dominoes – a fight to the death."

"We'll take you to the cleaners, Bateman. Wait and see."

After that exchange they waved goodbye and strode away. Dove swore Bowers tipped the wink at Penny.

"Not on first name terms as yet," Periwinkle quipped.

Penny detracted. "Poor Lizzie knew a little and closed her mind to it. She was a bonny woman, and damn good at her job." He chose not to mention his informers, the infamous now Fab Five who were a key to the little success they had.

The events of that night in the thick and difficult wood would stay buried for Hart and Raed. The broken tree with its amazing shards sticking out like a ribcage was a symbol of the circle of life and death; the skeleton, a *memento mori*. Periwinkle never heard another car. That was a conundrum. He had left the wood in the pouring rain and when it was possible had called Dove. Jim's car was gone.

Raed was with Hart in the station as they spoke. Her anger placed on the backburner; she finished on a low note. "Thanks, Hart. We'll let the grey suits follow it up. Jim Trout was responsible for the torture of a young man and God knows who else. It's out of our hands now."

"Yes, ma'am." At that, he left.

Raed considered the empty corridor where the two men sat that day and wished they were there. She closed her eyes. Her attempts to bring them back failed. She saw Penny glide along the floor on her prayer mat and couldn't laugh. She washed her hands at the small corner sink in her room and unwrapped her Misbaha and Koran from a bright coloured cloth. She placed them down, then picked up *Dark Art*, stuffed it in the drawer, washed her hands again. Satisfied, she returned to her Koran and her thirty-three prayer beads.

## Chapter 60

Periwinkle and Dove were back at Penny's place. They went food shopping. Penny cooked a splendid meal (as Periwinkle described it) from his curry collection – dishes from fish to chicken, with side dishes and pickles. He opened a bottle of Cabalié, a velvety red from the Côtes Catalanes, and poured a fizzy water for Periwinkle, a large glass of wine for Dove and another which he clutched without drinking.

Periwinkle wanted to ask Penny about his word list but expedience made him look up the words. He now knew what hypophora was. Penny exampled it so well. They began their personal debriefing, the real debriefing, as Dove referred to it. Both men had now read Penny's last chapter. Penny thought it might be his last! Both men were curious about his movements on the evening at Handale. Dove got no further than the word 'Jim'. He was dying to find out about Penny's movements on the night of Jim's death. Was he at the woods? Other questions fell aside as the major question arose. Why did he go there?

Penny looked around as if for support. "I walked to Handale. It's only two or so miles south of Loftus. In the dark

I took a wrong turning. I had a torch and a map, but the torch died on me."

"Did Jim pass you by?"

"No. All I can think of is he must have driven along when I took a wrong turn."

Dove eyed him in disbelief. "What were you going to do? You baited a trap for Jim and he followed you there. Were you going to kill him?"

Penny was sheepish. "No. When I got your email to lure him to the periphery of Handale Woods, I dropped everything and set off. It threatened rain, and I had my waterproof stuff with me."

"What?"

He regarded Dove with an anxious frown. "Not me. I didn't send you an email." He didn't say he was up on the hill watching. "You were duped." Penny's usual high colour faded. He tried to put his glass to his mouth, his hands shaking.

Periwinkle stepped in, "Let's return to the email later. I need to examine it."

"I deleted it."

"Not a problem."

Dove interjected. "Hell, it was probably Jim. Jesus Christ. You just dropped everything and went to the woods knowing a trained killer was out there? What did you have in the bag – cat food?"

Periwinkle reigned in the two with his usual sense of order. "I think I can explain. I got to the wood and found the green Ford, the one Jim hired which ended up in Skelton. I found Jim and a well-trained assailant. There was no sign of you. Jim lost. I withdrew."

Dove peered over his glasses. "Whoever did it would have left no evidence. There was no other car around. My guess is that the perp was taken there by 'others'. If he stole the green car to exit, he did us a service. Left there it would've led the police to Jim's body after a day or so."

Penny felt less uncomfortable. "That was me. I took the car."

Periwinkle resumed his story. "The man in the woods was carrying, though he chose a knife. Unless Oldman is young and black and very quick, we have a dilemma..." He eyed Penny. "Jim fired twice. I unsettled the cat and he fired a third random shot off, which allowed the young man to swoop." At this point, he reconsidered his reading of Penny's chapter. "It wasn't quite a tree stump the hitman hid behind in the way you described it, but damn close. Jim's opponent is highly trained and efficient. One cut to the throat. One of ours, Dove? The knife was perfect. He knew his stuff."

Penny was freezing. This was, as his pupils said, scary shit.

Periwinkle, continued. "It's not my job to theorise. However, in this case, Jim was becoming an embarrassment. His own people bumped him off. The fact that they used you was unscrupulous and frightening. I walked away. When I could get a signal, I called Dove. He picked me up on the road. As for you taking the car, that was a boon. They dusted it. Nothing came up, luckily."

Penny agreed by saying nothing.

Dove reiterated. "Ronnie-boy, he would have had no option but to kill you. The email was most likely from the black guy."

Penny took a breath. His wine glass was still full. "I arrived to hear shooting and hid. I wasn't sure who was shooting and from where. I crept into the wood from the outskirts and could see nothing. When it was quiet, I worked my way around the outside path and saw the car still parked up. I waited a while, then drove the car back to Skelton and ditched it near the green. The keys were in the ignition."

"I know," Periwinkle confirmed. "I saw them and nearly removed them, locked the door and threw them away."

Penny's colour faded further to white. "How did the other guy get away?" he stammered.

"It was an organised job and the perfect spot. A quick call and a pickup to who knows where, the probable answer is. These people can reserve a helicopter, if necessary."

Penny, who had been gripping his glass on the table, finally picked it up. The wine was warm and with hands still shaking he held it with both and necked it. "These people?"

Dove rounded off. "Enough is enough. We all lived to report back – this time. Raed and company never responded to my message at the police station. I wonder how it went astray. Any guesses? They did us a favour. Apart from witnessing an assassin at work, we are home free and have some more wine to drink."

Periwinkle raised his glass of juice. They clinked their glasses noisily.

After a drink or three, Penny told Dove and Periwinkle the backstory to Plan Rapport or Operation Empathy, he couldn't decide which, but it meant the beginning of the new and special relationship between two warring families. Penny part recounted the event, repeating as he recalled exact aspects of the conversation verbatim and other bits in precis.

"The Bowers were first. I called a key member of the Bowers family Kevin. He agreed to meet if only for his daughter Sara's sake. The idea of my visit to the house clearly caused Kevin a good deal of trepidation. Sara needed to talk to someone and 'it might as well be me' was the reply. That was my opening. Anything to help. I knocked on the door. Ms Bowers let me in. She was expecting me. She told me Kevin was walking the dog and wouldn't be long. Sara was upstairs putting on make-up. Her mam said she's not in great form and she'd like to keep her company."

As was usual with Penny, the tale was somewhat convoluted.

"Their house was small and comfortable. Ms Bowers offered me a cuppa. Kevin was bringing biscuits back. Ms Bowers explained he was prone to forgetting stuff or he might give them to the dog, the big daft thing. I think she meant the dog. Anyhow, I sat down. Ms Bowers put the kettle on. We chatted. The tea was on hold. She insisted I called her Jenny. Nice lass! Told her my name was Ronnie. With what I can only call a crooked smile, she said 'I know. We've heard your name in dispatches.' I found Jenny Bowers bright and conversational. Jenny is a working wife, and Kevin filling in by driving a van. In reply, I mentioned my own steelworks background."

At this point Dove was about to say get on with it but hung back.

"Jenny works full-time as a solicitor's clerk. She gave a different slant to unemployment in the area and a neglected aspect of such, that is the growing female employment. Jenny is quite well qualified too. She never thought she'd get to use her qualifications. Redundancy for one means work for the other. She explained, and this is a key issue, that Kevin was losing his self-respect. He wanted to work at a job that gave him satisfaction, and a decent wage. That grimy place did both. I concurred. My 'Plan Rapport' might work. Loss of self-respect for all was the way in. Before I had time to follow it up, Sara came clattering down the stairs and introduced herself. She appeared a confident young lady to me, though unsettled. Her excellent school results had guaranteed her a place at university to study psychology. The start date had gone. She was in limbo. I decided not to ask pointed questions. I needed to tread carefully as this could go horribly wrong."

Dove nodded his agreement. Periwinkle shook his head.

"Then Kevin arrived with the biggest dog I'd ever seen, the size of a Shetland pony. Harold, the dog, liked me. In truth I doubted Harold would dislike anyone. He showed it by flattening me against the chair-back. Kevin shook my hand. The skirmish with his brother didn't appear to be a problem. Then Jenny, aware that three was a crowd, excused herself. Kevin joined Sara on the settee. He'd forgotten the biscuits, but was quite laid back, despite his comment that he was in trouble. They both grinned at me. I started to relax a bit."

Penny breathed deeply. Dove resisted a comment.

"I told them I wasn't there to grill Sara but help. That was part one of the plan. I realised Sara couldn't recall much of what happened, but if she wanted to talk about it that would help. I mentioned that if it was difficult, no worries. Without looking at her dad for support, Sara told me as much as she told the police, though it was more nuanced than reading a police statement. The stress on certain aspects was apparent – that the attacker was agile and frenzied. The werewolf was small, all in black, its face covered. I could see why kids were suspect. Sara said she'd had a drink. Then came the interesting bit. She said neither her not her attacker spoke. She, she said she, was very strong. Kevin looked surprised. I'd heard enough. That's when I took a deep breath. I mentioned the fact she wanted to study psychology. I told her that my daughter Else is a psychologist. I always thought it was something she did to try and get an angle on her father!"

Dove took his chance to interject. "Going to prove difficult."

"Funnily enough Kevin said the same. Anyway, I asked her if her university place was still open. It was a no, but Sara wanted to reapply. She added that she wouldn't mind starting after Christmas. She nudged her dad as she spoke. Basically she thought it would divert her thoughts away from these horrible attacks and get her away from her 'doting parents'. Kevin added his tuppence worth. Jenny and he suggested Teesside as an alternative, but they wanted to get away. It's understandable. Teesside is a good university, but it is better to get away and experience life differently. It sounded like a question. At this point I felt more confident. I wondered if Leeds would be of any use. I told them that the BSc in psychology is highly rated; commended for their teaching."

It was clear to Dove and Periwinkle that Penny had pre-empted that and spoken with a close friend in the department.

He had. He's arranged a second semester start.

"Sara looked interested. In fact, she was positively animated. Kevin moved uncomfortably on the couch. I jumped in and responded that she didn't have to decide now. Best have a chat to her mam and dad, and mate Matty, first. Sara came alive. She excused herself in a hurry, her phone in her hand as she ran to ring Matty. Kevin explained that 'this business' had brought them closer together. It seemed that Sara and Matty had been mates since reception.

"Kevin offered me a brew. He was already on his way into the kitchen. I stressed the importance of letting the university staff know of her situation. I offered to do that. If anyone could help Sara, it was them. Kevin came back with the tea. He mentioned Raed had appealed for help for Sara and Matty, but there was no money in the pot. Still, his opinion was that she was 'sound'. When Kevin put the tea down, I couldn't resist saying 'no biscuits?'. Kevin's look was worth a fortune. Harold had trotted behind him into the living room and flopped down, taking a large part of the space up. Then he went to sleep."

Dove also felt as if he was going to sleep, but hung on in.

"Kevin raised the topic first and saved me the agony. I have to admit I was shitting myself at that point, but the subject required a change! Kevin thought the attack on his daughter was a family issue at first, just when we were beginning to think we were in the same boat – Bowers, Bateman, Smith, Jones, whatever. I threw a switch in the conversation to darts, dominoes, pool, snooker and cribbage. Pub games. I asked if he missed the Loftus Olympics, the two families playing against each other? He didn't answer directly. Rather he said something like 'we're both in the same boat now'. Out of work and isolated. I bit the bullet and raised the idea of a solution. Kevin was up for it, with some reservations. Fortunately, Sara interrupted. Neither of us had heard her coming into the room. We must have looked guilty. She asked him what he was plotting. She was spot on. He never replied."

Dove really hoped there was a point to this endless recollection.

"Then Matty turned up. I wasn't prepared for that. However, it worked. Matty, Sara and Kevin chattered and the atmosphere lifted. I still had to visit the Batemans. I wished Hart were there. He studied psychology. I kept Gran out of the conversation. Finally, Sara and Matty went out together, arms linked. Kevin and I sat quietly. Then we swapped stories for a while. I dived in feet first. I mentioned that his family were top at darts. I asked him when they last played a game against his rivals? I also said I'd heard that Batemans rule at pool. His hackles rose. Then he agreed that a game wouldn't be beyond them. But who would talk to the other family. I put my hand up. My visit to a member of the rival family was pending, and I did it then. As it happened, several of them were gathered. In for a penny... The fact Kevin has said his family could beat them at pool did it. At one point I thought they might hang me out of a window, but no."

Penny paused for effect, though the suspense was rather lost on Dove and Periwinkle.

"Instead, they agreed." Penny grinned. "Game on."

## Postscript

"I've read Ronnie-boy's manuscript."

"And?"

"It's very odd – the comparisons between events in Loftus and his fiction." Periwinkle eyed Dove, who was reading.

"How so?" Dove asked.

"Some of the events and references in his book may well have been prior to their happening here." He looked to Dove for a comment. "It's uncanny."

"Weird shit, you mean?"

"No, Dove, uncanny."

## Acknowledgements

Thanks to everyone at Cranthorpe Millner for their patience. From proofing to editing and cover design I felt involved and always in the loop. Thanks to Vicky for the latter. The cover design followed my ideas and developed them. Thanks Shannon. Michelle's suggestions and early proofing were excellent and helped me move on as a writer. Thanks too to Lauren and Kirsty Jackson. I hope I've not left anyone out!

The book was made possible in the early stages by a further list; above all Jonathan McAloon, who read early drafts courtesy of the Literary Consultancy. I sweated blood over your reports Jonny. Thanks. Still working on my 'issues'. Thanks to Josie Bland also who poured over very early rough drafts.

I must have quizzed and questioned a host of others on a host of things. Please add your own name...

Read on...